THE
GIRL'S
LAST
CRY

BOOKS BY ALISON BELSHAM

DETECTIVE LEXI BENNETT SERIES

The Girls on Chalk Hill

ALISON BELSHAM

THE
GIRL'S
LAST
CRY

bookouture

Published by Bookouture in 2023

An imprint of Storyfire Ltd.
Carmelite House
50 Victoria Embankment
London EC4Y 0DZ

www.bookouture.com

ISBN: 978-1-83790-113-5
eBook ISBN: 978-1-83790-112-8

ONE

MONDAY

The girl blinked but tears blurred her vision. She rubbed her eyes and the world came back into focus. The red-tiled roofs of Canterbury stretched away in every direction. She loved the view from the top of the Westgate Towers – it was one of her favourite places. And this was the last time she'd see it. A tear dropped from the end of her nose and she watched it glittering like a tiny diamond as it plunged to the pavement sixty feet below.

She could follow it down.

That was why she'd come here, wasn't it? To end it all. An escape from the pain. A refuge in darkness, instead of the bleak future that had turned her world the colour of ash. Her dad was gone – he had a new family now. Her mum had become a zombie. Always working. And when she wasn't working, always drinking. Her mum said she'd have to change schools. They had to move somewhere cheaper. Somewhere she wouldn't know anybody. She'd be alone, all the time. Everything was ruined.

The sound of a notification made her pull her phone from her pocket. She flipped it open and typed in the password that gave her access to the chatroom. She was surprised she had a signal up here. But she was in the centre of town – you could probably get a signal anywhere round here.

Yoshi: have you decided yet, lolly? you really gonna do it?

She typed furiously in response.

Lolly: i'm at the top of the towers. i don't know yet – it's all gone to shit

Yoshi: your parents won't care. your mum'll probably breathe a huge sigh of relief when you're gone

Trollster: yeah, go on, do it. kill yourself

Green letters blossomed on the tiny screen. Tears made them fuse together until the girl blinked. No one waited for her to respond. It was becoming a pile-on.

Ghoul: it'll be no loss to the world. most people probably won't even notice you're gone

Honey Box: you'll feel much better after it's done – it's the ultimate escape. lol

The girl leaned over the parapet with one arm dangling the phone over the edge. There was one person who might help her. She started typing again.

Lolly: nyx, i thought you were on your way up. where are you?

She paused, waiting for a reply. She'd thought Nyx was just behind her. They were meeting here, to talk things through.

Nyx was the sensible one in the group, the one who could shut the others up when they got too excited. They were like a pack of dogs, baying for blood, but Nyx was the alpha.

Nyx: yes, lolly, i'm just coming up. how are you feeling?

Lolly: it's bad today. i don't want to go on. i can't go on

Nyx: it's your decision – you know that, right?

Lolly: i don't know what to do

Trollster: don't be a coward

Nyx: trollster, shut it. comments like that don't help. it's a big decision for lolly. she needs some time. lolly, i'll be with you in a sec

The girl shoved the phone back into her pocket and brushed a strand of dark hair out of her eyes. Those people weren't her friends, were they? A moment of sharp regret stole her breath. Sam had knocked on her bedroom door earlier, when she'd sneaked up to her room to find some space instead of going to games. Like the good friend he was, he'd come looking for her. But she'd sat in silence, not answering when he knocked and called her name. Why not? Because he'd be able to persuade her not to do what she'd come here for?

She stepped back from the edge, crying again, confused and panicky. Life was so difficult and she didn't know where to look for the answers. The sun ducked behind a cloud and she shivered. But the grey sky suited her mood.

Her phone pinged, and then again. More notifications. Sometimes talking to the group online helped. Quite often it didn't. Nyx seemed to understand what she was going through, but the others were mental. It was better when she could talk to Nyx on her own, without Trollster, Ghoul and the rest of them.

She was scared witless by the thoughts in her head.

Where was Nyx?

She held out her hands. They were shaking. She didn't want to be here. She wasn't going to go through with it. It was time to leave. Get back to school. Find Sam. Rip up that stupid note she'd written. Nyx had told her it would help, but it hadn't.

The sun came out and she looked across the city, now bathed in light. The cathedral limestone glowed gold over a sea of red roofs.

She dialled Sam's number. It went straight to voicemail.

As she disconnected, she heard footsteps coming up the spiral stairs inside the tower.

'Lolly?' Nyx appeared in the small, arched doorway, holding a coil of red rope. 'How are you feeling?'

The girl stared at the loops of rope. She imagined what it might feel like against the skin of her neck and a wave of terror swept through her.

'I've changed my mind,' she said, practically tripping over the words. 'I can't go through with it.'

Nyx frowned. 'That's why I'm here. I'll help you.'

The girl shook her head. 'No. You don't understand. I don't want to do it. I've changed my mind.'

Nyx's lips twisted into a sneer. 'It's too late for that, Lolly. There's no turning back now.'

TWO

Detective Inspector Lexi Bennett shrugged out of her leather jacket and thrust it between the handles of her bag. It had seemed chilly when she'd left for work this morning, but now she could feel the May sun on her back and the breeze had a pleasant warmth. It was late afternoon and the unexpected spell of good weather had brought workers out of their offices early. The gardens which lay in the shadows of Canterbury's medieval city walls were packed with people – mums and kids dawdling on the walk home from school, men in shirtsleeves eating ice creams, women in gym kit or work clothes lounging on the grass.

Of course, she should still have been in the office, poring over a report from the Crown Prosecution Service about a case they'd wrapped up the week before, but she knew she'd be there till long after dark, so why not take advantage of the sunshine to run a couple of errands? She strode up Watling Street, then cut through the shopping centre to come out on the High Street. She needed to pop into the bank and then go to the pharmacy for some blister plasters – her new running shoes were taking longer to wear in than she'd expected.

She strolled up the pedestrianised section of the High Street, weaving between the shoppers, in no particular hurry. Her back was stiff from sitting too long on her uncomfortable office chair and the movement felt good. She would pick up a coffee and a piece of carrot cake on the way back. Or maybe not the carrot cake.

A flash of blue light and the yelp of a police siren coming from the other side of the Westgate caught her attention. She gazed up the street and through the arch at the base of the two fourteenth-century stone towers that formed one of the ancient gates of the city. In the distance she heard the blare of an ambulance approaching. She wondered what had happened. There was a small roundabout on the far side of the arch... perhaps a motorcyclist had been hit?

Picking up her pace, she walked towards the gate. The first responders had arrived, but if the incident was serious, it might be good to have someone of a higher rank in charge. Traffic accidents weren't her remit, but she could hold the fort until a more senior uniformed officer arrived.

As she reached the archway between the towers, a young PC blocked her way, holding up a hand.

'Sorry, love, you can't come through here – you'll have to go round.'

'What's happened?' said Lexi, slipping a hand under her discarded jacket to reach into her bag.

The PC started to shake his head but then he saw her police ID appear. 'Sorry, ma'am. PC Grafton.'

'Detective Inspector Bennett,' she said. 'Is there a more senior officer here yet?'

'It's just me and my partner,' said Grafton. He looked flustered as he waved her to follow him back through the archway. 'It only happened just a few minutes ago.'

'What?' said Lexi. He was blocking her view of the pavement beyond. And then as PC Grafton emerged from the arch and stepped to one side, she saw it.

Saw her.

The body of a young woman – a girl in fact, given that she was in school uniform – lay sprawled unnaturally with half her body on the pavement and half on the road. From the angle of her limbs and the spray of blood to one side of her head, Lexi had no doubt at all that she was dead. It appeared she'd fallen from one of the towers, a sixty-foot drop.

Lexi stepped out from the arch and walked around the body. She squinted up at the top of the towers, the sun in her eyes. A man's figure was silhouetted, leaning out through a notch in the lower-level battlements between the two towers. He stared down at the body below. Grafton turned and came to stand next to her.

'That's the manager of the Westgate,' he said. 'A Mr Bryant. I asked him to check if there's anyone else inside the building.' The towers, along with an ancient gaol next door to them, were one of the city's more popular tourist attractions.

'Good,' said Lexi. She looked down at the poor dead girl, her shoulder-length chestnut hair clumping in the spreading pool of blood, and her school blazer twisted unnaturally around her torso. She wondered what had happened to her – and she hoped to hell that it had simply been a tragic accident. The alternatives didn't bear thinking about.

Beyond the body, another uniformed officer was instructing people to stand back to let the ambulance through. It sped towards them, then half mounted the pavement to come to a stop where Grafton's partner waved it down. The paramedics ran to the girl, but they were only going to confirm what Lexi already knew. Another police car arrived from the opposite direction, parking across the mini roundabout and effectively blocking the traffic. As the siren died away, she heard someone crying noisily somewhere to her left. She looked around. A middle-aged woman was being supported by a young man at one side of the left-hand tower.

'Who's that?'

Grafton angled himself carefully so the woman wouldn't be able to make out what he was saying. 'Passer-by. Nearly got hit by the falling body.'

'My God!' Lexi took a deep breath. Things could have been so much worse. 'Get her name and address – she's probably the closest witness to what happened.'

Two more PCs emerged from the police car on the round-about, and Lexi beckoned to them.

She quickly introduced herself. 'Set up a cordon and start taking details from anyone who saw anything. Treat the area as a crime scene. Until we know precisely what happened, we've got to keep open minds.'

'Yes, ma'am,' said one, while the other nodded his agreement.

'PC Grafton, would you tell the manager I'd like a word. Somewhere private.'

'Yes, ma'am.' He disappeared around the left-hand side of the two towers. The way through the arch was now blocked by blue-and-white barrier tape, but the entrance to the complex was in the gaol building on the other side.

One of the paramedics, a woman in her mid-thirties, came across to her. She looked tired, and strands of mousy hair had escaped her unruly ponytail. 'You don't want us to take her, do you?' she said quietly.

'No. Until we know what happened, it has to be treated as a potential crime, so the forensic team and the pathologist will need to process the scene.'

The girl nodded. 'Okay, we'll write up our notes for you. We've got another call.' Her companion was already stashing their bags back into the ambulance. They'd covered the body with a white sheet, which would have to do until the CSIs arrived and could put up a proper shelter.

Lexi got out her phone while she waited for Grafton to return. First, she called Mort Barley, Kent's most senior forensic pathologist.

'Afternoon, Lexi.'

'Mort. I've got an unexplained death. Looks like a fall from one of the Westgate towers. A teenage girl.' She kept it clipped. Mort Barley wasn't one for chatter.

'And you need to know if it was an accident, suicide or murder.'

'Can you come?' He was based in Maidstone, about forty minutes' drive away.

'Sure.'

'And, Mort, would you mind calling Emily while you're in the car?' Emily Jordan was her preferred crime scene manager.

'I don't remember being promoted to your secretary.'

'Please. I've got a body, a crying witness and a crowd to manage.'

'Okay, okay.'

She could always count on Mort to be grumpy. Then she dialled the incident room back at the station.

DC Ridhi Kulkarni picked up. Ridhi was the most junior member of her team, but she was already showing the promise of becoming a fine detective.

'Hi, Ridhi, who's there with you?'

'Colin's downstairs interviewing someone, the support staff are here... Tom's out talking to a witness in that pub stabbing.' Tom Olsen was her sergeant, and in the five months since they'd started working together, they'd already forged a bond. He was solid, a down-to-earth guy with a good understanding of people and an affable manner when dealing with the public. DC Colin Flynn, on the other hand, could be sharp when questioning witnesses, and sometimes had an attitude to match. Lexi was still on the lookout for his particular strengths...

'Okay. Can you get down here to the Westgate?' She explained the situation and asked Ridhi to come and take witness statements. By the time she finished, PC Grafton was hovering at her side.

'Bryant's in his office. He's pretty shaken.'

As well he might be, she thought. After all, it happened on his watch. Maybe that was unfair. Maybe not. Time would tell.

Lexi's eyes swept the scene before her. Whatever it was, surely it could have been avoided? She looked down at the girl's body under the sheet. Someone's daughter. Maybe someone's sister. There was a family who would never be the same again. She knew what that felt like. She'd lost a sister when she was seventeen and when it happened, her parents had changed. She and her other sister, Amber, had changed, too. Everything was different after Rose disappeared.

But at least this family would have a body to bury, and the chance to mourn properly.

'What happened to you?' she whispered to the inert form at her feet. Her eyes rose to the top of the towers, and she vowed to herself that she'd find out.

THREE

As DC Ridhi Kulkarni hurried up the High Street, she thought about the first time she'd been called out to an unexpected death. It had been during her first week in uniform, her second day on the beat. She'd wondered why her more experienced partner had looked concerned and told her not to be nervous. Why would she be? It was only when she saw the woman's broken body, protruding from the smashed windscreen of a small Toyota, and had rushed to the side of the road to be sick, that she understood.

That had been several years ago. She'd probably seen more than a hundred dead bodies since then, and they didn't make her throw up anymore. But her nerves still jangled as she approached the scene – it was something that you never became used to. Each time, the circumstances were different, but the tragedy was the same. Someone had lost their life, and they'd had no warning. That's what got to her now. Not the blood and gore, just the sheer bloody tragedy of it. A life wasted, usually something that could have been avoided – if a driver had concentrated more or taken a break, if less alcohol had been consumed, if someone had managed their anger...

She approached the Westgate. Beyond the towers, she could see that the traffic was gridlocked where the mini roundabout fell within the cordon of police tape. A small group of people stood huddled on the opposite pavement, watching what was happening with serious expressions, whispering behind their hands.

As she came around the curved wall of the tower, Ridhi steeled herself for what she was about to see. Three uniformed officers were speaking with various civilians at the edge of the cordon, but thankfully the prone figure in the centre of the space was already covered by a white sheet. All she could see was a foot in a black trainer and white sock poking out at one end. Beyond the body, Lexi Bennett was walking towards the footpath that led around the other side of the towers.

'DI Bennett?'

Lexi turned around. 'Ridhi, great, you got here quickly.'

They moved together so they could confer.

'Check up that this lot—' Lexi waved a hand at the PCs '— are getting all the information we need from witnesses. Emily Jordan and Mort Barley should be here any moment – make sure they have everything they need.'

'What happened?'

Lexi shook her head. 'Hopefully, it's just a tragic accident.' She paused. 'But I don't know. There are some questions that need answering – what was she doing up there? Was anyone with her? How did she come to fall? It's to be treated as a crime scene until we have the answers. I'm just going in to talk to the manager.' There was another PC hovering, and Lexi followed him round the side of the towers.

Ridhi hurried over to the PCs and held out her ID.

'Hi, I'm DC Ridhi Kulkarni. DI Bennett asked me to supervise taking down the witness statements.'

Two of the three officers looked annoyed. It wasn't as if she outranked them, and they were probably doing a perfectly adequate job already. The third one continued his conversation with a woman leaning on a pushchair handle. She looked close to tears.

'Fine,' said one of the grumpy pair. 'Be our guest.' He tore a couple of leaves out of his notebook. 'Those are the details we've taken down so far.'

Ridhi took the pages from him, aware that she was frowning. But she needed to get them onside. 'Look, guys, I don't want to tread on your toes, but if this turns out to be something other than an accident, it's going to land in my in-tray. Did anybody see anything?'

'You might want to talk to that lady over by the other tower,' said the third PC. 'Mrs Glover.'

'Thanks.' Ridhi made her way over to the middle-aged woman the PC had pointed out. A narrow river ran along the foot of the old city walls and she was sitting on the low wall of the bridge across it. Leaning forward, her head in her hands, she was being comforted by a young man squatting down in front of her.

'Mrs Glover?'

She looked up. Her cheeks were wet with tears and she sniffed, before wiping her nose with a damp tissue.

'I'm DC Kulkarni. Would you be all right to answer a few questions?' She glanced at the young man, who'd now straightened up by her side.

He gave a small shrug. 'I don't know her. I was just coming in the opposite direction when the... the girl came down right behind her.' It sounded as if he'd been about to say 'the body' but thought better of it.

'And your name is?'

'Nathan Shaw.'

'Did you see what happened at the top? How she fell?'

He shook his head. 'I wasn't looking up. I was looking at my phone. It was the sound...'

Mrs Glover struggled to her feet. 'That was it. The noise –
just a small cry and rushing air... and before I could even look
round, she hit the ground.' Her face crumpled again.

'It was horrible,' said Nathan, also visibly upset.

Ridhi put a hand on his forearm. 'It's okay. You don't have
to describe it. But neither of you were looking up? You didn't
see her before she fell?'

They both shook their heads.

'Did you see anyone come out of the towers after it
happened?'

'No, but I think the door's on the other side of the building,'
said Shaw.

Ridhi glanced around. Of course it was.

'DC Kulkarni, do you know where DI Bennett is?'

Mort Barley, the pathologist, had arrived. He was already
wearing a white crime scene suit, and carrying his medical bag.
Beyond him, the CSI van was being ushered through the
cordon to park on the far side of the mini roundabout.

'She's inside somewhere, talking to the manager.'

Mort nodded, but his attention was on the body, just a few
feet away from them.

'Right-ho, I'll take a look now and talk to her when she's
finished.'

Checking that she had Nathan Shaw's and Mrs Glover's
details on the list the PC had given her, Ridhi followed him
across to the dead girl.

Mort pulled on a pair of latex gloves, then lifted the sheet.
'Here,' he said, thrusting it at her. 'Hold this up to give us some
privacy until the CSIs get one of their tents up.'

Ridhi did as she was told – Mort Barley wasn't a man she'd
want to get on the wrong side of – but she looked around for a
PC to palm the task off to.

'Know the school uniform?' said Mort, as he surveyed the
body.

Ridhi shook her head. But when he folded the flapping front of the girl's blazer shut, she saw a familiar emblem on the breast pocket.

'That's the choir school, isn't it? Where the cathedral choristers go.'

'I think you could be right,' said Mort. 'You'd better get onto them.' He slipped a hand into the girl's blazer pockets one by one, retrieving a chocolate bar wrapper, a leaky blue biro, a lip salve and a few pennies. He dropped them into an evidence bag, before pulling out one final item, a bus pass. He scrutinised the photo on the bus pass, then tilted his head to look at the side of the girl's face they were able to see. It was bruised and distorted. Ridhi looked away.

'Yes, that's her. Olivia James. Call the school and ask them for the parents' contact details, so Lexi can do the death knock.'

Olivia James. In a split second, the dead girl, still sprawled where she fell, half on the pavement and half in the road, had become someone. A young woman with parents, siblings maybe, friends, a busy life with school and hobbies and holidays and fun.

But there was one thing she didn't have anymore. A future.

FOUR

Mark Bryant didn't look like a well man, but Lexi couldn't work out whether this was down to the events of the past hour or if it was his default appearance. His complexion was mottled and grey, which might be down to the stale whiff of tobacco that hung around him, but there was a sheen of sweat on his forehead and a tremor to his voice that made him seem overly nervous. This she could understand – no one had suggested any wrongdoing or liability on the part of the Westgate or its staff. Yet. But his mind would be gaming all the ways in which he could be blamed for the girl's death. Of course he was worried.

'Can you tell me what happened, Mr Bryant?'

They sat opposite each other in his office, a small room on the first floor of the old gaol building. It suffered tired paintwork and a strip light, and no one would have guessed from the grey carpet tiles and veneered furniture that even this part of the building was nearly two hundred years old. The desk between them was untidy, and Lexi watched as one of Bryant's hands strayed towards a packet of cigarettes and a lighter at one corner.

'I was in here, working. I heard a scream from the other side of the towers, but I just ignored it.' He glanced down sheepishly. 'I mean, I thought it was school kids messing around. Then there was more screaming, some shouts, and I went across the corridor to look out of the window on that side. Just being nosy, till I realised...' He stopped abruptly and passed a hand in front of his eyes.

'What did you realise?'

'I saw the girl's body on the ground. A man was bending over it. Her. I thought she must have been hit by a car or something.'

'What did you do then?'

'I went out and ran round to the front, dialling 999. And then I saw that woman crying, the one she'd nearly hit, and the young man. He told me she'd fallen from the tower.' He shook his head, close to tears. 'She shouldn't have been up there. We close at three-forty-five, and either I or one of the ticket office staff usually walks through the building to check everyone has left.'

'That seems quite early in the afternoon.'

'The bar and café are open for longer, all evening in fact, and the escape room experiences run until half past eight, but the viewing point at the top of the towers closes then.'

'And what about today?'

He shrugged. 'It was a normal day. We closed on time, and there were no escape room experiences booked, so I locked up. The café has its own entrance, and there's a first-floor bridge between this building and the towers. Once that door's locked, there no access to the towers.'

'And you checked there was no one still up at the top?'

'Of course I did. And in the museum. Everywhere was empty. Monday afternoons are generally pretty quiet, at least until the school holidays start and the tourists arrive.'

'So how do you explain the dead girl being at the top of the towers at – what was it, approximately four-thirty?'

Bryant's face took on a fearful expression. 'I don't know. She shouldn't have been there.'

'Could she have hidden somewhere in the towers while you were checking?'

He shook his head, though he looked far from sure.

'What about the toilets?'

'They're located down by the café in this building, not in the towers.'

'Thank you, Mr Bryant.' Lexi stood up. 'Can you show me where she fell from?'

Bryant led the way out of his office and across the short, glazed bridge that connected the gaol to the towers at the first-floor level. They emerged into a large square room with ancient stone walls and, on one side, a pair of mullioned windows that let in precious little light. The walls were lined with display cabinets containing ancient weapons and instruments of torture.

'This is the Guard Chamber,' said Bryant. He didn't stop, but disappeared through a small arched doorway in one corner of the room.

Lexi followed him up a worn spiral staircase and then passed through another arched doorway to come out into the open air on a square battlement between the two towers. The stairs continued up, leading to the top of the east tower, while another set of stairs at the opposite corner gave access to the west tower. Lexi looked around. A wooden walkway lined the stone ramparts on all four sides of the square, while in the centre, the tiled roof of the room below formed a small, square pyramid. The ramparts themselves were about five feet high, but on each side there were wide notches cut through the stone – originally for archers, no doubt, but now allowing people to enjoy the views over the city. Each notch had cast iron fencing across it for safety.

As far as she could see, there was no sign that anything untoward had happened just a short time ago.

'I think this is probably where she fell from,' said Bryant, his voice betraying his discomfort at being at the spot. He pointed towards the notch in the centre of the north wall and started moving towards it.

'No, stay back,' said Lexi. 'This has to be treated as a crime scene.'

Bryant looked visibly shocked. 'What do you mean? She fell... Are you suggesting that someone else was involved?'

'At this point, I have no idea,' said Lexi.

'But I checked the tower afterwards. There was no one else in here.'

Lexi nodded, but she wasn't going to take Bryant's word for it. He'd failed to realise that the girl was in the tower after closing time, so how would he know if she'd been alone or not? Shock was making him an unreliable witness. 'How long after it happened did you check?'

'Two minutes? Five minutes at most, I'd say.'

'When PC Grafton asked you to? Surely that was more than five minutes after?'

'I'd already checked by the time he asked me, but I checked again. There was no one here, both times.'

'Okay. Let's go back down. The CSIs will need to come up here.'

Bryant nodded and led the way back down the spiral stairs. Lexi followed him, wondering exactly what caused the girl to plummet from the ramparts to the ground below.

'I'll probably need to talk to you again, so keep your phone switched on,' she said when they reached the Guard Chamber.

Bryant gave her another nod. He looked dejected, and it wasn't surprising. The press would get hold of the story, and this wasn't the sort of publicity the Westgate needed just before the start of the summer tourist season. Blame would be attached. Someone would be found at fault.

Lexi almost felt sorry for him, but at this point, she had to reserve judgement. He might have been the only other person in the building when the girl fell. Maybe the only person who could have prevented it. She didn't want to think anything worse than that – yet – but she had to keep an open mind.

FIVE

Bryant headed across the chamber towards the glass tunnel, but Lexi paused. The stone staircase carried on down. Could the girl have hidden there?

'Wait. Can you gain access into either of the towers at ground level?'

Bryant stopped and turned back to the room. 'There's a fire escape at the bottom of the west tower. There's no way of opening it from the outside, so no one could use it to get in, but I suppose someone could have left the building that way.'

'Could the girl have hidden at the bottom of stairs while you closed up?'

'I went down and checked. There was no one there.'

'Do you mind if I take a quick look?' It wasn't that she doubted his word, but... would they really bother to check a dead-end staircase each and every day?

'Go ahead,' said Bryant, a look of resignation on his face.

Lexi went to the archway in the opposite corner of the chamber and peered down the spiral stairs as Bryant came over and flicked a light switch for her. Clusters of dust on the sides of the steps attested to their infrequent use. She made her way down, careful to balance herself by resting one elbow against the wall, rather than grasping the thick rope handrail. She would get the CSIs to check it for fingerprints once they'd finished outside.

The bottom of the staircase brought her out into a circular room, the base of the tower. Another stone arch led to a small alcove where the fire door was located. In the dull light from the stairs, Lexi pulled out her phone and switched on the torch. There were footprints visible on the dusty floor, but she had no way of telling how recent they were. The small area smelled damp and musty, unused. Lexi pulled on a latex glove and then shone the beam of her torch on the fire escape door. It was definitely shut. She pushed her hand against it and it didn't move. It was the type with a bar that had to be pressed down to open. She peered more closely at the bar. It wasn't dusty.

Behind her, she could hear Bryant's noisy breathing on the staircase.

'Mr Bryant, do you happen to know when this door was last opened?'

He appeared on the bottom step, shaking his head. 'Some time last month, maybe. We do fire drills and check all the doors regularly – I'll have to look at the schedule in my office to tell you exactly when the last one was.'

Could the bar have been wiped to clear fingerprints? Another thing she'd have to get Emily Jordan's team to check.

Just as she was turning to leave, she saw something in the shadows at the base of the curved wall. Expecting to find just a piece of litter, Lexi bent down to take a closer look. A small sliver of pale wood, maybe a piece of pine – it looked as though it had been snapped off something. She didn't pick it up, but photographed it with her phone.

'What's this?' she said to Bryant.

He squatted next to her and squinted in the beam of her torch.

'I've no idea... a bit of wood.'

But Lexi had a suspicion. She looked more closely. There was an indentation across the middle of it, at a slight angle. The sort of mark that might have been made if it had been used to prop open a heavy door.

'This might be how she got into the tower after it was closed – she could have propped the fire escape door open earlier in the day, guessing that no one would notice.' She straightened up. 'I'll send the CSIs down here to process the scene and sweep for fingerprints. In the meantime, no one else is to come into the towers.'

Bryant nodded. 'Of course. I can lock the door by the bridge and it will be closed off.'

'Good. I'll send a PC to control access.'

She followed him back up the stairs. The timing of the girl's fall – after closing time – and the discovery of the little wooden wedge made it look less likely that the death was simply an accident. It seemed that there was definitely intent – but whose?

Outside, Lexi was relieved to see that Mort Barley and Emily Jordan had arrived. Emily's team was busy erecting a temporary shelter to protect the body from prying eyes until Mort deemed it ready for removal to the mortuary. She went across to where Mort was carefully placing a polythene evidence bag on one of the girl's hands.

'Thanks for coming out, Mort.'

He gave a small shrug. 'It's what I'm paid for.' Always the curmudgeon, particularly when thanked or praised. But she had a lot of respect for him – he knew what he was doing and didn't suffer fools, a trait they shared. No time-wasting, no prevaricating. He got on with the job and gave her results as soon as he had them.

'Any thoughts?' she asked.

'I don't know if you know yet, but we've got an ID. There

was a bus pass in her blazer – Olivia James. The uniform's for the choir school. I think your DC is on the phone to them now.'

Lexi glanced across the pavement in front of the towers. Ridhi had her phone pressed to one ear and a hand covering the other. She'd catch up with her in a minute.

'Any indications as to what might have happened?'

Mort glanced up at her with an expression that she knew only too well. It said: *Are you joking?*

'Sure, I get it,' she said. 'But I need to know if it was an accident, suicide or if she was pushed.'

'God forbid,' said Mort, with a frown. 'But the injuries would be the same, whatever. Blunt force trauma – collision with the pavement at speed.' He pulled another evidence bag out of his pocket for the other hand. 'What happened at the top is your department, Lexi, not mine.'

Lexi nodded. It was what she'd expected. She spun round, searching out Emily Jordan, the crime scene manager. Perhaps Mort's direct opposite in terms of temperament, Emily was a quiet woman and dedicated to squeezing every last drop of evidence out of a scene. She was a little bit older than Lexi, maybe someone Lexi could come to see as a friend over time. But so far, their relationship had stayed on a strictly professional footing. They worked together well and Lexi trusted her judgement.

Just as she was instructing Emily to send the crime scene team inside the tower to check on the various observations she'd made, the sound of a ruckus near one of the cordons made them both whip round.

A smartly dressed woman in her late thirties was trying to push her way past PC Grafton, shrieking loudly. There was a man trailing behind her, some years older, also smartly dressed. He reached forward to grip one of her arms, but she shook him off sharply. PC Grafton held his hands up in front of him.

'I'm sorry, ma'am, but you can't come through. There's been an incident...'

'But I think that's my daughter. You have to let me see.' The emotion in her voice made it break.

Lexi started walking towards them.

'Officer, can you tell us what's happened?' said the man.

'My daughter's missing,' said the woman, not giving Grafton a chance to answer. 'That must be her in there.' She pointed at the shelter that was shielding the body from view.

Her desperation gave her strength and, wrenching her arm from her husband's attempts to hold her, she ducked under the cordon and slipped past the PC. He didn't turn quickly enough to catch her, but Lexi had anticipated what was going to happen and moved swiftly to place herself between the woman and the shelter.

She spread both arms wide.

'I'm sorry, madam, but you can't do this.'

The woman changed her course to avoid Lexi, but Lexi dodged sideways.

'Please,' said Lexi. She was effectively blocking the woman's path. 'Talk to me. Why do you think this might be your daughter?'

As Lexi swept her into the circle of her arms, the woman's legs buckled underneath her, and she staggered. Lexi absorbed the fall and took her weight as PC Grafton rushed to help. Together, they gently lowered her to the ground, and the man ducked under the blue-and-white tape to come to her side.

'What's your name?' said Lexi.

'Sarah James.' It came out as a gulp – Sarah James was crying now.

'Rod James,' said the man. 'We think that might be our daughter.'

'Your daughter's name?'

'Olivia,' they said in unison.

'I'm so terribly sorry, but you may be right.' Lexi felt her heart breaking for them, sprawled on the pavement in front of the Westgate, crowds of onlookers staring, a man taking photographs. 'Get rid of the bloke with the camera,' she hissed in Grafton's ear.

Grafton straightened up and strode across to the cordon. Lexi turned back to the Jameses. Rod James had pulled his wife into an awkward hug, while looking anxiously over the top of her head at the ominous white shelter where he believed his daughter's body lay.

'Tell me how you knew,' said Lexi.

SIX

Mark Bryant, hovering close by, stepped forward.

'Do you want to bring them into the café?' he said quietly, directing his words at Lexi. 'I closed it when... when it happened.' He seemed slightly calmer now he could focus his attention on others.

'Thank you. That's a good idea.'

She helped the couple to their feet, but Sarah James was reluctant to be ushered away.

'I need to see her. I won't believe it's her unless I see her.'

'We found her bus pass in her blazer pocket,' said Lexi.

'But someone could have taken that.' Her voice was becoming shrill.

Lexi sympathised with her. She was a mother and she couldn't believe her daughter was dead until she saw Olivia with her own eyes. But Lexi was loath to let either of them see their daughter lying smashed on the tarmac.

'Don't we have the right to see her?' said Rod James.

Lexi drew him to one side. 'Mr James,' she said quietly, not wanting his wife to hear, 'it's not about rights. It's about the distress that seeing your daughter this way will cause your wife, and you. It would be better to see her later in the morgue.'

'Bloody hell – you don't get it, do you?' He was seething with anger. 'We don't even know if it's her. That's far more distressing for both of us.'

Lexi could see in his eye that he held a glimmer of hope that the body would turn out to belong to some other girl, not their daughter. But it wasn't the case. The body had matched the photo on the bus pass, and the bus pass said she was Olivia James.

'Give me a moment,' said Lexi.

She went over to the forensics tent and pulled back the flap to look inside. Mort and Emily were lifting Olivia's body into an open black body bag, gently straightening out her twisted limbs as they did so.

Mort looked up. 'We needed to move her before rigor set in.' He didn't need to explain further. If rigor mortis had been allowed to develop as she lay, they wouldn't have been able to move her until it had worn off – which could be up to twenty-four hours later, if not longer.

'That's fine,' said Lexi. 'Her parents are here. They want to see her.'

'How... did you call them already?' said Emily Jordan.

'Of course not. I would have gone to their house when I finished here.' She looked back over her shoulder, to where the Jameses stood huddled together in the shadow of the tower. 'They found out somehow – I'm about to talk to them. But can they come and take a look before you head off?'

'Of course,' said Mort. He sounded gruff, and it made Lexi wonder. Was the job finally beginning to get to him? There was nothing worse than having to bag up a young person who'd died unexpectedly and violently.

'We'll turn the head, so they don't see the worst of it,' said Emily.

'Thank you.' Lexi went back to the Jameses. 'You can see her now.'

Panic flashed in Sarah James's eyes, but then she reached for her husband's hand and steeled herself.

Lexi led them to the tent and held open the flap. Mort and Emily were both standing. The body bag was zipped up as far as Olivia's chest, and her head was angled to one side, so they wouldn't see where her skull had been crushed. Even so, it was a disturbing sight. Her skin was chalk white and her features had been distorted by the impact.

'It's not her,' said Sarah James immediately. 'That's not Olivia.'

Rod James slipped an arm around her waist. 'It is, Sarah.' He looked away, and Lexi saw tears sliding down his cheeks. 'That's our girl.'

'No...' Sarah gasped. 'No...'

Rod was ready and Mort stepped forward quickly as she collapsed. Lexi ducked outside. 'PC Grafton, call some paramedics, please.'

'Yes, ma'am.'

Supporting the distraught woman on either side, Mort and Rod James hurried her out of the tent. Ridhi appeared and exchanged places with Mort so he could remain with the body.

'This way,' said Mark Bryant, beckoning them around the side of the tower to the footpath which led through to the café.

It was too narrow to go three abreast, so they passed through the gap with an awkward sideways shuffle. Lexi followed them, having whispered to Mort that he could now remove the body. Sarah James seemed only half-conscious, her feet dragging along the ground.

Bryant held the door open and quickly ushered them through to the café. Outside it was overcast, but he didn't switch on the lights. Lexi understood why immediately – the opposite wall to the café entrance was made entirely of glass, overlooking the river. It made the place a fishbowl, and the crowd that was still loitering on the pavement opposite the Westgate would be able to see the Jameses quite clearly, as would the man with the camera. At the far end of the café, there was a small area of vaulted brickwork, beyond the range of the huge picture window, and Lexi led them to this more discreet corner. Bryant pulled a table out of the way so that Rod James and Ridhi were able to lower Sarah James onto a green leather banquette. She slumped sideways against the wall, but her eyes were open. She was in deep shock.

'I'll get some water,' said Bryant. Lexi shot him a grateful look – he was proving himself useful, despite being shaken by the day's events himself.

Rod James was pale, his hands visibly trembling, but he did what he could to comfort his wife. Lexi could hardly help but feel like an intruder on this very private moment of profound hurt. However, Sarah James glared at him and then pushed him away. Lexi heard her hiss something in his ear. She picked up the last couple of words: '...your fault.' Rod James responded as if scorched, jerking further from her as a look of deep hurt swept across his features.

Giving them a few moments to themselves, she quickly called the station to arrange for a family liaison officer to come out, so they would have someone to accompany them to the mortuary if they wanted to go with their daughter. Then she told Ridhi to go and check when Mort would be leaving, and how Emily and her team were getting on.

Mark Bryant appeared with a tray of both coffee and water, and offered them to the Jameses. 'I can get you something stronger, if that would help,' he said apologetically.

Both of them shook their heads.

Lexi came to the table and sat down opposite them. 'Once again, can I just say how terribly sorry I am?'

They blinked at her like owls, and Lexi noted that they

were slightly angled away from each other. Definitely not a united front.

'How old was Olivia?' Safe questions to get the ball rolling.

'Thirteen,' said Rod James. 'It was her birthday just a couple of months back.'

'And she was at the choir school?' Lexi knew this already from her uniform.

Sarah nodded. 'She sings in the Girls' Choir at the cathedral. We're so proud of her.' She started to cry again. Lexi pretended not to notice that she'd referred to Olivia in the present tense. It would take her a long time to get used to the past tense.

'My nephew is a chorister,' said Lexi. 'Perhaps they knew each other.'

Rod gave her a sad smile. 'Perhaps.'

'I know you won't feel like answering a lot of questions now, but can I ask you just one thing? How did you know that someone had fallen from the towers, and what made you think it might be your daughter?'

Sarah was still crying too much to answer, so it was down to Rod. 'Sarah had a call from the school,' he said, his voice shaky with emotion. 'Olivia was missing. She hadn't appeared for games in the afternoon, and then she didn't turn up for prep. That was when they phoned, and Sarah immediately called me.'

'Did they have any idea where she was?'

He shook his head. 'No, not at all. Neither did we. I went to Sarah's house straight away, and we decided to drive to the school – I don't know why. Maybe we thought it would better to be there when she reappeared...' His voice cracked. 'But then we got a text from a friend, a woman from Sarah's gym. She said she was here, she'd been walking by, and that a girl had come off the towers, and she was wearing a choir school uniform. What else were we supposed to think?' He was in tears now too, and even Lexi felt as if she wanted to cry.

But she'd noticed that Rod had referred to "Sarah's house", suggesting they were no longer together. There was far more that she needed to ask.

When had they last spoken to Olivia? Was she happy? Was she depressed? Did they know of any reason why she might have taken her own life? Was the Westgate a place that held any special meaning for her? Did she have any enemies? This last one seemed a ridiculous thing to ask about a thirteen-year-old.

Now wasn't the time. She would need to speak to them again, once they'd had a couple of hours to compose themselves.

Sarah James had managed to stop crying. She looked around until she saw Mark Bryant, who was standing some distance away, close to the bar.

'I think I'd like a brandy now, if that's okay?'

'Of course it is.' He went behind the bar to pour the drink. 'Mr James?'

Rod James shook his head.

Lexi cleared her throat. 'I've called a family liaison officer to come here and meet us. She'll be able to take you to the morgue if you want to see Olivia again, or she can accompany you home and explain what happens next.'

'Thank you,' said Rod.

'I'll leave you now.' She stood up, feeling helpless in front of the tidal wave of their grief. This was part of the job she'd never get used to. Tracking down killers – she could get excited about that – it was why she did the job. But witnessing what were probably the worst moments in a person's life...

She wondered how many more times she could bear it. The abduction that had resulted in her sister Rose's disappearance had ripped her family apart for almost two decades. The Jameses' suffering had only just begun.

SEVEN

It was another hour before Lexi got away from the Westgate, and even then she knew she faced a couple more hours in the office. However, an insistent message from her sister Amber reminded her that today was her nephew Sam's birthday and she was expected to put in an appearance, so she decided a short break would do her good. Particularly if it involved hoovering up a slice of the decadent chocolate cake Amber had described to her the day before. She felt drained after the time spent with Olivia James's parents, and seeing Amber and the kids would recharge her batteries.

She pulled into the Rileys' driveway and retrieved Sam's present from the boot of the Crossfire. Working out what her nephew might like for his thirteenth birthday had been difficult – especially as it was the first time she'd really had to apply her mind to it. Before she came back to Canterbury after four years working in America and an even longer estrangement from Amber, she'd simply done book tokens for Sam and his younger sister Tasha, for both birthdays and Christmas. But that was before she'd met either of them. Now she was back home and building bridges. She wanted to be part of their lives, and she was hardly going to earn favoured-aunt status by sticking with endless vouchers.

Luckily Amber had come to her rescue, and as she rang the doorbell she was clutching a giant box containing an electronic keyboard under one arm. It was twice the size of the one Amber had suggested, but if she couldn't spoil her sister's kids, who could she spoil?

The door opened and there was Tasha, dressed in full Wonder Woman regalia.

'Do I know you? Have I come to the right house?' said Lexi with a grin.

'Is that for me?' Tasha pointed at the box under Lexi's arm.

'Are you the birthday boy?'

Before Tasha could try and stake a claim, she was brushed aside by the cannonball that was her brother.

'Ouch!'

'Hey, careful, Sam!'

'Aunt Lexi, Aunt Lexi...'

He threw his arms around her and bundled her into the house. Still grumbling, Tasha closed the door behind them.

Amber appeared in the kitchen doorway. 'Please don't tell me that's for Sam. It's bigger than he is.'

'It is for Sam,' said Lexi, laughing. 'And I'll give it to him in exchange for an equal sized slice of chocolate cake.'

'You're lucky there's still some left,' said Amber as they all went into the kitchen. 'I thought you'd be here earlier.'

Lexi put the box down on the kitchen island, then swept a hand through her hair. 'Sorry. Grim day at work.'

'What happened?' said Tasha, fingering one corner of the wrapping paper.

'Not for small ears, sweetie,' said Lexi. 'Come on, Sam – open this up or Tash will do it for you.'

There was a frenzy of ripping paper and a full chorus of

'oohs' and 'ahs'. Sam was beaming. 'I love it, Aunt Lexi. I've wanted one for so long.' His voice cracked slightly.

Tash danced around behind him. 'Sam's voice is breaking.'

'Shut it,' growled Sam.

He started to plug the keyboard in on one of the kitchen counters, but his mother intercepted him with a hand.

'Kids, take it into the living room so Lexi and I can talk.'

'About your boring work?' said Tasha.

'It wasn't so boring today,' said Lexi, wrapping her hands around a mug of tea as Amber cut her a slice of cake. 'But it certainly wasn't pleasant.'

'Tell me about it,' said Amber, putting a plate down in front of her, and closing the door behind her children.

Seconds later Lexi could hear 'Für Elise' being played haltingly in the next room. 'He's good.'

'He's been having piano lessons at school for the last six months. He loves it. But you shouldn't have got such an expensive one.'

Lexi shrugged. 'Seeing your kids is a tonic after the day I've had.' She took a mouthful of a cake, then continued once she'd finished chewing. 'A girl came off the Westgate. She went to the choir school.'

Amber's hand went to her mouth. 'My God.' Her eyes darted towards the living room door. Thankfully it was firmly shut. 'Do you know her name?'

'Yes – Olivia James.'

Before Lexi could tell her more, there was an anguished howl from the beyond the door. 'Mum, Mum...' It was Sam's voice.

Amber rushed to the next room, Lexi following.

Sam was sitting in front of the new keyboard, but his attention was on the screen of his mobile.

'Mum, I just got a text saying Olly's dead. I don't believe it.

She can't be.' He was speaking very fast, his face turning scarlet as his eyes brimmed with tears.

'Olivia was one of his friends,' said Amber quietly over her shoulder to Lexi. She ran to her son and sunk down next to him on the sofa, putting an arm around his shoulder.

Lexi stood opposite them. 'I'm afraid it's true, Sam.'

'How do you know?' His voice was a hostile snarl.

She took one of his hands. 'I was near where it happened this afternoon.'

'But you don't know Olly. How can you be sure it was her?'

'It was her. Her parents came and they confirmed it. I'm so sorry.'

Sam's phone pinged with the sound of an arriving text. Amber reached for it, but Sam snatched it up first. He studied the screen and shook his head. Fresh tears coursed down both cheeks. Amber took the phone from his hand, glanced at it, then angled the screen for Lexi to see. It was another text from his friend, claiming that Olly had taken her own life.

Sam looked from Amber to Lexi. 'It's not true. It's so not true. Olly would never do something like that.'

'Did you know her well?' said Lexi.

'I've known her ever since I went to the choir school. She's been in my class all that time.'

'But I thought there were only boys in Choir House.'

'You're right,' said Amber. 'Choir House in the cathedral precinct is where the boy choristers board. The girls in the Girls' Choir don't have to board, but if they do, they board in the main choir school buildings on St Thomas Hill.'

'Where you go to school?'

Sam nodded. Then he looked down at his phone again as another message pinged. 'She wouldn't do that.' There was a desperate plea in his voice.

'Listen. So far, we don't really know what happened. It

could have been an accident. Do you know if there was any reason why Olly might have been unhappy?'

Sam shook his head vehemently, his lower lip jutting out.

'Her parents seem to have split. When did that happen?'

'Last holidays, I think.'

'Was she sad about it?'

Sam sniffed. 'Of course she was sad. But not so sad she'd kill herself over it.'

Amber pulled him into a tight hug against her chest. Over his head, Lexi mouthed the words, 'I'm sorry.'

'Not your fault,' mouthed Amber. 'Tash?'

Throughout the exchange, Tasha had been staring at the three of them, wide-eyed, perched on an armchair.

'You okay?' said Lexi.

Tasha nodded without speaking and slipped off the chair to join her mother and brother on the sofa.

Sam looked up. 'Aunt Lexi, will you be able to find out what happened?'

'I'll try my very best, Sam. Sometimes we can work it out, and other times we just can't be sure. But I promise you, I'll do all that I can.'

'I know she wouldn't kill herself,' said Sam. 'I just know it.'

For his sake, and for Olivia's parents' sakes, Lexi hoped he was right.

EIGHT

Seeing Sam so upset made Lexi feel absolutely wrung out. But it also galvanized her. She headed back to the police station with a grim determination to find out why Olivia James had ended up sprawled on the pavement at the bottom of the Westgate. Of course, as head of a Major Investigation Team, looking into accidental deaths and suicides wasn't really her remit. But she'd been the first senior officer on the scene, and now she'd promised Sam.

Tom Olsen looked up from his desk as she came into the incident room.

'You were down at the Westgate?' said Tom. 'I heard what happened.'

Lexi shook her head. 'Just horrible. Thirteen years old. And, it turns out, she was a friend of my nephew.'

'Is he okay?'

'No.'

'Of course not. I don't know how Billie would cope if one of her friends died.' Tom had a nine-year-old daughter with his husband Declan. 'She was so traumatised when Minki died...'

'Minki?'

'Our hamster. We couldn't face getting another.'

'This is probably Sam's first close brush with death and it's absolutely brutal.' Lexi wished she could protect her nephew and niece from things like this, but it was impossible.

Lexi felt a hand being placed on her shoulder from behind and spun around.

'Maggie, hi.'

'Hi.' Maggie gave Lexi a brief hug, followed by a questioning look.

Chief Superintendent Maggie Dawson might be her boss, but she was also a valued friend and mentor. Usually based at the Kent Police HQ in Maidstone, she put in regular appearances to support Lexi and the Canterbury Major Investigation Team. Tom gave her a nod of greeting, and the two civilian support staff working at the far side of the room seemed to sit up straighter in their chairs.

'Are you okay? You sounded upset just now.' Maggie took her pastoral duties for her staff extremely seriously, all too aware of what the job put them through.

'I'm fine. There was an incident at the Westgate this afternoon. Not nice.'

Maggie nodded and came further into the room, perching on the end of Ridhi's desk. 'What's the latest on that stabbing at the Swan?'

'Unfortunately, the victim died overnight, so we're now looking at a murder,' said Tom. 'We're getting conflicting reports from witnesses.'

'Because they were drunk when it happened or because they're partisan?'

'Both, I think. I've got a few more to talk to. I've asked Emily Jordan to take another pass over the scene, now it's more serious.'

Maggie nodded, then turned her attention to Lexi. 'So tell me about this thing at the Westgate?'

Lexi filled her in.

'Oh dear, that's unfortunate about the parents. What an awful way to find out your child is dead. Any thoughts yet on what happened?'

'As Mort pointed out, the injuries would be the same whether it was an accidental fall or if she jumped. She was in the tower, alone as far as we know, after closing time. It looks as if she might have propped a fire escape open to get in after it was shut and that suggests premeditation.'

'So you think it's suicide?'

'I think that's the most likely thing. It appears that her parents have recently split up – that could be contributory. And to be honest, I can't see how it was an accident if she was just up at the top on her own.'

'Assuming she was on her own,' said Tom. 'Any witnesses on the ground?'

'Ridhi was down there taking statements, but she hasn't alerted me to anything.'

'CCTV footage?' said Maggie.

'No. The only camera inside the complex is in the ticket office. I've asked Emily to give the whole tower section a thorough sweep, but scores of tourists go up to the ramparts every day, so of course there's going to be traces of other people.'

'The investigation will have to look elsewhere then,' said Maggie.

'I'll take it on,' said Lexi. 'She was a boarder at the choir school, and I was about to head down there to check out her room.'

Maggie looked surprised. 'Lexi, if you think it's a suicide, you should pass it to the crime squad to look into.'

'I was the first senior officer on the scene,' said Lexi, 'and I've got the capacity at the moment.'

'Sure, but it's considerably below your pay grade. I didn't

canvas for a Major Investigation Team down here so you could look into schoolgirl suicides.'

Lexi shrugged. 'My nephew knew the girl who died. She was a close friend, and he's taking it badly. I'd like to stay on it until we know for certain what happened.'

Maggie sucked in air between her teeth as she considered Lexi's request. Lexi silently willed her to say yes.

'Okay, stay on it until something bigger comes in. Then, if it's not resolved, hand it on to DI Gallagher.'

'Thanks, boss.'

As she left the incident room, Maggie beckoned to Lexi with a crooked finger. Out in the corridor, she took her to one side.

'Listen, are you sure you're okay to work on this one? You can pass it to Tom if you need to.'

'What do you mean?' Lexi knew where Maggie was going, but she wasn't going to make it easy for her.

'A young girl... perhaps a little close to the bone for you.' She was referring to Rose. Still missing, presumed dead now – and no one seemed to believe that Lexi could reach any closure. Particularly as the distant past had been stirred up by a recent case involving the man who'd abducted Rose. He was safely behind bars now, but refusing to give any information on what he'd done to Lexi's sister.

'Come on, Maggie. It's got to be worse for Tom. He's got a daughter to think about.'

Maggie sighed. 'Of course he has. Sorry, I wasn't thinking.'

'We're both fine. We wouldn't be doing this job if we didn't care – or if we weren't up to it.'

Maggie studied her face intently. 'Okay, I'll back off. But if it gets too much, you be sure to let me know.'

Lexi rolled her eyes, but inside it felt good that someone worried.

Lexi and Tom drove across town to the choir school in Tom's Jeep, calling Ridhi for an update en route.

'You're on speakerphone,' said Lexi, when Ridhi answered.

'I've pretty much finished,' she said. 'I've taken statements from nearing a dozen people who were on the street here when it happened, and I've got contact details from a lot more who were hanging around – though I don't think they'll have much to add.'

'Did anyone see her at the top?' said Lexi.

'Nah. No one walks around looking up. We all keep our eyes either to the ground or on our phone screens.'

'Going all philosophical on us?' said Tom, with a laugh.

Ridhi laughed too. Lexi felt relief that the team could keep things light, even in the face of such a shocking death. It was important that, while treating it seriously, they didn't allow themselves to be dragged down by their work.

'Okay, good work. You might as well head home now. You can type up the statements in the morning.'

Another five minutes brought them to the choir school, on the northern edge of the town.

Tom turned into the gravelled driveway, which quickly opened out onto a small parking forecourt in front of a sprawling gothic edifice. Lexi took in mullioned windows, arched doorways and ancient stonework, with a forest of tall, thin chimneys bristling from steeply pitched roofs.

Tom let out a low whistle as he parked the Jeep next to a spotless black Lexus saloon, the only other car on the forecourt. At the front of the car, a small wooden sign said 'Headmaster'.

'How the other half live, eh?' he said, looking round at the large L-shaped building as he got out of the car. The long end of the 'L' comprised an ornate chapel that was bigger than most country parish churches.

'Yes, but apparently it doesn't make them happy,' said Lexi, as they climbed out of the car.

Lexi had phoned ahead, and the sound of their tyres on the gravel must have alerted someone to their arrival, as one side of a double doorway opened inwards. Lexi peered into the darkness beyond as they walked across the forecourt, but she couldn't see anyone.

As she set her foot on the bottom of three stone steps leading up to the door, a man's voice from inside said, 'You must be from the police.' A figure stepped forward, his hand outstretched. 'I'm Toby Entwistle.'

Lexi recognised his name – he was the headmaster. He was wearing a well-cut Prince of Wales check suit and his swept-back black hair shone almost as brightly as his black Oxfords. Lexi thought his hair looked dyed, lending the impression that Entwistle was a vain man.

'I'm DI Bennett, and this is DS Olsen.'

'Please come through to my office.'

They followed him down the wood-panelled hallway and through a wide door into a spacious room overlooking a lawn. Lexi had seen no sign of any pupils so far, but perhaps the head-master of a school like this could keep himself well-insulated from them.

The room was part-office, part-sitting room, with a heavy oak desk situated in front of a wide bay window, and a pair of matching Chesterfield sofas on either side of the fireplace. A vast Persian rug laid on top thick wall-to-wall carpet made Lexi feel as if she was sinking with each step she took. Well, he had to spend the astronomical fees on something, she supposed. Entwistle pointed at one of the sofas. Lexi and Tom sat down as directed, while Entwistle went across to the opposite wall of the room where there was a console table with a silver tray of decanters on it.

He picked up a cut glass tumbler and gestured with it in

their direction. 'Grief – it's been a day and a half,' he said. 'Can I interest either of you in a snifter?'

Lexi coughed. 'No thank you, Mr Entwistle. Not while we're on duty.'

'Fair enough.' He went ahead and poured a hefty measure of what looked like whisky for himself, then came to sit on the sofa opposite them.

'Mr Entwistle...' Lexi started to say, but he interrupted her.

'Terrible business. Olivia was a lovely girl with a beautiful voice. So much ahead of her.' He shook his head. 'An absolute tragedy.'

'I agree,' said Lexi. 'But we need to find out exactly what happened.'

'She fell. I have no doubt that those battlements are too low, and ought to be fenced off properly. I expect your lot will be getting Health and Safety in to take a look?'

Whoever 'our lot' is...

'At the moment, we have to keep an open mind,' said Tom. 'That's why we're here – to have a look at Olivia's dormitory.'

Entwistle was definitely more attentive when Tom spoke and it rubbed Lexi up the wrong way.

'Bedroom,' said Entwistle. 'All our students have their own rooms. Dormitories have been consigned to history – it's not like Nicholas Nickleby anymore.'

'We'll need to see her bedroom, then,' said Lexi, working hard not to roll her eyes. Maybe it was a good thing that this headmaster seemed remote from his pupils. She hated the idea of Sam having Toby Entwistle as a role model.

'Do you mind me asking why?'

'We need to locate her mobile and check whether she left a note, or any other indication that she might have died by suicide.'

'I see. Well, I'm sure you won't find anything. Olivia was a happy girl, full of energy and grace. The idea that she might have taken her own life is ludicrous.'

'We hope so,' said Lexi. 'But I understand from her parents that she'd gone missing earlier in the day?'

'That's right. She failed to turn up for games.'

'What did you do?'

'The games master, Freddie Bartwell, followed protocol. He sent another of the girls to check the changing room – no sign of her – and then after the session, he reported to the office that she'd been missing.'

'But did anybody go looking for her?'

'Of course. Her housemistress, Sharon Porter, was immediately informed, and checked her room. By prep time it was clear to us that she was nowhere in the building, or on the grounds, so we took the decision to call her parents.'

'But not the police?'

'I wanted to involve her parents in that decision once they arrived here. But then, of course, they got diverted, and you telephoned us with the news.'

'Thank you,' said Lexi. 'Now, if you could show us to her room, please.'

Entwistle threw back the remainder of his whisky and stood up.

'Right, follow me.'

He led them out of his study and through a maze of thickly carpeted passages. They passed through a large fire door and the switch to a lino floor and painted walls implied they'd reached a part of the school where they might actually encounter pupils.

'Have you told the kids?' said Tom, taking the weight of the door from Entwistle as Lexi passed through.

Entwistle looked over his shoulder at them. 'Someone found out – it seems there were lots of WhatsApp messages going around, so we thought it best to call an assembly and announce it. There's nothing worse than when the rumour mill grinds into overtime.'

'When was that?' said Lexi.

'Just over an hour ago.'

They passed an open door and Lexi heard the noise of crying. She glanced into a large common room. Armchairs were grouped in a semi-circle in front of a television, but it wasn't switched on. A group of girls were clustered near the window, hugging and supporting each other, some crying and all looking shell-shocked. A couple of boys lounged across armchairs, not crying, but equally sombre.

Entwistle strode on, if anything a bit faster than before. So, not particularly comfortable with his charges, then? An ambitious man with a career in teaching rather than a vocation for it, perhaps.

Lexi increased her pace to catch up with him.

'We'll need to talk to Olivia's friends at some point,' she said.

The headmaster nodded. 'It's been a terrible shock to all the pupils.'

Olivia's room was a tiny shoebox in the middle of a row of similar tiny rooms with thin partition walls and cheap plywood doors. Obviously, the old-fashioned dormitories had been carved up to satisfy the modern demand for privacy.

Entwistle unlocked and held open the door for them, but didn't go in. It would have been far too crowded with three of them in there. Lexi stood in the middle of the room. If she stretched out her arms, she would be able to touch the walls on both sides. There was a single bed, a built-in desk under the window and a narrow wardrobe with drawers at the bottom. Despite the photos, cards and pictures of popstars Blu-tacked to the wall above the bed, there was something strangely impersonal about the space. Lexi had to wonder if the camaraderie of the dormitories might have been better than this.

'I'll take the desk,' she said.

Tom opened the wardrobe. 'Has anyone been in here since she was reported missing?'

'I can't say for certain, apart from Mrs Porter, the girls' housemistress. The bedrooms here are kept unlocked – we want the students to trust each other. I asked Mrs Porter to lock it after speaking to your colleague, but before that anyone could have come in.'

As Tom examined the contents of the wardrobe and the drawers, Lexi checked out the desk. It had a small shelf above it, which was stacked with textbooks. There was a pile of ring binders on the floor under the desk – Lexi guessed there was nowhere else to store them in this rabbit hutch. She flicked through some of the books and folders. Olivia's schoolwork was neat and her grades were good. Nearly all the teachers' comments were praise. There seemed nothing here to suggest why the girl might have wanted to end her life.

At the front of the desk, there was a small, shallow drawer. Lexi slipped it open. On top of a muddle of pens and pencils was a single sheet of folded paper.

Lexi's spine tingled.

She pulled on a pair of latex gloves and lifted it out, unfolding it on the surface of the desk.

'Tom, stop. We've got it.'

NINE

Life has become too difficult for me to bear. I can't see a way to my future or a way to make my dreams come true. I don't have it in me to achieve what everybody wants from me, and I'm finding every day is harder and harder.

My true friends will understand what I've been going through with mum and dad's divorce, and why I've come to this decision. Their kindness has given me hope in the past, but that has run out now. It's time for me to take the final journey alone, to find my peace and restfulness.

This isn't the end for me. I'm just going to another place. A better place.

The people I love know that I love them. Mum, I'll visit you in your dreams. You won't be lonely. I'll be always by your side.

Olly

Xoxoxoxoxo

Lexi read it through twice without saying anything, then stepped to one side so Tom could bend over the desk to see it.

Entwistle fidgeted impatiently by the door. 'Is it a suicide note?'

'Did Olivia's friends call her Olly?' said Lexi, not bothering to answer his question.

The headmaster shrugged. 'I... I really don't know.'

No surprise there.

Tom looked up. 'It's a pretty clear indication of intent, isn't it?'

Lexi turned back to him. 'Of course, we'll need to verify that this is Olivia's handwriting, but, yes, it certainly suggests that she took her own life.' A wave of darkness washed over her. Something in Olivia's life had brought her to this, despite what might look to outsiders like a gilded existence. Of course she would be depressed if her parents were breaking up, but Lexi believed there had to be more to it than that. And someone, at least one person, must have known she was in such distress.

She pulled an evidence bag out of her pocket, refolded the note along the existing creases and slipped it into the bag. Then she bent down and pulled one of the ring binders from the pile under the desk.

'What are you doing?' said Entwistle, stepping properly into the room for the first time.

Lexi straightened up, almost bumping into Tom. 'I'm going to need to take a sample of her handwriting for analysis.' She opened the file, snapped open the metal rings and took out the top couple of pages, both of which were covered with a meandering and curly cursive script. It looked the same as the writing on the note, but she would need to pass it to a handwriting expert to be one hundred per cent sure.

'But I'll need to give it to Olivia's parents.'

'Mr Entwistle, of course we'll show a copy to Mr and Mrs

James, but in fact, it's not addressed to them specifically. And the coroner will need it as evidence.'

'Even so...'

Lexi was finding his presence increasingly tiresome. She placed the handwriting sample in another evidence bag and turned to Tom. 'Did you find anything in the wardrobe?'

'Nothing that appears to be relevant. Clothes, shoes, games kit.'

'Devices,' said Lexi. 'We'll need to check Olivia's mobile and laptop.'

There was a closed laptop lying in the centre of the desk. Tom pulled on a pair of gloves and bagged it as evidence.

Lexi hadn't seen a phone anywhere, and they hadn't found one on Olivia's body. She saw that there was a small bedside cabinet they hadn't looked at yet.

'Excuse me,' she said to Entwistle, who was in the way.

He stepped back to the doorway with a frown. He seemed to resent their presence, but a shriek of girlish giggles further along the corridor caught his attention and he strode off.

Lexi heard him speaking to them in clipped tones, and decided she didn't like him. She sat on the edge of the bed and pulled open the small drawer at the top of the cabinet. It contained no surprises – hair scrunchies, sore throat lozenges, fruit-flavoured lip salve, a tape measure, nail scissors, a phone charging cable. She rifled through it, but there was no sign of Olivia's mobile. Tucked out of sight at the back corner, a lighter and a few shreds of tobacco. So she hadn't been the perfect student. The small cupboard underneath contained a wash bag. Shampoo, conditioner, shower gel, body cream, tampons.

Lexi stood up.

'Are we done?' said Tom.

She nodded, taking a last look around. She took out her phone and snapped a few pictures of the wall above the bed.

The photos of Olivia with her friends might help them decide who they needed to talk to. She realised that Sam was in a few of the pictures, pulling faces, laughing. Kids messing about without a care in the world.

Below the pictures, on the pillow, a small stuffed monkey was propped against the headboard. She might have felt the cares of the world on her shoulders, but Olivia James was still a child.

Someone had let her down somehow, and it broke Lexi's heart.

———

"'Life has become too difficult for me to bear.'" Rod James shook his head with disbelief as he read his daughter's words aloud. The photocopy of Olivia's letter shook in his hand so much that he had to stop reading. He looked towards his wife, and Lexi saw her slide her eyes towards the window to avoid his.

She hated that she had to show them the evidence that pointed towards their daughter having died by suicide. The death of a child was enough of a crushing blow, without having to learn that something, whatever it might be, had made her feel that life was no longer worth living. Since she'd told them, she'd seen shock, disbelief and intense pain written across their features. And now Rod was reading their daughter's actual words. Nothing could compare with their agony, and Lexi couldn't help but feel it with them.

'Then, "I can't see a way to my future..."' He started to break down.

Philippa Reid, the family liaison officer who'd been called out to stay with them, guided Rod to the sofa. Like a sleep-walker, he allowed her to lead him around the coffee table, and with a gentle pressure on his arm, she made him sit. Sarah

James tugged the note from her husband's hand so she could read it.

Lexi knelt down on the opposite side of the low table to ensure she was at eye level with the distraught couple.

'Is there anything in that note that makes sense to you?' she asked. 'Did you have any idea she was in such distress?'

Philippa Reid shot her a warning glance. Maybe it was too soon to be asking questions, but Lexi wanted their immediate reaction to the words, before their brains re-interpreted them to protect them from the harsh implication that they had been somehow to blame.

'She was home from school with me last weekend and she seemed fine,' said Rod. He turned to look at Sarah, maybe for confirmation, but she was too choked up to speak. 'She was quiet, mostly doing homework. Working on a history project...' Words failed him, and he looked down at the floor.

'Did Olivia ever suffer from depression?'

Both the Jameses shook their heads. 'Never,' said Rod, his voice cracking.

Philippa Reid frowned. Lexi understood and straightened up.

'Mr and Mrs James, I'm so sorry for your loss. I'll leave you in peace now but, please, if you think of anything that might explain why this happened, talk to Philippa or call me.' She held out two cards, but the Jameses sat like statues, unable to take them. She put them down on the table.

Philippa walked her to the front door.

'Stay with them until they get over the initial shock,' said Lexi, 'and keep in touch.'

Philippa nodded. 'But now you've got the note, it's case closed, right?'

'It might be,' said Lexi. 'But I'd like to know more. No one close to her seems to believe she was upset enough to do such a thing. But for some reason she did. It just doesn't make sense.'

'It never does,' said Philippa, quietly closing the door as Lexi returned to where Tom was waiting behind the wheel of his Jeep.

TEN

It was with a heavy heart that Lexi pulled up on Amber's drive again, but she felt she owed it to Sam to let him know that they had found a note in Olivia's bedroom. He was too young to have to deal with stuff like this, but it had happened and there was nothing she could do about it. Removing the question mark would be the first step in helping him come to terms with it.

Amber answered the door looking tired and drawn.

'Is Sam still up?' said Lexi, as she followed her sister through the house to the kitchen. It was nine o'clock, and Lexi realised that she had no idea what time her niece and nephew usually went to bed. After years of estrangement from her sister, she was only just learning about life in the Riley household.

'Yes, he's in the living room. I've put on a favourite film to try and take their mind off things.'

'Then I'm sorry to be the bearer of bad tidings,' said Lexi.

'Wine?' said Amber, opening the fridge.

'Better not – I need to go for a quick run when I get home.'

'Seriously? At this time of night?'

Lexi shrugged. 'Yup – only time I can fit it in.' With an Ironman event just a couple of months away, she couldn't afford to slacken up. Physical exercise was a non-negotiable in her life – it was like a palate cleanser after all the horrifying things she encountered in the day job. And she knew all too well the cost of neglecting it.

Amber poured herself a glass of white. 'So what's the news.'

'We found a suicide note in Olivia's room.'

'Oh no.' Amber put down her glass. 'Poor Olivia. Poor Sam.' Her eyes swung towards the living room door. 'Did she give a reason?'

'She mentioned her parents breaking up.' On reflection, the wording of the note seemed rather bland to Lexi – not so much a cry for help but what Olivia thought a suicide should sound like. 'I thought Sam should know, anyway.'

Amber grimaced. 'It won't make it any easier for him.'

'I realise that, but certainty helps. Shall I tell him, or do you want to?'

'You, then I'll be there to pick up the pieces. You won't show him the note, though?'

'Of course not.'

Amber took another large gulp of her wine, then led Lexi through to the living room. Sam and Tasha were curled up together under a duvet, eyes fixed on the screen. From the few seconds Lexi saw, she recognised it as one of the *Pirates of the Caribbean* movies.

Amber stepped in front of the screen.

'Mum!' cried Tasha.

'Can we pause it for a moment, kids?'

Sam had the TV remote lying on his lap. He zapped the film and the room became silent.

'Tash, will you go and get some biscuits?'

Tasha gave her mother a puzzled look, but emerged from under the duvet. 'Hi, Aunt Lexi,' she said as she padded out to the kitchen.

Sam looked at Lexi and Amber suspiciously. 'What's going on?'

Lexi squatted down in front of her nephew. 'Sam, I'm so sorry, but we found a note in Olivia's room that makes us quite sure she took her own life. I thought you should hear it from me, rather than from any rumours.'

Sam was shaking his head violently from side to side. 'No, no. It's not true. You're wrong.'

Lexi glanced up at Amber, who dropped onto the sofa and put an arm around Sam.

'It's true, love,' she said softly.

'Show me the note,' said Sam. 'You must have got the meaning wrong. She wasn't like that – it wasn't the sort of thing she would do.'

Lexi felt utterly horrible inside. 'I can't show it to you. It just said she didn't want to go on.'

'Go on with what?' He sounded angry, and there were bright flashes of scarlet on both of his cheeks. 'She could have meant anything.'

'I'm sorry. I know this is hard for you.'

'You know nothing.' Sam wriggled free from his mother's embrace and ran from the room.

At the same moment, Tasha came back in with a packet of chocolate biscuits, struggling to rip it open. She watched her brother leaving through the opposite door. 'What's happening, Mum?'

Amber was also watching Sam's disappearing form. She turned to Lexi.

'I'm so sorry,' said Lexi.

'Not your fault. I'll go up and talk to him. We thought it best to keep him off school for a day or two...'

'Not a bad idea. School will be a rumour mill in overdrive.'

'I should ring Olivia's parents, I think.' Amber looked pensive.

'You knew them?'

'Just in passing – I saw them at choir events and the like.'

'They're in shock. Maybe give it a day or two.'

Amber nodded. Tasha was pulling on her arm for help with the biscuit packet.

'I'd better go,' said Lexi.

She pondered on the case as she drove from Canterbury back to Wye, where she rented a small cottage. The note Olivia had written seemed to make her intentions clear – and if that was true, Lexi had no business being on the case. Her remit was catching killers. It was time to pass this one over to the coroner.

But... something was making her pause.

What was it?

Once home, she quickly pulled on her running kit, wishing she'd made it back before it got dark. That shouldn't be so hard now the days were longer, but work seemed to claim more and more of her time. She was beginning to wonder if she'd be able to keep her training up at the required level for competitions. However, she knew she'd regret it if she gave up. It was a way of challenging herself, and staying fit was essential to the job as well as for her mental health.

The village was quiet as she set off from her cottage. It was easy enough running on the pavements here, with the street-lights illuminating the way. But they didn't last beyond the houses, and she wasn't going to run along the verge of a busy A road after dark, even with her head torch and the luminous strips on her running kit. Before she reached the edge of the village, she took a turn up a rutted track. The ground was uneven, but at least there would be no cars.

As she ran, Lexi thought about Olivia James some more. Just thirteen years old. There was no way that she should have been facing the kinds of issues that might drive a person to take their own life. Her parents' relationship breakdown? Maybe she blamed herself. It wasn't unusual for kids to do that. But how had Olivia reached a place where throwing herself from the top of the Westgate seemed more desirable than facing the next day? And why hadn't anyone around her seen the distress she must have so clearly been in?

She thought about Sam. He was insistent that Olivia wouldn't do something like this. But he might easily have missed it. She should talk to Amber about what the welfare cover was like at the school.

The track led up a steep incline and Lexi could feel her breathing become more laboured as her heart worked harder. Thoughts about the day dissipated as she had to concentrate and dig deeper to make the climb. Her muscles protested and her chest heaved, but the burn of physical pain was cleansing. She did a stressful job which, at times, kept her awake at night. Sometimes only physical exhaustion allowed her to switch off her mind and get the rest that her body craved.

By the time she returned to the cottage, some forty minutes later, she was soaked in sweat and panting hard. A protein shake, a shower and then the blissful oblivion of her bed were all she could think about. If the handwriting expert could confirm that the note had definitely been written by Olivia, they could close the case and hand all the evidence over to the coroner, and she could turn her attention to something fresh.

The clean sheets on her bed felt like a cool balm.

But oblivion was interrupted by a shrill blast from her mobile. It wasn't one of the ringtones she had assigned to family or members of her team. She blinked at the screen: 02:45. Call from an unknown number. It continued to ring – it wasn't a mistake, someone was expecting her to answer.

'Lexi Bennett,' she mumbled.

There was a sharp intake of breath at the other end of the

line. Maybe whoever it was hadn't been expecting her to answer after all.

'Hello?' said Lexi.

A woman started to cry noisily, great gasps, almost choking. 'It's... I...'

Lexi waited, giving the woman time to compose herself. 'Take a moment,' she said gently, sitting up in bed and switching on her bedside light.

'That note...' The woman gasped and hiccupped. 'It's fake. It's false or something. I know it's not true.'

'Mrs James, is that you? Sarah?'

'She didn't... she didn't do it. She wouldn't. Someone did this to her.'

Lexi didn't know what to say. It seemed too harsh to tell this deeply grieving woman, this mother who was experiencing the sharpest pain possible, that she was wrong.

'Someone hurt my daughter. Someone killed her.'

'Sarah, I'm so sorry.' Even to Lexi, the words sounded hollow.

'I don't want your commiserations.' There was anger now in Sarah James's voice. 'I want you to find out who did this to her.'

'Sarah, do you have someone with you or are you alone?'

The line went dead.

Lexi replaced her phone on the bedside table and stared into the shadowy corners of her bedroom.

They had the note. Its meaning was clear.

But Sam and Olivia's mother were both adamant that Olivia wouldn't have taken her own life. Lexi sighed. It was hard enough to accept a loved one's death, but even harder to believe that someone close, someone you cherished, could do such a thing to themselves. It was normal.

She turned out the bedside light, but sleep eluded her until dawn painted a lattice across the opposite wall of her bedroom.

ELEVEN

I look at the black screen and start to type. Green letters march across it, forming into words, growing into sentences, with meanings that will find a place to settle inside a young reader's brain. Words with tiny hooks, ideas that take root. If nothing else, I know how to comfort the desperate. I am Nyx. It's my mission to help the lost and lonely teenagers who find their way to the Club Edicius chatroom.

An answer scrolls out on the line below, tentative at first, but then the words come quicker. Words that make me smile.

PopSpook: i keep asking people what i should do, but you're the only one who will talk to me, nyx

Nyx: because i can understand the pain you're feeling. i know what you're going through

Yoshi: we all talk to you, popso, but you don't listen

PopSpook: i mean people in RL, yoshi. Everyday gets harder and harder. Each night i make a wish that the next day can be my last

Nyx: be careful what you wish for popspook. It's a decision you can only make once

Trollster: unless he backs out of it. Then he gets to make the decision over and over. We've known a few like that, haven't we, nyx

Nyx: you're not helping, trollster

I wonder how long this dialogue is going to last. There are other things that need my attention. I switch from the chatroom to the WhatsApp group to see what's happening there. It's a bigger group, where I don't play a central role. But it's where I find the most likely candidates to invite into my small, exclusive club. All quiet on WhatsApp. I swap back to the chatroom, where PopSpook's still venting.

Nyx: listen, popspook, if you need to talk to me alone, let me know. Private chatroom or we could meet up in RL

PopSpook: Thanks nyx. i think that might help

Let me take you by the hand, PopSpook, and show you what you need to do, I think as I send him my contact details. I had a feeling he'd be an easy target and I've proved myself right.

He'll be ready for my help any day now.

And that's what I do. I help children like PopSpook to follow what's in their hearts.

TWELVE

TUESDAY

The knife fight that had gone down at the Swan the previous weekend was the type of case that bored Lexi rigid. Rival gangs of football supporters, far too much alcohol consumed, some muppet with a knife and a dead man in the morgue.

'They weren't even Premier League teams,' muttered Tom, as they climbed into Lexi's car to drive south to Folkestone to speak with another couple of witnesses.

'And that would have made it okay?' said Lexi with a dry laugh. 'Premier League matches are worth dying for, but League Two's only worthy of a black eye?'

'Not so sure – where would that leave the Southern Counties League?'

Tom supported a local team, but Lexi was clueless when it came to football, so she didn't bother answering. She had a feeling that the whole morning would be a waste of time. The witnesses they were going to speak to had been in the pub since lunchtime, and the stabbing had happened near closing time. They'd already heard at least five different versions of events, with very little overlap between any of them.

'You know what I'm thinking?'

Tom grunted as he scrolled through his phone while Lexi negotiated the outskirts of Folkestone.

'After this morning, we should hand the case to Colin and Ridhi. Good experience for Colin to take some responsibility.'

'Yeah, but I'm not sure how much Ridhi will learn from working with him.'

Lexi laughed. 'I think she could be a good influence on him.'

'Maybe.'

They arrived at a busy junction.

'Can you look at the map?' she said. She had no idea where she was going, and required a navigator.

'Sorry,' he said. He sounded distracted.

His phone bleeped with a text message.

'There's an all-units call for assistance from a first responder at a sudden death,' he said. 'Leas Cliff Hall, Folkestone.' He'd finally managed to open a map on his mobile. 'It's just round the corner. We could go – it's less than a mile from here.'

'Seriously?' Lexi shot him a look.

'Come on,' he said, replying to the text. 'It's going to be more interesting than speaking to Tweedledum and Tweedledee about what they remember after a twelve-hour session. Go right at the end of the road.'

Three minutes later, Lexi slowed down as they turned onto the Leas, a narrow road with sea-view hotels and apartments along one side and low cliffs tumbling down to the beach on the other.

'That's it,' said Tom, pointing at the only building on the cliff side of the road.

It was a glass pavilion with a green metal pagoda-shaped roof, nestling right on the edge of the escarpment. Cascades of fairy lights twinkled in the glass windows, seeming out of tune with the dull, drizzly morning. As the road passed in front of it, it narrowed to a single lane, and was already partially blocked by a police car. Lexi pulled up just short of the structure in a loading bay.

'Hall?' said Lexi, getting out of the Crossfire. 'I was expecting something larger than this.' It looked more like a glorified ice cream parlour with disco lighting.

'It's deceptive,' said Tom. 'Hangs out right over the cliffs. There's a huge auditorium inside.'

As they walked towards the entrance, a harassed-looking man in a too-tight suit came hurrying out towards them.

'Are you from the police?' he said, his voice shaky.

Lexi nodded. 'DI Bennett and DS Olsen. I understand there's been a sudden death?' She looked round but, apart from the police car, there was no sign of the first responders who'd requested help. 'Can you show us where?'

He nodded. 'I'm Vic Nesbitt. I manage the venue.'

Instead of taking them into the building, Nesbitt walked around the side of it, bringing them onto a wide expanse of terrace overlooking the sea. It was paved in cream tiles, apart from a large square in the middle of alternating black-and-white squares like a giant chessboard. He went to the far edge and stood peering over the railings.

'Down there, underneath,' he said, pointing dramatically downwards.

Lexi leaned over the edge and it became apparent how large the structure was – she was looking down over another, narrower terrace, below which she could just see the railings of a balcony, and even further down a second wide terrace, below which the land fell away to the beach, a steep, scrubby slope of perhaps fifty or sixty feet. At the bottom, where the gradient became shallow, there was a wide, paved path. A woman with a dog on a lead was staring up.

But she didn't see any sign of the first responders or, for that matter, a body.

'How do we get down there?' said Tom.

Nesbitt walked over to the side railing. 'See there?' he said pointing at the wooded slope to the side of the hall. 'That path will take you down.'

Lexi could see a winding path with timber steps and railings snaking down the hill between the trees.

'And what will we find?'

'Sorry, I should have said.' Nesbitt's face glowed pink with sweat, even though it wasn't a warm day. 'There's a body hanging underneath the lower terrace. A woman saw it and called the police, and they alerted me. There are two constables down there.'

As Lexi and Tom walked to the top of the path, an ambulance pulled up at the other end of the building.

'Send them down, would you, Mr Nesbitt?' said Tom.

Nesbitt scurried off to greet the paramedics.

As they made their way down the steps to the seafront, Lexi could fully appreciate the extraordinary nature of the Leas Cliff Hall. The building clung to the cliffside over four storeys, with each successive floor jutting out further. The wide terrace at the bottom was actually a broad balcony which extended at least thirty feet out over the slope, supported underneath by a series of angled steel struts set into huge concrete blocks further down the cliff. The overhang created an area of deep shadow, but as Lexi peered into the darkness from the timber steps, she could see something hanging from one of the beams. A body.

Below it, two uniformed officers, one male, one female, were unreeling Day-Glo yellow tape to secure the area.

She ran down the rest of the slope, Tom hard on her heels. As they approached the closest of the two PCs, she held up her ID. 'DI Lexi Bennett, answering your sudden death call.'

'DS Tom Olsen.' Tom was panting.

'PC York, ma'am,' one of the PCs replied, 'and PC Shepherd.'

Lexi gave her a questioning look.

PC York pointed up at the body, which was swinging slightly in the sea breeze. 'We got called here about fifteen minutes ago.' She turned slightly and nodded towards the woman with the dog. 'This lady was the first person to spot it and she dialled 999.'

Lexi climbed a few feet up the slope under the cover of the overhanging terrace so she could see better. The body twisted slowly on its rope. It was a young man, a boy possibly, dressed in dark colours – black tracksuit trousers, a dark grey hoodie. He was physically slight, and his hands were small and soft, with bitten nails. Black hair hung forward, obscuring his face, and the only thing with any colour was the rope. Bright red. His feet were a mere three or four feet above the steep ground. Not a long drop, but it had evidently been enough.

Another suicide. Two in two days. What were the chances?

She went back down to where Tom and PC York were waiting.

'You've called for a pathologist and the CSIs, I assume?'

'Yes, ma'am.'

'They're going to need a stepladder to bring him down, the sort that can be adjusted for sloping ground. Can you call the fire service – they'll have something appropriate.'

The second officer, PC Shepherd, had finished securing the scene with tape and came over to them. He looked almost as young as the dead boy, and his face was deathly pale.

'Ma'am, we weren't sure if we should have tried to cut him down straight away, or wait for assistance.'

'He was dead when you arrived?'

Shepherd nodded. 'I felt his ankle for a pulse.'

'Then you did right to leave him there for the pathologist to see.'

'What should I do next?'

Lexi looked around. A few more people had gathered on the path at the base of the hill.

'Close off that path for a couple of hundred yards in either direction, and the beach,' she said. 'We can't easily shield him until he's down, but he deserves some dignity.'

'Yes, ma'am.'

'PC York?'

'Yes?'

'Take a statement from the woman who spotted the body, and be sure to ask her if she saw anyone else around at the time. We need to do all we can to locate any witnesses.'

The PCs scuttled down the hill, their shoes slipping and skidding on the stony surface.

Lexi turned to Tom. 'Suicide? Or something worse?'

'Suicide, surely.'

She wished she could be as certain.

THIRTEEN

Lexi stared up to where the red rope had been tied over one of the steel beams on the underside of the wide balcony. There seemed to be no obvious way for the boy to have reached that high to secure the rope.

'I just can't make sense of it,' she said. 'There's no ladder, or stool, or rock that he could have stood on and then kicked away.'

Tom was standing next to her, also gazing up. 'And look, the gap above that strut is too narrow for him to have simply thrown the rope over it. It would have needed to be fed through quite carefully.'

Lexi studied the ground. The balcony extended out over the hill by about twenty feet, and underneath it the scrubby undergrowth that covered the slope had been starved of light. It was mostly stone and gravel, with patches of feeble vegetation and bare earth. She looked for footprints or any other marks that might suggest the use of a ladder, or something else the boy might have used to secure his rope to the beam.

'We need to be careful,' she said to Tom. 'This might be a crime scene.'

Tom stepped gingerly onto a patch of gravel where he was

less likely to disturb any evidence. Lexi got out her phone and started taking photographs of the ground as well as a couple of shots of the hanging body. Of course, when the CSIs arrived, one of them would take much better pictures, but the pathologist would want the body brought down as quickly as possible and that would disturb the ground underneath.

There was a flurry of activity down at the newly expanded cordon. A couple of firemen were talking to PC York, while PC Shepherd was lifting the tape to allow the arriving CSIs access to the site. Beyond them, coming down the timber staircase, Lexi spotted Mort Barley, the pathologist.

She and Tom walked down the slope to meet him on the lower path and, without bothering to even say hello, Lexi filled him in.

'We need to work out how he got up there, and whether he could have done it on his own.'

'You think he might have had assistance?'

'It's quite possible, maybe even likely – which would render this a crime scene.'

Emily Jordan came to join them.

'We'll treat it as a crime scene as a matter of course,' she said. She turned to Mort. 'Give me some time to document the ground under the body before bringing him down.'

Mort nodded. 'He's in no hurry,' he said, glancing up at the boy.

Lexi wondered who he was and whether his body would yield any clues as to why he'd ended up swaying in the breeze underneath Leas Cliff Hall. Two suicides in two days, she thought again – not so unusual, she supposed, but it was depressing to think that so many young people could find a reason to end it all.

The CSIs worked quickly and quietly, taking photographs and lifting samples or tiny fragments of potential evidence to take back to the lab.

Lexi went to speak to the two firemen who were still standing by the cordon. One of them was shaking his head and the other one was frowning. Lexi introduced herself and asked them what the problem was.

'Access,' said the older of the two. 'We'd usually use the hydraulic platform on the rig, but I don't think we'll be able to get the engine close enough.'

'Are you sure?'

'We've checked in both directions. No vehicular access – it's just too narrow.'

'So can you bring a stepladder down from the top of the hill?'

'Combination ladder should do it, if your CSIs can put some stepping plates underneath.'

A few minutes later, Emily Jordan indicated that they had got what they needed from the ground underneath the body. It took a while to position and secure metal plates, and then Mort directed the firemen where to position a folding stepladder of the type designed to use on stairs.

The firemen held it steady as Mort gingerly climbed up to inspect the body in situ. With a small camera in one hand, using the other to grasp the top of the ladder as tightly as he could, he photographed the hanging boy.

'Did I ever mention to you how much I hate heights?' he called down to Lexi, grimacing as he shifted from one side of the ladder to the other to take pictures from another angle.

'Only half a dozen times,' said Lexi. He hadn't, of course.

Tom smirked.

'You're lucky you don't do our job then, mate,' said one of the firemen with a wink.

Mort inspected the knot of the noose closely, and then climbed a rung higher to look at how the rope was tied to the beam above. Then he came down and instructed the CSIs to lay out a white rubber sheet for the body to be placed on once it was cut down. Lexi had instructed the two PCs to erect a screen so the gathering rubberneckers, now pushed back as far as the beach, wouldn't be able to see anything further.

Two scene of crime officers climbed up either side of the stepladder. A third one handed up a rope cutter and, as one of them took the weight of the boy's body, the other made a quick, sharp cut through the red rope approximately halfway between the back of the boy's neck and the beam above. The CSI who took the weight of the body gasped and the ladder creaked, but the rest of the team quickly stepped in, and they gently lowered him to the ground.

Lexi looked down and gasped. The sweep of black hair had fallen away from his face and he looked so much younger than she'd expected. His cheeks and chin were smooth, no stubble, and the tip of his tongue protruded slightly from between his lips. His features were Southeast Asian. The scarlet rope was still around his neck and as its position had slipped, she could see the deep grooves it had made in his throat. She turned away.

'What an awful way to die,' she said quietly to Tom, who was also studying the boy's face.

'I couldn't do it,' he said. 'I just wouldn't have the guts.'

Mort squatted down and took a temperature reading, which he recorded on his mobile, alongside observations about its condition, the visible signs of strangulation and how the boy was dressed.

'Can you check his pockets?' said Lexi. They needed an ID as quickly as possible so his family could be informed.

Mort investigated the pockets of the boy's hoodie and tracksuit bottoms but came up with nothing.

'No wallet, no phone, no money...' said Lexi in disbelief.

'No house keys or car keys?' said Tom.

'Too young to drive, but you might expect house keys. And what teenager goes anywhere these days without a mobile?'

'Wait a sec,' said Mort. 'There's something here.' He drew a hand out of the kid's tracksuit pocket and held up a padlock.

Lexi held up an evidence bag for him to drop it into. She studied it through the plastic.

Tom peered over her shoulder. 'That logo on it – that's a bike shop in Dover,' he said.

Mort waved a hand at one of the CSIs. 'Ready for a body bag.'

He would finish his examination of the body in the lab. Meanwhile it would be up to Lexi and Tom to try and find out who he was.

'Time of death estimate?' said Lexi hopefully.

'The body's cold, rigor's set in, tongue dry – that suggests he's been dead for maybe between five and eight hours.' He looked at his watch. 'It's ten a.m. now, so between two and five in the morning. I'll probably be able to narrow it down a bit more back at the lab.'

'Thanks,' said Lexi. She watched Mort and one of the CSIs gently lift the boy's body into the black vinyl bag.

'Come on,' she said to Tom. 'There's a lot to be done.'

FOURTEEN

The sun had vanished and a heavy charcoal cloud threatened to bring rain in from the sea. It wasn't cold, but Lexi still shivered. Mort and the CSIs were cautiously bringing the body down the slope.

She and Tom stood on the path at the bottom, looking up at the scene. 'Who was he and what brought him to this?'

It was a rhetorical question, and Tom seemed more interested in the structural elements that held up the balcony than a moment of silent reflection. He pointed up. 'The point where he hanged himself, the beam is about three metres out from where it meets the cliff.'

The balcony rested on a series of horizontal steel beams, which were supported by angled steel supports set in heavy concrete plinths. The point which Tom indicated was at least two metres above the sloping ground.

'How did he do it?' said Lexi, contemplating the physics. 'Could he have slung the rope over the beam closer to the building, then slid out to where he hanged himself?'

'I don't think that could work,' said Tom. 'How would he have placed the noose around his neck?'

Lexi looked at the sloping support pillars. 'Maybe he shinned up one of those,' she said, pointing, 'then put the rope around his neck and jumped.'

'Possible...' said Tom slowly.

'But not easy.' Lexi tried to picture the scene in her mind. A lone teenager, grappling with the rough, heavy rope. In the small hours it would have been pitch black. Had he used a torch or would that have risked bringing unwanted attention?

'That bike lock in his pocket.' Lexi was thinking out loud. 'Let's say he arrived by bike. He could have used it to clamber up to the beam, couldn't he?'

'But if he did that and then jumped, where's the bike now?' said Tom. 'Surely it would be lying underneath the body?'

Lexi shrugged. 'Maybe someone helped him, then moved the bike. Or maybe someone pinched it.'

'From under a hanging body? That's sick.'

'It might still be around somewhere.' Lexi spun round and Tom wandered a few metres along the path.

'There,' he said, pointing. 'Under that little bridge.'

Lexi looked. About thirty metres from where they were standing, there was a rustic wooden bridge where the main path through the coastal park passed over another one that led steeply down to the seafront. She could see the front wheel of a bicycle sticking out from under it.

They jogged over to it and found a red racing bike. Its crossbar sported the same logo as the padlock Mort had found. There was a bike chain coiled under the luggage clip on the rear rack, but no padlock in sight. Lexi snapped a few pictures of it with her phone.

'Emily,' she called to the CSM. 'Can you get someone over here to process this bike? It might have belonged to the victim.'

Tom shook his head. 'But why's it here? Who left it here? It doesn't really make sense.'

'Someone else must have put the bike there after the deed

was done, tucking it away out of sight, so it wouldn't be found immediately. Perhaps even hoping someone would steal it – an abandoned bicycle begging for a new owner.'

'What are you getting at?'

'The beam's quite high, but what if he used his bicycle to reach up to get the rope over. Standing on his bike, on the handlebar or the saddle, he could have put the noose around his neck. Then, kick the bike away – job done.'

Tom frowned at her, questions written across his face. 'But that would only work if there was someone with him to hold the bike steady while he did it. And then to remove the bike afterwards.'

'Exactly. I think this means there was someone here with him. Someone assisted him.'

Lexi walked slowly back up until she was right underneath the beam from which the body had been hanging. But she wasn't looking up – she was looking down at the ground. The path along the bottom was bounded by scrubby grass. Further up the slope, there were a few strategically placed boulders, perhaps to give the illusion of a natural rocky outcrop or perhaps to dissuade people from investigating the space under the balcony. A drift of gorse bushes created a further barrier, though not particularly effectively. The grass thinned out, giving way to rough gravel.

'Any tyre tracks?' called Tom from the path below.

Lexi shook her head. 'Nothing. The ground up here's too stony.' She came back down to where Emily was pointing out the bridge and the bike to her team. 'This whole area needs to be treated like a crime scene, now. Can you all be alert to any traces of another person being present and assisting the boy?'

'Of course,' said Emily. 'But it's a public park and it's used every day. It'll be virtually impossible to trace anyone who was here.'

She was right, of course.

But that didn't mean they couldn't try their best. They climbed back up the hill in silence.

Another young life cut short in its prime, for no apparent reason.

FIFTEEN

Of the two witnesses to the pub stabbing that Lexi and Tom had come to Folkestone to interview, one was missing from work and the other became hopelessly confused as to the date which they were questioning him about. They got nothing useful out of him and, driving back to Canterbury, Lexi felt deflated. This wasn't quite what she'd expected from the job as head of the Major Investigation Team – she couldn't help but feel that the investigative skills she'd learned from four years with the FBI were being wasted.

They'd tasked the Folkestone first responders, PC Shepherd and PC York, with checking recent missing person reports for the town and, if necessary, further afield. But she didn't think they would need to look far – the boy who'd hanged himself from the Leas Cliff Hall balcony couldn't have come from a long way off if he'd arrived by bicycle with no money or mobile.

Anyway, they'd done their bit. Hopefully they'd soon have an ID and, if someone had helped him, they would find out who. She wanted the team to focus on the stabbing at the Swan, given that it was now a murder case.

Halfway between Canterbury and Folkestone, Tom's phone rang.

'It's PC Shepherd,' he said to Lexi as he raised it to his ear. 'DS Olsen speaking.' He listened to whatever the PC was saying for a minute. 'Really? That was quick. Thanks. Stick it in an email.' He recited his email address and finished the call. 'He thinks they might have an ID on the body. A fifteen-year-old boy was reported missing this morning, fits the description.'

His phone pinged with a notification and he looked down at the screen.

'And?' said Lexi, impatient.

'Could be. Shan Liang, fifteen years old, American national, reported missing by his mother at six a.m. this morning. Mrs Liang. The picture definitely looks like him.'

'Where do they live?'

Tom glanced at his phone screen. 'Sandwich – Manwood Road – that's the address Shepherd sent over.'

They were halfway between Folkestone and Canterbury. Sandwich was in the wrong direction, and would mean driving cross country on narrow roads through a string of sleepy villages.

'Navigation,' said Lexi.

'To Sandwich?'

'Yes, where else?'

'Can't we dispatch Shepherd and York to do it?'

Lexi could perfectly well understand why Tom didn't want to go and do the death knock – it was probably every police officer's least favourite part of the job. Telling someone's family that they were dead, usually in shocking and unexpected circumstances, was always a distressing experience.

But that didn't make it okay to shirk it.

'What if it was Billie, and someone fobbed it off to a more junior officer?'

Tom bristled at the mention of his daughter. Lexi realised it was harsh, but it mattered to her that they did right by the dead as well as by the living.

Tom cleared his throat. 'Sorry. You're right.' He looked at the map on his phone. 'There's a turn coming up for Aylesham. Take it, then a right turn half a mile on.'

They drove in silence apart from occasional directions, and Lexi almost wished she could take back what she'd said.

Half an hour later, she turned the car into Manwood Road. Sandwich was a smart town and Manwood Road was in a smart part of it on the southwestern edge. One side of the road was bound by a park, while on the other they drove past a succession of large, detached properties. The houses varied architecturally, but the owners seemed to have one thing in common – a fondness for expensive German cars. BMWs, Audis, Mercedes and Porsches cluttered the drives. It was the sort of street where every house had a double garage, and a name rather than a number.

'Thornfield,' said Tom, peering at the name plaques as Lexi slowed down to a crawl. 'That's it. Stop here.'

She pulled into a space between two cars, and they got out. She paused for a moment before striding towards the house. This was the worst kind of family visit to make. They suspected the dead boy was Shan Liang, but they would need someone to come to the mortuary to make a formal identification. Of course, any parent would cling to the hope that the police had got it wrong and that it wouldn't be their child. Lexi didn't want to give them false hope, but at the same time she couldn't categorically tell them that their son was dead. It meant walking on a knife edge.

Tom rang the doorbell and Lexi's stomach fluttered with nerves as they waited.

After half a minute, the door opened and a blonde woman in a paint-daubed smock looked them up and down.

'My name is DI Bennett, from Kent Police. I'm looking for Mrs Liang.' She wondered if they'd come to the wrong house.

But the colour drained from the woman's face. 'You've found Shan?' She spoke with a strong American accent. 'Where is he?' She moved her head to look between them, as if expecting him to be there, standing on the drive behind them.

'Mrs Liang?'

'Yes, I'm Shan's mother.'

'Can we come in?'

She seemed to realise that this meant the news wasn't good and as she stepped back to let them in, her knees let her down. Lexi put out an arm for her to grab and Tom quickly came around to her other side to offer more support.

'Is your husband home?'

She shook her head, but words failed her.

Lexi looked around. They were in a wide double-height hallway, lit from above by a domed skylight. There were doors leading off it, and she saw the corner of an armchair through one of them.

'Over here,' she said to Tom, gesturing towards the doorway.

They helped Mrs Liang into a large room. The furniture was modern and boxy, and they led her to a wide sofa upholstered in pale blue velvet.

'Tom, can you fetch a glass of water?'

Mrs Liang shook her head. 'Please tell me he's not dead. Please...'

Lexi sat down next to her and Mrs Liang clutched at her arm. 'He's not, is he?' Her eyes drilled into Lexi's, searching for the answer she wanted.

Lexi took a deep breath. 'This morning a body was found near the seafront in Folkestone. We have reason to believe that it might be your son.' Opposite the sofa, on the far side of the room, her eyes alighted on a baby grand piano. The top of it was populated with photos in silver frames. A small Asian boy. The same boy a few years older. A wedding photo that showed a younger version of Mrs Liang with a handsome Asian man in some sort of military uniform.

'How do you know it's him?' The anguished question dragged Lexi back to the moment.

'The police in Folkestone have the photo that you emailed when you reported him missing. Also, we found a red racing bike nearby. Did he have one?'

It was as if she'd punched the woman in the stomach. Mrs Liang struggled to breathe. Her eyelids fluttered and her eyes rolled back. For a moment Lexi thought she was going to faint.

'Mrs Liang, can I call your husband?'

This brought her back from the brink. She leaned forward and rubbed her eyes with both hands. They came away wet with tears. 'No... we won't reach him. He's on a training mission.'

'But...'

Mrs Liang looked up. 'He's a flight instructor with the RAF at Manston. He's flying today.'

Tom came back into the room with a glass of water. He offered it to Mrs Liang, but she pushed his hand away, slopping water onto the plush velvet of the sofa.

Lexi rose to her feet. 'Tom, Mr Liang is flying at RAF Manston. Can you call them and ask them to get him onto the ground as soon as possible.'

'Of course.' He left the room and Lexi heard his footsteps go in the direction of the kitchen.

She turned back to Mrs Liang. 'Is there someone else I can call?'

'You said he drowned? He was a strong swimmer.'

Lexi shook her head. 'No, I said the body was found by the seafront. But he didn't drown.'

'So how...'

'We think your son took his own life, I'm afraid.'

'No!' She was up on her feet. 'No, no. Dammit, not my Shan.'

Lexi reached out to her, but Mrs Liang pushed her roughly away. She ran from the room. Lexi followed, and practically knocked her over in the hall where she appeared to have thought better of her flight.

'Mrs Liang, please let us call someone.' She let Lexi lead her back into the living room.

'I don't really know anyone here.'

'No neighbours or work colleagues even?'

'I'm an artist. I work alone, here at home.'

'Another parent from Shan's school?'

'We home-school. We don't mix much with other people.'

So what had made Shan leave the family home, cycle to Folkestone and hang himself in a place he probably barely knew? And if he was home-schooled and didn't mix with other people, who might have been there to assist him? It was only the first of many questions springing into her mind.

SIXTEEN

Mrs Liang drank the glass of water.

'Excuse me,' she said, placing her hand under her nose, 'I need a tissue.'

She left the room on unsteady feet, but Lexi decided against going with her. It was more likely that she needed a moment alone. The news of a sudden death stripped dignity and hit people physically in ways they didn't expect.

Instead, she went over to the piano and examined the photos. They quickly extinguished any doubt as to the identity of the body they'd seen. Shan Liang had been a beautiful child who had grown to a handsome teenager, and even the grim physical effects of what had happened to him hadn't obscured that. She picked up the wedding picture and thought of Mrs Liang, probably screaming into a pillow somewhere upstairs or taking the chance to breathe in her son's clothes while they still retained his smell. Then she thought of Mr Liang, as yet unburdened with the knowledge that would cause his world to implode. Turning to the window, she gazed up into the blue. Was he up there somewhere, his only concern the pilots he was instructing?

Tom reappeared in the sitting room doorway. 'They're calling him back to the base and they'll have someone drive him here. His CO will tell him what's happened as soon as he lands.'

Lexi's heart clenched.

'Look at this,' said Tom. He walked across to the fireplace, and pointed up at the abstract painting hanging above the mantelpiece. 'I think it's by her.'

'Her?'

'Mrs Liang. She said she was an artist.'

Lexi went over and squinted at the signature in the corner of the picture. It looked like it said *Cindy Liang*. 'You're right.' She stepped back so she could take in the whole of the canvas. Blue, green and grey shapes seemed to float over a pale horizon. The brushwork was bold and the colours sang. 'It's good,' said Lexi.

'If you like that sort of thing,' said Tom, pulling a face. 'Have to say I prefer something more traditional.'

They heard footsteps out in the hall, so Lexi didn't answer him. Cindy Liang came in. Her nose was red, and she was clutching a box of tissues in one hand. She seemed to have composed herself.

'Mrs Liang,' said Lexi, gesturing for her to sit down again, 'can we make you some tea?'

Cindy Liang, halfway down, sprung up again. 'Oh goodness, no. Let me make *you* some tea.'

'We're fine, thanks,' said Lexi. But a sweet tea would do Cindy Liang the world of good for the shock. Lexi desperately needed to ask her a few questions, not least if she could see Shan's bedroom. They needed to check whether his bicycle was missing and if he'd left a note. She looked at Tom and jerked her head towards the kitchen. He got the message and went out.

'You reported Shan missing at about six a.m. this morning?'

Cindy Liang nodded.

'Is that when he would normally get up?'

'No. I was up early to paint – it's an urge I have to follow whatever the time. I walked past his bedroom and the door was open. He wasn't in his bed. I checked the rest of the house, but I didn't find him.'

'And this surprised you? You didn't think he could have just gone for an early walk or out cycling? Did you check his bicycle?'

Cindy Liang put a hand to her mouth. 'No, I didn't think of that.'

She got up and went out of the room. Lexi heard a door being unlocked and opened. Seconds later, she was back.

'It's gone.' She looked crestfallen – perhaps imagining that if she'd realised this earlier she might have somehow been able to stop him or save him. 'I should have realised. He was a teenager. He's never usually up before ten or eleven. We let him sleep the hours that suit him and start our school day later.'

'So when was the last time you saw him?'

'Last night, when I went to bed, he was still up playing games on his computer.'

'What time was that?'

Cindy shrugged. 'About midnight, I think.'

Tom came back in carrying a tray with three mugs of tea on it. He put it down on the coffee table, but nobody picked one up.

'And your husband, when did he last see him?' said Lexi.

'Tao wasn't here. He stays at Manston, depending on his shifts.'

'But you told him Shan was missing?'

'I phoned him this morning, of course. He said not to worry, that Shan would probably turn up later.' Her lower lip quivered. 'He was wrong.'

Lexi had one more question. This would be the hardest one for Cindy Liang to answer.

'Mrs Liang, I hate to have to ask you this, but it's important.

Do you know of any reason why Shan might have taken his own life? Was he depressed about anything?'

Cindy Liang's face quivered between anger and heartbreak. Then tears welled from her eyes and she snatched a tissue from the box. 'How can you ask me that? He's my only child.'

The last thing Lexi wanted to do was add to her pain, but she had little choice. 'May I see Shan's room? He might have left a note.'

Her anger flared again. 'I already went into his room, just now. There's nothing out of the ordinary there. There's nothing that would have made my son take his own life. You've made a terrible mistake.' She rose from the sofa, glaring at Lexi. 'I'd like you to go now.'

It didn't feel right, leaving her alone, but they couldn't persuade her to let them stay until her husband got home. With great reluctance, they set out back to Canterbury.

'Don't you think it was odd that she didn't ask how he died?' said Tom, as Lexi accelerated on the main road out of Sandwich.

'That struck me as well, but perhaps she couldn't bear the thought of it. And let's face it, people don't always think logically when they're in shock.'

'True.'

'But what a weird life for a teenage boy – at home with just his mother for company, not knowing anybody locally.'

Tom frowned. 'Sounded like she didn't want to get to know the neighbours.'

'He must have been horribly lonely.' But would that have been enough to make him take his own life? And why in Folkestone, rather than closer to home? The more Lexi thought about Shan Liang, the stranger his death seemed to her. Something wasn't right.

When they got back to the office, she left Tom in the incident room logging the interview with the one witness to the stabbing they had found, and trying to track down the missing one. Colin was checking CCTV footage of the area immediately surrounding the Swan for the hours after the incident and Ridhi was buried under a pile of the interminable paperwork that had to accompany virtually everything they did these days.

Lexi retreated into her office and called Amber to check up on Sam.

'He's gone into school for a couple of hours,' said Amber. Lexi heard a slight note of regret in her voice. 'He needed to be with his friends – they're putting together a memorial service for her and the choir will sing at it.'

After that, Lexi spoke to PC Shepherd. 'How far is it from Sandwich to Folkestone?' she asked him.

'It's about twenty miles,' he said.

'And could someone do that on a bicycle, after dark?'

'There's a cycle route right along the coast, but it's not lit at night. I reckon it would take a couple of hours.'

Shan was definitely home at midnight. He probably would have had time to cycle to Folkestone, but why go that far? What had made him choose the Leas Cliff Hall? Lexi rang Mort.

'Time of death for Shan Liang?' she said when he picked up.

Mort grunted disdainfully. 'Same as I already told you – between two and five.'

'You were going to narrow it down.'

'And I will, in due course.'

But between two and five. That meant he had time to get there.

'I'll let you carry on.'

Just as she was debating with herself whether to risk a canteen sandwich or to venture further afield to find some lunch, her phone rang. She didn't recognise the number.

'DI Bennett speaking.'

'Inspector Bennett, this is Cindy Liang.' She sounded out of breath.

'Mrs Liang, are you okay? Has your husband arrived yet?'

'Yes, they just brought him here.' She gulped air. 'I found something. I found what I suppose you might call a suicide note.'

'Where did you find it?'

'I opened the piano keyboard – I wanted to play, to touch the keys that Shan's fingers had last touched.' She paused, perhaps trying to get control over her emotions. 'Stupid really – it can't bring him back. The note was on the keyboard.'

Lexi couldn't ask Cindy Liang to read her son's suicide note over the phone, but she needed to know what it said, and they would have to have it to pass on to the coroner.

'Can you photograph or scan it and email me a copy of it?'

Cindy Liang said yes but it was barely audible.

Ten minutes later, Lexi received an email with a scanned image in it. She opened it on her laptop and called Tom into her office.

'Mrs Liang found this,' she said, and they both leaned forward to read the handwritten note that now filled the screen.

Mom, pop,

Believe me when I say I don't want you to be reading this, but there's no other way for me, and I know you'll understand when you learn what happened.

I've done something wrong, something that can't be made right and it leaves me with only one course of action. I've brought great shame on our family and I can't even look you both in the eye to ask for your forgiveness. Instead, I will go to our ancestors and ask for their forgiveness.

Each day is harder and harder, and I can't see the way

*forward. You tried to make my dreams come true, but I set fire
to your efforts and I hang my head in shame.*

Know that I love you always.

Shan

Lexi scrolled down the page.

'Wait, what's that?' said Tom as something else came into
view underneath the message.

'Chinese characters?' said Lexi. 'He's written something in
Chinese as well. We'll need to get this translated, but that's
unequivocally a suicide note. It shows he had the intent to take
his own life. But I can't help wondering about the way he did it.
Even using his bicycle, could he have got up there without
help?'

Lexi continued to stare at the Chinese characters long after
Tom had left her office. In two days, two teenagers had taken
their own lives. Was that so unusual? It was a tragedy that was
becoming all too common. Today's teenagers seemed to be
under levels of stress unlike anything experienced by previous
generations. Social media. Peer pressure. Exams. Society's
expectations. Or perceived expectations... God, she wouldn't
want to be a teenager now.

There was nothing suggesting a link between them.
Different locations. Different methods. A girl of thirteen, a boy
of fifteen, who probably didn't know each other.

But still something niggled at the back of her mind.

SEVENTEEN

If Shan could write in Chinese, Lexi decided it was a safe assumption that his father also could. If she went to pick up Shan's note, she could ask Mr Liang to translate the Chinese portion of it, which would almost certainly be quicker than tracking down a police translator.

It was only half an hour's drive, and she ate a petrol station sandwich on the way that was neither better nor worse than whatever she might have grabbed in the police canteen. Brushing breadcrumbs from her black trousers, she rang the Liangs' doorbell. This time it was answered by a slim Asian man wearing an American air force uniform, jacket undone and tie knot pulled loose. He had a cut glass tumbler with a couple of fingers of amber liquid in one hand.

'Mr Liang?'

He gave a slight nod, his expression blank.

'I'm DI Lexi Bennett – I spoke to your wife earlier.' He continued to stare at her. 'Can I come in?'

'Yes, yes, of course,' he said, snapping into action. He also had an American accent, but it wasn't as pronounced as his wife's, and there was the ghost of a Chinese accent blended with it. He led her inside.

The sitting room was almost the same as when she'd left it little more than an hour earlier, but instead of the tea tray on the table, there was now a decanter and a second tumbler. And when she looked round, she saw that all the photos had been swept off the top of the piano and scattered on the floor in a jumble.

There was no sign of Cindy Liang.

'Is your wife okay, Mr Liang?'

Liang took a slug from his glass, then nodded. 'She's resting.' He sat down in an armchair and nodded towards the sofa opposite.

Lexi sat too. 'I'm so sorry for your loss.'

Liang acknowledged this with another nod. 'I have some questions. Where is my son's body?'

'He's been taken to the mortuary in Maidstone. I'm afraid as it was a sudden death, there'll be an autopsy to determine the cause. Once the coroner has finished his inquiries, the body will be released to you.'

'I think we will probably want to repatriate Shan's body to America.'

'That's fine. I'll ask a member of the coroner's team to talk to you about the procedure for that. However, more immediately, we'll need you to come and officially identify the body.'

'There's some doubt about this?' He looked shocked.

Lexi shook her head. 'No. I'm sorry – I have no doubt that it's Shan, but it's required that the body is identified by someone who knew him well, usually the next of kin.'

His face fell, and he took another sip from his glass. 'When will I have to do that?'

'It's up to you, but as soon as possible.'

There was silence for a moment. Then he looked up at her. 'Please tell me how my son died.'

Lexi had expected this question, but it didn't make it any easier to answer. 'He hanged himself underneath the balcony at the back of the Leas Cliff Hall in Folkestone. Did he have any connection to the building?'

'A connection? No. I don't even know if he knew about it.'

'Did he know Folkestone? Had he ever been there?'

Liang thought for a minute. 'He plays music and sings with a group. They go around old people's homes and hospices, entertaining them. I think they went to Folkestone once or twice.'

'Can you give me the name of the group?'

Liang shrugged. 'I have no idea. I can ask my wife for you when she feels better... or maybe you could find it on Shan's Facebook page.'

'I understand your son was home-schooled?'

Liang glanced conspiratorially towards the sitting room door, as if worried his wife might be listening there. 'Cindy grew up in a closed community, a very strict religious order. She left them, but even now she doesn't like strangers or large groups of people. It was her decision to home-school Shan, but we always let him join musical groups. He was so talented...' He shook his head, lost for words. 'Cindy will never get over this.' Then he dropped his head forward and Lexi could tell he was crying. 'Nor will I.'

Lexi went across to the window to give him a few minutes' privacy. The Liangs' garden was large, but simply laid to lawn with a few trees along the far perimeter – there was nothing to suggest the presence of a keen gardener in the house. But she supposed if they were here with the military on a temporary basis, why would they invest the time?

'Sorry.' Mr Liang sniffed, and Lexi turned back to him.

'I'm afraid I have a favour to ask of you,' said Lexi. 'Your wife sent me a scan of the note Shan left. Would you be able to translate the part he wrote in Chinese for me?'

'Of course,' said Liang.

He pulled the original from his jacket pocket and studied it for a moment. Then he started to speak falteringly as he translated: 'Honoured parents who gave me the gift of life, I'm full of shame that I'm now taking that gift from you forever. But I do not cling to life in the face of another shame that would be far worse.' He became too choked up to continue.

'What does he mean by "another shame that would be far worse"?' said Lexi.

Liang shook his head and handed the note to Lexi. 'I don't know.'

'Did he seem depressed recently?' she said.

'He was always a quiet boy. Self-contained. But he loved music and nothing made him happier. I hadn't noticed any change in him.'

'Did he have any close friends?'

'That's something you will need to speak to my wife about.'

Lexi nodded. She didn't want to disturb Cindy Liang now, so the answer would have to wait. She asked Liang for a sample of Shan's handwriting for comparison, and he gave her one of his son's schoolbooks. Then, feeling unnecessarily cruel, she swapped the scanned copy of Shan's note for the original, which she put into an evidence bag. Mr Liang seemed to understand but looked devastated nonetheless.

Bright. Talented. Loved. Olivia James and Shan Liang had plenty in common. Lexi felt profoundly depressed as she contemplated the fact that both of them felt desperate enough to end their lives. But suicide was no longer a crime and, unless she could show that someone had helped or encouraged them, Lexi knew she should pass both cases to the coroner.

So why did she find herself searching Facebook for Shan Liang's page as soon as she got back to the office?

It only took a couple of minutes, and she recognised the profile picture immediately as one of the framed photos that had stood on the Liangs' piano. He had nineteen friends, and he hadn't bothered to fill in any of the 'About' details. She scanned the pictures of the friends. As she scrolled over their pictures, a small pop-up box gave details of what they did and their location. The majority of them seemed to be American, living in America, presumably people he knew from before the Liangs' relocation to the UK. However, there were three teenagers, two boys and a girl, who were Kent-based. Perhaps they would be worth talking to. She continued to look at Shan's page. He didn't post very often, and most of them were just reposts of widely shared funny memes.

There were a few pictures of him with a group of young people gathered around a piano, some holding musical instruments, against various backdrops. Studying them, Lexi recognised the three Kent-based Facebook friends. This must have been the musical group that Mr Liang had told her about. Most of the pictures appeared to have been taken in institutional settings, and one post featured a selection of pictures that were almost certainly from an old peoples' home. She scrolled back up towards the top of the page again, stopping when one particular picture caught her eye. It was an image of the group, bunched together, no piano, and there, right at the side of the frame... it was the edge of a full height window. With strings of fairy lights hanging in front of the glass.

It was the Leas Cliff Hall. Did this have something to do with why he'd picked it as the place for his final act?

She called Tom into her office and pointed it out.

'But so what?' he said. 'What difference does his having been there before make?'

'Put it together with what he said in his note, about something shameful happening. He did something that he didn't want his parents to find out about, badly enough that he chose to end his own life rather than face them.' Lexi shrugged. 'Perhaps it happened at that event at the hall. And maybe one of those kids knows something about it.'

Tom gave her a look that said 'So what?' again, and maybe he was right. But she wasn't quite ready to give up on Shan Liang.

EIGHTEEN

Reading the posts, Lexi found the name of the group – the Kingsdown Singers – and she quickly found a link to their Facebook page. It seemed there were fifteen or so members, mainly teenagers, a few of them looking as if they might be in their early twenties. An older man featured in a few of the shots and Lexi guessed he was the page administrator, Paul Arbuthnot.

The group page had an events calendar, so Lexi clicked through to it.

'What are you doing?' said Tom.

'Look – they've got a rehearsal this afternoon. Five o'clock in Walmer Parish Hall.'

'What of it?'

'They'll all be in one place. Let's go and talk to them – catch them on the way in and find out what was going on with Shan.'

Tom shifted his weight from one foot to the other while he considered it.

'I'll go,' said Lexi. She glanced at her watch. 'I should just make it. Can you sort Colin and Ridhi to track down that stabbing witness again? Then everyone back here for a team briefing at six thirty.'

The route from Canterbury to Walmer was less direct than driving to Sandwich, but the cross-country roads weren't busy in the late-afternoon, and Lexi jammed her foot to the floor in a way she wouldn't have if Tom had been in the car with her.

It was five to five when she pulled up outside the parish hall in the small village of Walmer. The lights were on in the squat Arts-and-Crafts-style building and through the open door, she could hear someone practising scales on a piano. As she walked towards the hall, two young men cycled past her, got off their bikes and locked them together to a fence at one side.

'Excuse me,' she said, 'have you got a moment?'

One of the boys, wearing tortoise-shell glasses, glanced at his watch. 'Not really, miss.'

'What for?' said the other. He was the taller of the pair.

Lexi had to be careful. The news of Shan's death hadn't been released to the press yet, so they wouldn't know.

'Do you know Shan Liang?' Although Shan's father had introduced himself as Liang Tao, using the traditional Chinese way of putting the surname first, Lexi had noticed that Cindy and Shan seemed to put their first names before their surname in the western style.

They both nodded and the one with glasses frowned. 'Are you police?'

'Yes.' Lexi flashed her ID.

The taller boy glared at her. 'He didn't do it, right? The whole business stinks.'

'I'm sorry – what exactly are you talking about?'

'At Sunny Oaks, in Deal. Last month, someone pinched an old guy's medal. They said it was Shan,' said the taller one.

'Who accused him?'

'If you're the police, don't you know what's going on already?' said Glasses.

A noise from the doorway made all three of them turn towards the hall.

'Jack, Kieran, you're keeping everyone waiting.' The older man that Lexi had seen on the Facebook page emerged onto the tarmac forecourt in front of the building. He looked mid-sixties, his hair grey and thinning on top, and despite being skeletally thin, his cheeks had formed heavy jowls that made his jawline sag. He eyed Lexi suspiciously. 'Who are you?'

'DI Lexi Bennett, Kent Police. You are?'

'Oh.' He sounded surprised. 'Paul Arbuthnot. Look, I'm sorry, but we've got a rehearsal scheduled, and I can't ask people to stay late because these two are chatting.'

'I understand there was a theft reported at Sunny Oaks recently?' Lexi was winging it.

Arbuthnot frowned. 'They reported it to the police? But they got the thing back and everything was sorted.'

'You found out who did it?'

His frown turned to suspicion. 'Inspector, this is beginning to sound like a fishing expedition, and I really don't have time to talk to you. I only have access to the hall for an hour, so I need to get my rehearsal going.' He turned to go back inside. 'Kieran, Jack, come on.'

Glancing quickly at Lexi, the two boys followed him inside and the door closed. Lexi could have gone after them and demanded more information, but to what purpose? It seemed clear that whatever had happened at Sunny Oaks was quite petty, and she couldn't blame Arbuthnot for wanting to protect a member of his group against an unfounded accusation. But however it had played out, it seemed to have been enough to push Shan Liang to the brink.

As she unlocked her car, the door of the parish hall opened and the taller of the two boys emerged. He hurried across the pavement towards her.

'I told him I needed to get something from my bike,' he said. There was an edge of panic in his voice.

Lexi closed the car door and leaned against the bonnet. 'How can I help you?'

'Shan did it, didn't he? He's dead.'

She nodded slowly. 'How did you know?'

'Why else would you be here?' His face crumpled as he struggled with his emotions. 'He said he was going to. I begged him not to, and I thought I'd got through to him.'

'I'm so sorry...' She paused, realising she didn't know whether he was Kieran or Jack.

'Kieran.' He filled the gap, roughly wiping a tear from his cheek.

'Did he do it because he'd been accused of stealing?' That would make sense of the note he'd written – the great shame that he couldn't bear his parents to know about.

'There was no theft – the old man misplaced his medal and accused one of the carers of taking it. Because it happened on the day we'd been singing at Sunny Oaks, they wanted to pass the blame onto us. Arbuthnot was called in by the manager and, at the next rehearsal at the Leas Cliff Hall, he accused Shan of taking it in front of everyone.'

'But the medal was found, so surely Shan was exonerated?'

'Arbuthnot's a bully. He picked on Shan and he threatened to tell his parents.'

'Why Shan in particular? Or is he a bully to all of you?'

'Mostly just Shan,' said Kieran, sniffing. 'But sometimes other people. No one stood up to him.'

'So why did Shan stay?'

Kieran shrugged. 'I think his parents made him. At least, he didn't want to tell them that he wanted to leave.' He paused for a second. 'And, also, he liked being with the rest of us. He didn't go to school, and we were his friends.'

Behind them, Lexi heard the sound of the hall door opening.

'Kieran?' Arbuthnot's voice was sharp.

'I gotta go.'

'One more thing – did you ever play a gig at the Leas Cliff Hall?'

'Yes...' But another shout from the doorway cut him off.

'Tell him that I waylaid you,' said Lexi quietly, so Arbuthnot wouldn't hear. She didn't want Kieran to get into trouble for talking to her.

He nodded and jogged back to the hall.

Lexi started the car and sat lost in thought for a moment. Arbuthnot had made an accusation against Shan at the Leas Cliff Hall. Was that the event that Shan had found so shaming he didn't want to live anymore?

Had Paul Arbuthnot bullied Shan Liang to his death?

NINETEEN

I monitored the local news websites all morning, but it's only now, late in the afternoon that the news of Shan's death has surfaced, and the information is scant. It's just a small paragraph on a local news website, and it doesn't mention Shan by name. It certainly hasn't come from a police press release. But it's enough. I know from the details it's Shan they're referring to.

Better head back to the chatroom and calm everybody's nerves.

Nyx: hi, how's everyone doing today? who's here?

Trollster: here. but wishing i wasn't

Doobie: hello everyone

Nyx: i don't know if any of you have heard, but popspook checked out earlier today

Yoshi: boo hoo. me sad

Trollster: can't believe he did it, man. didn't think he had the nerve

Nyx: hey, trollster. don't speak ill… he obviously felt the time was right

Doobie: you mean he did it?

Doobie's the new kid and I'm watching him closely. It won't do if somebody spooks him too early. I've spent months slowly gaining his confidence and I don't want that work to go to waste.

Nyx: he did what was right for him. now he's found the peace he craved

Yoshi: i kind of liked him, even though he was so quiet

Nyx: he was brave and thoughtful

Doobie: brave for sure. i'd be much too scared to go through with it

Nyx: you'll find your courage, doobie. and we're all here for you

Gently does it. No hurry. I won't let him down. Not like I did before.

Nyx: you'll find your peace when you're ready for it. we all do in the end. your time will come soon enough

TWENTY

Ridhi picked up the phone in the incident room. It was Lexi calling ahead as she drove back from Walmer.

'Ridhi, can you check up for me if there was ever a report of a theft at a Sunny Oaks old people's home?'

'Do you have a date?'

'It would have been pretty recent I think – the last month or two.'

'On it.'

'Let me know what you find. Oh, and see what you can find out about a bloke called Paul Arbuthnot. I'll be back in my office in fifteen minutes.'

Ridhi jotted down Lexi's requests, then looked across the room to Colin. He was scanning more CCTV footage from the pub stabbing. His eyes were glazed over and he looked stupefied.

'Coffee, Colin?'

'Could murder one.'

When she came back into the incident room with two cardboard cups of brown water from the machine, his demeanour was sullen. He was lounging back in his chair, staring at the screen with drooping eyelids.

'I've watched this footage ten times. Gary Ross comes out of the pub alive. Less than a minute later he's bleeding out on the forecourt.' He tapped on the screen with the end of a ballpoint. 'But the quality's too shitty to make out exactly how it happened. Bloody cut-price security cams.'

Ridhi put the two coffees down on the side of his desk and peered at the blur of moving images. He rewound the footage again. The camera covered the car park at the side of the Swan that had spaces for about twenty cars. The incident had happened at closing time, after a rowdy night of football on the big screen. An argument had spilled out of the main entrance and onto the pub forecourt – a paved area in front of the Swan that was also picked up by the car park camera. Most of the screen was taken up by the cars, but the left-hand third of the footage showed what was happening on the forecourt.

Grainy figures moved jerkily across that corner of the screen – rather than film footage, it was stop motion made up of successive stills. Without sound, it looked like an elaborately choreographed dance, but the reality was that members of two groups of rival fans were coming to blows. Some of their friends tried to hold them back, and pull them off each other, while others stood by shouting, egging them on and laughing.

All perfectly normal for a Saturday night, until some idiot had pulled a knife.

'There,' said Ridhi, tapping on what looked like a small, white blur moving across successive pictures. 'What's that?'

Colin's eyebrows went up and he rewound a few seconds. He shrugged, but Ridhi leaned in closer to the screen, squinting.

'That's the blade, isn't it?' she said in a low whisper.

She followed the small white flash in the next few pictures

until they reached the point when the victim dropped to the ground. Colin paused it.

'Damn, you might be right.' He glanced up at her, and Ridhi got the distinct feeling that he was somewhat annoyed that she'd spotted it when he hadn't. 'Before, when I looked at it, I was always looking at the people. But when it actually happened, he has his back to the camera and the view of who's in front of him is blocked by these guys here.' He indicated a group of three men that were moving towards the melee just as the stabbing happened.

Ridhi nodded. 'Sure – in these last few images before he went down, you can't even see the blade.'

Colin pressed rewind again and Gary Ross seemed to magically spring back to his feet. The three men went backwards, as the whole group shifted in reverse. Colin paused it. 'Look – this is where we get a final glimpse of the knife before Ross is stabbed.'

There was just a tiny white line in the midst of the blurred group of people. It was no wonder that Colin hadn't picked up on it before. As he let the images scroll back, they watched it moving towards the outer edge of the group. It jumped position in each still image, sometimes disappearing from sight for a split second before reappearing somewhere else in the scuffle.

'Hold on,' said Ridhi. 'Pause it again.'

Colin did as she asked.

'That's it, isn't it?' she said, pointing at the still. 'You can see the blade clearly and you can see the hand on the handle.'

'And you can see whose hand it is.' Colin put his finger on a blurred face in the crowd. 'It's this guy. And when we follow him through the fight to what happened afterwards...' He fast forwarded. 'He makes a run for the car park.'

'It looks like he's stashing something into his pocket,' said Ridhi. 'It could be the knife, explains why it hasn't been recovered.'

'These two men here look like they're coming after him, but in fact they're his mates. All three of them get into this car and...' Colin fast forwarded again. 'When it drives out of the car park, we can get the plate.'

'You've already checked the reg numbers of all the cars, haven't you?'

Colin grinned. 'Yes. We know whose car this is. We've questioned the driver. We just didn't realise he had the killer in the back.'

'Time to talk to the driver again.'

'You're not kidding. Want to come along?'

'Wouldn't miss it. But shouldn't we run it past Tom first?'

Colin shrugged. 'He's not here. The boss isn't here. Let's just do it ourselves – no need to let those two grab all the glory.'

TWENTY-ONE

Maggie Dawson was sitting at her desk when Lexi walked in. It was always a pleasant surprise to see her slumming it down in Canterbury rather than her sleek office at the Kent Police HQ in Maidstone, but it meant that Lexi would need to have all her ducks in a row.

'Hello you,' said Maggie.

Lexi nodded. 'Good to see you.'

'Tom told me you were out checking details on another teen suicide.'

'There seems to be an epidemic of them.' Lexi hazarded a guess where this was going. 'I know – no crime committed. At least ostensibly. But it seems like this kid might have been hounded to his death by a false accusation of theft.'

'Still no crime. Not unless someone actively encouraged him to take his own life, or helped him do it.'

Lexi's mind flashed up an image of the red rope tied around the steel strut on the underside of the Leas Cliff Hall balcony. She realised she needed to urgently speak to Emily Jordan to see how likely it was that Shan could have rigged it up himself.

'There are questions to be answered about the viability of

the way he did it. And coupled with the questions I still have about Olivia James's death, I want to keep looking into both of them for just a little bit longer.'

'Fair enough then. Keep me updated. What about the murder at the Swan?'

'I was just going in to brief the team. Join us?'

The incident room was quiet when Lexi and Maggie came in. Tom was at the coffee machine and several of the civilian staff were working at their desks.

'Tom, where are Ridhi and Colin? You did tell them we were having a briefing?'

Tom turned to face them, a pained expression on his face. 'Yes, I told them and no, I don't know where they are.'

Great. Maggie was going to think she had no control over her team. Which apparently she didn't. 'Text them, will you?'

She addressed the rest of the room. 'Okay, guys, let's hear what progress everyone's made so far, then we'll discuss next moves.' It was early evening now, but there were still a few useful hours left in the day. 'Michelle, has your team got anything useful from the CCTV footage or ANPR?'

Michelle was head of the Major Investigation Team's cohort of civilian researchers. She shrugged and pointed at her computer screen. 'Couple of cars parked near the pub left very quickly after the stabbing. I've got names and addresses from the reg numbers, and I gave them to Colin.'

'Great. And, Tom, what about our disappearing witness? Any luck?'

'I spoke with him briefly and he told me where I could get off. We'll have to pull him into the station.'

'Is this person a suspect in the stabbing?' said Maggie.

'He wasn't, but now I'm beginning to wonder. Either a suspect or he knows more than he's willing to let on.'

'Tell Colin and Ridhi to go back over the footage and pictures from inside the pub,' said Lexi, 'and see if you can map out exactly where he was when it all kicked off and who he was there with.'

One of the civilian research staff raised a hand. 'I think Colin and Ridhi were doing that before they went out.'

'Thanks.' Lexi turned to Tom. 'Can you get either of them on the phone and see when they'll be back.'

There was a clatter of footsteps from the top of the stairs, then Lexi heard Ridhi's distinctive giggle.

'I'm not joking,' said Colin. 'We did the right thing.'

'I'll be the judge of that,' said Lexi, stepping out of the incident room and directly into their paths.

Ridhi's smile vanished in an instant, but Colin didn't seem at all fazed.

'Boss,' he said, giving her a nod.

'Where have you been?'

'Long story.' Colin held up both hands to pacify her, which made Lexi even more annoyed, but she ushered them into the incident room and over the next five minutes extracted the details from them.

The man who'd driven the getaway car out of the Swan car park was a photocopier salesman called Rolly Weaver, and he'd already been interviewed once. Colin and Ridhi had tracked him down again at his place of work, a business machines supplier located next to the Wincheap Park and Ride.

'He recognised me as soon as we walked into the showroom,' said Colin. 'Nervy as hell. Kept looking towards the door at the back. Either his boss was somewhere behind it or he was looking for a quick getaway.'

'Yes, but why did you go to question him again?' said Tom.

'Because when we watched the pub's security footage for the ninety-ninth time, we actually spotted a knife,' said Ridhi. 'The murder weapon.'

'You mean *you* spotted the knife,' said Colin. 'Bloody amazing. I'd watched that bit over and over, but Ridhi saw a small white flash and realised it was a blade.'

Colin Flynn singing someone else's praise? That was a turn up for the books.

Ridhi flushed, but she looked pleased with herself. 'The guy with the knife got into the back of Rolly Weaver's car, but when we questioned him the first time, when we checked the plates of all the cars in the pub car park, he never mentioned a third passenger.'

'And this time?'

Colin gave a snort of laughter. 'Couldn't lie to save his grandmother's life. We threatened him with perverting the course and he rolled over on his mate straight away. He gave us a name, Kevin Stewart, and a partial address. Then we arrested him as an accessory after the fact. Custody sergeant's just checking him in.'

'He was a bit shocked when we did that,' said Ridhi. 'Thought he'd be cut loose for giving up his mate's name.'

What should she say? *Good work, team*, or *why the hell didn't you run this by me first?*

'Great work,' said Maggie. 'Presumably this Stewart is the knife wielder?'

Ridhi nodded, grinning again.

'Excellent. As soon as we've finished the briefing, you can bring him in for interview,' said Lexi. She'd decided there was nothing to be gained by showing them up in front of Maggie. She'd have a word with them later about checking in before acting on impulse. After all, she'd wanted this case off her desk, and that seemed to be what they'd presented her with. Showing a bit of initiative wasn't a bad thing.

'Yes, boss,' said Colin.

'Ridhi, before all this kicked off you were looking at Paul Arbuthnot and Sunny Oaks, weren't you? Got anything?'

'Sunny Oaks. Private nursing home in Hythe for up to

sixteen residents. Looks smart from the website. But no record of any thefts being reported recently. The only contact we've had with them was when one of the night manager's cars was stolen, but it was parked on the street nearby, so not much to do with the home itself.'

'That fits with what Paul Arbuthnot claimed – that they'd agreed not to report the theft to the police.'

'Yeah, but why's Ridhi looking into this?' said Colin, He seemed emboldened by their recent success. 'Surely a theft from an OAP's place isn't on our remit.'

'One of the kids that died by suicide had been accused of the theft,' said Tom.

'Can't you hand it off to the coroner?' asked Maggie.

Lexi took a breath. 'We've had two teenage suicides in two days, and neither of them sit right with me. I just want to give them a bit more time and effort.' It was a tactful way of saying there was no way she was palming these cases off till she felt certain that no one else had been involved.

Colin's eyebrows went up. Some days he really seemed to have had an empathy bypass.

Ridhi ignored him and handed Lexi a sheet of paper. 'This is what I found out about Paul Arbuthnot,' she said. 'He's a retired music teacher and he leads the Kingsdown Singers in his spare time. He works four days a week at a garden centre on the edge of Ramsgate and he lives at Minster, a few miles inland.'

Lexi took the sheet of paper. It had Arbuthnot's address and the rest of the details Ridhi had dug up. 'Thanks.' She turned back to the whiteboard and pointed at a photo of Gary Ross, the victim of the pub stabbing. 'Okay, get this wrapped up so we can concentrate on the two suicides.'

She didn't miss the look Tom gave her, but she didn't care. Even if Olivia James and Shan Liang were only victims of themselves, they deserved her full attention. And she had a strong feeling there was more to it than that.

Maggie trailed her back to her office, then stood leaning against the door jamb. 'I don't think these suicides are worth any more of your time, Lexi. After all, there's nothing concrete on either of them to suggest assistance or coercion, is there?'

'Just being thorough. It would, at the very least, have been tricky for Shan Liang to hang himself without some help.'

'Leave it for the coroner. If he spots anything untoward, he'll toss it back to us quickly enough.'

'But he won't spot anything unless we present him with all the evidence.'

Maggie came in and shut the door behind her. 'Lexi, tell me this isn't about Rose.'

'What are you talking about? There's no connection.'

'Not on the surface, I agree. But any case involving the death of young woman is like a red rag to you.'

'Of course it is. It should be to every policeman or woman in the country.' She could hardly keep the anger out of her voice.

'But it's personal for you. And that worries me.'

'Why?'

'I don't want you to burn out. I've seen it happen. If you put too much of yourself into your work, you'll run dry. And when you haven't got anything left in the tank, you won't be able to do the job.'

'That's not going to happen, Maggie. Not to me.'

Maggie went to the door. Her expression told Lexi she didn't believe her.

TWENTY-TWO

After Maggie had left, Lexi sat her desk, eyes closed, considering what she had said. Perhaps she was right – perhaps there was no logical reason for her to keep digging. She needed another opinion.

She dialled Emily Jordan. 'Tell me these suicides are okay to pass on to the coroner,' she said as soon as Emily was on the line.

'Yes, in my opinion,' said Emily.

So why did she feel so uneasy about them? Something was nagging in the depth of her lizard brain. Something not right. But the logic of her frontal cortex was clear – of course it wasn't right that two young people, thirteen and fifteen, felt distressed enough to do what they had done.

She chewed on her lower lip. Whenever she'd trusted her intuition in the past, it had proved to be the right thing to do. Which meant, for Olivia and Shan's sake, she couldn't afford to ignore it now.

She pulled the copies of the two suicide notes out of her desk drawer. She wanted to be one hundred per cent sure that they were genuine. She called the incident room and Ellie answered the phone.

'Ellie, did we get anything back from the handwriting expert with regard to the two suicide notes?'

'Not yet, boss.'

'Right, give me her number.'

Two minutes later, she was on a Zoom call with Georgina Griffiths, a handwriting expert based in Hull.

'Sorry to ambush you like this,' said Lexi, once they'd introduced themselves, 'but I just want to draw a line under these two cases.'

Georgina Griffiths smiled. 'Not a problem. I was looking at them earlier this afternoon and I was about to email you anyway. But let's talk it through.' She held up an enlarged photocopy of Olivia's note. 'I would usually insist on comparing the original documents, and definitely if I had any doubts, but comparing this letter with the sample of handwriting from the schoolbook, I feel satisfied that they were written by the same individual.'

'How can you be sure?' said Lexi.

'There are various things to consider – the shape of the letters, how they curve and how angular they are. With experience, you learn to discern the stroke direction. This is really hard for someone to change, even if they're trying to disguise their handwriting.' She pointed at the word 'difficult' on the first line of the letter. 'For example, the way the double F has been formed can be compared with the double F halfway down the page in the schoolbook sample.'

Lexi looked at the two copies she had in front of her, and nodded. 'They're just the same,' she said. 'Same loops above and below the line.'

'That's it. And if you look at how she writes "I", it's identical on both samples. It always makes a good comparison as people are quite idiosyncratic about the capital I they use.'

'So they were both written by the same person?'

'Yes. I looked at lots of smaller features of the writing, too, and I can say with one hundred per cent certainty it's the same hand.'

'And the other one?'

They both shuffled the papers in front of them to look at Shan's letter to his parents.

'This one was even easier. The characteristics suggest that whoever wrote it went to school in America.'

'Well, he was home-schooled, but his mother's American and he lived there until recently.'

Georgina nodded her head. 'His writing's very even, with very curvy letters. No variation in stroke direction, super neat.' She glanced down at the photocopy. 'Of course, I couldn't say anything about the Chinese writing – there isn't a sample to compare it to. So I can't tell you if the same person wrote the upper bit of the letter and the bottom part. But the English section of the letter matches with the sample writing you sent me.'

'Thank you for your help,' said Lexi.

'No problem.'

As they finished the Zoom, Lexi stared down at the two letters, lying side by side on her desk. Her eyes darted from one to the other, reading different sentences.

Then she snatched up a pen and started to underline words and phrases, her heart beating wildly in her chest.

Life has become too difficult for me to bear. I can't see a way to my future or a way to <u>make my dreams come true</u>. I don't have it in me to achieve what everybody wants from me, and I'm finding <u>every day is harder and harder</u>.

My true friends will understand what I've been going through with mum and dad's divorce,, and why I've come to this decision. Their kindness has given me hope in the past, but that <u>hope has run out now</u>. It's time for me to take the final journey, to find my peace and restfulness.

This isn't the end for me. I'm just going to another place. A better place.

The people I love know that I love them. Mum, I'll visit you in your dreams. You won't be lonely. I'll be always by your side.

Olly

Xoxoxoxoxo

Mom, pop,

Believe me when I say I don't want you to be reading this, but there's no other way for me, and I know you'll understand this when you learn of what has happened. The well of <u>hope I had for the future has now run dry</u>.

I've done something wrong, something that can't be made right and it leaves me with only one course of action. I've brought great shame on our family and I can't even look you both in the eye to ask for your forgiveness. Instead, I will go to our ancestors and ask for their forgiveness.

<u>Each day is harder and harder</u>, and I can't see the way forward. You tried to <u>make my dreams come true</u>, but I set fire to your efforts and I hang my head in shame.

Know that I love you always.

Shan

The same phrases, appearing in both letters. Could that simply be a coincidence? She listed them, side by side. Apart from *make my dreams come true,* they weren't absolutely identical. But the other two were incredibly similar.

She called Tom into her office and handed him the two notes with the underlining.

'Tell me I'm being stupid or overly suspicious.'

He studied the photocopies, then said slowly, 'You're not.'

'How likely is it that they would use the same words in that way? Once perhaps. But that's a substantial overlap.'

He nodded. 'Do you think they knew each other?'

'I should have seen it sooner.' Lexi was furious with herself. 'I didn't think to compare the two notes.'

'But why should you have? There was nothing to suggest any link between them. People take their own lives every day.'

'It's my job to spot patterns in people's behaviour – that's the basis of profiling. We need to find out if they knew each other.'

Tom dropped into the chair opposite Lexi's desk and put down the two pieces of paper. 'If they did, what would it show? That they collaborated on their suicide notes? It seems pretty far-fetched.'

'Right – it's hardly a group activity.' Lexi pursed her lips, trying to work out what the similarities could mean.

'How do people write a note like that?' said Tom. 'I can't begin to imagine the process you'd go through.'

'If they didn't collaborate, maybe they used the same source material. Examples of suicide notes on the internet?'

Tom shrugged.

It sounded bizarre, but no more bizarre than the two of them writing the same phrases in isolation.

'Can you make it a priority to find out if Shan Liang had a laptop, and take possession of it if he did.'

'Yes, but...' Tom looked at her askance. 'I thought Maggie wanted us to wrap these up.'

'She did,' said Lexi. 'Don't you see? This changes every-thing.' There was no way she wasn't going to follow where the two notes led. No way in hell. Her instincts had told her some-thing was off, and this had just proved her right. 'We're not backing off.'

TWENTY-THREE

'Put Sam on the phone, could you?'

The traffic was light as Lexi headed out of Canterbury. She was heading towards Minster – she had questions for Paul Arbuthnot, but first she wanted to check something with her nephew.

Amber didn't sound so keen. 'Is this to do with Olivia?'

'I've just got a quick question for him.'

'Listen, Lex, this whole thing has knocked him for six. Please don't force him to dwell on it any further.'

Lexi felt instantly bad, but she had to think of Olivia and the family she left behind, too. 'I wouldn't if it wasn't important. But he might just have a scrap of information that would be helpful.'

'Helpful for what? Nothing can bring her back.'

'It's complicated.' She didn't want to confide her growing hunch. 'Just a quick question, then I promise that'll be it.'

Amber grudgingly agreed and put Sam on the line.

'Hey, Sam, how're you doing?'

'Could be better.' His voice sounded dull and deflated – not her usually cheerful nephew, excited to be speaking with his recently discovered aunt.

'I get it – it's rough when we lose someone we were close to.'

Sam sighed but didn't say anything.

'I've just got a quick question. Do you know if Olivia was ever a member of a group called the Kingsdown Singers?'

'Why d'you need to know that?'

'Just trying to work out if she knew someone who's also a member.'

'She went for an audition for a singing group some time last year, I think. It might have been them – I don't remember.'

'But she didn't get in?'

'They offered her a place, but she didn't want to join. She said the guy who ran the group was a bit creepy.'

'Okay, thanks.' It sounded like it could be Arbuthnot. 'Listen, if you remember anything else she said about it, give me a ring.' She was pleased Amber couldn't hear this request.

'Sure.'

'Back to school properly tomorrow?'

'Yup.'

After checking when she could see him next, she hung up.

It was a link. Tenuous, at best – but now she was going to follow it all the way. If there was a common element in both of their deaths, it would be worth digging into. And if that element was actually a person... It was a horrible thought.

She called the office. 'Ridhi, can you get me a list of all the young people who are currently or who have been members of the Kingsdown Singers?'

Paul Arbuthnot lived in a small, modern bungalow in a quiet cul-de-sac on the edge of Minster, itself a small and quiet village a few miles inland from Ramsgate. As Lexi parked on the road outside, she reflected that the front garden didn't exactly look as if it belonged to someone who was working out his retirement in a garden centre. There were weeds in the scrappy flowerbeds and coming up between the paving stones of the front path.

She rang the bell and waited. She could hear classical music playing inside and wondered if Arbuthnot had heard the bell. It was late now, and no doubt he wouldn't expect someone to be calling at this time of night. Just as she was about to press it again, the door opened a crack and his face appeared in the space.

'Mr Arbuthnot, you remember me? I'm DI Bennett...'

The door slammed shut, making Lexi inadvertently step backwards.

Bloody rude!

But then she heard the rattle of a security chain being drawn back, and the door opened. However, the look on Paul Arbuthnot's face was still hostile.

'What can I do for you?'

'I wonder if I could come in and ask a couple of questions?'

Arbuthnot's eyes went from side to side as he scanned the road. There was no one around. 'I'm sure I can answer them here.'

'As you wish,' said Lexi. It was a little offhand, but she was developing an intense dislike for him. 'Were you aware that a member of your singing group was found dead early this morning?'

'The Chinese boy, Shan Liang? I heard a rumour to that effect.'

'He took his own life.'

Paul Arbuthnot was a tall man and he gazed down his nose at Lexi for a couple of seconds. 'It's terribly sad, but I'm not sure why that would bring you to my door.'

He didn't look very sad.

'How long was he a member of your group?'

'A few months... I seem to remember he joined us last September.'

'You didn't particularly like him, did you?'

'He had a beautiful singing voice and that was what mattered. The Kingsdown Singers isn't a social group. I don't give people a spot in the group because I like them.' He hadn't denied disliking Shan.

'Did you know a girl called Olivia James?'

'No.'

He answered that too fast. 'Are you sure? I understand that she auditioned for you.'

'As do lots of people. If she did, she obviously didn't get in.'

'From what I heard, you offered her a place, but she declined. Do you remember?'

'Possibly... yes. There was a girl who did that.'

'Why do you think she declined to join?'

He let out a frustrated sigh. 'I wouldn't know. Personal issues, maybe. Not enough time. Those are the usual. But I really don't remember her.'

'So it's happened more than once?'

'What exactly are these questions driving at?'

'Did you bully Shan Liang?'

'No.'

'Did you accuse him of stealing something from a resident at Sunny Oaks?'

'No.'

'And humiliate him in front of the rest of the group at the Leas Cliff Hall?'

'I don't care for your tone or your implications, Inspector. What happened with Sunny Oaks was a misunderstanding, and I managed to persuade them not to involve the police. I did everything I could to prevent Shan from getting a criminal record.'

'What made you think that Shan was the culprit? Did you find the stolen medal in his possession?'

'No. It wasn't like that. It turned out the medal was misplaced, not stolen – but for a short while the manager at Sunny Oaks believed a member of the group had taken it. Like I said, I requested that they didn't go to the police – but it looks as if they told you about it. Anyway, it's water under the bridge now.'

The visual image that this brought to Lexi's mind blended with the memory of Shan hanging under the balcony of the Leas Cliff Hall – and it wasn't a good combination.

'I have nothing else to say.' Paul Arbuthnot started to close the door.

'Thank you, Mr Arbuthnot. I'll let you know if I need to talk to you further.'

The door was slammed in her face before she'd finished speaking.

TWENTY-FOUR

It was well past knocking off time and Kevin Stewart was now in custody for the stabbing at the Swan, but Ridhi still needed to check out the Kingsdown Singers before she called it a day. She typed the group's name into the search bar and the relevant page popped up immediately, thanks to her earlier visit. The header showed a bunch of youngsters standing around a grand piano, with song sheets in their hands, mouths open. She squinted at the pianist – it looked like it was Shan Liang – while at the other end of the instrument an older man, a head taller than any of them, had a hand in the air conducting. There was a huge Christmas tree in the background, so she guessed they'd probably been singing carols.

The page was marked as public, so anyone could see what was posted and Paul Arbuthnot was listed as an administrator, along with someone called Maddie Scott. The group had 185 followers. Ridhi scanned through them – they included singers she could see in the picture, but plenty of others. Friends, relatives and audience members, she supposed. The About section described them as a group of enthusiastic singers who volunteered to perform at old people's homes, hospices, church gatherings, community concerts and schools. When they could, they raised money for a local music charity. There was also an events calendar that listed when and where the group would next be singing as well as a rehearsal rota.

It all seemed completely wholesome, but the boss suspected there might be some connection to the reason Shan had taken his own life. She'd asked Ridhi to dig a bit deeper into the dynamics of the group and see if anything stood out. Ridhi couldn't help but feel she was somehow being tested, so if there was anything of interest, she was determined to find it.

There didn't seem to be a list of the members anywhere on the page, so she typed a quick message to the admins, asking one of them to give her a call as soon as possible.

Within five minutes, just as Ridhi returned to her desk with another cup of coffee which was sure to disappoint, her mobile rang.

'DC Kulkarni speaking.'

'Hi, this is Maddie Scott. You sent a message asking one of the admins to call.' Her voice sounded young and a little nervous.

'From the Kingsdown Singers?'

'Yes...' The woman paused. 'I should tell you straight off that I've actually left the group, so I don't know if I'll be able to help you.'

'But you're still getting messages?'

'Paul doesn't really know how to run the page and he never removed me as an admin, so I keep an eye on things – make sure the rehearsal schedule goes up in the right place and so on.'

'Then you might be able to help me.'

'Is this something to do with Shan?' Ridhi could tell by the sombre tone of Maddie's voice that she knew about his death.

'Not exactly,' said Ridhi. 'I suppose you've heard what happened?'

'Yes – Kieran Williams, one of the group, messaged me.'

'What did he tell you?'

'Just that Shan was dead, that he'd killed himself at Leas Cliff.' Her voice cracked with emotion.

It appeared the news was spreading fast, including some of the details – but once a story was out, there was no way of controlling how it spread.

'I wonder if you have a list of all the members of the group – current and maybe going back a bit as well?'

'I can easily tell you the current members,' said Maddie. 'And I'll be able to remember some of the more recent ones who've left.'

'Can you jot them down in an email?' said Ridhi. She gave Maddie her email address. And then, as an afterthought, she said, 'Don't tell Paul Arbuthnot, please.'

'I barely speak to him,' said Maddie, with disdain in her tone. 'I just check up on the Facebook page every now and again. More for the sake of my friends who're still in the group than for Paul.'

'Do you mind my asking why you left?' said Ridhi, her curiosity piqued.

'I don't mind at all. Paul Arbuthnot is a bully – anyone who doesn't live up to his expectations for the group, he singles out. To be honest, I'd seen enough of it.'

'He picked on you?'

'Not me. But he bullied lots of others. People who weren't as lippy as me – Shan... and a black girl called Suzanne. She left. A couple of young gay guys joined the group, about eighteen months ago this was, and he was vile to them too. Kept saying their voices weren't up to scratch.'

'But if he thought that, why did he let them join the group in the first place?'

'He constantly invited new people to join, but then he'd needle them until they left. He's just not a very nice guy.'

'So there's a significant turnover of singers?'

'Yes, which is why he pretty much has to let anyone in. He's running out of people who can sing.'

It gave Ridhi plenty of food for thought, but was it what the boss was looking for? 'Well, if you could email that list of people, it might be useful.'

'Sure.'

Ridhi finished the call and sighed. There was half a cup of cold coffee on her desk, and no one else left in the incident room. As she cleared the drink away, she thought about what Maddie Scott had told her. Paul Arbuthnot had accused Shan of stealing, until it was later cleared up, and had apparently picked on him as well. Would that have been enough to push Shan over the edge?

Just as she was leaving, Colin came into the room carrying two laptops.

'You're working surprisingly late, Colin.' She raised her eyebrows at him.

'Get lost, Kulkarni – I put in more hours than you, any day.'

Ridhi stifled a snort and Colin grinned at her. 'I'm always thinking about my cases – when I'm in the gym, down the pub, even in bed. It's all work.'

'Yeah, right. Anyway, thanks for telling Lexi that I spotted the knife on the CCTV.'

'No biggy – sure you'll return the favour some time.' Ah, now she got it. There was a price attached to Colin's seemingly selfless action, and at some point she'd have to pay up. Or at least that was what he thought.

'What have you got there?' She pointed at the laptops, which he was now logging into evidence.

'Olivia James and Shan Liang's laptops. I'll just do the paperwork, then send them over to Greg.' Greg Chambers was their contact in the tech department. 'The boss wants to know if they knew each other or ever had some kind of contact online.'

'I suppose it makes sense,' said Ridhi. 'Might explain what the boss said, about their notes being really similar.'

'Then, talking of the pub, fancy a drink?'

'Why not?' Ridhi knew there were plenty of reasons why not, given Colin's fast and loose reputation, but it had been a long day and a quick G&T wouldn't go amiss. Colin Flynn wasn't anything she couldn't handle. 'Meet you in the lobby in five.'

TWENTY-FIVE

The pub was busy for a Tuesday evening. It had surprised Lexi that when she called Ed Harlow to see if he could spare a minute or two to brainstorm, he'd suggested meeting for a drink. But despite being tired, she'd agreed – Ed was one of the country's top forensic psychologists, and she always had time to hear his views.

Professionally, they had a lot in common. They'd both spent time training and working with the FBI's Investigative Support Unit in Virginia – the unit responsible for evolving the art of behavioural analysis in relation to tracking serial sex offenders and murderers – though they hadn't been there at the same time. It was in fact Lexi's old boss, Harry Garcia, who had put them in touch with each other when Lexi had first arrived back in Canterbury. Over a couple of cases, they'd forged a good working relationship, despite having initially rubbed each other up the wrong way. Lexi was still a little wary of Ed. Because of what had happened to her sister, Rose, she sometimes felt that he viewed her as another case to be studied. And, at times, he could be moody, but his wife, Charlie, was seriously ill with breast cancer, so Lexi understood why he could be tired and prickly.

'Hey,' she said, as she sidled up to where he stood waiting at the bar.

'Lexi, good to see you.' He gave her a swift embrace, before turning back to the bar to make sure he didn't lose his spot in the queue. 'What'll you have?'

'A glass of red, whatever they've got.'

Once the drinks were in, they elbowed their way through the crowd and found a tiny, secluded table in a cramped corner.

'I was surprised you agreed to come out in the evening,' she said, glancing at her watch.

'You're right,' he said. 'I would normally keep to work hours, but Charlie's staying with her sister for a few days.'

'How is she?' said Lexi. Ed's wife, Charlie, was receiving a second round of treatment as her cancer had proved unresponsive to the first attempt.

Ed sighed, and not for the first time Lexi noticed how exhausted he was looking. There were dark rings under his eyes, and the few wrinkles he already had seemed to be carved deeper than when she had last seen him just a few weeks ago. 'She's not great, which is why she's staying at Mel's – it's nearer to the hospital and she's in the middle of a round of chemo.'

'I'm so sorry. Must be tough.'

'Tough on her – the side effects are horrendous. But they think it could make all the difference, so she's determined to go through with it.' He shook his head. 'She's so brave. She didn't deserve for this to happen.'

'No one does,' said Lexi. 'It's like Russian roulette.'

Ed took a long draught of his beer. 'So what are you working on that needs unpicking?'

Lexi rested both hands on the base of the wine glass on the table in front of her and looked Ed square in the eye. 'Two suicides with nothing in common. Girl, thirteen, boy, fifteen.

One in Canterbury yesterday, one in Folkestone early this morning. Different methods.'

'Different methods are to be expected. The data shows that men are one-and-a-half times more likely than women to choose hanging as the way of killing themselves, while women favour poison or overdose, or jumping from high places.'

'I get it – and if the girl, Olivia, didn't have access to pills, jumping off the Westgate might seem the most logical means. Not that it's something you can really apply logic to.'

'Where are you going with this? Did they know each other?'

Lexi shook her head. 'No, there's nothing to suggest that.'

'But?' prompted Ed.

'But they both left notes behind and when you compare them...' She pulled folded copies of the two suicide notes from her jacket pocket and put them down on the table in front of Ed. These weren't the versions that she'd underlined. She wanted Ed to look at them clean to see if he spotted what she'd seen.

Ed's eyes shifted from one piece of paper to the other. 'You've verified that they were written by the individuals that died?'

'Yes.'

'It's the phraseology, isn't it?'

Lexi nodded. 'It seems like a weird coincidence that they would use so many similar phrases.'

'Are you looking for a crime?'

'The boy, Shan Liang, was bullied by an older man in a singing group he was in. It might have contributed to how he was feeling.'

'But not the girl?'

'We think Olivia James auditioned for the same group – the man who bullied Shan runs it, and would have auditioned her. According to one of her friends, she took a dislike to him so she didn't join when offered a place.'

Ed glanced back down at the notes. 'If they didn't know each other or collude on these, they could have sourced the language from the same place. Have you considered that?'

'Both their phones are missing...'

'A bit odd, isn't it?'

'Very. Most teens are glued to their phones – you'd have to prise it out of their cold, dead hands.'

'Maybe someone did.'

'We can't exclude that possibility. Anyway, I've requested their laptops for analysis. That way we can check if they knew each other via social media and whether they accessed any pro-suicide sites.'

'Those sites are abominations, but they get shut down pretty quickly whenever they pop up.'

'I suspect they find a home on the dark web, don't you?' It wasn't really her area of expertise, but she knew there was a whole lawless flip side to the internet where criminals and conmen did their business.

'And the people who want to visit them tend to find them.' He finished off his beer.

Lexi was only halfway through her wine, but she went to the bar to get him another.

'Thanks,' he said, as she put it down in front of him. 'Tell me how they did it.'

'Olivia jumped from the top of the Westgate.'

Ed grimaced.

'And Shan hanged himself under the overhanging balcony of the Leas Cliff Hall.'

'That's more usual for a boy.' He paused. 'You think there's something not right, don't you?'

Lexi nodded. 'I've got a hunch. The way Shan hanged himself, he needed to climb up on something to reach the beam he tied the rope around. He arrived at the site on his bicycle, and he might have been able to use that. But I don't really see how he would have balanced on it without someone holding it, and if he had used it, it would have still been lying on the ground underneath him when he was found.'

'And it wasn't?'

'No – we found it propped up, several metres away.'

'So someone moved it after he was dead. Someone who helped him or someone who came upon the scene later?'

'That last one wouldn't make sense. I could understand if someone had stolen the bike from under the body, repugnant though it would be. But who would simply move it?'

'Which leads you to think his suicide was assisted.' Ed paused for a moment to drink his beer. 'And that tenuous link between them via the singing group? Does it tell you anything?'

'It's probably too tenuous. But it's a crime to encourage someone to commit suicide and it's a crime to help them and, for my own peace of mind, I need to rule out that either of those things happened. Or find the person responsible.'

'Then you're going to have to keep digging, I think,' said Ed. 'There's a weird motivation involved when one person helps another to take their own life – apart from when someone's terminally ill. But helping teenagers to kill themselves – you're going to have to consider the motivation for that really carefully.'

'Suicide by proxy? Playing out their own death wish, without having to die? Or trying to resolve a trauma from their past by projecting it onto others?'

'Whatever's driving them, it's going to be complicated – but I'm pretty sure you're onto something.'

In other words, she wasn't going mad. She knew there was something about the two cases that didn't add up. She took a last sip of her wine.

'Another?' said Ed.

'No, but thank you. I have to drive.'

Ed stayed seated and didn't go for another round. But he

didn't seem that keen to get home either. 'Tell me, how are you finding it back in Blighty after four years in the States?'

Lexi considered the question. 'Don't get me wrong – I loved my time in America, but it's great to be back. I hadn't realised quite how much I'd missed my sister, and her kids are amazing.'

'But the work was more exciting across the pond. And you must miss working with the great Harry Garcia?'

After what he did to me at Diamond River?

But she kept her thoughts to herself and nodded. 'I learned so much over there.'

Ed's expression perked up. 'Listen, we still haven't sat down to talk about what happened at Diamond River. You promised to tell me about it.'

She hadn't promised anything of the sort. She hardly had her thoughts in order about her final case in America, and she certainly wasn't ready to let Ed Harlow pick over the bones of it. He'd already taken far too much professional interest in her past. She liked him, but that didn't mean she was willing to subject her life to his academic scrutiny.

Luckily, she was saved by the bell. She picked up her phone, glancing at the screen to see that it was Greg Chambers.

'Hey, Greg, what can I do for you? Did Colin get those two laptops to you?'

'An hour ago.'

'And?'

'It's pretty safe to say that if your two kids knew each other, it wasn't online. They're not friends on any of the socials, not in each other's contact lists... I didn't even find a single overlap in their contact lists so they're not friends-of-friends, or anything like that.'

'Thanks so much.' Lexi tried to keep the disappointment out of her voice.

'But I've just found a couple of interesting things.'

'Yes?'

'Firstly, both of them had Tor installed.'

'Tor?'

'It's short for The Onion Router. It's a browser that gives you access to the dark web. You know what—'

'Yes, I know what that is. Can you find out what they were looking at?'

'Apart from porn?' said Greg, with a dry laugh. 'That's the most likely thing for Shan, at his age. But without his password, I won't be able to get into his accounts. However, it's a different story on Olivia's laptop – she left her Tor browser open, so we can see what she was up to.'

'Can you meet me at my office and show me what you've got?'

'Sure.'

Lexi turned back to Ed. 'Shan Liang and Olivia James were going on the dark web.'

His eyebrows went up. 'That opens a whole new can of worms.'

'Exactly what I was thinking.'

TWENTY-SIX

Greg was already waiting in her office when Lexi arrived back at the station.

'Thanks for staying on late,' she said.

'I need the overtime,' he said with a grin. 'Second baby incoming.'

She smiled back at him. 'Then I'll try to keep you here as long as I can.'

Greg opened one of two laptops he'd placed on her desk. 'This was Shan's.' He tapped a few keys to wake it up. 'We were able to bypass his password to get in, and then I found his Tor browser. But I can't access it, as he logged out.'

The screen was showing the Tor login page – intense purple, with drawings of onion halves along the bottom of the screen. At the centre, *Explore. Privately.*, with a search bar underneath it.

'Tell me how it works,' said Lexi.

'If you search for something, Tor will encrypt the data and route you through its private network. This means the sites you visit won't be able to track you, and when you finish it deletes all the cookies and browsing history.'

'So how will you be able to tell what he's been accessing?'

'We use something called NIT malware to retrieve the information, but it will take time.'

This was getting technical enough for Lexi. 'What about Olivia?'

Greg pushed Shan's laptop to one side and pulled the other laptop towards him. 'She's been using it too, and she left it open. She didn't log out.'

'Can you use your malware now to see what sites she's been visiting?'

'I can.'

Lexi went to fetch coffee, leaving Greg to get on with it. When she came back, he showed her a list of sites on the screen. It wasn't long, but the URLs didn't really give Lexi any idea of what she was looking at. Greg took a mouthful of coffee and flicked from screen to screen, too fast for Lexi to make head or tail of what he was doing.

Until he stopped.

'Here,' he said. 'I think this is what you're looking for.'

Lexi squinted at the screen. The type was so small she had to move in closer. The URL was just a random stream of letters and numbers. There was no page heading, just a stream of messages between chatroom users that slipped silently down the screen.

Not real names.

Doobie. Trollster. Yoshi. Nyx.

There was a small logo at the top of the page. An emoji-sized noose and the words *Club Edicius*.

She read some of the chat as it dropped down the page.

Trollster: i still feel amazed he did it

Yoshi: props to the guy. i didn't think he had it in him

Nyx: no, i could tell he was serious, right from the start. he just needed a bit of help to inch his way over the edge

Doobie: OMG – you guys seem so calm about popspook's death

Nyx: because we know it was what he wanted

Masher: poor guy

Doobie: how did he do it

Doobie: it's okay to ask that, yeah?

Yoshi: he said he was gonna use the big red rope

Trollster: what a dude

Siren: what's the big red rope

Nyx: it's our sign, to each other, when we take the big exit. so we know who someone is in RL when they go. btw, guys – meet our new girl, siren

Masher: hi, siren

Trollster: hey, siren, how's it hanging? (pardon the pun!)

Yoshi: god, man, that was lame

Nyx: what are you thinking, doobie? are you nearly ready

Lexi's blood ran cold. 'This is live, right?'
'Yes,' said Greg. 'That's the chatroom in real time.'

'And Olivia was a member of this group?'

'I can't say,' said Greg. 'If she'd been using a normal browser, we would have been able to see how often she accessed the page. She left it open, so we can be certain she came here once at least, but that's all.'

'Is there any way of finding out who these people are?'

'No. That's the point of the dark web. It protects their anonymity. I can't even tell you where in the world they are. They could literally be anywhere, so even if you think they've committed a crime, chances are they won't be in your jurisdiction.'

'And you can't tell me if Shan accessed this site?'

The person called PopSpook in the chatroom had apparently hanged himself that morning using a red rope. It had to be Shan, didn't it?

Greg shook his head. 'No – Shan closed his dark web browser and each time you do that, it deletes all trace of where you've been.'

Lexi looked at the screen again and rubbed her eyes. They were gritty. She was tired. But here was a bunch of kids discussing the best methods of killing themselves, and she had no way of finding out where they were, no way of intervening in what one or more of them might be about to do, no way of saving a life.

Club Edicius. The penny dropped – Edicius was suicide spelled backwards.

'We can shut this club down, right?'

'Sure. I can pass on the information we have to the cyber-crimes unit and they'll be able to close it. But there's nothing to stop it popping up at another IP address in some other dark corner.'

Lexi thought for a moment. 'What if we keep Olivia's browser open? Will that give us ongoing access to it?'

'It should do, at least in its current incarnation.'

But what was the good of that? Watching the conversation unspool with no way of finding the participants or preventing another death would be slow torture.

'There's nothing more we can do, Greg?'

'I can't see it at the moment, boss. Let me sleep on it, and chat with some of the guys in the cyber team tomorrow.'

'Thanks.' Lexi checked her watch. It was gone ten. 'Get along home now. We'll catch up in the morning.'

Once Greg had gone, Lexi turned back to the screen.

It appeared to be just Nyx, Siren, Masher and Doobie now. Nyx was encouraging Doobie to share whatever problems were distressing him. Or her? Lexi didn't even know if Doobie was a girl or a boy.

Doobie: i hate my life. I don't want to go on

Siren: i know how you feel

Nyx: stay strong, doobie. you're ready for this decision

Doobie: it's not fair

Nyx: listen, you've got to be the author of your own story. and that means you get to say when it ends

Nyx: the group is here for you. we're rooting for you

Doobie: that at least feels good

Nyx: and we can help you – whatever you decide

Lexi felt a tide of anger surging through her. Whoever this Nyx was, he or she was enticing someone into making a decision that could result in suicide. Encouraging or assisting the suicide or attempted suicide of another person was a crime. Nyx was breaking the law, and in a way that could result in another dead teenager. But why? What could this person get out of pushing a vulnerable young teenager to the brink? Yes, it was someone seriously disturbed, but she needed to understand the motivation. Something had caused Nyx to behave in this abhorrent way. Maybe if they could work out what it was, it might lead them to Nyx's identity.

Whatever Greg said about not being able to tell where the players in this drama were, Lexi had a feeling they were somewhere close to home. If Olivia and Shan had both been in Club Edicius, perhaps there was some basis for assuming that the other members of the club were somewhere in Kent, too. Or at least in the UK. She scanned the screen. UK spellings, UK vernacular. It didn't seem likely these were American kids.

But what the hell could she do?

Doobie: thanks, nyx. you're giving me the courage to make the right decision

'No!' Lexi yelled at the screen. 'Don't do it. For God's sake, Doobie...'

But it couldn't do any good. Doobie wouldn't be able to hear her. All Doobie was hearing was Nyx, glamorising the idea that taking his or her own life would be the solution to all his or her problems.

She stared at the screen, waiting to see what Nyx would come back with. At the top of the page, the cursor flashed in the dialogue box.

'Yes.' Of course she could talk to Doobie. It would just look like a message from Olivia.

Olivia James, back from the dead. With a message to Doobie that it wasn't worth it.

She knew she shouldn't. She knew she'd be blowing her

cover. But Doobie's life literally hung in the balance. And she wasn't sure that the group members even knew Olivia was dead, so maybe she could get away with it...

She began to type.

TWENTY-SEVEN

At first, it looked like Doobie was going to be a tough nut to crack, but then he crumbled. He fell under my spell, and I can already see how he'll look on the end of a length of red rope.

Nyx: i have a feeling you'll both be making your decisions sometime soon

Doobie: so do i

Masher: i don't know yet

Doobie: i'm almost ready to do it

Lolly: no, doobie, you mustn't. it's a decision you can never reverse

Lolly: it's not worth it

Lolly: there's always something to live for

Masher: WTF? who are you?

Lolly? Olivia James has checked out. She's dead. So who the hell is this?

Damn!

Olivia must have left the browser open on her computer. What a bloody idiot. The instructions have always been clear. Log out of the chatroom. Log out of your browser. Log off your computer, and make sure it's password protected.

But someone's found a way in, using Olivia's login.

I slam my fist on the desk, and the laptop jumps.

What shall I do?

Talk to the new Lolly? Recruit whoever it is into the group, and then send them on their way?

But those messages from the new Lolly are unequivocal. Anti-suicide. Pro-life. They're probably not going to succumb to my charms in a hurry, and I don't want them poisoning the others. And what if it's an adult, someone who knows their way around the dark web? Security has to be my priority.

First things first. I eject Lolly from the group with a couple of keystrokes, then take the necessary steps to protect its integrity. I set up a new URL and send a coded message to trusted members. It takes me about an hour to get it all sorted, time which could have been better spent doing something else.

This might be a huge setback – a stranger breaking into the group – but I'll take it as a timely reminder to be ever vigilant. There's someone out there sniffing around. I'll need to look into who's taking an interest. All I'm trying to do is help these kids, and we don't need any interference. But at least this fake Lolly, whoever they are, won't be finding their way back in anytime soon.

TWENTY-EIGHT

The screen went black.

'What?' Lexi jabbed at the keyboard – the return key, the space bar, the escape key – but nothing happened. 'No... No, no, no.'

What the hell had she expected? She'd barged into the conversation, under the guise of someone who was dead, and it had been a mistake. She'd been shut out. That meant they knew Lolly was dead, so they knew who Olivia was in real life. She'd learned something, at least. But now they wouldn't have a chance of finding out who Doobie was. They wouldn't be able to intervene. If Lexi ever saw him or her at all, it would probably be with a red noose around their neck – and the trade-off definitely wasn't worth it.

She slammed the laptop shut, swearing loudly, and reopened it. It showed the Tor home page. She'd been ejected from Club Edicius and, if what Greg had told her was true, they would have no way of getting back to it. And somewhere in a solitary corner of the dark web, a person called Nyx was leading a teenager called Doobie inexorably closer to death.

In her book, that was as good as murder.

But she would be just as culpable. She'd thrown away whatever slim chance she might have had of saving his life.

If Doobie turned up dead somewhere, it would be her fault.

'You stupid bloody woman,' she hissed at herself.

It was too late to ring Greg now. It was too late to ring Ed. It was too late to ring Maggie.

All she could do was pray that it wasn't going to be too late to save Doobie.

No, that's not good enough.

She dialled Greg's number and it went to voicemail.

Damn! Damn! Damn!

But she shouldn't be surprised.

He picked up when she dialled for a second time.

'Yeah?' His tone wasn't friendly, but it didn't sound as if he'd been asleep. In fact, he must only just have reached home.

'Greg, I'm sorry, I really am – the chatroom shut down and I don't know what to do. We need to get back in.'

'Shut down? How exactly?'

'The screen just went black. It was my own fault – I typed a message.'

'You what?' he exploded.

Lexi had to pull the phone away from her ear sharply.

Then a moment's silence.

'I'm sorry. I realise it was a stupid thing to do.'

Greg sighed. Lexi got the feeling he might have wanted to say more, but she was a superior rank to him, so he had to keep it in check.

'This Nyx character was goading someone else to take their own life. I wanted to stop them. You've got to get us back in, Greg.'

'I'll come to your office first thing in the morning and see what I can do. But I don't hold out much hope. He'll have changed the IP address and moved on.'

It was all she could expect. And by then Dobbie might be dead.

TWENTY-NINE

WEDNESDAY

Someone was banging on Lexi's front door. Even though she closed her eyes tight and hoicked the duvet up over her head, they wouldn't go away. A shower of pebbles on the glass of her bedroom window infuriated her enough to throw back the covers and scrabble out of bed. She stared down into her front garden. Tom was staring back up at her.

How did he manage to look so wide awake and chipper at this hour in the morning?

'You turned your phone off?' he said accusingly when she opened the front door twenty seconds later.

'I turned off notifications,' she said. 'Even I have to get some sleep.' She pulled her dressing gown more tightly round her body, and ushered him inside. 'What is it?'

'Another teenage boy has died by suicide. I thought you'd want to check it out.'

It wasn't something they'd be routinely called to, but Tom was right. It came like a kick in the gut, and she wondered if it was the boy who had called himself Doobie in the chatroom. How could it be anybody else? She pressed her palms against her eyes. This was her fault. Another kid was dead. She'd known it was going to happen and she'd let him down.

'You okay?'

'No, I'm bloody not. We should have been able to stop this.'

Tom blinked at her, uncomprehending. 'You're not super-woman, you know.'

Too damn right. He didn't know about her mess up in the chatroom. She'd have to fill him in, but now she needed to get into work mode and get going. She was determined not to let Nyx get to anybody else.

'Make an espresso,' she said as she sprinted back up the stairs to get dressed. 'In fact, make it a double.'

She could hear Tom clattering in the kitchen as she took a ten-second cold blast under the shower, then quickly pulled on whatever clothes were to hand. Her hair was a mess, but she could fix that in the car.

'You drive,' she said, as Tom handed her a small cup of thick, black liquid at the bottom of the stairs. She threw it back with a grimace and put the cup down on the hall table, following Tom out to his Jeep.

She looked at her watch – it was only just nudging seven a.m. 'Tell me what we have,' she said as Tom drove slowly through the village, obeying the twenty-mile-an-hour speed limit.

'A boy found hanged in the woods in the grounds of Griffin Elms.'

'That's a school, isn't it?' The cold shower and the caffeine jolt were starting to kick in.

'Posh boarding school. Just boys, about five hundred pupils.'

'And the victim was a student there?'

'Yes. He was discovered by one of the housemasters on an early dog walk. They've given us his name – Neil McGowan. He hadn't been flagged as missing, so he must have sneaked out in the night.'

After she'd been shut out of the chatroom. That would have been between eleven and twelve. Nyx must have convinced him to go ahead with it in the small hours.

Damn! Damn! Damn!

'Did he hang himself with a red rope?'

'I have no idea. Why?'

Lexi told Tom about how she and Greg had discovered Club Edicius the previous evening, and how the mysterious Nyx had clearly been grooming the kid called Doobie for suicide. And about how she'd acted on impulse and been thrown out of the chatroom.

'Encouraging suicide is a crime – up to fourteen years,' she said. 'But if we find that Neil McGowan and Doobie were one and the same kid, in my view Nyx as good as murdered him. He's got to be stopped before another person dies.' She remembered Siren joining the group – was she next in his sights?

'Yeah, but we'll have to find him first,' said Tom, turning off the main road into a small lane. 'I think the body's in the woods just down here from the information dispatch gave me.'

Lexi could see a blue light flashing through the trees ahead, meaning that the first responders were already here. As soon as Tom pulled up, she was out of the car.

She flashed her ID at two uniformed constables that were leaning on the bonnet of their police car. 'I want this treated as a crime scene,' she snapped at them. She looked round. 'Where is he?'

One of the PCs pointed. There was a small, wooded hillock to one side of the road, overgrown with a tangle of hawthorn and yew, a narrow path winding around one side. At the top, Lexi could see crumbling flintstone walls.

'There's an old keep up there – he's just on the other side of it.'

'Right, get the whole area cordoned off, including all of the path, and the road here, as well as any other access points to the site.' It struck her that if the boy had come from the school, he could have walked through the woods without coming anywhere near the road. But if anyone had come to assist him, they might well have driven up the lane she and Tom had just used. She pointed up the road in the other direction. 'Where does that go? Is it a dead end, or does it come out somewhere?'

One of the PCs must have been local, because he said, 'It brings you out on Baker Lane, a T-junction – back to the village or out to Boyton.' His colleague scurried round to the boot of their car to get the crime scene tape for the cordons.

Of course, out in a backwater like this, there would be no ANPR cameras to pick up the number plates of passing vehicles.

She turned to Tom. 'Come on, we'd better take a look.'

Lexi felt sick as she trudged up the sloping gravel path. Attending a sudden death was an integral part of the job – she'd viewed scores of bodies – but that didn't make it any easier. This one felt particularly close to the bone. Was it the boy from the chatroom she'd tried to save? If it was, she'd failed. She'd let down him, his family, his friends...

She felt Tom's hand on her shoulder. 'You can't think like that, you know,' he said.

'Like what?'

'I can see it on your face. You're blaming yourself.'

'Of course I am. I might have had a chance to prevent this.'

As they reached the top of the hillock, they came round the corner of the keep. The path petered out – and they were looking at the three-sided ruins of a small rectangular building on the grassy dome of the hill. There was an archway in one of the three standing sides and Neil McGowan was hanging from the centre of it.

On a red rope.

Realising her worst fears had been right, Lexi stumbled and had to put a hand out to the nearest wall to steady herself.

Sharp flint dug into her palm – the mortar had long since eroded away, leaving a rough and jagged surface. Regaining her balance, she glanced down at her hand. Blood. The same colour as the rope.

She let out an involuntary gasp.

'Can we at least get him down now?' It was a man's voice, angry and exasperated. Its owner appeared, framed in a lopsided window in the wall opposite where they stood. Lexi couldn't judge his height because she couldn't see the ground he was standing on, but she got the impression from his top half that he was a big man. A rugby type, and indeed he was wearing a rugby shirt underneath a quilted puffa. He had a beard, shot through with grey, and an almost white mane of hair.

'Who are you?' she said.

'I might ask you the same thing, but I assume you're from the police?'

'DI Bennett and DS Olsen.'

'I'm Christopher Appleby. Housemaster here. I came across Neil when I was out with Flanders, my dog.'

Lexi looked around, but there was no sign of a dog. She supposed he'd had time to take it away.

'I'm sorry – we can't bring him down until the forensic pathologist has arrived and seen him in situ. It will help him determine the exact cause of death.'

'It's bloody obvious, isn't it?'

'We have to be exact about these things,' said Tom. Lexi could hear annoyance in his voice.

Time to calm things down. 'Mr Appleby, you're sure of the boy's identity?'

There was a moment's pause as Appleby walked round from the far side of the keep to where Tom and Lexi were standing. He looked up at the hanging body, and despite being a huge brute of a man, Lexi saw that he was blinking back tears. 'Yes. It's Neil McGowan. I've known him for three years – I'm his housemaster at Griffin Elms.' He wiped a hand across his face, to stem the flow or perhaps wanting to hide the fact he was crying. 'Neil was a good kid.'

'How old was he?'

'Seventeen.'

Lexi looked up at him. Though ugly in death, she could see the features of a handsome boy with spiky, sandy hair and a sprinkling of freckles across a square face. He was wearing a tracksuit with the school logo on its chest, and trainers, one of which lay on the ground beneath him. He must have kicked it off in his last moments – a realisation that cut Lexi to the core.

'Looks like the rope is the same as the one Shan had,' said Tom.

Lexi let her eyes travel up it, from the knot at the back of Neil McGowan's neck to where it was looped and tied over the crumbling stone structure of the arch. She didn't know the exact name of the knot he'd used to secure it, but it was identical to the one Shan had used. To one side of the archway the wall was crumbling away at an angle, almost like steps. It would have been easy for him to climb high enough to secure the rope so, unlike Shan, he probably wouldn't have needed help. But that didn't mean to say he didn't have any.

The sound of a vehicle drawing up on the road below signalled the arrival of Emily Jordan and her team of CSIs in their van. Mort followed immediately behind them.

Lexi turned to Chris Appleby. 'I wonder if you could go and wait for us back at the school. We need to clear the scene.'

'Of course,' the housemaster answered, taking a last look at the dead boy.

'I or one of my colleagues will come and take a statement from you in a little while.'

As Appleby disappeared through the woods, Lexi's phone buzzed in her pocket. She pulled it out and checked the screen.

'Yes, Maggie?'

There was a tight intake of breath at the other end of the line. 'Greg Chambers just called me.'

Shit!

'I know, I messed up. We've lost access to the site on the dark web and it was my fault.'

'I'm not questioning your motives, Lexi, but you can't afford to act on impulse. Not on something as serious as this.'

'I'm sorry. I'll apologise to Greg as soon as I'm back in the office.'

'Where are you now?'

'Another death by hanging.' She didn't add, *and it's probably my fault.* She didn't need to. Maggie's heartfelt sigh was all the remonstrance required. She dropped her phone back into her pocket, feeling worse than ever.

Mort and Emily appeared coming up the path, so she pulled herself together quickly. The process was the same as before – examine the ground directly beneath the body, put down footplates, photograph the body, the ground and everything in the surrounding area, a fingertip search of the wider crime scene. Tom and Emily helped Mort to cut the body down, and the boy was laid out on a black rubber sheet on the ground. Mort examined him more closely, while Lexi and Tom hovered at his side.

'Yes, he died of hanging,' said Mort before Lexi had even asked him. 'Body temp suggests it's been a few hours. Rigor setting in.'

No surprises, then.

But whatever Mort discovered about Neil McGowan's death, Lexi would hold Nyx responsible. And, as far as Lexi was concerned, that put the two of them on a collision course.

THIRTY

.

Lexi went over to talk to Emily. 'I've reason to believe that someone is using the dark web to push these kids towards taking their own lives.'

Emily's eyes widened. 'Jesus, what sick bastard would do that?'

'That's what I mean to find out,' said Lexi through gritted teeth. 'I want you to treat all the sites where teenagers have died by suicide as major crime scenes. This person has already committed a felony by encouraging them, but I need to find out if he's actually assisting. He goads them into action in a chatroom. But I'm wondering whether he's also involved with them in real life.'

'Right, I'll brief the team to look for any signs of third-party involvement.'

'I also think that the rope might be from the same source as the rope that Shan Liang used.' She explained what she'd seen in the chatroom about the 'big, red rope' being a signal to other members of Club Edicius.

'We'll compare the fibres from the two ropes and track down where they've come from.'

'That would be useful. Especially in case someone's giving the rope to them, rather than the boys buying it themselves.'

'Leave it with me and I'll come back to you as quickly as possible.'

Lexi turned back to Mort. 'Have you checked his pockets?' The chances were that Neil McGowan would have left a note, and that some of the phrases would match those used in the notes written by Shan and Olivia.

'I've checked. Nothing in them except a locker key.' He held up an evidence bag in which Lexi could see a small silver key. Presumably for his classroom or changing room locker, and the school would hold a master key. Whoever went to interview Chris Appleby could check up on whether McGowan had a locker, and also search his bedroom for a note.

'No mobile?'

'No. Just the key.'

Olivia didn't have a mobile on her when she was found. Neither did Shan. It could no longer be a coincidence. So who had the missing phones? She had to assume it was Nyx.

She signalled to Tom that they should go back to the car. The fewer people trampling the site the better – the CSIs knew what they were looking for now and could get on with the job. But as she started down the uneven path on the side of the hillock, she saw a skid mark in the mud that bordered its lower edge. Telltale grooves suggested that someone wearing shoes with a heavy tread had veered a little off the gravel and slipped in the mud.

'Was that you on the way up?' she said to Tom, glancing down at his feet.

But he was wearing flat-soled lace-ups that wouldn't have left a mark like that.

He shook his head. 'Probably one of the early responders or the CSIs,' he said.

'Possibly,' said Lexi. 'But we need to be sure.' She turned to face back up the hill and called out to Emily.

Emily jogged down to where they were standing and Lexi pointed out what she'd seen.

'That looks pretty fresh,' said Emily. 'It was dry yesterday, but it rained in the night, and this mud is wet.'

'In other words, it could have been made within the time frame that Neil McGowan died?'

'Yes, it could, but it could also have been made by one of us.' She beckoned one of her team. 'Can you compile a list of anyone who's been up here since the body was discovered and get details of the shoes they were wearing for elimination purposes. And maybe take a cast of this in case we need to match it up to a shoe.'

'Thanks,' said Lexi. She had a thought and went back up to the keep.

'Mort, have you got McGowan's shoe? The one that was on the ground?'

'One of the CSIs has bagged it.'

It took a moment, but Lexi returned to the skid mark with Neil McGowan's left trainer in an evidence bag. It looked muddy, but that was no surprise if he'd walked here through the woods while it was raining. Emily took it from her and compared the tread pattern on the sole with the grooves in the mud.

She shook her head. 'Not a match. The ridges on this sole are narrower.'

So that ruled out McGowan. But it would take a while for the CSIs to check up on the shoes of everyone who'd come up the path once the body had been discovered.

She and Tom left Emily in charge and headed back to Canterbury. It was time to upgrade this investigation and to do that she needed to get Maggie fully up to date on McGowan's death.

'You spoke to Greg?' said Maggie, as Lexi and Tom adjusted their chairs so they both appeared on the screen.

'Yes,' said Lexi, 'all fine now.' She'd just called him and he'd been almost more apologetic for getting Maggie involved than she'd been for messing up. So, all fine with Greg. But that did nothing to assuage the guilt that still churned through her guts.

'Good,' said Maggie. 'Now, tell me about this new death.'

'I have reason to believe it's linked to the other two.'

'Linked? In what way?'

'It's my belief that this chatroom is actually some sort of suicide cult and the group's moderator, Nyx, is inciting young people to take their own lives. I'm reasonably sure Shan Liang was assisted in the act, and while I'm not so sure about the other two, it's certainly possible. We've got an unidentified footprint where McGowan died, and none of the three of them had mobile phones on them – that seems unlikely enough for me to think someone might have taken them. I want to upgrade the three cases into a joint murder investigation.'

'Woah, hang on a moment,' said Maggie. 'Murder? That's a stretch, Lexi. The most you've got so far is encouraging suicide. I think you'd be hard pushed to make a case for even assisting, as things stand.'

'That all depends on the legal interpretation of "assisting", doesn't it?'

'You really think Nyx is present when they take their own lives?'

Lexi shrugged. 'It's not certain, but it's not beyond the realm of possibility. But if Nyx is telling them how to do it, supplying the rope or telling them what rope to buy, or coaching their suicide notes, then I would argue he's assisting – over and above encouraging. We know from the time we spent in the chatroom that he's absolutely encouraging them, so he could be charged with both of those offences and a jury could decide if he's guilty of one or both. And all their mobile phones are missing, as if someone's taken them.'

'So far I'm with you, but you mentioned murder.'

'If I can prove that he was with them when they died that, to my mind, tips it into possible murder.'

'I'm not sure I agree,' said Tom. 'It would still legally fall under the definition of assisting.'

'But surely it comes down to intent?' said Lexi. 'If he goes to meet a teenager with the intent that the outcome of that meeting is the death of the teenager, that strikes me as more than just assisting. The guy's running a suicide cult and we can't let him carry on. Three dead already...' She stopped talking, realising that her voice had been steadily rising.

'Fair enough,' said Maggie. 'I agree – whatever he's up to, he's got to be stopped, and then it will be up to the CPS to determine what he's charged with. But for now, run it as a joint investigation.'

'Thank you,' said Lexi. She'd been given the green light to go at this hard and fast.

'But...' There was always a 'but', wasn't there? 'How do you intend to apprehend this person? You only know of him in the dark web, and doesn't that mean you won't be able to track him down? No real name, no address, no photo, no age... Do you know anything about him? Or even her?'

As if this hadn't been swirling around at the back of Lexi's brain every waking moment since she'd been ejected from the chatroom.

'I propose a two-pronged approach. I'll brief Greg Chambers in tech to do what he can online, while I'll use the rest of the team to investigate the links between the three victims. The fact that all the young people he's groomed so far appear to live in Kent...'

'But we don't know that,' said Tom, 'because we don't know

if there are other suicides linked to that one site. Or whether he might be running other chatrooms.'

'True,' said Lexi. 'Maybe Greg will be able to shed some light on that. But in the meantime, I've got to go with a first assumption that he's based in Kent, given that he seems to have known Olivia's real-life identity, and the disappearance of the mobiles. Then if we get any information that he's working a wider area, we can expand our focus.'

'Good,' said Maggie. 'But don't let other things drift. Tom, why don't you take over the Swan stabbing file and make sure it's ready to pass to the CPS?'

'Of course.'

That was fine by Lexi.

'Right, I won't keep you any longer,' said Maggie. 'Let's get this Nyx, whoever he is, into custody.'

'Easier said than done,' murmured Tom, as Maggie vanished from the screen in front of them.

'When isn't it?'

But Lexi was under no illusion. She had her work cut out to find Nyx before he lured another young neck into a noose.

THIRTY-ONE

First on their agenda was to learn more about Neil McGowan, so they headed back to Griffin Elms. Chris Appleby showed them into a study that Lexi would only be able to describe as 'cricket themed'. An ancient and cracked cricket ball in a wooden cradle was afforded pride of place on the mantelpiece, while the walls were adorned with a couple of scuffed bats, each signed by the team, framed newspaper articles and team photos which appeared to date back to the eighties and nineties. The hearth was decorated with a pair of grass-stained batting pads and even the carpet was grass green.

Appleby smiled apologetically as Lexi and Tom took it all in. 'Harking back to my glory days, I'm afraid.'

The statement invited questions, but none were forthcoming. Cricket wasn't Tom's scene and Lexi couldn't have cared less what the man did in his teens and twenties.

'Mr Appleby, can you tell us everything that happened this morning when you discovered Neil McGowan's body?'

The change of subject seemed to catch him unawares and he frowned. 'I've already given a statement to one of your PCs.'

People hated having to tell their story twice, but Lexi wasn't sympathetic. 'I know, and I've read it. But I'd like to hear it first hand, please.'

Tom sat down on a sagging leather sofa in front of the fireplace, perhaps in an effort to make Appleby more relaxed, but Lexi remained standing.

'I was taking Flanders for his early morning walk...'

'What time was this?' said Lexi.

'We try to get out by six thirty,' said Appleby. 'I have to be back here by seven ready for reveille – I make sure all the boys get down to the refectory in time for breakfast. This morning, when we reached the keep, Flanders started barking.'

'Is that unusual?'

'It happens, mostly when he's seen a squirrel he thinks he can get. He was off the lead, and he galloped straight up the hill. When I reached the top, he was sitting under Neil's body.'

'He knew Neil?'

'Flanders knows all the boys in the house. He's sort of a mascot to them.'

'What did you do?'

'I dialled 999, of course. Then I tried to climb up and let him down, but I couldn't undo the knot at the top of the arch.'

Just as well, thought Lexi. He would have totally compromised the crime scene.

'Do you always walk the same route?' she said.

'We alternate between a couple of favourite walks, both in the school grounds.'

'Which extend as far as the keep?'

'Yes. That's Griffin Castle, after which the school was named.'

'So, just chance really that you came across him?'

'I suppose so.'

'Do you think there's any reason why Neil chose that particular spot?' said Tom.

Appleby shrugged. 'Honestly, I have no idea why he chose to do it at all.' His features sagged.

'You're his housemaster, so you know him pretty well?'

'I see him every day.'

'And you hadn't noticed that he was depressed, or knew of any reason that he might be unhappy?'

'No, nothing had come to my attention. But I'm housemaster to forty boys – I can't gauge all their moods every day.' He swept his white hair back from his forehead. 'Look, I need to speak to his parents – no one has been in touch with them yet.'

'It's all right,' said Lexi. 'We'll be going to tell them in person.' She'd called Philippa Reid and asked her to be ready to meet them at McGowans' family home.

'I meant someone from here, from the school. He was in our care, after all.' Appleby sounded angry and Lexi understood why – he was dreading making the call.

'Tell me about Neil,' she said, to distract him.

'He was a brilliant cricket player and a very bright boy. Good marks in exams, musical, a prefect. He was in with a chance of being head boy next year.' He looked away, pursing his lips. 'One of the best.'

'And you really have no idea what might have made him do this?' Now wasn't the time to share with Appleby their suspicions that someone else was involved.

The housemaster shook his head. No one likes being asked the same question again, but in Lexi's experience it was an effective way of getting answers.

'He hadn't seemed depressed or upset by anything in recent weeks?'

'No, not upset. Maybe a little quiet – exams are coming up. All the boys are busy revising.'

'But he had no academic worries?' said Tom.

'None. I was expecting him to sail through.'

'Thank you,' said Lexi. 'Could we take a quick look around his bedroom, just in case he left a letter or a note?'

'Of course.'

They followed him out of his study and up two flights of stairs. Griffin Elms was a sprawling Victorian mansion that had probably been too ugly to attract attention from the National Trust. Now it was uglier still, with a plethora of cheap class-room constructions in what would have been its gardens and a 1980s postmodern sports complex to one side, with a vast acreage of rugby and cricket pitches stretching out beyond. The boys were housed in the main building, and Neil McGowan's room, shared with two other boys, had a sloped ceiling and was cramped under the eaves. Probably the servants' quarters in days gone by.

Appleby stood watching them as they quickly checked through Neil's belongings. There was no sign of a note, or anything else suspicious, but Lexi made a note to herself to ask Emily Jordan to send a CSI to give the room the once over.

'Where are his roommates?' said Tom.

Appleby glanced at his watch. 'In class. We haven't said anything to the boys yet, and they wouldn't have come back up here after breakfast, so no one will have touched Neil's stuff.'

'Thanks,' said Lexi, taking a last look round. 'We'd better go and speak to his parents. Maybe you could give them a call later on?'

Appleby nodded, still looking distraught.

Lexi wasn't surprised.

A boy had committed suicide on his watch. She had no doubt there would be some who would point the finger of blame before too long.

THIRTY-TWO

Neil McGowan's parents, Steve and Linda McGowan, lived in a swanky executive new build on the outskirts of Maidstone, part of a gated community which overlooked a golf course and where every garden was manicured to within an inch of its life.

Tom snorted as he parked. 'Wouldn't live in a place like this if I had all the money in the world,' he said.

Lexi agreed, but she still asked, 'Why not?'

'Utterly soulless. And what about the kids? Bet there are no football matches in the street around here.'

'There aren't kids playing in the street anywhere these days,' said Lexi. 'Next you're going to tell me things were so much better when you were a nipper – rationing, air raids, evacuations to the country.'

'Oh, get lost. I'm a millennial, not a baby boomer.'

Lexi laughed. 'Baby boomers were after the war.' Then, getting out of the Jeep, she remembered why they were there and adopted a more serious demeanour. There was no sign of Philippa Reid yet, the FLO, but she was coming all the way from Canterbury, whereas it hadn't been far from Griffin Elms to Maidstone.

On the other side of the road, a Waitrose van was delivering the weekly shop. A few doors down, a woman in fancy gardening gloves was weeding her rose beds. A perfect slice of suburbia. With two disruptors incoming.

Tom rang the bell and Lexi held her breath as they waited.

The door opened almost instantly and a man in his mid-forties, wearing an expensive suit, looked them up and down.

'Mr McGowan?'

'Yes. Who are you?'

Before they could answer, a woman called out from somewhere in the house behind him. 'There's an email in from Neil...' Her voice faltered.

He looked over his shoulder. 'Give me a minute, love.' He turned back to them.

'I'm DI Bennett and this is DS Olsen, Kent Police.'

'I hope this is something quick – I need to get to the office.'

A woman appeared at his shoulder – Linda McGowan, Lexi assumed. 'This email is weird. What's he talking about?' She thrust her mobile at her husband.

As Steve McGowan gave an exasperated shake of his head, Lexi realised what the woman must have received. A final message from her dead son. She reached out to grab the phone from her, desperate for them not to learn the news in such a brutal fashion, but Linda McGowan pulled the phone back and was already reading it.

'It's like he's saying goodbye or something.'

'Wait!' said Lexi.

'Why?' said Steve McGowan.

But his wife ignored the warning. She didn't even seem to realise Lexi was addressing her. Lexi watched in what seemed like slow motion as the woman scrolled down the screen.

Lexi's breath caught in her throat as Linda started to read out loud.

'"Dear Mum and Dad, by the time you read this—"' her voice suddenly wavered '"—I'll be gone." What does he mean?'

'What?' Steve, snatching the phone from his wife. 'Is this some sort of sick joke?' His anger seemed to be directed at Lexi and Tom. He scanned the email and went pale, but Lexi was watching Linda. Her eyelids fluttered and she was swaying on her feet.

'Catch her!' Lexi said.

Tom pushed past Steve McGowan just in time to put an arm out to stop Linda McGowan's fall. He took the brunt of her weight, stumbled slightly and lowered her gently onto the hall floor.

'What the hell is going on?' said Steve McGowan, squatting down by his wife's side. 'Linda, are you okay?' He patted her cheek, but her eyes were closed and she didn't respond.

'I'll call an ambulance,' said Tom.

Lexi picked up the phone from where Steve McGowan had dropped it. As Tom and Steve McGowan busied themselves with Linda, she quickly scanned Neil McGowan's final missive.

Dear Mum and Dad,

By the time you read this I'll be gone.

I'm so sorry. I'm so sorry. I honestly can't express how bad I feel, but that's all part of it. Every. Single. Day. Is. Harder. Than. The. Last.

Every breath is harder to take. I want to keep living. I want to be happy, to feel joy. I want to look forward with hope. But there's a cloak of darkness descending, heavy folds of black, that I can't find my way through. I can't find my way back to the light.

I've reached the end.

My dreams for the future are shattered and I'm a useless burden to you. I can't bear to be such a disappointment.

Mama, I'll visit you in your dreams, I promise.

Yours, with enduring love,

Neil

xxxx

Lexi knew what she was looking at. She had no doubt the email came from Neil. But she also had no doubt that the words belonged to Nyx.

THIRTY-THREE

The incident room fell silent when Lexi and Tom walked in. They'd left the McGowans in the capable hands of Philippa Reid. Both of them were too shocked to talk about what had happened, and any questions as to why Neil might have been suicidal would have to wait.

The team had heard that a third teenager had died by suicide, and Lexi had phoned ahead to make sure they were all present for a briefing. Ridhi had tacked pictures of the victims onto the whiteboard, giving details of their names, ages and where their bodies had been found. She'd also phoned Greg Chambers and asked him to come along so he could explain the issues surrounding the dark web.

'Olivia James. Shan Liang. Neil McGowan.' Lexi said the three names slowly, looking around the room as she spoke. 'They were groomed, encouraged, possibly assisted. On the surface, it seems like they took their own lives.' She paused. 'There was no reason for any of them to die. They were bright, talented youngsters with the world at their feet.' She looked at the photos on the board and felt a tide of anger sweeping through her.

Some of the assembled team nodded their heads in sympathy.

'They all crossed paths with an individual who goes by the name of Nyx. He – or possibly she – appears to be operating a suicide club on the dark web. Club Edicius, where teenagers meet to talk about killing themselves – and Nyx is in there, egging them on.'

'Can we close it down?' said Ridhi.

'In theory, yes,' said Greg Chambers, getting up to stand beside Lexi at the board. 'Sites on the dark web can be disabled, but they simply tend to pop back up using another IP address. And because of the level of encryption, we can't trace who's behind them or where they're physically located.'

'So how do we find this character?' said Colin.

'In the real world,' said Lexi. 'As far as we know, all the teenagers he's groomed have lived in Kent. Two of them, Shan and Neil, used what we suspect is rope from the same source – in both cases it was red, and this red rope has been referred to in the chatroom. If Emily can confirm that the ropes used came from the same source, it will be one of the key directions for the investigation. I have a hunch that Nyx is present when the suicides take place, so we're also looking for physical evidence of another person at each site.'

'But what about Olivia James? She didn't hang herself, so how do you know she's connected?' Ridhi was clearly thinking out loud.

'It was through her laptop that we found the club – she'd left her browser open,' said Tom.

'Also,' said Lexi, 'they all left suicide notes. Written themselves, but in all three cases using the same or extremely similar phraseology. They were either being coached by someone or using the same source material.' She had compared Neil's note with the copies of the other two she had on her phone, and there was no doubt in her mind.

A murmur of disapproval swept the room.

'The problem we face,' said Lexi, 'is that Nyx will already be grooming his next victim. We need to move fast if we're going to prevent another life from being lost.'

Tom stepped forward. There was a map at one side of the whiteboard and Ridhi had put red pins in it to indicate each of the sites where the bodies were found. Tom pointed to them. 'Michelle, can you co-ordinate your researchers to check CCTV and ANPR to see if there are any vehicles showing up near all three scenes within the relevant time frames?'

'Yes, of course.'

'It's going to be harder with the Griffin Elms site – it's in the back of beyond. I'm not sure where the nearest road cameras are.'

'We'll find them,' said Michelle.

'Great.' Tom turned to Ridhi. 'Can you liaise with Emily to get the latest on the rope, the shoe print and any other physical evidence they've been able to turn up?'

'On it,' said Ridhi, tapping the details out on her keyboard.

Lexi took over. 'Colin, would you go to the Westgate and find out how many people bought tickets on Monday? Get names from credit card payments, though if Nyx was there, he would probably have used cash. And both of you, check the street CCTV for the area surrounding the towers.'

'What are we looking for?' Colin sounded disgruntled. Lexi knew how much he hated sitting in front of a screen checking CCTV – they all did. But it was an important part of the job. And it needed doing, even though it was the weekend.

'Anyone you can spot who's around before Olivia died and also visible in the crowd afterwards. And anyone who seems suspicious for any reason, I suppose. See if you can pick up Olivia on her way in. She might have been there earlier in the day to wedge the fire exit door open, or maybe Nyx did that for her. Let me know what you find.'

'Yes, boss,' said Ridhi. Chances were that she would be the one to do the donkey work here.

Another thought came to mind. 'Ridhi, have you got that list of people who were members of Arbuthnot's group?'

'Yes, it's on here.' She waved a hand at her laptop. 'Do you need it now?'

'Just see if Neil McGowan's on there, could you?'

Ridhi started typing, then scrolled her finger down the screen. 'No, he's not showing up.'

It didn't mean anything. Maybe he'd auditioned without joining, like Olivia. Lexi grabbed a marker pen and wrote Paul Arbuthnot's name on the whiteboard. 'Paul Arbuthnot. Director of the Kingsdown Singers. Shan was a member, and Olivia auditioned for it. We know from one of the other group members that Arbuthnot bullied Shan.'

'Are you saying he could be Nyx?' said Colin.

'I've got to consider that possibility.'

'Do you want me to bring him in for questioning?' said Tom. 'We could check his alibis for the times when the victims died.'

Lexi shook her head. 'Not yet. Let's wait and see if Emily comes back with any physical evidence that might link him to one of the scenes. That'll give us much more justification for getting him in, possibly even holding him.'

But could it really be Paul Arbuthnot? Working in a garden centre, retired, taking a bunch of singers around old people's homes. And running a virtual dark web suicide cult on the side. It didn't really seem to add up. Why would he want to draw young people to their deaths? What would he possibly get out of it?

'You think he's the number one suspect?' said Ridhi.

'He's *a* suspect, but it's weak. We need to do the work and come up with some more lines of inquiry. We don't know why he's doing this, but if we could work out the motivation, it might make it easier to find an identity.'

Nyx was out there somewhere, lurking in the darkest corners of the web – and at the same time hiding in plain sight as he lured vulnerable teenagers to their death on the end of a rope for reasons unknown. This was what she had to get a handle on.

THIRTY-FOUR

'So what's the plan?' said Tom, as he followed Lexi from the incident room to her office.

She grabbed her jacket from her chair and patted it to make sure her car keys were in the pocket. 'We're going back to Griffin Elms.'

'What for?'

She led the way out and headed for the stairs. 'Remember what Appleby said about Neil McGowan?'

'Bright, good at exams. Brilliant rugby player. Head boy material.'

'And?'

'That was it, wasn't it?'

'Musical. He also said that Neil was musical. So was Olivia. So was Shan. Olivia was in the cathedral choir. Shan played the piano and sang with the Kingsdown Singers. I want to know what Neil McGowan did. I'm wondering if there's some sort of overlap somewhere between the three. We'll talk to his music teacher, maybe his friends. If we can find a real-life connection between the victims, I think we can find Nyx.'

Chris Appleby didn't seem altogether thrilled at their reappearance. They were directed to where he was officiating a cricket game between two of the school's houses. Appleby, wearing a tracksuit in the school colours, was bellowing loudly to keep the game moving, but the boys were lethargic and when one of them hit a long shot, the fielder sauntered after the ball rather than ran.

Lexi's boots, already muddy from their visit to the keep earlier in the day, were getting a new drubbing, and her heels, although not high, kept sinking into the soft ground. She was as relieved as the boys were when the final batter was caught out.

Appleby directed the two teams back to the changing rooms, then came over to where Lexi and Tom were waiting. He gave them each a weary nod.

'Mr Appleby, would you be able to spare us some time? We've just got a few questions,' said Lexi.

Appleby looked at the backs of the two disappearing teams. Bickering voices could already be heard among them.

'Give me a moment.' He turned and looked round the pitch. There were a couple of older boys, in similar tracksuits, pulling up the stumps. 'Porter, Simmons, can you go and supervise the changing rooms – make sure World War Three doesn't break out among that lot.'

The two boys nodded their heads and jogged away.

'How can I help you?' Appleby started slowly walking off the pitch, so Lexi and Tom fell into step with him.

'When we spoke to you earlier, you mentioned that Neil was musical. Can you tell us more about that?'

The housemaster gave them a puzzled look. 'He was very musical, though more passionate about his sport. He was a really excellent bowler, too.' The man seemed obsessed – reliving his youth, no doubt.

'His music?'

'What? Oh, yes – he played the saxophone in the school orchestra and in the sixth form jazz club.'

'Do you know if he ever sang with a group called the Kingsdown Singers? They went around old people's homes giving concerts.'

'Never heard of them. It's not something that he would have done while he was here.' He shrugged. 'Perhaps in the holidays, but I wouldn't know about that.'

'What about the jazz club?' said Tom. 'Who runs that, and what do they do?'

They'd reached the sports complex at the side of the pitches now. Appleby pulled open the door and gestured for them to go inside. 'The boys run it themselves. It started as an informal thing, but they've built quite a little ensemble. They play at school events, and they've started entering competitions. The loss of Neil will be quite a blow to them, although he wasn't the driving force behind it.'

'Who was?'

'Two lads – Dave Kelly and Bobby Pisano. They're not in my house, so I don't really know them.'

'Could we speak to them?' Lexi wasn't sure what information these boys might be able to give them, but if they knew Neil well, they might have spotted that things weren't right with him. More than his housemaster had apparently managed to do.

Appleby made a call and then directed them to the sixth form common room, where the two boys would be sent to talk to them. They didn't have to wait long. Five minutes later, they appeared.

'Hi, I'm Dave,' said the first through the door, a handsome boy with blond curly hair, and at least a head taller than Tom. 'This is Bobby,' he added as an equally tall, dark-haired boy followed him in. 'You wanted to ask us about Neil?' There was a slight tremor in his voice, betraying how upset he was at the loss of his friend.

'Sit down,' said Tom. The common room offered an array of

battered armchairs and sagging sofas. The boys did as they were asked, and Tom and Lexi took seats opposite them.

'I'm so sorry about your friend,' said Lexi. 'It must have been a huge shock to you.'

Dave nodded, but Bobby took a breath as if to speak. Lexi gave him a nod of encouragement.

'He said something last week.' He paused.

'Something?' said Tom after a long moment.

'It was a joke. At least, at the time I thought it was a joke.'

Dave was looking at him, aghast. 'What?'

'You were there. It was at practice. He was playing something slow and mournful, and I asked him what it was. He said, "It's what they're going to play at my funeral." Do you remember?'

Dave nodded. 'Of course, but what of it? It didn't make me think he was going to top himself.'

'Not at the time. But now, when I think about it...' Bobby Pisani's voice cracked and Dave looked uncomfortable.

'Did he seem depressed at all in recent weeks?'

'No, not depressed. I think he was feeling the pressure of exams. His parents wanted him to go to Oxford or Cambridge. He wasn't sure what he wanted to do,' said Dave.

'But it's like that for everyone,' said Bobby.

'He'd been going on about crypto coins a bit,' said Dave. 'Spent a lot of time on his computer.'

'Yeah, he was getting into programming as well,' said Bobby. 'Was even talking about it as a career.'

'When you say he was spending a lot of time on his computer, this was a recent thing?'

Bobby nodded. 'A couple of times we had to go and find him for rehearsals. Never used to be like that. But now, he'll be on his computer, and he'll shut it down quickly when anyone comes near.'

Lexi exchanged a glance with Tom. 'Do you know if he was accessing the dark web at all?'

Both boys shrugged.

'He never said anything about that,' said Dave.

She had one last question. 'He was found at the old keep in the school grounds. Do you know if that location had any special meaning for him?'

Bobby shrugged. 'Everyone goes there to smoke or drink sometimes. Neil was no different.'

Lexi stood up. 'Thanks for your time, boys. You've been very helpful.'

Bobby showed them the way back to Appleby's study and when they knocked on the door, Appleby's voice shouted, 'Come in.'

He was out of his tracksuit now, back in a shirt and jeans, and his hair was wet.

'Sorry to keep bothering you,' said Lexi, 'but could we go back to Neil's room and pick up his laptop?'

'Why do you need that?'

'We just need to check what websites he was accessing,' said Tom.

Appleby nodded. 'Okay.'

'And one other thing, can we talk to whoever taught him computer science?' It was an afterthought. Might not prove useful, but as they were here...

'That would be Mr Cotter. He's housemaster of one of our junior houses, so he should be around.'

Chris Appleby made another call, took them to Neil's room where they picked up his laptop, and then pointed them in the direction of Eric Cotter's office. Lexi's thanks were heartfelt – he'd been incredibly patient with their repeated demands and he seemed genuinely upset about the boy's death.

'D'you think Appleby could be involved?' said Tom, as they

climbed a spiral staircase up to Cotter's office, at the far end of the building from Appleby's.

'That he could be Nyx?' Lexi paused on the top step. 'No, I don't get that vibe at all. Not sure he'd have a clue as to how to use the dark web. He's got one obsession – cricket – and probably no room for anything else inside his head.'

'True – plus, no links to the other teenagers.'

'That we know of so far. Maybe we shouldn't rule him out just yet, but he's not setting off any red flags.' Lexi's training with the FBI had taught her to look out for certain markers that might suggest a predator or potential killer, and Chris Appleby didn't fit the picture. He seemed confident, entitled even, in the way he interacted with other people. There was no hint of past trauma or PTSD, at least on the surface.

The door at the top of the stairs opened before they knocked, curtailing their conversation. Eric Cotter was younger than Lexi would have expected a housemaster to be, and was dressed in skinny jeans and T-shirt with an xkcd graphic on the front. He greeted them in a strong American accent.

'Hi, you're the guys from the police, right?'

'We are,' said Lexi and did the introductions.

'Come on in and grab a seat.'

Cotter's cramped, untidy office looked like an eight-year-old's dream of a mad inventor's den. Across his desk was a bank of huge computer screens, in front of which sat a couple of games consoles as well as a keyboard. The screens showed a variety of gaming worlds, while the desk chair looked like something designed for the bridge of a spaceship. Anime posters covered the walls. On a flat table close to the window, there were a number of miniature robots in various stages of assembly, two of which were actually marching round in circles. As Lexi and Tom watched, distracted, the two robots crashed into one another and fell over.

Cotter laughed. 'They have sensors that are supposed to

make them turn away rather than bump into something, but it doesn't work if they both turn the same way.' He walked over to them and flipped switches on each of the robots' backs.

There were no additional chairs in the office, but a cluster of mini bean bags in one corner – possibly fine if he had a bunch of nine-year-olds in his room, but it didn't look too appealing to Lexi. She decided to remain standing.

'Mr Cotter, we just wanted to ask you a couple of questions about Neil McGowan, if that's okay?'

His expression became serious. 'Of course. It's a hellish thing to have happened. What can I tell you?'

'You taught Neil computer science, right?'

Cotter nodded. 'I did.' He sighed. 'He was so promising, and I'd spoken to him about the possibility of taking it further – studying it at university. He was even considering applying to do it in the States, MIT possibly.'

'That all sounds really positive,' said Lexi. 'Did you have any idea that he was depressed or that he had problems?'

'Not at all. He seemed fine when I saw him last week.' Cotter rubbed the stubble on his chin. 'Really, all seemed okay. Do you know why he did it?'

'It's what we're trying to find out,' said Lexi. 'Did he ever express an interest in the dark web?'

'Yeah. I cover it in class.'

'Seriously?' said Tom. 'Surely it's not appropriate to teach kids how to go on the dark web. It's far too dangerous.'

The look Cotter gave him was full of disdain. 'Listen, most of the kids I teach have already been there before I get them. And, yes, you're right – it can be dangerous in places. So it's my job to make sure they know how to stay safe there. But you also need to realise, it's not all bad. For people living under regimes who control the internet, the dark web is a way they can make their voices heard without the fear of persecution. And that's super important.'

It seemed an unorthodox stand for a teacher to take – Lexi would have thought the dark web should have been strictly out of bounds. 'Do you have any idea what sort of sites he might have looked at?'

'No. That's the whole point of using Tor. Even if I had access to his laptop, I wouldn't be able to trace any activity.'

'And he didn't discuss any with you?'

'We looked at a few sites in class. Political platforms for dissident voices. It excited him to see that the internet had value beyond social media and games streaming.'

'Did he ever mention a chatroom called Club Edicius to you?'

'No.' Cotter didn't even pause for thought. He seemed immediately sure.

'Thanks for your time,' said Lexi.

'You're welcome.' He held the door open for them as they left. 'I hope you find out why it happened. Such a waste – he was a great kid. Big hearted.'

'And what about him?' Tom whispered in Lexi's ear as the door closed behind them and they went back down the spiral stairs. 'He knows his way around the dark web.'

'So do millions of people,' said Lexi. 'But let's take a closer look at him, see if we can dig up any links between him and the other victims, or find anything in his past that would give him a reason to groom his pupils for suicide.'

THIRTY-FIVE

It was getting late and the incident room was quiet when Lexi and Tom got back to the station. Most of the civilian staff knocked off at five, and Lexi tried to make sure that her team didn't work later than they had to, too.

'You should go home,' she said to Tom. 'Billie will be missing you.'

'And then I'll lose my position as Number One Dad.'

'I suspect Declan already holds that crown.'

Tom laughed. 'You could be right.' He grabbed a few bits and pieces from his desk. 'Okay, see you tomorrow. And don't work too late.'

'No, sir,' said Lexi, giving him fake salute. 'Wouldn't dream of it.'

He was right. She shouldn't stay too late. She needed to get out for a run if she was going to keep her training on course. And God forbid that she might actually take some downtime. She couldn't remember the last time she'd slobbed out in front of the television or met a friend for a drink. And dates? Forget it. When was she ever likely to meet anybody? A run was the best she could hope for.

But there were a few bits and pieces she wanted to tidy up before knocking off. She added Chris Appleby and Eric Cotter's names to the list of witnesses on the right-hand side of the whiteboard. She didn't see Chris Appleby as any more than a witness – he'd had the misfortune of finding Neil's body – but Eric Cotter clearly had the technical know-how to run a chatroom. It would have been incredibly easy for him to draw Neil into Club Edicius. But what about the others?

Back in her own office, she logged Neil's laptop as evidence and left a message for Greg Chambers that it would be coming his way first thing in the morning. And she asked him to check Olivia and Shan's laptops for any online links to Neil McGowan or Eric Cotter.

All valuable and necessary, but where was the progress? She drummed her fingers on her desk in frustration. She needed access to the chatroom to see what Nyx was up to and so far Greg hadn't been able to find a way of reconnecting. More than that, she needed to discoverer the identities of the teens that were meeting there. She couldn't bear the thought that somewhere, possibly nearby, another boy or girl was considering ending it, writing a note to their parents, selecting a location...

She had to do something. Maybe she should talk to Paul Arbuthnot after all. She sent two PCs to pick him up, and then decided to recruit some extra help.

A phone call and half an hour later, she was talking to Ed Harlow in her office. No, he hadn't minded her calling him so late and, yes, he was at a loose end because Charlie was still at her sister's.

'I want to get your opinion on a suspect,' she said, as he sat gazing at her from the other side of the desk.

'Suspected of?'

'Incitement to suicide, possibly assisting.'

'But you think it could be more than that?'

Lexi shrugged. 'I'm not sure exactly where the CPS would

draw the line between assisting someone to die and actually murdering them. In my view, if you help a healthy young adult take their own life, that's as good as murder. It's not the same as assisting someone who's terminally ill.'

'Different standards for different victims? That's a dangerous path to tread.'

'I know. So luckily I don't have to make that decision. It will be up to the prosecutors. I just need to get enough evidence for at least one of the lesser charges to stick.'

'Okay. Who's the suspect?'

'Paul Arbuthnot, the guy who runs the singing group that Shan Liang was a member of. Remember I told you about him and how he was picking on Shan. We have a statement from a woman who used to help with the Facebook group that he bullied several group members, forcing them to leave.'

'But you don't think he's the one running the suicide club?'

'Why d'you say that?'

'If you were convinced of his involvement, you wouldn't have called me in to give you an opinion. You're dithering.'

'It would be good to either rule him in or out.'

'My opinion won't do that for you.'

'Maybe not. I'm waiting for Emily to come back to me with physical evidence, too. And at some point I'll need to take a view on the way forward.'

'Fine. If you want to consider him, let's look at what his motive might be.'

'That's what I'm finding problematic. Why would anyone encourage others to take their own lives?'

'Financial gain, personal grudges – it's the sort of thing that happens in families or between spouses. In relationships where one person might have something to gain from the other's death. Whisper in someone's ear long enough that they should do it themselves, and you don't end up a murder suspect.'

'But not in these cases,' said Lexi. 'Three teenagers with no ostensible connection. I can't see how the person who's grooming them gains from their death. I think we're looking at something more like a Munchausen syndrome by proxy type of thing. If the guy – I have a hunch it's a man – is helping these kids to die, and is actually present at the deaths, then it's satisfying some sort of urge for him.'

'A sexual motive?'

'Possibly, although if it was sexual, I'd expect them all to be the same gender. Maybe he's using them as stand-ins for his own suicidal urges. He feels he should be the one dying, but of course he doesn't want to die. So he finds others to take his place. Maybe it assuages some long-held guilt?'

'But never for long, so he needs to do it again, and again – and we know where that leads.'

Lexi nodded. 'Which is why I need to close this down fast. Three kids are dead, and I've no idea who's next on his list.'

'But you think it might be Arbuthnot?'

'It's one theory. Not much of a theory, I know, but I've sent a couple of uniforms down to collect him for a voluntary interview in the station.'

'What if he doesn't volunteer?'

'I have a feeling he will. He's arrogant enough to think that he can see us off by answering our questions.'

She was right. A minute later, one of the two PCs she'd sent to fetch Paul Arbuthnot called her mobile and said they had him ready for her down in the interview room.

'There are two things I want to find out,' she said as they went down the stairs. 'Firstly, if there's some trauma in his past that might have given rise to a sense of guilt or suicidal tendency.'

'And the second thing?'

'I'm going to ask him about the dark web. On the face of it, he doesn't seem like the type who'd have the level of computer literacy to set up chatrooms and switch IP addresses at the drop of a hat.'

'You're being ageist, you know?' Ed grinned at her. 'I know plenty of OAPs who're competent silver surfers.'

'So maybe I'm wrong – perhaps he's a tech genius, but I don't think so.'

'And I guess for the same reason, you would assume that your suspect is male? Women spend far less time on the dark web.'

'That might be a factor, but if Arbuthnot isn't who we're after, I can't afford to make assumptions. Anyway, can you focus on his answers? If he denies knowledge of it, and whether the denial is plausible.'

'Sure.'

It was good to have Ed here. Whether it was down to the similar training they'd had at Quantico, or just because their brains worked the same way, she felt she could bounce ideas off him, without having to explain her thinking. They were on the same wavelength, but he could also spot weaknesses in her theory or help her come at things from another angle, and she was beginning to value his help more and more with each case.

They stepped into the interview room. Paul Arbuthnot was sitting on his own on one side of the table, and they took the two seats opposite him.

'Thank you for coming in, Mr Arbuthnot,' said Lexi. 'This is Ed Harlow. He's a forensic psychologist and he'll be helping me to evaluate your answers, if that's okay?'

Arbuthnot nodded. He looked resigned to the fact that he probably didn't have much choice.

Lexi switched on the tape recorder and stated who was present. 'Please could you confirm, Mr Arbuthnot, that this is a voluntary interview and that you're happy for us to record it.'

'I can confirm both those things.'

'Thank you.' She took a sip of water from the paper cup in

front of her. She would lead off with questions about the dark web. Tackling Arbuthnot's past might prove less straightforward and was best left till later in the interview. Clearing her throat, she said, 'We'd like to ask you a bit about the dark web. Do you know what that is?'

'The dark web?' His face looked blank.

'The dark internet – it's part of the deep web,' said Ed.

'I don't know what you're talking about.'

'Do you know what the Tor browser is?' said Lexi.

Arbuthnot shook his head.

'So we wouldn't find it installed on your computer?'

'I have no idea. Is it something that the computer could have come with?'

'Definitely not,' said Ed.

'I'm sorry, computers aren't really my thing. Try to avoid them as much as possible, apart from sending emails.'

Lexi believed him, and it tied in with Maddie still keeping an eye on the group's Facebook page. She glanced at Ed and a slight movement of his mouth told her that he did too. Of course, Lexi would still have his computer checked by Greg or one of his colleagues, but it told her that she probably needed to move the investigation in another direction as far as finding Nyx was concerned.

However, as she had him here, Arbuthnot's bullying of the group members still deserved scrutiny.

'Mr Arbuthnot, we have reason to believe that the accusation of theft against Shan Liang at Sunny Oaks wasn't an isolated incident.'

'How do you mean? There weren't any other thefts reported.'

'I mean that someone who was a former member of the Kingsdown Singers told us that you have a track record of bullying group members that didn't meet your exacting standards or who questioned your leadership.'

Arbuthnot looked aghast. 'That's absolutely not true. Who told you that?'

'Did you take against Shan Liang for some reason and try to push him out of the group?'

'No.' He was getting angry now. Lexi didn't mind – uncontrolled anger led to slip-ups.

'So you can assure us that you treated all the members of your group equally? No favourites?'

'Has someone made any sort of formal complaint against me? Or are you going on the word of just one person who's no longer a member of the group?' His face had turned red and his hands on the table had clenched into fists.

'As far as I know there hasn't been a formal complaint, but that doesn't mean it's not happening.' Lexi kept her voice calm and her tone measured.

Ed cleared his throat. 'Mr Arbuthnot...'

Arbuthnot switched his glance from Lexi to Harlow. 'Yes?'

'Have you ever in your life considered suicide or had suicidal thoughts?'

At first Arbuthnot looked puzzled, then he stood up. 'I've had enough. If you want to talk to me again, you'll have to arrest me and I'll want a lawyer present.'

'That is, of course, your right,' said Lexi, also rising to her feet.

But Arbuthnot wasn't interested in hearing more and was already heading towards the door.

'One last thing,' she said.

He turned to look back at her.

'Do you know a boy called Neil McGowan? Was he ever a member of the Kingsdown Singers?'

He stopped in his tracks, his anger dissipating. 'The name... maybe rings a bell.' He paused. 'But, no, I don't think I do. Sorry.' He shut the door behind him.

After he'd gone, Lexi sat down next to Ed.

'Well?'

'He hadn't heard of the dark web, he's probably a bully, though he wouldn't recognise it in himself – and I believe he knew who Neil McGowan was.'

Lexi took her phone out of her pocket and pressed one of the speed dials. 'Hi, Colin, can you apply for a warrant to search Paul Arbuthnot's house and car. We need to check his shoes against the shoe print made at the keep at Griffin Elms. And we'll want to confiscate his computer.'

She didn't believe he was Nyx, but that didn't mean she wasn't going to double check whatever she could. Peter Sutcliffe, the so-called Yorkshire Ripper, had been interviewed by the police nine times before they finally arrested him, killing several more women after his first interview.

There was no way she was going to let the same thing happen in this case.

THIRTY-SIX

Ridhi ran her finger down the list of names, all of them past or present members of the Kingsdown Singers. She'd phoned, or tried to phone, most of the current members, with varying degrees of success. Some she'd left messages for, a couple of others were too traumatised by Shan's death to talk to her, and at least two of the phone numbers were out of date. She'd spoken to three, all of whom supported Maddie Scott's claims that Paul Arbuthnot was a bully. But, of these three, none had been particularly friendly with Shan. The general impression she got was that he kept himself to himself, turning up at rehearsals and performances on time and leaving promptly afterwards. One of them had invited the whole group to her birthday party, including Shan, but he hadn't put in an appearance.

Conclusion? Shan was a loner. Maybe because he was home-schooled and wasn't really used to large, noisy gatherings of young people. He was probably socially awkward and maybe found it difficult to make friends.

The only useful thing she'd gleaned was that if Shan was friendly with anyone, it was a boy called Tyler Morgan. The girl who told her seemed to think Tyler was 'a bit of a weirdo' without really being able to clarify what she meant. He'd left the group several months ago after a row with Arbuthnot over being late for rehearsals.

She found his name and number on the list and dialled.

'Yo?'

'Excuse me, are you Tyler Morgan?'

'This is he.' He had an American accent. Perhaps that's what they had in common – strangers in a strange land.

'My name's DC Ridhi Kulkarni of Kent Police. Do you have a minute?'

'I didn't do it, okay?'

Ridhi stared at the phone. 'You...?'

His laughter sounded strained. 'It was a joke. You know, what people always say to the police.'

'Right, yeah, very funny.'

'Sorry.'

'It's fine. You knew Shan Liang, didn't you?'

'Shan the Man, I know him, of course I do.'

He used the present tense. Didn't he know?

'When did you last see him?'

'Couple of weeks ago. We were supposed to meet up yesterday, but he didn't answer my text.' There was a long pause before he spoke again. 'What's going on? Why are you calling me?'

Ridhi took a deep breath. 'I'm sorry, Tyler. Shan's dead. He took his own life yesterday.'

There was a gasp of surprise. 'No way. No, please tell me he didn't.'

'I'm so sorry.' Ridhi waited for a while, allowing Tyler to get his emotions under control.

'That bastard – it was his fault.' Shock had given way to absolute venom.

'Who are you talking about?'

'Arbie – the group Führer, Paul Arbuthnot.'

'What did he do?'

'He never liked Shan and he was always trying to push him out of the group.'

A thought came to Ridhi. 'Was it because he was racist?'

Tyler paused. 'No, Paul Arbuthnot isn't racist – he's married to a Filipina care worker – she's actually really nice, nicer than him. The people he picks on, it's not about the colour of their skin.'

Ridhi wondered. Just because he was married to a person of colour didn't mean he couldn't be racist.

'Maddie Scott suggested it was people who questioned his authority.'

'Ah, Maddie... that girl has her own issues. But sure, that's a fair assessment.'

Ridhi didn't want to get sidetracked by asking what Maddie's issues might be. 'Was Arbuthnot's bullying enough to drive Shan to do what he did?'

'Are you sure it was suicide, officer?'

'What do you mean?'

'When I last saw Shan, he was upset. At first, he wouldn't tell me why. He kept saying it was too dangerous and that he didn't want to involve me. But I kept pressing and he relented. He told me when they'd been at Sunny Oaks a few weeks previously he'd overheard something bad.'

Ridhi waited.

Tyler filled the gap. 'He heard Arbie talking with a member of the staff, one of the carers, about one of the residents. Arbie was asking how long she'd got and if the carer had managed to persuade her to make the changes.'

'Changes to what?'

'At first Shan couldn't work it out. But later, when he thought about it, he figured that Arbie and the woman were going to pressure the resident to change her will. He confronted

Arbie and that's when Arbie and the care assistant accused Shan of stealing. Their word against his, and there were two of them, adults, against just him. He agreed to shut up, so they said the accusation had all been a big misunderstanding. But Shan hated himself for caving into their demands. I think he was going to make it public, what he'd heard them discussing. So are you sure it was suicide?'

'Did Shan ever say anything about a suicide club on the dark web, Club Edicius?'

'They're just a bunch of creepy teenagers, egging each other on. Nobody ever does anything – it's pretty lame.'

'But you know of it?'

'Shan showed it to me one time. I told him to get out of it. I wasn't really interested.'

'But he was?'

'Shan had a dark side. He was a bit obsessed with his own death and how it might happen. I guess he'd flirted with the idea of suicide – but you still need to check up if that bastard Arbie was involved.'

THIRTY-SEVEN

THURSDAY

Lexi banged a teaspoon on the side of her coffee mug to bring the incident room to order.

'No, Colin, we are not about to arrest someone on the basis of one teenager's accusations. But what we are going to do is look into this further. If what Tyler Morgan says is true, whether or not he has anything to do with the suicide cult, Paul Arbuthnot might be engaged in a serious case of organised fraud.'

The chatter which had broken out when Ridhi had repeated Morgan's accusations simmered down.

'So how do we verify what he says?' said Tom. 'Do we need to get Paul Arbuthnot back in here?'

'Not yet – he'll just deny the accusations and claim that Morgan has a grudge against him. Let's see if there's any evidence.' Lexi looked around the room. Ridhi had done good work over the last couple of months. It was time to give her some responsibility. 'Ridhi, you can take point on this part of the investigation. Check the Kingsdown Facebook page and compile a list of nursing homes that they visited. Look at the wills of any residents who died recently and see if Arbuthnot was a beneficiary of any of them.'

'On it,' said Ridhi.

'Also, find out his wife's name and the names of any charities that he might be on the board of or employed by – the bequests could go to other people or organisations on his behalf.'

Ridhi nodded, scribbling in her notebook.

It seemed that Colin didn't want to be left out. 'Boss, I've got a list of the most recent deaths by suicide across the county.'

'Good – Greg Chambers has emailed us a series of cached pages from Club Edicius chatroom, the pages we saw. Cross reference the dates and any other details you have about the suicides with anything that was said in the chatroom. It's almost certain that Nyx had earlier victims, so we need to identify them. And can you also get hold of the missing mobile phone numbers and request access to their accounts?'

Colin nodded.

She raised a hand and tapped on the whiteboard next to the photos of the victims so far. 'Olivia James, Shan Liang, Neil McGowan. Three deaths. Two with the same MO. Three suicide notes, written by each of the victims, but sharing too many phrases not to have come from the same source. Olivia James was accessing a chatroom called Club Edicius on the dark web – we know this from her computer. We suspect we saw Neil McGowan conversing with Nyx live when we had access to the chatroom for a short time. Neil McGowan hanged himself using the same type of rope as Shan Liang, from which we can conclude they were both visiting Club Edicius. Greg Chambers is looking at Neil's laptop now, and will hopefully confirm it.' She paused. Every eye in the room was fixed on her. 'What we don't know is the thread they had in common that drew them into the cult. We've found no online connections between them, so we suspect the link is something that they share in the real world.'

'I think we need to dig deeper into music being the connection,' said Tom. 'There's no link between Neil and the Kingsdown Singers, but all three were musical.'

'Look into that, will you?'

Lexi's phone rang. She looked at the screen, but didn't recognise the number. 'DI Bennett.'

'Sergeant Maplin, Dover Police here, ma'am. I was told that you wanted to be informed of any suicides around the county.'

'Yes, that's right.' A sudden adrenalin rush made her heart hammer.

'We've just been apprised of a body at the bottom of the cliffs at Langdon Bay.'

Langdon Cliffs was a section of the famous White Cliffs of Dover.

'When?'

'A few minutes ago. First responders are on their way. No other details yet.'

'Do you really think someone going over the cliff edge could be one of ours?' said Tom, as they sped down the A2 towards Dover. 'I mean, it could just be an accidental death.'

'You're right. It could be.' Lexi glanced in the rear-view mirror before pulling out to overtake a lorry. 'But it could be a suicide. And it might be the work of Nyx and his little gang of trolls – so we need to get down there and rule it out. And I need to make sure they treat both the top and bottom of the cliff as crime scenes.'

She spoke firmly, but inside she was terrified. She didn't want to see another mother crushed and broken, because their child had strayed into the orbit of pure evil that surrounded Nyx. Drawn to the rocks, where the wrecker waited, watching for carnage. In her mind's eye she saw a shadowy figure observing from the sidelines as teenagers died.

'He's there when they do it.' She was practically driving on autopilot.

'What?'

'Nyx – I think he watches them commit suicide. That's why he does it. He's with them at the end, I'm almost certain of it.'

'That skidding footprint up at the keep?' said Tom.

'Exactly – it must have been his. Emily hasn't managed to match it to any of the first responders or the CSIs, and it wasn't a match for Neil's trainer. It must have been him.'

She drove on in silence, passing the huge queue of lorries waiting to get through the port at Dover, then skirting the edge of the city to where the cliffs reared up on its eastern flank. They'd had instructions to drive as far as the road went and park at the Coastguard Maritime Rescue Co-ordination Centre – a satellite station used by the coastguards.

The wind was blustery at the top of the cliffs, and Lexi could taste the faint tang of salt on her lips as they made their way along the narrow path towards Langdon Bay. She could see a uniformed PC several hundred metres away from them at the top, and veering off the path towards the edge, she looked down to see more activity on the shingle below him.

'Stay on the path,' said Tom. 'The edge can be crumbly.'

He was right, of course, and they couldn't rule out that the person at the bottom had simply trodden on unstable ground and skidded over the edge by accident. Lexi quickly stepped back onto the gravel track and they hurried on.

When they reached the uniformed PC, Lexi instructed him to cordon off the path and the whole area at the top of the cliff for twenty metres on either side where the body had fallen. Then she had him radio down to the team at the bottom to treat the area with the tightest crime scene protocol.

'How do we get down there?' she asked him.

The PC pointed further along the cliff. 'About fifty metres on, there's a path that winds down the cliff.'

'Thanks.'

The cliff path was steep and twisty, and the crumbling chalk underfoot made it hazardous in the extreme. Lexi skidded a few times, as did Tom, once nearly bowling her over as he was unable to stop his slide.

'Sorry, boss,' he said, grabbing for one of the scant tufts of grass that grew on the vertiginous slope.

'No worries.' Usually she would have come up with a jokey response, but seeing the dark form of the body lying a little way along the beach, with a paramedic bent over it, made it feel inappropriate to mess around. She carried on down in silence, then crunched across the shingle beach to the small cluster of first responders. There was a sergeant who seemed to be in charge, so she introduced herself and Tom.

'Bring me up to speed,' she said, looking down on the body. It was a woman, mid-thirties she guessed, limbs splayed unnaturally. Lexi could see blood from a head wound seeping into the pebbles.

'We got the call just over an hour ago,' said the sergeant. 'A walker at the top of the cliff spotted her. It was quite clear from the moment we arrived that she was dead.'

'Any ID on her?' said Lexi. The woman looked too old to be one of Nyx's victims, but they would need to check her out.

'She had this in her pocket,' said the sergeant. He held out a clear plastic evidence bag.

Lexi took it and studied the contents through the plastic. It was a letter from the NHS – the oncology department of the local hospital, addressed to Ms Kara Pope. She read in silence, Tom peering over her shoulder to see what it said. Apparently, Kara Pope had stage 4 breast cancer. The letter didn't say much, some details of upcoming treatments, but reading between the lines the woman's prognosis didn't look good.

'I think it's safe to say this suicide isn't going to be of interest to our investigation,' she said, handing the letter back to the sergeant. 'But thank you for alerting us.'

She looked down at the woman and wondered about her life. Did she have children, a family who loved her? Maybe she didn't want them to witness a long, drawn-out ordeal. Or was she was alone in life and simply couldn't face what was coming? Someone would know, but it wasn't for Lexi to find out. Her job was to track down Nyx.

She turned back towards the cliff path.

'Come on,' she said, and they set off back to the top.

THIRTY-EIGHT

Financial investigation left Ridhi cold. She knew it was an expanding branch of police work – forensic accountants and auditors on the track of money laundering and fraudsters – but it seemed dry and dull compared with the excitement of hunting down killers. Maybe that was a naive way of looking at it, but she was already bored with digging into the financial affairs of the Kingsdown Singers.

It was a registered charity and that meant that its annual report and accounts had to be filed with the Charity Commission. The information she found was unremarkable. The annual report showed a list of the locations where they'd performed – six nursing homes, the Leas Cliff Hall, a hospice and a couple of schools. They'd also attended the first round of a singing competition, but had been eliminated before progressing any further. The accounts detailed the small amount of money they raised each year to cover the running costs of an ancient minibus which Arbuthnot used to drive them to gigs and to pay a peppercorn rent for the use of the church hall for rehearsals. But there were also several larger deposits, sometimes up to several thousands of pounds, which were paid into the group's bank account, with similar amounts being withdrawn as cash, in smaller chunks, over subsequent weeks.

'Not dodgy at all,' Ridhi muttered under her breath.

'What's that?' said Colin from across the office. He was scrolling through the cached pages that Greg had sent them, trying to find links with a list of other teenagers that had died by suicide in Kent in the past year. Ridhi had become aware of his fidgeting as he grew increasingly bored with the task.

'Strangely large and unaccountable sums moving in and out of the Kingsdown Singers bank account.'

'So maybe the accusation that the guy's fleecing the old people is true.'

'Gotta think so.'

She jotted down the dates the money came into the account and wondered how she could find out the source of it. The most obvious thing would be to get a warrant to allow them to examine the group's bank account – that would certainly shed more light, but it would take time. The other thing she could do would be to look at the nursing homes and the hospice. If she could find out the names of people who'd died in each of them and check their wills, she might find out if the group or Arbuthnot had been a beneficiary. Not that that in itself was a crime – of course old people left money to charities – but if it was the case, it would give them grounds to investigate further. If Arbuthnot was in cahoots with care home staff to put pressure on lonely residents to change their wills, that certainly would be worthy of their attention. And where was all that cash going?

Rather than approach each of the establishments individually, she emailed a request for information to the Births, Deaths and Marriages Registration office which was based in Maidstone.

She sat back in her chair and yawned. Financial investigation seemed to move more slowly than an octogenarian on a zebra crossing. But at least she wasn't stuck looking at traffic cams all day.

They say yawns are catching, and Colin caught hers.

'Open the window, would you?' he said to Ellie, who sat closest to it. 'We're dropping off to sleep over here. We need some action – can't you come up with anything, Ridhi?'

'I wish,' she said. 'Once I've got the names of people who died in the care homes the Kingsdown Singers visited, we can look into their wills – and that's when things'll get interesting.'

Once probate had been granted, wills became documents of public record and they would be able to gain access to them. Arbuthnot couldn't have received any legacies unless probate had been granted.

'And what about his wife?' said Colin. 'She works in care homes, too. She's gotta be in on it, hasn't she?'

'Already on it,' said Ridhi with a grin. 'Her name's Kim Ramos – she doesn't use her married name. She works shifts at several different homes, and I'm digging into those too.'

'Turning into quite the detective.'

She couldn't tell if this was a compliment or if Colin was being sarcastic, so she shrugged. She'd take it as a compliment. And it didn't really matter what Colin thought of her work. It was the boss she was out to impress.

THIRTY-NINE

Lexi closed her office door, sat down at her desk and rested her head on folded arms. She shut her eyes and took a few deep breaths. If this morning's little expedition had taught her one thing, it was that they couldn't go haring off every time there was a report of a suicide. She would make a checklist to narrow things down and have it circulated to all the stations in the county – the victim's age, the MO, the presence of red rope in two of the cases, the missing mobiles... she didn't have much more than that, and it probably wouldn't be enough.

Anyway, arriving on the scene once somebody was dead meant they were already too late. They needed to find a way to intervene before it happened, a way of stopping Nyx from drawing more vulnerable teenagers into his sick cult.

That meant venturing back onto the dark web.

She had to get back into the chatroom somehow, so they could monitor what was being said. Greg Chambers had already made it clear to her that they wouldn't be able to trace anyone's identity if they were using the Tor browser. But perhaps, if they could just listen in on the chat, someone would drop a clue to their identity.

She phoned Greg.

'What can I do for you, Lexi?'

'I know you're going to tell me it can't be done, but I need you to gain access to the Club Edicius chatroom again.'

'You're right – it can't be done.'

'It could mean saving someone's life.'

'If I could do it, I would, believe me. But the whole point of running it on the dark web is to keep people like us out.'

'And you can't get any additional information from those few pages we have cached?'

'Like what?'

Lexi was stumped. 'When we were in the chatroom, Nyx introduced a new girl, Siren. I'm scared that he'll be pushing her towards the edge.'

There was silence at the other end of the line, and she realised she'd spoken out of turn.

'I'm sorry. That sounded like I was piling on the emotional pressure.'

'It did.' Greg's voice sounded tired. 'Look, I'll go back in and dig around, but don't get your hopes up.'

'Thanks, Greg.'

She felt bad for a minute, but not as bad as she knew she would feel if she got called out to attend Siren's body somewhere.

An email pinged into her inbox, and she looked up. It was from Tom, and by the time she'd opened it, he'd appeared in her office doorway.

'Just emailed you all the information Ellie's team have dug up on our victims.'

'Have you gone through it yet?'

He shook his head. 'Wanted to get it to you straight away. It's a long list of activities, events, social media references, absolutely anything they were able to find about them online.'

Lexi opened the email and speed scrolled down more than

thirty pages of cut-and-pasted screenshots and snippets. She would get Ridhi to go through all the details and find any correlations that existed between Olivia, Shan and Neil. There had to be something that linked them all to Nyx, the thing that had given him access to them and the opportunity to recruit them.

She scrolled back up more slowly, pausing to read some of the information. All three of them had uploaded videos onto TikTok – Olivia singing advertising jingles with the words slightly changed, Shan playing the piano and Neil jamming with the members of the school jazz band. None of them were on Twitter. They all appeared to have Facebook pages, but mostly unused. Neil shared comic strips from xkcd occasionally, and Lexi remembered that Eric Cotter had been wearing an xkcd T-shirt when they'd spoken to him. Just a sign that they were both geeks, or indicative of a more sinister connection?

Tom was still leaning on the doorframe, looking at the email on his phone.

'Tom, I'm wondering if we need to take a closer look at the computer science teacher, Eric Cotter. He would certainly know how to run a chatroom on the dark web.'

'Sure, but what's the link between him and Olivia and Shan?'

Lexi shrugged and carried on scrolling, half her attention on the screen and half wondering how they could find out if Eric Cotter was Nyx. Even if they confiscated his computer and phone to see if he was on the dark web – and he'd already admitted that much to them anyway – they wouldn't be able to access anything he didn't want them to see. He was far too clever to simply leave his browser open to show others the way.

'We need to find someone who has the current IP address of the chatroom so we can get access to it,' she said, her eyes glazing as more pictures of Shan seated at the grand piano in his parents' house slid down her screen.

'I don't see how we can do that,' said Tom. 'You can't put

out a public appeal asking members of Club Edicius to step forward and make themselves known.'

He was right.

A picture caught her eye. It was Neil, playing his saxophone on a small stage inside a marquee. At a wedding maybe? She'd seen it somewhere before though. She reversed her scrolling and went back, more slowly, over what she'd just seen.

'Look!' She pointed at another picture further down. It was of Olivia singing, with two other girls, and they were on the same stage in the same marquee.

Tom came over to her desk, and she scrolled up and down between the two images for him to see.

'Same place,' he said.

She stopped at one of them and looked for the context. There was a caption underneath:

Neil McGowan on saxophone in the final round. © Tenterden International Music Festival

'Ever heard of it?' said Tom.

'No.' Lexi typed the name of the festival into Google, and clicked through to the page at the top of the search results.

There was a bird's-eye photo showing a red-brick Tudor manor house with red roofs and tall, spiral chimneys. It was surrounded by grounds, and dotted around the gardens were several marquees in varying sizes. The paths between them were crowded with people, and there were food vans, outdoor seating areas and, discreetly located behind a hedge, a row of grey plastic portaloos. The words *Tenterden International Music Festival* ran across the image in yellow italic type.

Lexi scrolled down to find the explanatory text.

The Tenterden International Music Festival, held every May at Winterhythe Place, Tenterden, draws together the country's finest young musicians and singers for three days of competition which showcases the breathtaking raw talent of tomorrow's stars.

We celebrate the best classical music has to offer – orchestral masterpieces, solo virtuosity, heaven-sent voices and exquisite composition – until one young singer and one young musician have been crowned the overall winners.

The page went on with explanations of how to enter and where to order tickets. Lexi clicked through to the gallery and skimmed the pictures.

'There.' She jabbed a finger at the screen, where Shan was pictured sitting at a grand piano, eyes closed in concentration and one hand raised above the keys. 'Shan's been there too. This could be our link between the victims and Nyx.'

'You think he could have made contact with them here?'

'It's the only link we've seen between them. Tenuous, I know.' Tom looked doubtful. 'The thing is, it opens up new avenues for us to look at. Who played or sang here? We should be able to get a list of participants from the organisers, and perhaps we could canvas them to see if they've heard of Nyx or Club Edicius. And who was in the audience – perhaps not so easy to establish. We could get information on tickets bought in advance by credit card, but not when people pay cash at the gate.'

'I'll send Colin to retrieve the information.'

Lexi closed the email and snapped her laptop shut. 'No, we'll go ourselves.'

Tom looked askance at her.

'This year's festival kicks off this afternoon – heats for a few days, finals on Thursday – and I have a feeling we should be taking a closer look at exactly what goes on there.'

FORTY

Tenterden could easily claim the title of Kent's prettiest village. It had a high street of Tudor and Georgian shops with bay windows, an Anglo-Saxon church named after St Mildred, and a fine choice of coaching inns, all of which made it popular stockbroker territory with house prices to match. Winterhythe Place lay five miles north of the village, and even without satnav, they would have found it easily enough by following the stream of cars, coaches and vans winding through the narrow lanes towards it.

They were in the Jeep, which meant Lexi could peer out of the passenger window as they were directed past the driveway of the main house to the festival car park in a nearby field. She caught a glimpse of red brick splendour at the end of an avenue of smartly pollarded lime trees – mullioned windows, purple wisteria and spiral brick chimneys that could have come straight out of a period drama. They followed the car ahead of them another hundred metres down the road and then through a five-bar gate into a field. The recent rain had left the ground soft and the first few metres were a muddy churn.

Tom winced. 'Back to the car wash after this.'

'At least we're not in the Crossfire,' said Lexi. Her low-slung sports car definitely wasn't built for off-roading.

They followed directions from a man in green overalls, and five minutes later found the way from the car park to the festival ground along a rutted gravel track.

Lexi outlined her plan. 'We'll ask to have a word with whoever's in charge. We want a list of participants for this year and the last couple of years. I assume that will be easy enough – they should all be listed in the programme each time. Getting a list of ticket holders probably won't be so straightforward, but they're going to have to dig it up for us.'

Tom glanced around as they emerged through another gate into an open space at the side of the manor surrounded by a semi-circle of catering vans. People were queueing for coffee and doughnuts, vegan burgers and cheese toasties, Pimm's and beer. 'One of these people could be Nyx, and there's no way of knowing.'

Lexi shared his frustration. 'They walk among us.'

'Who?'

'Killers. And they look just like us.' She could have done with a coffee, but they needed to get on. The clock was likely ticking on another young person's life.

A sign pointed them to the ticket office, which seemed the logical place to start. They walked past a row of large marquees, from one of which issued an achingly melancholy string piece, winding down to thunderous applause. Passing another, a cacophony of sounds assaulted them, like three orchestras tuning up at once. A sign pinned onto its canvas flap indicated it was the rehearsal space. Musicians came and went, carrying instrument cases, some dressed in black tie or long dresses, others entirely casual. Finally they reached a small white tent with a green-painted sign declaring 'Tickets' above the entrance. They went in. While the girl behind the desk dealt with a woman with an overly complicated ticket collection, Lexi picked up the programme and flicked through it.

A familiar picture leapt from the page.

'Sam!'

'I'm Tom, in fact,' said Tom, with a wry smile.

'No, here.' She showed him the programme. 'This is my nephew. Look, he's going to be in round one of the singing competition this afternoon.'

'He's the one in the cathedral choir, right?'

Lexi nodded. But her bubble of pride was popped as she remembered why they were there. What if Nyx was wandering around on a recruitment drive?

The woman at the counter became free and they stepped forward. Lexi showed her ID, and Tom followed suit.

'I wonder if you could help us. We need to talk to whoever's in charge here.'

Thankfully, the woman wasn't curious. She just gave a nod and detached a handheld radio from her belt. It crackled to life as she pressed the transmission button.

'Barry, have you got a moment? Kent Police are here and want a word.'

Lexi couldn't make out the answer, but the woman assured them her boss would be along shortly. They moved to one side to allow her to get on with her job.

A few minutes later a man came into the tent and up to the desk. 'Bethany, you said someone was here to see me.' Lexi noticed that he didn't mention the police. Probably didn't want the punters to think something might be wrong.

Bethany jerked her head in their direction and the man came over to them.

'I'm Barry Gray, Festival Director. How can I help you?' He spoke with a public-school drawl and was dressed in accordance

– pale blue shirt with an embroidered logo, crisp chinos and brown loafers without socks. It came as no surprise to Lexi. The whole event smelled of wealth and privilege. It was certainly not the sort of thing she'd ever been involved in when she was at school.

'DI Lexi Bennett. We're working on an investigation and we have reason to believe that a number of victims of a crime might have performed here in past years. Would it be possible to have copies of your past programmes?'

'I'll have Bethany email them to you once things are quieter,' he said. 'May I ask about the crime? I'd like to know why the fact that the victims might have attended Winterhythe could be of any importance.'

But Lexi wasn't about to share their thoughts with Barry Gray. They had no idea who he might tell, and she didn't want Nyx to get wind of their investigation. 'We'll also need to see the names of any ticket holders who paid using a credit or debit card.'

Gray's eyebrows went up. 'I'm afraid that's altogether more complex.'

'I appreciate that, but we need it, and if you're unwilling to co-operate, I'll get a warrant to seize your records.'

'No, I don't mean to be uncooperative at all,' he said, sounding flustered. 'All I meant was that we won't be able to provide those instantly. We'll have to request the details from our ticketing agency, and then there's GDPR to consider.'

'We'd appreciate if you could move as fast as you can to get them to us,' said Tom. 'It's extremely important.'

'I'll do what I can.' Gray glanced around the ticket tent, as if he was hoping someone would come to his rescue.

And a thought struck Lexi.

What if Barry Gray is Nyx?

The festival would give him plenty of access to potential

victims. He was an authority figure, someone they might look up to. His mention of GDPR as a way of quickly dodging their request showed a level of legal savvy...

Had they just shown their hand to the one person they needed to keep it from?

FORTY-ONE

After leaving their details with the harassed-looking Bethany, Lexi and Tom left the ticket office. Barry Gray had slipped out just ahead of them, and as they emerged into the sunshine, Lexi looked around for him.

'Where did he go?'

'Why?' said Tom.

'I don't know. Just feel like keeping eyes on him.' She thumbed through the programme she'd picked up to see if there were any details about the man. On the inside page, there was a welcoming letter with his picture above it and his signature beneath. He looked younger in the picture, making her wonder when it had been taken. Not recently. Underneath the illegible signature it said: *World-famous violinist and Tenterden International Music Festival founder Barry Gray.*

'World-famous violinist?' mused Tom. 'I've never heard of him.'

'Listen to much classical music?'

'Nah, more into the Foo Fighters myself.'

Lexi laughed, but she listened to Radio Three quite often and she'd never heard of him. But of course his own festival would puff him up. He'd probably played second fiddle in a regional orchestra back in his youth.

'Let's grab a coffee,' she said, 'and scope the place out. See if we spot any suspicious behaviour. See what Mr Gray gets up to.' She knew it was a long shot, but they were both due some caffeine.

It was a pleasant enough place to wander around, but Lexi couldn't let herself get distracted by the music. The bitter taste of an espresso on the back of her tongue sharpened her senses as they filtered through the swirling mass of people drifting between the various venues. Large boards announced the programme for the day – concert performances, workshops and the competition heats. As far as she could gather, winning one of the competition categories or the overall festival award was enormously prestigious. But of course, the festival publicity would imply that.

They caught odd glimpses of Barry Gray, walkie-talkie glued to his ear, hurrying from place to place with a self-important air.

'Far too busy to be grooming teenagers,' said Lexi, as he rushed past them for the umpteenth time.

'And too high a profile in this particular arena,' said Tom. 'But look who else is here.' He nodded his head in the direction of one of the food kiosks.

Lexi looked round. It was Paul Arbuthnot, chatting with two teenagers as they waited in the queue for snacks. She recognised one of them as Kieran, the boy she'd spoken to outside Walmer Parish Hall. The other was a girl she'd never seen before. She wondered if she could be Siren, the new girl in the chatroom.

'Take a couple of pictures,' she said to Tom in a low voice. 'You keep an eye on him, and get pictures of any young people he talks to. We might be able to find Nyx's next victim among them – which means we might be able to prevent the next death.'

'Gotcha.'

She looked in the programme. There was the first rounds of a singing competition for groups and soloists taking place – the Kingsdown Singers were listed among the entrants. 'But keep an eye out for anything else that looks like grooming. It's still my opinion that Arbuthnot hasn't got the technical skills to be a lord of the dark web.' Of course, with countless young musicians taking pep talks from music teachers and mentors, anything could look suspicious. She wondered if they were clutching at straws.

Arbuthnot had reached the front of the queue. He bought himself a drink, but didn't buy anything for the two kids he was talking to. They were left to get their own snacks as he wandered away. Tom followed in the same direction, leaving Lexi to finish her coffee on her own.

She sat down on an empty bench and let her gaze sweep through the throng of people. Could Nyx really be here? They knew so little about him – just a few minutes' chatter before he'd shut her out of Club Edicius. She didn't feel she had a fix on him and she couldn't get inside his head, which was a critical part of being able to profile. What were his motivations? What was he getting out of it? Where did he come from and what was his background?

'Aunt Lexi, Aunt Lexi.'

She looked up to see Sam running towards her down the path.

'Sam – hi.'

As she was sitting down, he towered over her. He'd reached the age at which boys seemed taller every time you saw them. She stood up and gave him a brief hug.

'I saw your name was in the programme. I was going to try to find you.'

'Amazing. We're on at three p.m. – we're going to sing a requiem for Olly. Will you still be here?'

'Of course. I wouldn't miss it for the world.'

'Did Mum tell you about it? She and Dad are coming to listen.'

'No. It's just a coincidence. I'm here looking into something for work.'

'To do with Olly?'

Lexi shook her head. Sam was far too young for her to discuss cases with. It didn't seem like he was that interested anyway.

'Will it be a competition entry or just a memorial?'

'It's part of the competition, too.' His expression changed. 'I'm singing a solo verse. Man, I hope I don't let the others down.'

'You won't. You'll be great.'

A woman came and sat down at the other end of the bench. She was young and studious-looking.

Sam looked around sharply. 'I've gotta go. We're having a final rehearsal in a minute.'

'Good luck,' said Lexi, as he bounded off at full speed. 'You'll smash it.'

But a twinge of unease ran through her to see him disappearing between the marquees. At least he'd be back with the rest of the choir in a minute. She didn't like the thought of him wandering around here on his own.

'Don't talk to strangers,' she called after him, but he was long gone.

Lexi dialled Tom. 'Where are you?'

'Round the back of the manor.'

'I'll find you.'

She followed a gravel path around the sprawling building, then climbed a set of stone steps onto a raised rear terrace. There was a temporary bar here. People were buying Pimm's

and huge gin and tonics in plastic beakers. It was a sunny afternoon and there was a buzz of chatter rising from around the
small circular tables overlooking the manor's perfect lawn. She
spotted Tom at the far end of the terrace. He was taking photos
– there was a rose garden to one side of the lawn, a glorious
splash of colour absolutely worthy of a picture. But as Lexi
came up to him, she saw what he was really focused on.

In the centre of the rose garden, under a wrought-iron
pergola tangled with climbing roses, two people sat together on
a curved bench, heads bowed low and together. One she
quickly recognised. Eric Cotter, the computer science teacher
from Griffin Elms. The other was unknown to Lexi, a teenage
boy who might or might not be one of his pupils. They were
speaking animatedly, the boy shaking his head vigorously on
occasion.

'What's he doing here?' she said, reaching Tom at the stone
balustrade that marked the edge of the terrace. 'He's not a music
teacher.'

Tom lowered his camera. 'Exactly what I was wondering.
Shall we go and ask?'

Lexi thought for a moment. 'I think we'll keep our powder
dry,' she said. 'If he's Nyx, we don't necessarily want him to
know we're onto him. Just keep an eye on him.'

As she spoke, a woman walked across the lawn towards the
rose garden. She was carrying a couple of cans of coke, and a bar
of chocolate. The two beneath the pergola looked up as she
reached them, the boy stretching out a hand to take one of the
drinks. Cotter looked up and laughed at something she said, and
then stood up to take his leave. Seconds later, he was striding
back across the lawn, leaving the boy and woman in the rose
garden.

'Curiouser and curiouser,' muttered Lexi. She checked her
watch. 'My nephew's singing in a minute – I just met him and
promised I'd go and listen. Maybe you could keep eyes on

Cotter for a bit and, as soon as I can get away, we'll head back to the station.'

Tom nodded, his eyes following Cotter as he skirted round the far end of the terrace.

Lexi made her way to one of the larger tents where the choir competition was in progress. As she slipped in at the back, she spotted Amber and Grant sitting in the second row. As if suddenly aware of her arrival, Amber looked round, and their eyes met. Lexi raised her hand in a wave as Amber's eyebrows went up, no doubt wondering what her sister was doing here. Then the Canterbury Cathedral Choir walked out onto the stage in two columns, and Amber turned back to the front. The requiem they sang was haunting and beautiful. The audience was mesmerised. When it came to the second verse, Sam stepped forward and sung a solo, his treble voice soaring above the audience like quicksilver. Lexi was surprised to find tears building in the corners of her eyes.

His talent was extraordinary, and he didn't even seem aware of it.

She couldn't bear the thought of anything ever happening to him, and as applause erupted at the end of the performance, her eyes scanned the crowd.

Nyx, are you here?

FORTY-TWO

I saw the way the two pigs were sniffing around, though luckily their interest seemed to be focused elsewhere. But it's a big site and the cops won't be there all week – plenty of time for making connections once they're out of the way.

It was great to catch up with Masher again. I wonder if he'll show up in the chatroom later. I told him to check in. And I've got my eye on a couple more in our WhatsApp group who might be ready to graduate to the club.

Time to go online.

Nyx: hey, who's here this evening? how u all doing?

Trollster: in the house

Ghoul: doing okay in dark times

Nyx: we're here for you, buddy

Ghoul: it helps

Trollster: you know what to do when it gets too dark, don't you

Nyx: careful, trollster

Trollster: i just say what we all think

Trollster can always be relied on to push the boundaries and give the extra nudge. I've worked hard to get the group dynamics just right to achieve the best results.

Nyx: anyone else lurking in the shadows?

Siren: always happiest lurking

Nyx: hey, siren - glad you came back

Siren: feeling a bit shit actually. had to cut myself this afternoon to keep a lid on it

Nyx: be careful when you do that, siren.

Masher: hi

HoneyBox : there's a familiar voice. been a while

Nyx: hey masher. how's it going? how was the competition?

Ghoul: hi to you, masher

Masher: thanks for asking, nyx. it went pretty badly. i'm having trouble with my voice

Trollster: here for you kid - we're one big happy family here

Honeybox: happy isn't the word i'd use to describe you lot

Trollster: depressed as fuck, that's us

Masher: I feel like i fit right in

Good. They're all playing nicely together. A nice choice of recruits to lead through the funnel towards their grand finales. Perhaps Masher and Siren could have a joint final act.

First, though, there's a bit of housekeeping.

Nyx: guys, you might not have realised this, but a couple of days back our security was breached

Yoshi: who done it?

Nyx: someone – not necessarily someone here right now – left their browser open. we had a visitor who tried to sneak in under their identity

Trollster: so ding em out the club

Nyx: they're already gone. they won't be back

HoneyBox: oh god, you mean lolly, right?

Nyx: it doesn't matter who it was. just keep by the club rules – tell no one, show no one – got it?

HoneyBox: listen, lolly was a drag. why's it no surprise she left the door open when she checked out

Siren: where's lolly gone

Trollster: lolly took a dangle

Yoshi: she jumped, man

Siren: wow, guys, show some respect. you're pretty harsh, you know

Nyx: she's right. you should be respectful of a fallen comrade

Ghoul: so, masher, what's your problem? why d'you feel the need to join an exit club

Nyx: hey, masher – you still there?

Trollster: don't worry – he'll be back

Siren: don't be so sure – you know sometimes you guys make this a pretty hateful place...

But that's the whole idea, isn't it?

FORTY-THREE

Ed looked ragged. The stress of Charlie's illness was drawn on his features and even his movements lacked their usual vigour. It wasn't surprising, given the circumstances, but it worried her. Despite having suffered her own losses over the years, the prospect of losing a life partner so young was something she could hardly imagine.

'You sit. I'll fetch coffee,' said Lexi. It seemed a pitiful gesture of support.

He complied without protest, and Lexi went up to the counter and ordered an espresso for herself and a flat white for him. As well as a large slice of carrot cake. She was guessing his mind was on things other than food at the moment, and at least carrot cake would give him an energy boost.

She'd called him on the drive back to Canterbury. Initially she thought it would be a good idea to get him over to Tenterden, to see if he could spot any suspicious behaviour. But when she spoke to him he'd sounded wiped out, so she'd suggested meeting for coffee instead, if he could spare the time. He said he could, so half an hour later here they were, in a small café on St Peter's Street.

'I'm sorry if this wasn't a good time for you.' She put the cake down in front of him, but he was more interested in the coffee.

He took a sip and let out a long sigh. 'Sorry, Lexi. I'm a bit all over the place. We found out yesterday that Charlie's cancer has spread to her lymph nodes.'

Lexi put a hand to her mouth. 'Oh no, I'm so sorry. What happens next?'

'They're going to explore various treatment options – we'll know more in a couple of days.'

'Listen, I didn't mean to drag you away from her. If you want to get back...'

'It's okay. We get on each other's nerves if we're together twenty-four-seven. She needs time to process this and so do I. And the world doesn't just stop when someone's ill.'

Lexi couldn't shake off a feeling of guilt at having called him out, so the least she could do was make it quick.

'I'll try not to keep you. I just really wanted to run over a few thoughts about the guy running the chatroom. I believe he recruits his victims in real life.'

'What makes you think that?'

'There's nothing on any of the kids' laptops that sets off alarm bells over grooming or inappropriate contact, which we might expect to see if he was recruiting them online – before he diverted them onto the dark web.'

'That makes sense.'

'And there are no online connections between the three victims whose identity we know – Olivia, Shan and Neil. Naturally, we don't know the real names of the other members of the chatroom.'

'So your theory is that Nyx engineers meeting these kids in real life and persuades them to join his chatroom?'

'That's what it looks like to me. Does that align with any experience you've had with suicide cults?'

Ed picked up the fork and toyed with the carrot cake for a moment before finally taking a mouthful of it. He chewed slowly, obviously weighing up his next answer.

'It's good.'

'My theory?'

'No, the cake. But your theory's got legs as well. The fact that the victims live relatively close to one another suggests a real-life connection. And I think you need to look at how his motivation fits in.'

'The geographical proximity lends support to him being present when deaths occur. Perhaps he gets some sort of voyeuristic pleasure out of watching, or perhaps he needs to see them die to get closure.'

'Your Munchausen theory?'

'Yes, he's using them as proxies to feed his suicidal urges.'

'So where do you go from here?'

Lexi took a mouthful of her coffee as she pondered. 'What I don't have is that place of connection – where they meet in real life and how those meetings are arranged. Who picks the sites – him or his victims? When do they discuss the timing, the method, all that stuff?'

'Presumably in the chatroom. You don't have full access to it, do you?'

'No. But another thing – all the victims' mobiles are missing. I suspect Nyx is taking them – possibly to stop us seeing messages they exchanged.' She made a mental note to chase Colin – she'd asked him to request access to accounts of the missing mobiles so they could see what text messages had been sent and received.

'What you need to look at is what the kids in the chatroom have in common in real life,' said Ed, 'and then you'll find the connections that brought them into Nyx's sphere.'

'Like I said, we haven't found any direct connections between them at all so far. They're musical and might have met at the Tenterden music festival, but we don't have evidence of this.'

'No direct connections, but what is it that makes Nyx single them out?'

Lexi thought about what she knew of Olivia, Shan and Neil. 'One girl, two boys. They all live in Kent. Age range thirteen to seventeen. They're all bright, from families that value education. Olivia and Neil were at boarding schools, but Shan was home-schooled...'

'Wait – stop at that. Shan is taught at home, alone. Very isolating. Boarding school can be isolating, too, for some kids.'

'So Nyx is looking for loners. Teenagers who aren't part of a strong friendship group perhaps – so more likely to spend their time in a chatroom?'

'And not have anyone around persuading them not to.'

'Kids that can sneak out to Nyx's choice of location... It makes sense,' said Lexi. 'If he shows up to watch his victims take their own lives, he needs to find kids that are within reach.'

Ed offered her a forkful of cake and when she nodded, instead of passing the fork to her, he fed it to her directly. It was a strangely intimate gesture, given theirs was a professional relationship.

'Thanks.'

Ed's eyes met hers. 'You know why I like working with you, Lexi?'

'Why?' Her mouth was still full of cake.

'Your superpower.'

She laughed and was then embarrassed as crumbs sprayed onto the table.

'No, seriously.' He held up a hand, though he was smiling with her. 'You and I, we've been through the same training. We know all the theories, we've got the experience. But you bring something extra to the table.'

'Yes, crumbs.'

He ignored this. 'Your empathy. Very few people have such a high level of empathy. Not only with the victims, but with the perps, too. It's what makes you such a good profiler. You get right inside the doers' minds and your empathy allows you to understand what they're thinking when they act out their urges.'

'Maybe,' said Lexi, 'but I can assure you, it's not a great place to be.'

'I don't doubt it.' He paused, as if weighing up his next observation. 'I think it's because of what you went through, with Amber and Rose.' He was referring to when Lexi and her sisters were abducted at the age of seventeen. It had been a truly harrowing experience. She and Amber had managed to escape, but leaving Rose behind, injured, was the biggest regret of her life. They'd fetched help, but when they returned to the spot where they'd left her, she'd disappeared. Lexi had never seen her again.

She hated talking about it, even to Ed. Especially to Ed, given that he taught her case on his forensic psychology course at Kent University. Time to change the subject.

'But so far, getting inside Nyx's head has proved difficult. We know nothing about him. In fact, we don't even know if he's a man or a woman.' It was far too easy to slip into referring to Nyx as him, as that was most likely – but it was dangerous. Confirmation bias could lead to missing important clues.

'Have you found evidence of his or her presence at the scenes?'

Lexi shrugged. 'Nothing concrete. There was a footprint we haven't managed to identify where Neil died. Nothing at the Westgate and nothing at Leas Cliff Hall.' It reminded her that she needed to catch up with Emily Jordan in case the CSIs had managed to find more evidence.

'And do the scenes have anything in common?'

'They're all in public places. So Nyx could be there – which he couldn't if the victims were doing it in their own bedrooms or other private spaces.'

'In other words, the circumstances in all three cases would allow for that theory to be true, but don't actively support it in terms of evidence.'

Lexi nodded. 'That's why I wanted to run it by you, in case you'd seen the like before.'

'Nothing exactly like this. Most suicide cults are about mass suicides – you know, like Jim Jones and the People's Temple.'

'Kool-Aid in the commune...'

'In fact, it was a drink called Flavor Aid, but when has the press or the internet cared about accuracy? Anyway, that was nine hundred people, all committing suicide simultaneously, and Jones died with them. Your Nyx is playing an entirely different game, and I don't suppose it includes his own suicide.'

'In which case, he's actively inciting suicide in victims he's identified and targeted. Surely pushing it across the line to manslaughter.' Lexi wanted to be sure Nyx could be charged with something more than just incitement.

'I'd have to agree with that.'

'And if he's turning up at the scene and physically assisting them, could that be construed as murder?'

'That's one for the lawyers to argue over in court but, sure, I'd view it as murder. Current case precedent would definitely allow for a manslaughter charge on that.'

Lexi absentmindedly helped herself to another mouthful of the cake.

'But he's escalating – pushing his victims ever quicker towards the final step. What's his end game?'

'Hard to say – but I'm not sure we want to find out.'

'Making it all the more critical that I find the evidence that proves what he, or she, is doing. And more importantly, I've got to catch him, before another kid dies.'

And she would – for Olly, for Shan and for Neil. And in time to save Siren and the other nameless teenagers Nyx was drawing into the web.

FORTY-FOUR

It was time to catch up with Emily Jordan. After expressing well wishes for Charlie as she and Ed parted company, Lexi turned back towards the Westgate and dialled Emily's number. She wanted to see the crime scene manager face to face, so she could really stress the importance of finding some evidence of another person at each of the murder scenes. Because, in her opinion, that's what they were – murder scenes. These kids didn't need to have died. They were pushed into it by an unscrupulous manipulator, and if she couldn't catch him via the dark web, she would damn well catch him out in the real world.

Although it was past five thirty, she was confident that Emily would still be working.

She wasn't wrong. 'Lexi, sorry – I know you've been waiting to hear from me.'

'No worries. No point in phoning unless you have something for me. But I wondered if we could meet? I wanted to talk to you about where I think this case is leading.'

There was a second's silence on the other end of the line. 'I have to follow where the evidence leads – you know that.'

'Of course.' Emily had misunderstood her. 'I'm not trying to sway your view of the evidence. I just need you to know what I'm looking for.'

'Which is?' The CSM's voice was distinctly frosty.

'Look, I'm pretty sure that someone is not only inciting these kids to take their own lives, but I suspect they're actively helping. Will you meet me at the Westgate, so we can analyse how Olivia might have fallen and whether there might have been someone else present?'

'It sounds like you don't think we did a proper job first time round.'

'No, it's not that.' She wasn't explaining herself well. 'But when Olivia died, we really had no idea that someone else might have been part of it. I just need someone to knock heads with, someone who understands the principle of Locard's exchange.'

'Every contact leaves a trace,' said Emily. 'Something taken away from the scene, something left behind.'

'Exactly. If my perp was actually present, you're the one person who'll be able to confirm it.'

Emily sighed. 'Okay. It'll take me half an hour to get there.'

'Thank you a thousand times,' said Lexi.

She checked her texts and emails while she waited and was pleased to hear from Tom that the suspect in the Swan stabbing had been charged and the files were being prepared for the CPS. Colin and Ridhi were turning into quite a formidable little team – and she seemed to bring out the best in him, which was no mean feat.

Thinking of them, she allowed herself a smile as she walked up the High Street, but as the two dark towers loomed above her, their long black shadows falling to one side in the early evening sun, her thoughts turned to Olivia James. This case was far more complex. She walked through the arch between the towers to come out just where the girl's body had been sprawled on the pavement several days before.

Of course, there was no sign of it now, apart from a small pile of fading bouquets that had been left at the foot of the east tower.

She stared up to the top. The ramparts from which Olivia jumped – or was pushed – were silhouetted against a grimy sky, its blue giving way to a bruised grey to the northeast. It seemed a little cool for May and Lexi wondered if it was going to rain. Not that it mattered – it had rained several times since Monday, so any evidence that was weather-susceptible would have already been compromised. But there still had to be something – a fibre snagged somewhere inside the towers, a scuff of rubber from the sole of a shoe, a fingerprint on a surface not often cleaned. She needed to be able to see the place through Emily's eyes. She was the expert on discovering the traces a person left behind and Lexi was certain that Nyx must have left evidence at all three scenes.

She went back through the archway and towards the tower's reception area in the old gaol. Inside, she could see Mark Bryant, the manager, talking to a girl who appeared to be reckoning up the till. She pulled open the door.

'Hello Mr Bryant, you remember me – DI Bennett?'

He turned around and smiled as he recognised her. 'Of course. What can I do for you?'

'I'm glad I caught you.' She didn't add that if he'd already left for home, she would have had him called back. 'I wonder if it would be possible for me and my crime scene manager to take another look at the top of the tower. Just in case we missed anything.'

'Of course,' he said. He looked at his watch. 'I've got an escape room experience booked in, kicking off at seven. You've got an hour – will that be enough?'

Lexi nodded. Of course, the towers had visitors to its museum all day and experiences in the evening. How likely was it that a small piece of trace evidence from Nyx could be found and identified?

A minute later Emily arrived with raindrops spangling her hair. 'Hi,' she said.

Lexi introduced her to Bryant.

He nodded. 'We met on Monday, I think?'

'We did,' said Emily.

'Let's start at the top,' said Lexi.

They left Bryant in the old gaol and made their way up the stairs and across the glass bridge into the towers. As they emerged into the open air of the viewing platform at the top, Emily turned to Lexi.

'The footprint at Griffin Elms...'

'What about it?'

'We're fairly certain it's not Paul Arbuthnot's.'

'How so?' They hadn't had access to all of Arbuthnot's shoes yet.

'We took a cast. The skidding meant the pattern of ridges on the sole were distorted, but we made some experimental skids on the same slope to see how they matched up. What those told us was that the shoe that slipped there was a pretty standard size-nine trainer, suggesting an individual approximately five feet eight, average build. Arbuthnot is quite a way over six foot, and his feet will be correspondingly larger – I would guess at least a shoe size eleven or twelve.'

'Could he have been wearing shoes too small to disguise himself?'

'Two sizes too small? It would make it hard for him to walk.'

'Small feet for his height?'

'That small would look weird and I think you would have noticed it.'

Lexi made a mental note to get Tom or Colin to confirm the size of Arbuthnot's feet. 'Thanks,' she said to Emily. It was something of a disappointment, not really the sort of information Lexi was hoping to hear. It just seemed to rule out one suspect without pointing the finger at another. But it was in line with what Lexi had always felt about Paul Arbuthnot. Perhaps instead they should be looking at the shoe size of Eric Cotter.

'Got a match for the rope, though,' said Emily. 'It's made from natural hemp fibres, and I'm about ninety-nine per cent certain that it was made in Chatham – there's a rope walk there at the old naval dockyard, and it's still operational.'

'Brilliant. Perhaps we'll be able to trace who bought it.' She made a mental note to get Ridhi or Colin to follow up on this.

Emily started to make a careful inspection of the wooden railing that ran along the inside of the stone ramparts. 'You know, even if I find something now, it's not going to carry weight in court. Too much time has elapsed and the place has been open to the public.' She pointed at some more bunches of flowers that had been left just between the railing and the outer wall. 'God knows how many people have traipsed through.'

'I get it,' said Lexi, unable to contain her irritation. 'But what if we find trace evidence that links all three sites? Especially if, at some point, it can be tied to a suspect.'

Emily turned away to examine another section of the railing. 'It's fine, Lexi. I'll look for more. But it's up to the courts how much weight they place on it.'

'And I won't even get this to court if I don't know who's behind it.' Lexi hated arguing with colleagues, but she had to put the case first – and if she had to push the boundaries to catch a killer, she would do it.

She waited in silence while Emily carried on her inspection. At one point she went to her bag and pulled out a small spray can. She sprayed the top of the wooden railing and then stepped back.

'Luminol?' said Lexi.

'It'll emit pale blue light if there are any traces of blood or other body fluids on the surface.'

They both stared at where she'd sprayed, but there was no luminescence.

Emily shrugged. 'I didn't expect it to show anything. After all, we've had some heavy rain over the last couple of days.'

Disappointment fuelled Lexi's anger. Not with Emily – she was just doing her job as requested. But with her own inability to find Nyx. She left Emily to it and went back to the top of the spiral staircase. There was a thick rope handrail attached using iron rings to the outer wall of the spiral, essential when climbing the worn and slippery stone steps. Lexi donned a pair of latex gloves, and examined it closely using the torch on her phone. The rope was black and smooth with the grease from hundreds of hands. She couldn't believe that it would have anything to offer, but still she had to look.

There was nothing to see on the top of the rope, or the side that faced out from the wall, but she realised she could twist it round in the iron rings which secured it. The underside was less grimy, the individual strands making up the rope less worn smooth. But there was still nothing to see. Then she looked at the individual iron rings, each hanging from a hasp set into the stonework of the wall at intervals of approximately three feet. They'd obviously been in place for a very long time, regardless of whether the rope had been replaced over the years. Some of them were showing signs of corrosion and flakes of rust, while one or two had worked a little loose in their settings.

She examined each one of them closely from every angle.

'Emily! Emily!' One of the hasps had a row of tiny white flakes clinging to its outer edge. 'Come here – there's something you need to see.'

Emily hurried down the steps to where Lexi was standing.

'Could this be skin? Could someone have grazed their arm or hand on this hasp as they made their way up or down the stairs?'

Emily looked more closely, and pulled a magnifying glass

out of her pocket. She sprayed a tiny amount of luminol onto some of the flakes.

Lexi immediately saw a blue glow. It lasted less than thirty seconds, but it was long enough for Emily to quickly photograph it with a small camera.

'Yes, that's skin and, I think, a tiny trace of blood as well. But it could be anyone's. It would be easy enough to knock your knuckle against these, don't you think?'

Lexi took the spray can from where Emily had put it down on one of the steps. She sprayed it in a broad sweep across the stone wall above the rope banister. Emily stopped what she was doing and looked up.

'Jesus!' Emily scrabbled for her camera.

Blue luminescence blossomed in a wide arc across the wall, a curve that stretched from the hasp they'd been looking at to a point a few feet further down the staircase.

'That looks like the person grazed their hand or arm against the wall,' said Lexi.

'Someone falling down the stairs?' said Emily. 'Or trying to keep their balance after stumbling?'

'If it was a fall... I think the arc would be lower, probably under the level of the hand rope. Maybe someone pushing past another person... Or, if someone was running down the stairs as fast as they could, they might have brushed an arm against the wall to keep their balance.'

'Hard to say.'

'I need to call Mort,' said Lexi. 'I'm sure Olivia had a graze on one of her forearms. If these specks of skin and blood match her DNA, it'll tell us something about what happened up here.'

'How do you mean?' said Emily.

'If the DNA matches Olivia – and that's a big if – depending on which arm the graze is, we'll be able to surmise whether she was moving up or down the staircase when it happened. Did she stumble as she came up the stairs, or was she trying to run away down them? Can you tell from the skin which direction the hand or arm moved across the wall?'

'Possibly, once I enlarge the photos. But Olivia didn't go back down the stairs, did she?'

Lexi looked up towards the doorway that led out to the viewing area from which Olivia had dropped to her death.

'No, she didn't. But maybe she tried to. Maybe someone pulled her back up.'

FORTY-FIVE

After the excitement of solving the pub stabbing, Ridhi now faced a thankless task. On the left side of her desk, she had a list of the witnesses that she and the first responders had spoken to at the base of the Westgate just after Olivia's death. On the other side, she had a stack of grainy images printed out from the various CCTV cameras in the immediate vicinity, ranging from half an hour before the girl fell to the point several hours later when the body was taken away and the onlookers cleared.

She was painstakingly matching the two – identifying the people in the pictures and checking them off on the list of witnesses from whom they'd taken statements. Lexi had asked her to track down anybody that they hadn't already spoken to who might have seen something, before or after the event. The boss seemed to think that someone had been with Olivia at the top of the tower. In which case someone else must have seen that person, either at the top or entering or exiting the tower before or after it happened.

Ridhi wasn't quite so sure. Surely if there'd been someone with Olivia at the top, they'd have stopped her? Not just stood idly by and watched. Even someone who might have been inciting kids to take their own lives wouldn't be as stupid as to stand right next to them when they did it, in a public place, where they might be seen. Besides, she felt pretty sure they'd spoken to everyone who'd been there at the time.

But she carried on diligently, only stopping to refill her coffee mug and nip down to the vending machine for another bar of chocolate. This was now sitting unopened in front of her. She'd had two already, earlier in the afternoon, and the thought of more sugar was making her feel sick.

She picked up her red marker pen again, working through the pictures by placing a red X over the face of any of the bystanders she knew they'd interviewed. She had to admit, there was a level of satisfaction when she could put an image aside because all of the people in the picture had been seen.

But she had a long way to go – the pile was high. She pulled the next one onto her blotter and studied it, quickly crossing out three witnesses that had already featured in earlier shots. As she worked, she was thinking about her sister. Meera was waiting for the results of her online assessment with the College of Policing – the start of the long and rigorous application process to become a PC. And while Meera was bubbling over with excitement at the prospect, Ridhi had some reservations. She remembered the things she'd seen and the incidents she'd been called to as a uniformed PC, and she wasn't at all sure she wanted her baby sister to be subjected to the same experiences. She sighed. She remembered how excited she'd been at this stage of the process. She should be excited for Meera, too.

Blinking, she realised her concentration had lapsed so she reapplied her mind to the task and moved on to the next picture in the pile. But her breath caught, as in this image, for the first time, she spotted Olivia walking in at the very edge of the picture, on her way to the Westgate. She was dressed in her school uniform – as she had been when she'd died – and the time stamp on the image put her arrival at the Westgate some twenty-five minutes before the alarm was raised that someone had fallen. She was alone and she didn't have a bag.

Of course, she'd seen the image before – it was one of the first things they'd checked for in the first few hours after she died. But realising now the person almost disappearing from the edge of the frame was actually Olivia carried an emotional punch. The picture quality was grainy, but Ridhi could see the defeated expression on Olivia's face, the way her shoulders were bowed as if she was carrying the weight of the world. The series of images showed that she was walking funereally slowly, almost as if she didn't want to reach her destination.

In the next picture, she was a few metres closer to the tower, and in the next one, closer still. Ridhi screwed up her eyes and looked more closely. There was something... different going on. A barely perceptible change in Olivia's body language – back straighter, foot raised slightly, but not stepping forward. Ridhi studied her face. Her eyes were wider. Her mouth, which in the previous image had been set in a grim line of determination, was slightly open in this one. And before, bent arms, hands balled into fists, while here her arms were straight, hands flat, fingers splayed.

What had she seen?

By the time the next image had come around, she'd disappeared into the tower.

Ridhi went back to this one picture. What had made Olivia's mood change so dramatically?

In all the pictures of her walking, Olivia's gaze had been fixed straight ahead, as it was in this wide-eyed image. Had she seen something further along the pavement? Someone coming towards her? Ridhi hurriedly checked the list of the CCTV camera locations to work out which one would have pointed in the same direction, and would show what was ahead of her.

She identified the relevant camera and leafed through the printed images to find the one that carried the same time stamp on the bottom left corner – this one would show her what Olivia had seen that had had such a dramatic effect. When she got to it, she pulled it from the pile and smoothed it out on the desk in front of her.

An empty pavement.

There was no one there. Nothing that might have spooked Olivia. She checked the images before and after. A car passed on the road, driving away from Olivia, meaning she wouldn't have seen the driver's face. About twenty metres away from where Olivia was when her demeanour changed, between her and the towers, there was a pair of old-fashioned red phone boxes. They looked unremarkable in the earlier picture, when Olivia was further from them. But in the critical image, one of the phone box doors looked as if it was swinging open. Ridhi couldn't see anyone going in or coming out, until she looked closer and saw a hand, pushing the door open from within.

Someone was in the phone box, about to emerge.

By the next shot in the sequence, Olivia was past the phone boxes and disappeared into the tower.

Had she been able to see who was emerging? Was it someone she wasn't expecting to see? Someone she was maybe afraid of?

She grabbed the pile of images from a camera that faced the phone boxes from a different angle and, yes, several cycles earlier, there was someone coming from the direction of the towers and going into the phone box. Dressed in dark clothing with a black or navy baseball cap, peak pulled low, there would be very little chance of identifying the person in the footage. Ridhi looked at the time stamp. Whoever it was had stayed in the phone box for almost fifteen minutes. Someone innocent making a lengthy call or someone waiting for Olivia to come down the road on her way to the towers?

Then they'd vanished in the few seconds or so between one picture and the next.

Had they stopped to speak with Olivia? Gone to the tower with her? Or simply gone on their way, nothing to do with the girl at all?

Ridhi thought not. Olivia's demeanour had changed when she'd seen them – and that very definitely made them a person of interest.

FORTY-SIX

As Emily Jordan scraped samples from the stone staircase wall, Lexi answered her phone.

It was Ridhi.

'I've been checking the CCTV images round the Westgate to sweep up any witnesses we missed and I found something.' She explained the sequence of images which showed Olivia approaching the Westgate and her apparent panic at seeing whoever was emerging from the phone box.

'Email them to me straight away,' said Lexi. She turned to Emily. 'Are you nearly done?'

'Here? Yes, but I want to do a full sweep of the rest of the staircase and the glass bridge over to the gaol, plus the stairs from there down to reception.'

'How long will that take?'

'A couple of hours at least.'

That was no good. 'Right, maybe call some of your team in. We need to check out a couple of phone boxes outside on North Lane.' She explained what Ridhi had just told her, and together they looked at the grainy images that Ridhi had emailed across.

Not that they could discern much from them on the tiny phone screen.

'They seem to be in the phone box nearer to the towers,' said Lexi. 'We need to get it cordoned off and processed.'

While Emily phoned for some CSIs to come and take over at the Westgate, Lexi explained to the manager, Mark Bryant, that she would need the entire complex closed down until after they'd finished.

'But I can't do that,' he said, ruffling his hair distractedly. 'I've got an escape room booked, and they'll be here any minute.'

'Then I'm afraid you'll have to turn them away,' said Lexi. 'I'm sorry, but information has come to light that suggests Olivia James might not have been alone when she was at the top of the tower. It puts a whole new complexion on the case and we need to do another sweep for evidence.'

'But loads of people have been up and down since then.'

'Unfortunately, yes, but that doesn't mean we can afford to ignore it.'

He looked furious, but he went down to reception in preparation to turn his punters away.

Ten minutes later, Lexi and Emily were standing in front of the two phone boxes on North Lane. Lexi had called in a bunch of uniformed PCs to secure the area around them and cordon off the entrance to the Westgate in preparation for the arrival of the CSIs. She wondered if they'd find anything useful – three days had passed, and even though public telephones now seemed like an anachronism, other people had probably used it in the intervening period.

'It was the one on the right, wasn't it?' said Emily.

Lexi knew it was, but doubled checked against the image on her phone, just to be sure.

'Yes,' she said. 'There's the hand, pushing open this door.'

Emily took photos of the two phone boxes, doors still shut,

then pulled open the left-hand door by its edge with a gloved hand, being careful not to touch the brass indented handle. Lexi took the door from her, so she could photograph the interior of the phone box. The door was heavy and the self-closing hinges meant it would swing shut if she let go of it.

She grimaced as the smell of stale urine wafted out of the confined space. 'Didn't realise these things still operated,' she said.

Emily lifted the phone's receiver and carefully held it close enough to her ear so she could listen for the dial tone, without actually letting it touch her hair or cheek. 'It doesn't – the line's dead. Just used as a public urinal, I suspect.' Her nose wrinkled as she said it.

She quickly got out her fingerprint kit and dusted down the receiver, the keypad, the coin slot and the refund tray, as well as the door's outer handle and the inside edge where people would push the door open.

'It's a mess,' she said, peering at the silver smudges on the surface of the phone apparatus. She got out a roll of clear adhesive tape. 'I can lift a few partials, but I don't know how useful they'll be.'

She worked in silence, with Lexi watching over her shoulder, wondering if one of the prints could belong to Nyx. Hoping.

'Let me see the picture again,' said Emily. 'I want to see exactly where that hand was pushing the door open.'

Lexi pulled it back up onto her screen. 'Gloved.'

'So this is a bloody waste of time,' said Emily.

'What about other traces? Hairs, fibres? I know it'll be a long shot – given that we don't even know who to match them to.'

Emily shrugged. 'It's always a long shot, but sometimes we get lucky.' She put away her fingerprinting kit and took a magnifying loupe out of her bag. Then, using a strong torch and the magnifier, she set about examining the few flat surfaces inside the box, including the floor.

'Ugh, I sometimes really hate this job.'

Where the sides of the phone box met the floor, the red paint was rusting and flaky – testament to the legions of drunk men who had used the place for something other than its original purpose.

'Wait, I might have something.' She handed Lexi the torch and pulled a clear evidence bag and a pair of tweezers from her pocket. 'Keep the beam just down there, in the corner.'

Lexi craned her neck, trying to see what Emily had found, but whatever it was, it was far too small for her to see. Using infinite care, Emily lifted something from the floor and popped it into the bag. She straightened up and held out her find.

Lexi peered at it but couldn't see anything. 'I swear, I need glasses.'

'Use this.' Emily handed her the loupe.

Lexi looked through it and Emily's hand became that of a giant. She could see every ridge on the side of her finger pads, every ripple in the surface of the crumpled bag. And inside the bag, she could see a fibre that looked as thick as a length of thread. Rough and hairy.

And red.

'It's hemp fibre,' said Emily.

And Lexi knew what it was from.

'The big red rope.'

FORTY-SEVEN

FRIDAY

Sleeping in a small, lumpy armchair in someone else's office had nothing to recommend it. When Lexi woke up, she was cold and stiff, and her neck hurt from having rested against the not particularly well cushioned arm of the chair. She opened her eyes and blinked – it was light already outside. Her watch told her it was half past five and she groaned.

'Back in the world of the living?' Emily Jordan was sitting at her desk, peering at an oversized computer monitor on which there were two enlarged images of fingerprints.

Lexi straightened herself and rubbed her neck with one hand. 'Have you slept at all?'

'Uh-uh.' Emily shook her head – and it showed in her face. Dark rings shadowed her eyes and her skin looked dry and tight. Her eyes were red-rimmed and she blinked a couple of times as she focused on the screen.

'Sorry,' said Lexi. 'I should have stayed up to keep you company.'

'Nothing you could have done to help. You should have gone home and got some proper sleep – I'm sure you've got a long day ahead of you.'

She wasn't wrong. Lexi knew she wouldn't let up for a minute until she'd discovered Nyx's identity and put him out of action.

'Point me to where I can get some coffee,' said Lexi.

Caffeine and a splash of cold water on her face made Lexi feel more human again, and Emily also looked better for the insertion of strong, black coffee.

'Please have some good news for me,' said Lexi, taking the chair opposite Emily's desk. She'd had enough of the armchair by the window to last her a lifetime.

'Right, this is where we are. I couriered the blood and skin samples from the staircase for fast DNA testing – the results should be back with us any minute.'

The advent of express DNA testing, though expensive, had made a material difference to solving cases over the last few years – instead of waiting weeks for the results, detectives could now identify suspects from trace evidence in a matter of hours, while the trail was still hot.

'What about the fibres from the phone box?' said Lexi.

'We've compared them in the lab here. They're a match for the type of rope that was used by both Shan and Neil.'

'Yes!' Lexi punched the air with her fist. This gave them a solid connection between the three deaths. 'So the person in the phone box was carrying the rope, presumably to give to Olivia. But something happened, and things didn't go according to plan.'

Emily shrugged. 'Not for me to speculate. But one thing you might need to consider… if the plan was for Olivia to hang herself – or be hanged – using the rope, where exactly would it have happened? By which I mean, where would they have secured the rope?'

Lexi considered the question. 'Over the parapet itself? Or somewhere inside the tower?'

'You don't need a very great height to hang from – after all, people hang themselves on door handles, so there could be any number of possible sites inside the building, up the staircase, somewhere on the top of the towers.'

'But this killer seems to have a taste for the dramatic. Underneath the Leas Cliff Hall, hanging from the ruins at Griffin Elms... I think to have Olivia hanging over the edge of the battlements would be in keeping with his style. Anyway, wherever it might have been, things clearly didn't go to plan. Olivia wasn't hanged. So, did she fall or was she pushed?'

'You seem certain she didn't jump.'

'More and more certain of it, the deeper we dig.'

It was too early to call Ridhi, but Lexi quickly sent her a text to keep scouring the CCTV footage when she got in. She needed to work back in time to track where the phone box individual had approached from, and then also move forward in time. Whoever it was must have left the scene after Olivia was dead, and they needed to find out where he or she went.

She looked up. Emily had turned her attention back to the fingerprints on her monitor.

'There's nothing here,' she said. 'The CSIs swept the whole tower for finger marks and we've fed them all into the system. So far, it's just a multitude of random prints and the only thing the computer has flagged up are a couple of partial prints from the underside of the wooden railing on the viewing platform that match Olivia.'

Finding Olivia's prints wasn't a surprise, but it made Lexi feel unaccountably sad – the last physical traces she left before she fell to her death.

'What about the ones you collected in the phone box?'

'One match to a fifty-six-year-old male who's on the system for a couple of counts of being drunk and disorderly. I checked his file – he's homeless, so I think we can guess what he was doing in there.'

'You're probably right, but can you email the details to me –

I'll get one of the team to check him out, just so we can rule him out definitively.'

Emily's phone pinged with a notification, and she picked it up.

'It's here,' she said. 'The result of the DNA analysis.'

Lexi held her breath as Emily scrolled down her screen.

'No.' She shook her head. 'The skin and blood samples from the staircase aren't a match for Olivia.'

Lexi felt immediately deflated. 'Are they a match to anybody?'

'No – person unknown. Female. Could be anybody. Those steps are so worn and uneven – someone will have slipped and could easily have grazed their arm as they reached for the rope.'

'Damn.' Lexi pressed her hands to her eyes and took a deep breath. Why did working a case have to be so frustrating all the time? One step forward, two steps back.

'Do you have a DNA sample and fingerprints from Paul Arbuthnot?' she said.

Emily shook her head.

'I'll get them organised,' said Lexi. 'And from Eric Cotter.'

'Who's he?'

'A teacher at Griffin Elms. Tom and I saw him yesterday at the Tenterden International Music Festival. It's a long shot, but if you got a match to either of them at the tower, even though it would just be circumstantial, we could use it to justify digging deeper.'

'Okay, if you get them to me, I'll process them as a matter of urgency.'

'Thanks, Emily. It could make all the difference.'

'Just doing my job.'

Lexi stood up to leave, but then had one final thought. 'Did you ever check Olivia's clothing for trace evidence?'

'No – we weren't asked to. I believe that after the autopsy, it was simply logged into evidence as, at that point, her suicide note meant her death was being taken at face value as just that, a suicide.'

'Would you check it for me? Particularly for rope fibres.'

Something had happened at the top of the Westgate. Lexi felt sure Olivia hadn't been up there alone. Someone had been there with her, someone who was pushing her to take her own life.

Had that person literally pushed her over the edge?

FORTY-EIGHT

I open up a private chatroom and send an invitation to Masher. The boy is in need of some encouragement, a little extra help. Things are moving fast and if there's one thing I've learned, it's that you have to strike while the iron's hot.

A flashing notification announces Masher's arrival in the chatroom. He seems a biddable individual. I've been massaging his ego for several months, and it's been a couple of weeks since I upgraded him from the WhatsApp group to the chatroom. I get the feeling we're reaching the sweet spot.

Nyx: hey masher

Masher: hey

Nyx: i thought you might like to unburden away from the rest of the crew

Masher: thanks

Nyx: i got the feeling you're going thru some tough times

Masher: i had a bad day yesterday

Nyx: what happened? why was it bad?

Masher: a thing i had to do didn't go as well as i'd hoped

Masher: i felt empty afterwards. it wasn't what I was expecting

Nyx: i understand that feeling

Masher: it's like some days the world isn't listening to me

Nyx: do you feel sad?

Masher: sad and broken and angry

Nyx: do you wish you could be somewhere else?

Masher: all the time

Nyx: there's a place you can go

Masher: ?

Nyx: where it's quiet and no one can hurt you

Masher: i dream of a place like that

Nyx: but it's a one way ticket

Masher: sign me up

Is he ready? Because I don't want to stop now. I know she'll be coming for me and I want to help as many lost souls as I can in the time I've got left. I wonder... I wonder if I could lead her down that magic path, if I had enough time. It would be my perfect finale.

I'm getting carried away.

Nyx: what about your family?

Masher: they don't care

Masher: they wouldn't miss me if I was gone

Nyx: you can dream your dreams without them

Masher: where's this place you mentioned?

Nyx: i think you know where it is

Nyx: maybe you know people who've gone there already

Masher: if we're thinking of the same place, then yes

Nyx: do you think they're at peace now?

Masher: for sure

Now's the time. Masher needs me.

Nyx: we need to meet

Nyx: in RL

FORTY-NINE

'Lexi, love, you look like shit.'

'Wow, Maggie, don't hold back.'

Maggie put out a hand and brushed Lexi's cheek. 'I know you're going at it one hundred per cent, but you must take care of yourself.'

Lexi had thought about heading home for a shower once she left Emily's office, but somehow she'd found herself driving straight back to the station. She needed to brief the team on the latest developments. Thoughts crowded her head as to which way to steer the investigation. As well as checking Olivia's clothes for red hemp fibre, she'd asked Emily to send CSIs back to the Leas Cliff Hall and Griffin Elms to see if they could have missed anything. Could the footprint at the ruined keep have been left by the person from the phone box?

She'd bumped into Maggie at the top of the stairs on her way in.

'I'm fine, honestly,' she said, suddenly self-conscious. She hadn't even stopped to run a brush through her unruly hair.

'Burnout is real, and the last thing I need is for the head of my Major Investigation Team to flake out in the middle of a case.'

'That's not going to happen.' Lexi glanced towards the door of the incident room. 'I need to brief the team.'

Maggie nodded and followed her into the room.

Tom and Ridhi were already at their desks, as were most of the civilian staff. Colin arrived seconds later with a Greggs bag and takeout coffee. Lexi checked the time – they were all early, as determined to prevent another young person's death as she was. Maggie perched on the side of Ridhi's desk, while Lexi grabbed a pen and went across to the whiteboard.

'Morning, everyone,' she said, receiving nods and murmurs in return. She quickly explained how Ridhi had come across the figure in the phone box and the subsequent discovery of hemp fibres of the same type as the red ropes used in the deaths of Shan Liang and Neil McGowan.

'Way to go, Ridhi,' said Colin.

'Thanks.' Pink cheeks.

'Yes, excellent work,' said Lexi. She turned back to the whiteboard and pointed at the grainy image of the person in dark clothes coming up North Lane towards the phone boxes. 'Here's our problem. We can't find a bridge between the online character of Nyx and this unidentified individual, who I now presume to have been present when Olivia died – and who may have been instrumental in her death.'

'By instrumental, are you implying that this person murdered her?' said Maggie.

'We've got to consider it a possibility. I believe that this person, Nyx, met her at the tower and brought a length of the so-called "big red rope". Something happened up there. Olivia didn't hang herself, but she still ended up dead. Could she have changed her mind? Otherwise, why not go through with it as planned, in the same way that Shan and Neil did?'

'What happened at the top of the tower is guesswork for now, so where do you go next?' said Maggie.

'Nyx is an online persona. But his or her counterpart exists in the real world – and I think we've caught sight of them now. We need to do some lateral thinking to join the dots and identify the individual.'

'Yes, but you need a concrete plan of action,' said Maggie.

Although Lexi knew that Maggie wasn't intending it, she felt undermined.

She cleared her throat. 'It's now my firm opinion that all three of these deaths certainly qualify as manslaughter, and quite possibly as murders. In terms of suspects, we've been looking at Paul Arbuthnot, director of the Kingsdown Singers, and Eric Cotter, the computer science teacher at Griffin Elms. Arbuthnot has a known connection to Shan Liang, who was in the singing group, and there have been allegations that he bullied Shan. Cotter has a known connection to Neil McGowan, having taught him. However, neither of these two men have an obvious connection to Olivia James.' She pointed at the three pictures of the dead teenagers. 'As far as we can tell, the three victims didn't know each other – we've asked their family and friends, and scoured their laptops and social media pages for links, and we haven't found anything. They only had one thing in common that we know of – they had all attended the Tenterden International Music Festival over the last couple of years, which happens to be on this week. Yesterday, Tom and I went there and we spotted both Cotter and Arbuthnot. Arbuthnot because his group was singing, but I'm not sure why Cotter was there.'

'But what's the music festival got to do with Nyx?' said Colin.

'Nyx is operating Club Edicius – his suicide club – on the dark web. All three of the victims had Tor, the dark web browser, installed on their computers, but because their phones are missing, we don't know of any initial communication with Nyx via social media or text messaging. I think that Nyx recruits in person, and an event such as the music festival might be just the right place.'

'Why the festival?' said Ridhi.

'Lots of young musicians wandering around unsupervised – they might be just the type of young person he would target – bright, insecure, vulnerable, in a competitive environment. Then he starts grooming them, possibly over the phone. All their mobiles are missing. If Nyx was present when they died, he could have taken the phones to cover any evidence. Colin, could you chase their mobile records as a matter of priority? It could give us a number for Nyx.'

'Makes sense,' said Tom. 'And it means Nyx is able to recruit kids that are relatively local to him. If he made first contact on the dark web, they could be located anywhere.'

'Moving forward,' said Lexi, 'Paul Arbuthnot looks weak as a suspect. According to Emily Jordan, the partial footprint found at the scene of McGowan's death would suggest someone smaller than Arbuthnot – he's over six feet – so Ridhi, will you get an accurate height assessment of the person spotted on North Lane.'

'Yes, boss.'

'Having seen Arbuthnot in person, I would suggest that it's not him anyway,' said Tom. 'That figure in the pictures looks shorter.'

'It might depend on the camera angle,' said Maggie.

She could be right, but Lexi was feeling more and more certain that Arbuthnot wasn't their man. 'Arbuthnot is the least likely suspect, but we have discovered that he might have been scamming old people into leaving him money. Tom?'

'I've passed all the information on that over to the fraud team – they're going to be looking into it.'

'Brilliant. Colin, can you bring in Eric Cotter and see if he has alibis for all three times of death?'

'Yes.'

'But if he does have alibis, would that rule him out from being Nyx?' said Maggie.

'I think so,' said Lexi. 'We've got the phone box individual likely present when Olivia died, and we've got the skidded foot-print at the ruin where Neil died. It points to someone else being present at both of their deaths.'

'And Shan's?' said Maggie.

'We don't have concrete evidence of another person being there, but I think it would be very hard for Shan to have set up the rope without another person's help.'

'And what are you doing about re-locating the chatroom?' Maggie again.

'Greg Chambers is working on it, but he admits it's going to be difficult, unless we can find a way in via one of the victim's laptops. With Nyx recruiting in person, we can't set up a fake online ID to go phishing with.' She glanced up at the white-board for inspiration but all she saw was three young people lost, three families devastated and three communities ripped open. 'That's all we've got for now, so let's get on. Nyx is out there, grooming another victim – we need to act fast.'

'Thanks very much,' said Maggie. 'Keep me posted with whatever you get.'

After she'd gone, Lexi exchanged a look with Tom, and he shrugged. She might have talked a good talk about all they'd found so far and what they were going to do next, but she knew Maggie would have seen through it. The clock was ticking and Lexi didn't know what to do next.

Tom was on his phone, fixing up for two PCs to bring Cotter in for questioning.

As he finished, Lexi's phone sounded in her pocket.

'DI Bennett speaking,' she said.

'Lexi, it's Greg Chambers.'

'You've got something?' Her head jerked up to meet Tom's gaze.

'I'm back in.'

'The chatroom? How the hell did you manage that?'

Greg laughed. 'You really want the details?'

'No, of course not.' She wouldn't understand a word of it. 'Can you come to my office?'

'Sure.'

'Is he online now?'

'He is – and it's pretty bloody disturbing.'

'Don't waste a second.'

FIFTY

A secret breaktime meeting behind the bike sheds!

It isn't quite like that, but it reminds me of being back at school. This time, though, the assignation is in an out-of-the-way spot at the furthest reaches of the school grounds. I'll give him a ten-minute pep talk, words of reassurance, a pledge of support and guidance through a difficult decision. Important instructions, too.

I enjoy these meetings with my lost souls. It's my way of giving something back.

Masher arrives. He's a little late and out of breath.

'I'm sorry,' he pants, 'had a problem getting shot of a couple of mates.'

'No worries,' I say. 'I'm just glad you made it. It's so much better to talk about these things in person.'

He smiles wistfully and nods. He seems nervous. 'Now I'm here, I don't really know what to say.' He looks at his feet, twisting his fingers together nervously.

'Just tell me why life's getting you down.'

I listen for nearly twenty minutes, nodding, offering reassurance. Masher's family don't understand him. His schoolwork's going badly. He's scared about climate change. He thinks he might be gay and he's worried what other people will think, especially his best friend. He's scared of the future, upset by things in the past.

I've heard so many similar stories. And I know that I can offer him the guidance he needs. Since Siren backed off, this boy with his fragile ego and shattered dreams has become the focus of my attention. He'll be next.

'I understand.'

'I've been there too.'

'I know what you're feeling. Some days it's hard not to feel that way.'

'I can help you.'

This to Masher's declaration that he wants to end it all.

'I can help you, I promise.'

Masher twists a thumb and forefinger against his eyes, embarrassed at the tears that threaten to overflow. He looks at his watch.

'I've gotta go. I'll be late.'

'We'll meet up again later on,' I say, giving him details of when and where.

The boy nods, but he looks distraught.

'Don't worry.' I give him a small smile of reassurance as he walks away. 'It'll all be okay, Sam.'

FIFTY-ONE

'Ridhi, you be good cop, I'll be bad.' Then Colin grinned at her. 'Or d'you want to play it the other way around?'

'Thanks, Colin, but I think you'll be just right as bad cop.'

He laughed, but there were days when Ridhi thought that had a slight ring of truth to it. Not that she believed he was corrupt or anything. Not that bad. But he could be a lazy little sod, and he was always manufacturing reasons to pass on his tasks to the civilian investigators. While she could understand that he wanted to be a man of action rather than stuck behind a screen looking at CCTV images and checking ANPR reports, she wasn't impressed. They were a team, and that included the civilian staff, so it wasn't right to palm off all the rubbish jobs on them. And the boss wasn't stupid – she had to realise what was going on. Still, it wasn't Ridhi's problem to sort. She'd make sure she did everything the right way.

Eric Cotter had been brought in and placed in one of the interview rooms. Colin and Ridhi spent ten minutes working out what they needed to ask him, then went in and took the two seats opposite him at the table. Cotter glared at them – he'd been pulled out in the middle of a lesson, and the PCs who brought him in reported that he had been surly and abusive for most of the drive to Canterbury.

Ridhi pressed play on the recording device and, after the long bleep that indicated the beginning of a recording, she named all those present in the room.

'Hang on,' said Cotter, interrupting her, 'why are you recording this? Don't you need my permission for that?'

'Are you unhappy for it to be recorded, Mr Cotter?' said Colin.

'Look, I don't even know what I'm doing here or on what basis I've been brought in. Let's start with that, shall we, DC whatever-she-said-your-name-is.'

'Flynn, DC Flynn.'

'Right, DC Flynn, am I here as a suspect or a witness?'

Ridhi decided the conversation needed to be dialled down a notch or two if it was going to be at all useful to them.

'We just need some help with our enquiries,' she said in a soothing tone. 'No one is accusing you of anything – we've just got a few questions to ask.'

'For which you had two of your officers pull me out of class. You couldn't even wait until I'd finished teaching?'

He must have felt humiliated in front of his students.

'I apologise for that,' said Ridhi, 'but this is a fast-moving investigation.'

'And what exactly are you investigating, that you think I might be able to help with?'

Colin had had enough. 'If we could get on with the questions, the sooner you'll be back to teaching classes.'

Cotter didn't say anything, but glared at him.

'I understand that you taught your pupils how to access the dark web?' said Ridhi.

Cotter sighed. 'Not how to access it. I taught them about its dangers. It's a thing. It exists. The kids all know what it is already, so I feel it's important to make sure they understand how dangerous it can be.' He glanced from one to the other of them. 'I already went over this with your DI.'

'Did you teach Neil McGowan how to use the dark web?' said Colin.

'Just rewind and listen to my previous answer.'

'Were you aware that he was a member of a suicide club on the dark web?'

'No.' Cotter shook his head as he spoke. It consolidated his answer, so Ridhi felt inclined to believe that he was telling the truth. 'If I'd known about it, I would have spoken to him... directed him to the right sort of help.'

'The right sort of help? What's that?' said Colin.

'The school employs the services of a mental health nurse to counsel any students who need it. I could have referred him to her.'

'But you didn't?'

'Because I had no idea he was in such distress.'

'Mr Cotter, are you gay?'

Ridhi looked round sharply at Colin. This hadn't been on their agreed list of questions. What the hell was he getting at?

'Are you implying something? Because my sexuality is none of your business.' Cotter seemed shaken by the question, and she wondered if that had been Colin's intent.

'Can you tell me where you were last Monday afternoon between two p.m. and seven p.m.?'

Cotter's eyes widened and Ridhi noticed him starting to breathe more quickly. Fight or flight reaction kicking in. 'You said I wasn't a suspect for anything.'

'Did I say that a crime had taken place then?'

'That's when that girl died at the Westgate, isn't it?' So he'd been following the story.

'You haven't answered the question.'

'I expect I was teaching most of the afternoon, then supervising computer club.'

'And between midnight on Monday and eight a.m. on Tuesday?'

'In bed, sleeping.'

'On your own?'

Cotter hesitated a fraction too long. 'Yes, on my own.'

'So no one can corroborate that?'

He shrugged.

'And during the same hours, Tuesday to Wednesday?'

'In bed.'

'Alone.'

'Yes.'

'Can you tell us what you were doing at the Tenterden International Music Festival yesterday afternoon?'

This question took Cotter aback. 'Pardon?'

'You were seen at the music festival,' said Ridhi. 'What were you doing there?'

'I work with a group of students who are interested in synthesizers and synthesized music. We entered the composition competition at Tenterden. Yesterday was the first round of heats.'

'How did you do?' Ridhi didn't realise that synthesized music was still a thing.

'We didn't get through to the next round.'

'Was Neil McGowan in that group of students?' said Colin.

'Sure, for a while. But he left a few months ago to concentrate on his saxophone.'

'Very musically talented?'

'I would say so, though I'm probably no judge.'

They'd lulled him back into a false sense of security.

Colin drew a breath. 'Mr Cotter, did you help Neil McGowan take his own life on Tuesday night?'

Without answering the question, Cotter stood up so abruptly that his chair toppled over behind him.

'You want more? Charge me.' His anger was an electric current in the air.

'That's fine, Mr Cotter,' said Ridhi in her most reasonable tone. 'Feel free to leave if you want to.'

He was out of the room before she finished speaking.

'Thinks he's clever, doesn't he? Threatening to get a lawyer,' said Colin, as the door swung shut behind him. 'Been watching too many cop dramas on TV.'

'Why'd you ask him if he was gay?' said Ridhi. It had been bugging her all through the rest of the interview.

Colin smiled at her. 'You'll learn – it's an old trick we've been using for years. Ask them something unexpected and it disrupts their chain of thought. Then they're off guard for the next question. It's a way of making suspects slip up.'

In other words, what she'd suspected. But not very subtle.

'I have to say, I don't like him one little bit,' he added.

Ridhi shrugged. She neither liked him nor disliked him – that would tell her nothing. What interested her was whether or not he was a killer.

FIFTY-TWO

Lexi stared at Greg's laptop screen, cold fear crawling across the surface of her skin.

They were looking at the page of a private chatroom. It had the same tiny noose emoji at the top of the page as the main Club Edicius chatroom, but there were only two participants.

Nyx and Masher.

'He's shut out all of his little acolytes,' said Tom, reading over her shoulder.

'He wants to be the only voice Masher hears at this stage,' said Lexi.

'What stage is that?' said Maggie, who was crowding in from the other side.

'The end game.'

And that's certainly what this seemed to be leading up to.

Nyx: have you written a note to leave behind

Masher: ive been working on it

Nyx: using the examples on that link i sent you

Masher: they're useful, but i have to say what i have to say in my own words

Nyx: that's fair – it'll sound more genuine that way

Masher: it is genuine

Nyx: of course. we know that but the police twist things

Nyx: are you ready

Masher: i think i am

Nyx: it will be a blessed relief, believe me

Masher: that's what i need

The words kept tumbling down the screen and there was no way that Lexi could stop them.

'Who the hell is Masher and where is he? How are we going to stop this?' She was furious and frustrated. Powerless.

Maggie looked across at her with concern. 'We've got to stay calm.'

'I'm sorry, Maggie, but calm is useless. I need to take action.'

She could hear Tom breathing more rapidly behind her. 'Come on, Greg – there's got to be a way of knowing where this kid is.'

Greg shook his head. 'It's the dark web. It was built for secrecy.'

Lexi's fists were tight balls, her fingernails digging hard into her palms.

She heard the door opening and looked up. It was Colin and Ridhi.

'We've just questioned Eric Cotter,' said Colin.

'And?'

'He seemed pretty shifty.'

'But did he have alibis for the times of death?'

'He claims to have been teaching on Monday afternoon, but he seemed a bit vague about it. We'll follow up with witnesses at the school.'

'What about for Monday and Tuesday nights?'

'In bed, alone.'

'Mmmm...' Lexi chewed on her bottom lip. Pretty inconclusive. 'Where is he now – are you still holding him?'

Ridhi shook her head. 'He just left. We only interviewed him as a witness. He got pissed off by the end and stormed out.'

'Just now?'

'Yes.'

Lexi's eyes went back to the laptop. The words were still sliding down the screen.

Masher: tonight

Nyx: you remember the plan we made

'This is live, happening right now, isn't it, Greg?'

'Yes.'

'Which means... Eric Cotter can't be Nyx. Not unless he's in two places at once. Sorry, you two, looks like that interview was a waste of time.'

Masher: of course

Nyx: will you be able to get to the meeting place

Masher: i'll be there

Nyx: i won't let you down. i'll show you how to do it quickly.
you won't feel any pain

Lexi gasped. 'Shit, he's going to kill Masher this evening.'
Her heart was pounding. If they didn't do something immediately, the kid would probably wind up dead within a few hours.
The body would be discovered, cold and lifeless, hanging from a
thick red rope. The family, whoever, wherever they were, might
already have seen him or her for the last time. Barring that
moment when they'd have to identify his body in the morgue.

The wheels were in motion, and Lexi had never felt so helpless in her life.

FIFTY-THREE

If anything, Ed Harlow was looking even worse than when Lexi had seen him the previous day. It was as if a phantom sculptor was slowly chipping away at him – cheeks hollowed out, wrinkles deeper – and the dark rings under his eyes seemed to be spreading like ink on blotting paper. Another sleepless night, she guessed, feeling immediately guilty for calling him away from Charlie's side.

'How is she?' she asked, as Ed settled into the chair opposite her desk with a tired sigh.

'She's at home now. She's sleeping.' He pursed his lips for a second. 'I think it's her way of escaping what's happening.'

'Is she in pain?'

'Good and bad days, but she has effective medication for it. We've got some time in hand and I think we might try and go away for a while, if she feels up to it.'

Lexi could hardly imagine what it must be like for him. A ticking clock hanging over the head of the woman he loved. 'Till death do us part.' Usually, that was an unknown, but not so much for Ed and Charlie.

'I'm sorry.'

Ed gave a small shrug of one shoulder. 'What did you want to talk about?' It was clear he wanted to change the subject.

'I'm running out of time. This afternoon, we got back into the chatroom and Nyx was grooming some poor kid for a meeting tonight. A murder's going to take place – but I don't know where, and I don't know the identity of either the killer or the victim. All I know is that I've got to stop it.'

'And how do you think I can help?'

'Greg Chambers of our tech department has managed to download some cached pages of the Club Edicius chatroom. I want you to help me scour them for details and, adding them to what we know about the three victims so far, build a profile of who Nyx might be or identify a location or some clue about the next victim. Anything that can point us along the right path...'

'It's a big ask.'

'I know – I'm sorry, and I'll understand if you don't have the time to give to this.'

Ed shook his head. 'It's not the time. Of course I'll help you, Lexi – I don't want to see another child die. It's whether we can find anything useful. It's an anonymous chatroom. No one knows who anyone is, so there's nothing to stop people lying, omitting facts, making stuff up. That's sort of the point of places like that. We'll find it very difficult to discern anything concrete.'

Lexi knew all this already. 'I don't have anything else to go on, and you're the best profiler this side of the pond.'

'Then we'd better get to it.'

Lexi printed out the cached pages that Greg had managed to scrape from the dark web and distributed them between Ed, Tom, Colin and herself. She wiped clean a segment of the whiteboard that had been used for the Swan stabbing case.

Kevin Stewart had been charged, and the file had now been passed on to the CPS.

'Ridhi, we'll call out any facts we find for any of the people in the group – you record them under each name.'

Ridhi grabbed a marker pen and drew a column for each name that appeared in the chatroom – Nyx, Yoshi, Trollster, Lolly, PopSpook, Doobie, Siren, Masher, Ghoul, Honeybox.

'We know that Lolly was Olivia. The timing of when Nyx mentions that PopSpook is dead fits with him being Shan, and when we last saw the chatroom, Nyx was grooming Doobie. I think that was Neil. But with the rest of them, we have no idea – and we especially need to identify Masher before it's too late.'

They settled down in silence to scour the endless stream of conversations in the chatroom. The bit Lexi was reading was heartbreaking – Olivia, as her online persona Lolly, was clearly distraught, while the others in the chat pushed her for details of her life, then mocked her. Each time, Nyx would step in and tell them to back off, with words of reassurance for the desperate girl. But the more of it she read, the more Lexi realised exactly how manipulative Nyx was being, how he was framing everything he said to fall in line with what she wanted to hear while pushing his own agenda of inciting her to take one last desperate act.

'It makes me sick,' she said out loud without thinking. 'He's leading her around as if she's got a ring in her nose.'

'He's using classic manipulation techniques,' said Ed. 'He gets the rest of the group to pile on, then he rides in to rescue her. Whoever Nyx is, he's a master manipulator.'

'Is that something you can learn or just an innate skill?' asked Colin.

'A bit of both,' said Ed. 'It comes naturally to some people, but you can learn it as well. Classic sales techniques put to nefarious purposes. If you compare Nyx's interactions with different members of the group who went on to take their own lives, you'll probably find that he takes them on the same journey – creating a funnel through which he steers them towards his ultimate goal.'

'It's sick,' said Ridhi.

'He's definitely clever,' said Lexi. 'From the outside, we can see the pattern, but for his targets, the bigger picture is obscured, and they have no idea they're being played. The question we need to address is what does Nyx get out of it?'

Tom raised a hand. 'I think I might have found something concrete.'

'What?' Ridhi stood ready with the marker pen.

'Here.' He held up one the pages he was looking at. 'Nyx is commiserating with Lolly about her parents making her do piano practice. He says: "I used to play an instrument but the constant practice ruined it for me." So he's musical, which fits with him using the music festival to recruit victims.'

'He understands what they're going through because he's been through it all himself,' said Ed.

'Let me see,' said Lexi, holding out a hand for the sheet of paper. '"I must have played Bach's Chaconne a thousand times for one competition. I thought I would die." Chaconne... that's a violin piece, isn't it?'

Tom shrugged, but Ed nodded. 'A beautiful piece of music. If he can play that, he must be good.'

'Okay, Ridhi, add it to the board – we're looking for a violin player,' said Lexi. The team were pulling together and they were making progress. Tiny steps, but that was all it took.

Their heads went down, back to studying the pages. Silence reigned. It seemed to Lexi that there wasn't much to be found in the chatroom's ongoing litany of mocking interspersed with encouragement. Lolly, PopSpook, Doobie – they were all dead, apparently having been manipulated into the painful decision to take their own lives. Lexi was convinced that Nyx was culpable. But what about the others? Who were Trollster, Honeybox,

Yoshi and Ghoul? Where were they? They popped up in conversations with each of the three victims. Siren had been around for a shorter spell of time, then seemed to disappear. Was there another suicide that they had missed, perhaps further afield? And now Nyx was working on Masher.

What was she missing?

'Everyone, take particular note of anything Siren says. It seems like he was grooming her but maybe she stepped back from the brink, at least for now. If we can identify and find her, she should be able to tell us who Nyx is.'

'Not very forthcoming, is she?' said Colin, after they'd all spent several minutes working in silence.

He was right. In every interaction, Siren seemed stand-offish. She never stayed in the chatroom for long, despite Nyx's repeated attempts to engage with her. And Lexi noticed that the others, Trollster and Yoshi in particular, who could usually be relied upon to say something brutal, started to tone it down a bit when she was around. Was that at Nyx's bidding? Was he communicating with them somewhere else, by text maybe, instructing them how to interact with whomever he was grooming?

And he never actually seemed to be grooming *them* – Troll-ster and Yoshi...

Realisation struck like a lightning bolt.

Ed was the first to notice Lexi's frenzied leafing through her stack of pages. 'You've found something, haven't you?'

'It's just—'

Tom interrupted with a yelp. 'I think Siren knew Shan in real life – the way she talks about him on a couple of occasions. And it seems like it was after his death that she started to pull back from the group.'

'Brilliant,' said Lexi. 'Ridhi, Colin, can you two speak to his friends and track her down?'

'Absolutely,' said Ridhi.

'Right now,' said Lexi.

Ridhi grabbed her bag from beside her desk, but Colin seemed much slower in getting going.

'What is it, Colin?'

'Shan was home-schooled, and he didn't really have any friends, did he? So how would he have known Siren?'

Lexi shrugged. 'That's for you two to work out. Get on his social media pages, ask his parents. Back on it, everyone else.'

Ed reached out and touched her forearm. 'You had a thought just now, didn't you?'

Lexi looked up. 'It might be nothing – I was just taking another look.'

'Tell me.'

Tom looked up, interested.

'Okay, I've got a theory.' She stood up and went across to the whiteboard. 'We have no doubt that Nyx is running the group – he, possibly she, picks out targets and manipulates their feelings until they believe the only thing they can do is take their own lives.'

Tom and Ed nodded.

'But what about the group dynamics? I think it splits neatly in two.' She started listing the names of the members into two groups.

Yoshi
Trollster
Ghoul
Honeybox

Lolly
PopSpook
Doobie
Masher
Siren

'In the second group – those are the kids that Nyx chose to target. And in the first, his little gang of cheerleaders, always there, always ready to undermine the confidence of the targets while giving them a sense of belonging to the group. Always dishing up just what might be needed to drive a vulnerable person into Nyx's embrace.' Ed and Tom were watching her closely, following every word, and she could tell from Ed's expression that he knew what was coming next. 'Thing is, I don't think they exist at all. I think all four of them, Yoshi, Trollster, Ghoul and Honeybox, are just Nyx's alter egos. I believe he's using these fake personas to run the show.'

'Spot on,' said Ed.

'Of course,' said Tom. 'It makes perfect sense. So how do we prove it? Do you think Greg can show that they all logged on from the same IP address?'

Lexi shook her head. 'Not if he was using Tor and a different login for each one.'

'Uh-uh,' said Ed, shaking his head. 'It's easier than that. Linguistic fingerprinting.'

'What?' said Tom.

'You did it informally with the suicide notes – the same phrasing kept cropping up, which led to the conclusion that the victims had been coached in what to write. If you want to show that all the characters in the chatroom are one and the same, give a selection of the chats to a forensic linguist and they'll be able to tell you.'

'We don't have time for that – it could take weeks,' said Lexi. 'Nyx has Masher all lined up.'

Ed raised a placatory hand. 'Let me reach out. I know someone, a forensic linguist I've used before. She owes me a favour and if she's not busy, maybe she'll look at them right away.'

Ten minutes later, they were gathered around Lexi's desk on a Zoom call to a woman called Stephanie Hunt, a linguistics expert at the Aston Institute for Forensic Linguistics at Aston University.

'Hey, Steph,' said Ed. 'Thanks for doing this.'

She looked up at them from the chatroom samples they'd emailed across to her. She wore oversized, black-framed glasses, and her hair was pulled up in a messy bun. 'Anything for you. It can only be a first impression,' she said, 'but if I find anything, I'd be happy to follow up with a full report.'

'Thank you,' said Lexi. 'I think we'll definitely need one.'

They waited in silence while Steph studied the chats. Ed had instructed them not to tell her which characters they thought were being role-played by Nyx. It was important that she should be able to spot them without any prompting. After what seemed like forever, but was probably less than fifteen minutes, she spoke.

'Okay, it's pretty clear what's going on here. Every individual has his or her own speech pattern – a unique way of using language that's as individual to them as their fingerprint. In written text, we expect to see what's known as inter-author variation, the way in which we tell the difference between individual writers.'

'And what do you see when you look at the samples?' said Lexi.

'Nyx is the lead author in this group, and it's clear to me that this one individual is also writing the entries of several other members of the group.'

'Can you say which ones?'

Steph glanced down. 'Yes. Nyx, Honeybox, Yoshi, Ghoul and Trollster are one person. I'm absolutely sure of it, and I'll be happy to send you a written report setting out my reasons. They use identical phrasing and the same vernacular, and while this can happen to a certain extent between people who spend a lot of time together, say family members, what I'm seeing here is almost certainly the work of just one person.'

'That's brilliant – thank you so much, Steph. You absolutely rock.' Ed was delighted.

So was Lexi. It would be a huge help in proving that Nyx was inciting his victims to take their own lives. Tom suggested sending her the suicide notes as well, to see if they were also created in collaboration with Nyx, and they ended the call feeling like they'd achieved something good.

But not good enough.

They still didn't know who or where Nyx was.

And Masher was still in danger.

FIFTY-FOUR

It was possible that finding Siren was their only hope, and then only if they found her straight away. It seemed unlikely. In fact, it seemed impossible. But Lexi knew she couldn't afford to let despondence take the upper hand.

'I'd better get back to Charlie.' Ed was leaning against the doorframe.

'Of course.'

'What will you do now?'

Lexi sighed. 'The only concrete information we have on Nyx is that he plays the violin and hangs out with a bunch of imaginary friends. Not much to go on.'

'I wish I could do more.'

'I wish you could, too. Maybe if we can find Siren, and if Siren knows who he is and where he is, and chooses to co-operate with us, then just maybe...'

Ed gave a look of sadness and regret. They both knew that whatever she tried, it was likely to be too late to save Masher, and that the call would come announcing that another teenager had been found dead.

'See you,' he said. Then he was gone.

Lexi dialled Tom. 'Where are you?'

'With Ridhi, on our way to talk to Shan's mother.'

'What happened to Colin?'

'He's scouring Shan's social media.'

'Call me if...'

'Sure.'

Masher's time was ticking away, minute by minute.

She pressed her fingertips against her temples.

Think, damn it.

Shan knew Siren in real life. He'd arrived here recently. Probably knew no one in Kent before he got here. Didn't go to school. Joined the Kingsdown Singers. Until they discovered otherwise from Shan's mother, the singing group seemed to be the only social outlet he had. She thought about ringing Paul Arbuthnot, but it seemed unlikely that he would be co-operative. Then she remembered the girl Ridhi had spoken to, the former member... What was her name?

Lexi ran round to the incident room and sat down at Ridhi's desk, firing up her computer. It only took her a couple of seconds to find the case files Ridhi was working on. Witness statements. She scanned the list of names... Maddie Scott, that was the one. She knew the members of the group. Perhaps she'd know who Shan had been close to, who might have joined Club Edicius as Siren. Perhaps it was even her.

It was a long shot.

Dead in the water straight away – the girl didn't answer her phone.

But there was an address and five minutes later, Lexi was in her car, driving towards Deal. She checked in with Tom and Ridhi on the way. They had nothing. She slammed the heel of her hand against the steering wheel and drove faster than she should have.

Her satnav guided her to a run-down bungalow on a grotty estate on the edge of the town. The front garden had been covered over with concrete and two cars were parked on it – the cheap version of a Japanese boy racer's wet dream and a dented Ford Fiesta. Paint was peeling off the front door. A dead plant in a plastic pot sat on the red tiled doorstep. Lexi pressed the doorbell and heard chimes sounding inside.

A young woman in skinny jeans and a checked shirt opened the door. Lexi would have guessed she was about nineteen or twenty, but there was something shifty or fearful in her expression that made her seem younger.

'Are you Maddie Scott?'

She shook her head without speaking, and tried to close the door.

Lexi put a foot in the way. 'I'm DI Bennett from Kent Police and I need to talk to Maddie Scott. Is she here?'

'Why?' said the girl, so quietly that Lexi lip-read the answer rather than hearing it. It made her sure this was Maddie Scott.

She raised her arm to push back against the door and Lexi saw a fresh blood stain on the sleeve of her shirt. A graze on her arm? Acting on impulse, Lexi pushed up the sleeve – could she have been the person at the Westgate with Olivia?

'No!' The girl let go of the door and stepped back into the hall.

But what Lexi saw on the girl's arm wasn't a graze at all. There were three fresh cuts, each one about an inch long, in a parallel row across the soft flesh of her pale forearm. One was still bleeding, and looked deeper than the other two. Further down her arm were more rows of cuts at various stages of healing – some still red and angry, others pink and some that had faded away to white lines. Too many to count.

'Oh, Maddie,' said Lexi. 'Did you do these yourself?' It was heartbreaking to see.

The girl pulled down her shirt sleeve. Her eyes brimmed with tears.

A flash of intuition burned a single word into Lexi's mind.

'Siren?'

The door slammed shut, leaving her with the impression of fleeting expressions on the girl's face. Fear, guilt, anger.

'Maddie, please open the door.' She banged on it with her fist.

'Go away.'

'Please. I need your help to save a boy's life.'

Silence.

'Maddie, you're not in trouble. But I need to know who Nyx is.'

Slowly, the door opened a crack. 'I can't tell you that.'

'But you know?'

'No.'

'But you've met Nyx, in real life?'

Maddie shook her head vehemently, but she allowed the door to open further. She was thin, way too thin, and with her bleached hair pulled back from her forehead into a scruffy ponytail, her face was almost skull-like, her eyes big and dark.

Lexi took a breath. 'Maddie, do you know who Masher is?'

The girl shook her head again, glancing beyond Lexi to the road, as if she expected someone to be there, watching her. She ushered Lexi inside and slammed the door. From somewhere further inside the bungalow came the sound of a noisy computer game – thrashing music, gunfire, squealing tyres.

'I never met Nyx,' she said, speaking so fast she tripped over her words. 'Shan told me about the club and I wanted to join. He introduced me to Nyx online.'

'So you are Siren?'

Maddie nodded. 'But I don't go on the site anymore. It scared me, what Nyx was doing. What happened to Shan.' She burst into tears.

'What exactly did happen to Shan?'

Her eyes widened. 'You know already. He killed himself.'

'But Nyx helped him?'

'I guess. It seemed to be what he wanted.'

'Nyx or Shan?'

'Nyx. Nyx is all about people being free to make their own decisions, even if it's the choice to end it all.'

'But that wasn't what you wanted?'

Maddie sobbed loudly and wiped her nose on the sleeve of her shirt. Lexi realised the question had been inappropriately harsh. But she was focused on saving Masher.

'Listen, Maddie, Nyx is going to push someone else to the brink. Maybe Masher.'

Maddie looked terrified.

'Please help me save him.'

There was a lull in the noise. 'Who's there, Mads? What you doin'?'

'No one, Dad. It's nothing,' yelled Maddie back into the house. 'You'd better leave,' she hissed at Lexi.

'Let us help you,' said Lexi, almost pleading. She was desperate. 'Please help us. Apart from the chatroom, how does he communicate with the people in the group? Does he send texts?'

Maddie ushered her towards the door. Then, as she opened it, she leaned in close to Lexi. 'Not texts – they're not private enough. There's a WhatsApp group with lots of members, teenagers mostly, into playing music. Nyx is on there sometimes.'

Of course – Lexi understood what was going on in an instant. WhatsApp messages were encrypted and could only be seen on individual devices, whereas texts could be accessed via phone records. Nyx kept to WhatsApp, then took his victims' mobiles. 'Can you show me the group?'

'My phone's not here. It's at my mum's.'

Lexi could tell she was lying, but there wasn't much she could do. They'd have to get a warrant to seize it.

'Anything else?'

'Mads?' The man sounded more impatient.

Maddie dropped her voice to a whisper. 'Nyx plays the violin – really well, he was almost famous, then it all went wrong. That's what Shan said.'

He.

'Do you know where he lives?'

'Somewhere near Margate. That's all I know, I promise.'

Lexi wasn't sure if she believed her, but there was nothing else she could do.

'Maddie?' shouted the man.

'Please go,' whispered Maddie.

'Are you okay?' said Lexi, stepping back onto the front doorstep. 'I can try and get some help for you.'

The door closed in her face.

FIFTY-FIVE

It was after five thirty by the time she got back to the station. Tom and Ridhi had arrived just before her. She went into the incident room and let the civilian staff go, but she asked Tom, Ridhi and Colin to stay late.

'This is what we know,' she said. 'He was a gifted violinist, almost famous according to Maddie Scott, until something happened that ruined his career. He lives somewhere in the Margate area. We need to identify him quickly.'

'That's it?' said Colin. 'That's all we've got?'

'Yes. Stop moaning and get to it.' Her temper was short – she hadn't eaten since... she couldn't even remember. She went back to her office and found an opened packet of digestives in the bottom draw of her desk. That would do. She bit into one as she opened her laptop. Stale, crumbly. It didn't matter.

Where to look?

She picked up her phone. 'Tom, did Barry Gray ever send us the earlier Tenterden programmes?'

'I sent a uniform over to collect them. They arrived about half an hour ago.'

Three minutes later, he came into her office carrying a

brown envelope. He tipped the contents on the desk – a stack of programmes for the music festival slid out. Lexi picked them up and flicked through them. The details of every musician who'd appeared there for the last seven years.

'He's got to be in these somewhere,' she said.

'But that could be one of hundreds of kids.'

She picked up the pile and led the way back to the incident room, then divided the programmes between the four of them. 'Go through each year. Make a list of the male solo violin players. Then we Google them. We're looking for a celebrated young player, career cut short. He apparently now lives near Margate, but we can't know if that was the case when he was playing. Let's get a shortlist.' She spoke fast, the urgency of their task carried in her voice.

It took them twenty minutes to come up with a shortlist of seventeen possibles, then an hour spent on Google to whittle it down to a list of five names. They were able to rule out any that were deceased – one – or who lived abroad – six. Five had gone on to have successful music careers, either solo or playing in an orchestra, so they were ruled out. The remaining five seemed to have dropped away from the professional music scene at one point or another – and these were the ones that Lexi deemed most interesting.

Ridhi fed the names into the Holmes 2 computer database to check whether any of them had previous touch points with the police, but this, not surprisingly, drew a blank. Colin matched the names against the electoral register and DVLA and came up with addresses for three of them. One had moved away from Kent and appeared to be living in a small town in Scotland's central belt.

'Rule him out for now,' said Lexi.

'What about the two with no addresses – Austin Bell and Lee Costa?' said Tom.

'Ridhi, see if you can track them down over social media.'

'Yes, boss.'

'That means we have two current possibilities with known addresses in Kent. Kai Epson, twenty-seven, living in Westwood, a music teacher at a secondary school in Dover, and Edward Mason, twenty-five. Mason's last listed address appears to be his parents' house in Birchington-on-Sea. Both of those places are reasonably near Margate, which is in line with what Maddie Scott told us.'

She looked at Tom and jingled her car keys. 'The rest of you, keep digging. Find out all you can about Bell and Costa. If you dig up addresses for them, let me know straight away.'

She took the stairs at a run. 'We've got no time to waste,' she called over her shoulder to Tom. 'Nyx has a meeting set up with Masher, so we need to get to him first.'

As they drove east out of the city in the direction of Margate, Tom called the town's police station and asked them to watch the two addresses. 'At least if he makes a move, we'll have someone on him.'

'Assuming he hasn't already made a move.' Lexi's heart was in her mouth as they sped along the busy A road, flashing past the cars and lorries coming in the other direction. It was dusk, making the headlamps seem brighter, blurring the outlines of the road in the shadows beyond.

'Slow down,' said Tom, sounding more irritable than alarmed.

Lexi shook her head, but she had to as the road dog-legged into a small village. A flashing speed sign told her she was going at thirty-seven in a thirty zone, so she reluctantly applied more pressure to the brakes.

They took the Birchington address first as it was the closest. Tom reviewed the information they had found online on Edward Mason so far. 'He was a gifted violinist, apparently with a huge future in classical music ahead of him. But then he got tendon problems in his left shoulder and wrist. He had to take a break from playing and it appears that he never recovered his previous form.'

'Leaving him bitter and twisted enough to incite other young musicians to cut short their own careers?' It was speculation but it sort of made sense.

Birchington-on-Sea was a sprawling village that bled into Westgate-on-Sea, which itself bled into the suburbs of Margate – a North Kent coastal conurbation. They took a left from the main road that led past the railway station and into the centre of the village.

'We need Reculver Avenue, fourth on the left,' said Tom as they left the station behind them.

Birchington was bungalow land, and Reculver Avenue was no exception. A wide street with grass verges and neat front gardens, squat bungalows with cars on the drives and on the road in front. Quiet and comfortable.

'This is where his parents live,' said Tom. 'But Edward is mid-twenties now, so how likely is it that he's still here?'

They found the house they were looking for, and Lexi was relieved to see an unmarked police car parked on the other side of the road, a couple of doors down. She walked across to it and flashed her ID. The passenger window slid down and the officer inside looked up at her.

'Anything?'

'All quiet.'

'Thanks. Can you hang on while we check it out – then I'll let you know whether to stay or go.'

'Sure.' He closed the window again.

Tom and Lexi went up to the house. The front garden was laid to lawn, with a drive to the left and a garage with a green-painted wooden door. A white Volkswagen Polo sat on the drive. A light inside shone through the windows, showing a tidy sitting/dining room, crammed with furniture but no sign of the inhabitants.

Lexi pressed the doorbell with her forefinger.

Inside, she felt a mixture of grim determination and nerves. What if he wasn't here, if he'd already gone to meet Masher and lead him to the darkness?

The door opened to reveal a black-haired woman of about thirty, dressed in a brown corduroy shirt dress that seemed a size too large and moved stiffly when she did. She was too young to be Edward Mason's mother, but the way she was dressed reminded Lexi of someone.

'Can I help you?'

Lexi flashed her ID. 'Detective Inspector Bennett, Kent Police. May I ask your name?'

The woman still looked puzzled. 'Of course. I'm Donna Mason.'

'We're looking for Edward Mason. Does he live here?'

Donna Mason's face creased into a frown. 'Edward Mason was my brother,' she said quietly. 'He's... he's no longer alive.'

'Edward Mason, the violinist?' said Tom.

Donna nodded. 'What's this about?'

'Would you mind me asking when and how he died?' said Lexi.

'You'd better come in.' Donna pulled the door open and they followed her into a spacious hallway. There were a number of dark wooden doors leading off it, all closed, but Donna made no move to invite them further inside. She turned and looked at them.

'Ed committed suicide three years ago. He couldn't play anymore and when that happened, he felt life wasn't worth living.' She blinked to avoid eye contact with either of them. 'He was my kid brother.'

'I'm sorry for your loss,' said Lexi, but inside her heart was thumping. Could Ed Mason have been one of Nyx's earliest victims?

Tom was obviously thinking along the same lines. 'I hate to ask this, but do you mind telling us how he did it?'

Donna looked away from them towards a narrow console, on which stood a framed photo of a young man holding a violin. 'He took pills, mixed with alcohol.' There was a tremor in her voice, matched by a trembling lower lip. 'Why are you asking these questions?'

'We have reason to believe that someone has been encouraging young musicians to take their own lives.'

Donna's hand flew to her mouth. 'And you think...?'

'It might be a possibility.' Lexi wasn't going to admit to her that their original reason for coming was because they thought her brother might have been the perpetrator. But now they needed to get out and get to the address for Kai Epson. 'We're sorry to have bothered you, Miss Mason. If anything further comes to light, we'll make sure we keep you informed.'

'Thank you. Please do let me know what you find. I... I always felt something was off. He shouldn't have died. He had so much to live for, but...' She stopped speaking and Lexi sensed there was more that she wasn't saying.

Neither she nor Tom spoke, waiting for the silence to do its work.

'There was a man, a friend of my parents...' She faltered again. 'He abused my brother.'

'Was he ever charged?'

'No, he got away with it. I think he pushed Edward to the brink of suicide to keep him quiet.'

'Can you give us his name?' Lexi fought to keep the excitement out of her voice. This was progress – this man could be Nyx.

But Donna shook her head. 'I only ever knew him by his first name. Barry.'

'Barry Gray? The man who runs the Tenterden International Music Festival?'

Donna shrugged. 'I don't even know for certain what happened. It was all years ago and I was away at uni on and off.'

'What about your parents? Maybe they could help us?'

'They're both dead. My dad died during the pandemic, and my mother never really got over it.'

'I'm so sorry,' said Lexi. They would need to check out Barry Gray – whether he had alibis for the times of death, and where he was right now. And whether there had ever been any formal complaints or charges against him.

Donna glanced towards the front door. It seemed she wanted them gone as much as Lexi wanted to go, so they said their goodbyes and beat a hasty retreat, dismissing the police car which had been watching the house before they arrived.

'Weird that our searches never flagged up his death,' said Tom.

Lexi shrugged. 'We didn't search that far back.'

'Kai Epson or Barry Gray?'

'Epson's relatively nearby, isn't he? While we go there, get Ridhi to locate Gray and have him brought to the station.'

As they got into the car, Tom pulled out his phone. 'Back to the main road, but go straight across it. We'll go cross country to Westwood – it's more direct.'

As the engine roared to life, a tingle ran down Lexi's spine. She had a feeling they were closing in on Nyx.

She just hoped they would get there on time.

FIFTY-SIX

Ten minutes later, they drew up in front of the address they had for Kai Epson. It was on the main road connecting Westwood to Ramsgate, a flat above a run-down chippy in the centre of a small parade of shops. Once more, they had a quick chat with the occupant of an unmarked car that was watching the premises in advance of their arrival.

'Doesn't look like anyone's home,' said the unshaven officer behind the wheel. 'No one's been in or out since I got here, and there are no lights on.'

'Thanks,' said Lexi.

They crossed the road and rang the bell for Epson's flat. It shared a front door with the flat above, and both bells went unanswered. The smell of fried food pervaded the air, despite the fact the chippy had no customers, and the other shops in the parade – a newsagent, a pharmacy and an estate agent – were all closed.

'Come on, let's ask in here.' Lexi pushed open the door of the chip shop and was immediately enveloped in warm, greasy steam. She felt hungry, but the smell was anything but appetising. Tom followed her in.

Lexi flashed her badge at a short barrel-chested man who was half-heartedly attending to the friers.

'Do you know the bloke who lives upstairs?' she said. 'Kai Epson.'

'Yeah. What of it?'

'He a regular customer?'

The man nodded. He wasn't going to volunteer any more information than he had to.

'D'you happen to know where he is?'

A shrug. 'Been away for a while, 'bout a week. Said something about going on holiday the other day.'

'Do you know when he'll be back?'

'No.'

'And the flat above?'

'That's been empty these last months.'

They went back to the car, dismissing the officer in the car. Tom called the station and Ridhi told him that Barry Gray was being brought in for a voluntary interview.

'He wasn't happy about it at all.' Ridhi's voice came over on speakerphone inside the car. 'They've got evening performances on at the festival, and he was furious at being called away.'

Or was he furious at being taken to the police station when he had plans to meet Masher later? 'Tough,' said Lexi. 'We'll be back in half an hour – hold him for our arrival, if you can.'

'One other thing, boss,' said Ridhi.

'Yes?'

'I checked him out on Holmes. There was an accusation against him – a young violinist accused him of inappropriate behaviour at the festival a few years back. It was investigated and he was exonerated.'

'The name of the alleged victim?'

'Edward Mason.'

Exonerated because he didn't do it or due to a lack of evidence?

Lexi took the journey back to Canterbury at a more sedate pace – she didn't need any more remonstrances from Tom.

'Looks like we can strike Kai Epson off the list,' she said. 'If he really has been away on holiday for the last week, he would have been gone when all three of the victims died.'

'I'll sort someone out to verify that,' said Tom.

They arrived at the station, and Lexi gulped down a black coffee from the vending machine. It was disgustingly bitter, but the caffeine hit the spot.

Ridhi had Barry Gray in one of the interview rooms, and reported that he was far from happy at being kept waiting, but Lexi took a few extra minutes to go over her strategy with Tom before they spoke to him.

The festival director stood up when they came into the room.

'Good evening, Mr Gray,' said Lexi.

'It certainly isn't,' he said, failing to keep the frustration out of his voice.

'You remember us from yesterday?' said Tom.

'Of course I do. And I expect you to remember that I co-operated fully.'

Lexi nodded. 'You did. However, we have some questions we'd like to put to you.'

'Do I have any choice?'

'I'm sure DC Kulkarni told you this is a voluntary interview, but it would really be in your own interests to talk to us.'

Barry Gray sat down. He wasn't a stupid man, and he appeared to recognise the implication that Lexi would have her questions answered one way or another.

Tom pointed at the recording device. 'We'd like to record this interview, if that's okay?'

Gray nodded. He seemed to know the form – clearly he'd been subject to police interviews before.

Lexi dove straight in. 'Olivia James. Do you recognise that name?'

'No.'

'What about Shan Liang?'

Gray shook his head, but he seemed to be thinking.

'Neil McGowan?'

'Plays the saxophone, I think. He did well at the festival last year.' He fixed Lexi with an angry intense stare. 'Why should I know these people?'

'They're all dead. Their deaths were made to look like suicide.'

Gray processed the information. Tom was watching him closely. Lexi had told him to make note of any reaction when he heard the names.

'You're implying they were murdered?'

'Can you give me details of your whereabouts last Monday afternoon, between two p.m. and seven p.m.?' Barry Gray was a short man, slight of build. So was the person who emerged from the phone box.

'I was on the festival site. Monday was when we had all the marquees erected and I was there all day, until after nine p.m. There are plenty of people who can vouch for my presence. It was organised chaos and I was directing operations.'

Chaotic enough for him to have slipped away for a couple of hours? They would need to talk to people who'd been there and establish a timeline of sightings. She'd put Colin onto it right away.

'What about last Tuesday, from midnight until eight a.m.?'

'Home in bed. My wife will verify that for you.'

'And the same hours on Wednesday?'

'Again, my wife will confirm that I was at home.'

'Is it just you and your wife? Do you have children?'

'Not living at home anymore. I'm afraid it's just me and Sandra – and of course, that won't do for you, will it?'

'Tell me about Edward Mason.'

'I wondered how long it would be before that name was mentioned.' His eyes narrowed. 'I really have nothing to say on the subject, apart from to tell you to check your own files.'

'You do know that Edward Mason also died by suicide?'

Gray looked genuinely surprised. 'I didn't. I suppose you'll be wanting an alibi for whenever that happened too?'

'You're right. We will.'

Gray shrugged. He didn't look worried. 'When was it?'

'Who's Masher?'

'I have no idea.'

'Have you ever been charged with the sexual assault of a minor?'

He didn't blink. He didn't break eye contact. His breathing remained unchanged.

'No.'

It meant nothing. Donna Mason had told them he'd never been charged, that he'd got away with it.

Lexi reached out a hand to flick off the recorder.

She had no reason to hold him, and every reason to follow him to wherever he went next.

'You can go, Mr Gray. I'll save the rest of my questions for another time.'

Tom looked at her, eyes wide with amazement. But Gray's answers were too slick, too practised. He wasn't telling them anything, except that he had something to hide.

Barry Gray didn't waste a second.

When he was gone, Lexi turned to Tom.

'Come on. He's going to lead us to Masher.'

FIFTY-SEVEN

'You follow him out front, see which way he goes, and I'll come round with the car,' said Lexi.

A minute later she pulled out of the station car park to find Tom waiting on the pavement.

'Left on the ring road,' he said as he concertinaed himself to get into the Crossfire's low-slung passenger seat.

'Who am I following?'

'The Jag,' said Tom, pointing to a maroon Jaguar just clearing the junction. 'She was waiting for him outside the station. I assume it's his wife.'

He phoned Ridhi and gave her the car's registration number to check. A couple of minutes later she came back to him and confirmed it.

'Damn,' said Lexi. 'He's not going to meet Masher with the wife in tow.'

They still had the car in sight, heading in the direction of Tenterden. The grey-haired woman driving it stuck assiduously to the speed limit.

'Give Ridhi another call,' said Lexi. 'Get her to send us the

details of the accusations against him made by Edward Mason. I
want to know why no charges were brought.'

It only took Ridhi a couple of minutes to pull up Barry
Gray's file from the online archives, and by the time Tom was
reading the details on his phone, they'd arrived back at the
music festival. The Jaguar turned up the main drive, rather than
heading for the public car park, so Lexi pulled up on the road
just beyond the entrance gate. It was gone nine p.m. now, so
Gray was only going to catch the end of whatever performance
he'd expected to attend.

As they walked up the driveway, keeping in the dark
shadows along the edge, Tom summarised the details.

'Edward Mason's parents brought an accusation against
Gray on behalf of their son – the claim was that they'd been
alone in one of the rehearsal spaces and Gray touched the boy
inappropriately.'

'When was this?'

'A few years back, before the pandemic. Just months before
Mason died.'

'And?'

'According to the report, at the time when Mason claims it
happened, Gray was on stage introducing the finals of the
choral competition. Literally hundreds of witnesses. The
parents then claimed there had been some confusion over the
time and it basically became Mason's word against Gray's. The
CPS decided there simply wasn't enough evidence to secure a
conviction.'

'But Mason could have got the time wrong. A simple
mistake and the bastard got off.'

'That's what he and his parents claimed – a mistake. But
after that, Edward couldn't come up with a convincing alterna-
tive time. He killed himself a couple of weeks later.'

Lexi watched as Barry Gray, holding hands with his wife,
went around the corner of the main house. She walked faster,

and rounding the corner, she saw the couple go into the largest of the marquees, from which she could hear the strains of a familiar opera aria.

'What do you think?' said Lexi. 'Could he be Nyx?'

Tom thought for a moment. 'You think Edward Mason was his first victim?'

'If he pushed Edward towards taking his life, that could have been the trigger for what he's doing now. Trying to repeat the excitement he felt the first time he exercised that power over someone.'

'The power of life and death,' Tom mused.

But Lexi couldn't square the circle. For some reason she wasn't quite convinced. She didn't think Barry Gray was Nyx. That didn't mean he wasn't a child abuser – and it didn't mean she wouldn't investigate him further. But when she asked herself if he was the person responsible for the deaths of three teenagers, her inner voice said 'No'. There was something about the way Nyx spoke to the teenagers online that didn't fit with Gray's middle-aged, middle-class persona.

'How old is Donna Mason?' she asked.

Tom called Ridhi to find out. 'Twenty-three.'

'She seemed older.'

'Maybe it's the way she was dressed – a bit frumpy. Why d'you ask?'

'I just don't feel we've got to the bottom of what's going on yet.' The singer in the tent moved on to a new aria. 'Tom, can you sort a couple of guys to come out here to follow Gray once the performance finishes, and tell them if he meets up with anyone at all, they're to intervene and arrest him.'

'What are we going to do?'

'I think we need to have another word with Donna Mason.'

Tom's eyebrows went up. 'Do you think she was lying about Edward Mason being dead? That would explain why it didn't show up in any of our searches. Could he still be alive and she knows it? Do you still think he could be Nyx?'

It seemed far-fetched, but Lexi was practically running to get back to the car.

'She definitely knows more than she told us.'

The forty-mile run back across the county to Birchington was fast – the roads were empty. It was a dry night and the sky was clear – if Lexi's mind hadn't been racing from one possibility to the next, she would have enjoyed the challenges of the dark country roads. As it was, she gave Tom a white-knuckle ride that had him muttering about bringing his own car next time they went anywhere.

'We don't have time to waste on the niceties of the speed limit,' said Lexi, accelerating out of a corner and picking up pace on a long, straight stretch of road.

There was a little bit of traffic as they drove through Birchington, and they turned into Reculver Avenue less than an hour after they had left Tenterden. But something was different this time. The lights inside the house were out and the white Polo no longer sat on the drive.

'Shit,' said Lexi.

'What now?'

'Half past ten. Wonder where she is?'

'Do you want try the village pubs?'

'Would she drive, if she was drinking?'

Birchington was a small place, and there were several pubs within walking distance of Donna Mason's house.

Lexi got out of the car. She looked around. No sign of any neighbours out on the street. Most of the front rooms were lit, curtains drawn or the incessant flicker of the television holding people's attention. She walked slowly up the path at the front of the Mason property. Donna's parents were dead, her brother was supposedly dead, and she just kept on living in the family home on her own. Lexi wondered why she'd never moved away, especially if this was the place where her brother had died.

She stepped off the path onto the small patch of lawn so she could stare in through the dark window. Something on the floor glinted in the light of the streetlamps. She could just make out the shape – it was the body of a violin. But the neck had been snapped and lay close by at an angle, the twisted strings still holding the two pieces together.

Her brother's violin? But why lying broken?

She switched on the torch on her phone and shone it through the window, sweeping the room in a giant arc of light.

She felt Tom stepping up behind, his breath warm on the side of her neck.

'What can you see?'

The light showed that the violin had been violently smashed against the side of a small table – splinters of lacquered wood lay on the tabletop and scattered across the floor.

And then, beyond the broken violin, Lexi spotted something else.

Dark fluff on the pale carpet.

She focused the beam of her torch onto it and saw it clearly.

A small piece of twine.

A trimming from the end of a rope?

It was red.

FIFTY-EIGHT

'What does it mean?' said Tom, as Lexi turned abruptly and stormed back towards the car.

What does it mean?

'I...' Lexi stood by the driver's door, rifling through her bag for the car keys.

'Do you think Edward Mason is still alive? Do you think he's Nyx?'

'No... yes... no, that doesn't make sense at all.' She finally located the car keys in her trouser pocket. 'A faked death? Somehow living in hiding? Or living somewhere else and coming back here to murder people?'

They got into the car.

'I can't believe Edward could have remained off the radar for so long,' she said, furious and scared at the same time. 'But that leaves Barry Gray or Eric Cotter.'

'Or someone we don't know yet,' said Tom.

That was her biggest fear.

She looked around the street before starting the engine, trying to calm herself down.

'If Nyx is someone else, he knows Donna Mason. He's been

here. At least, that's what that snippet of red rope suggests.' Tom was gaming the possibilities.

'And what about the broken violin?'

'An argument? A struggle?'

Then she got it. 'He's taken her. But if Nyx has taken Donna, they've gone in Donna's Polo. So how did he get here?' She couldn't remember which cars had been parked in the street when they'd arrived earlier. And what if he'd come on foot, or on a bicycle which he could have easily hidden?

She pulled away from the curb, still deep in thought.

Tom made a call. 'Ridhi, we're looking for a white Volkswagen Polo, registered to Donna Mason. Last seen in Birchington-on-Sea earlier this afternoon. Put out an APB on it. We have reason to believe that Donna Mason has been abducted, identity of the abductor unknown.'

Lexi interrupted. 'Tell her to get some uniforms up here to go house-to-house and work out who owns what vehicle. If they find an unknown one, I want it checked out.'

It wouldn't help them find Donna in a hurry, or Masher either, but it could still be critical information.

'And what are we going to do?' said Tom, as soon as he'd finished talking to Ridhi.

Lexi realised she was driving back towards Canterbury on autopilot. 'I don't know.' She spoke through gritted teeth, hardly able to admit that the case was running away from her.

Her phone sounded from inside her bag, but she didn't answer it.

'Where would he take her?' she said.

'And why?' added Tom.

'Because she spoke to us? She knows who he is – she would if he's her brother – and he's scared she'll spill the beans. So he wants to shut her up.'

'That would make sense if it is Edward, but what if it's not?'

'And either way, it doesn't help in terms of location.'

Her phone rang again.

'Do you want me to get that?' said Tom.

'No, leave it. If it's important I'll call them back when we're in the office.' She didn't want her concentration broken while she was thinking through what might have happened to Donna Mason. Ironically, they might have bought some time for Masher, but if it was at the expense of Donna Mason falling victim to Nyx, it wasn't a good trade-off.

Lexi drummed her fingers against the steering wheel.

Where? Where? Where?

The ringtone of her phone fell in with the beat.

Tom glanced at her, but she was staring at the road ahead.

'This rules out Barry Gray,' she said finally.

'What about Arbuthnot and Cotter?' said Tom.

'Arbuthnot – we've practically ruled him out already. And Cotter was in custody while Nyx was online. I think we've got to face the fact that Nyx is someone we haven't identified yet.'

'Back at square one, in other words.'

The rest of the drive passed in silence. Lexi's phone rang again.

'Maybe you should get that,' said Tom.

Lexi pulled a face and ignored the insistent ringing. She was trying to work out where to go next. Things were coming to a head but, at the moment, they were shut out. She couldn't bear the thought that their only way back in might come with the discovery of another dead body.

She'd let down Masher and now Donna Mason as well.

Things couldn't get worse, could they?

They walked back into the station slowly, shoulders slumped, a grim silence hanging between them. It was late, but with a woman missing and likely abducted by an unknown killer, there was no doubt in Lexi's mind that the night was far from over. It was her intention to go up to the incident room and collate everything they knew. If they were lucky, they'd get an ANPR hit on Donna Mason's car. If they weren't, they'd have to work out some other way of finding her.

'Check with Greg Chambers if the chatroom is still active,' she said, mentally compiling a list of tasks as they reached the bottom of the stairs.

The door that led through to the front part of the station swung open.

'Lexi, someone here for you.' There was something guarded about the desk sergeant's tone.

'Who?'

'You should come with me.'

Giving Tom a shrug, she followed the sergeant out into the public reception area.

Amber rushed towards her. 'Lexi, oh my God, I've been calling you and calling you.'

The phone ringing in the car.

'Why? Has something happened?'

'It's Sam.'

'What about him?'

'He's missing.'

Sam. *Masher*.

Fear crashed over her body like a tidal wave.

FIFTY-NINE

'School called me half an hour ago. I've been trying to get you ever since.'

'How long has he been gone?'

'They're not sure.'

Shit!

'Come on. We need to talk to them, find out who saw him last.' Bundling Amber through the door to go back to the car park, she turned to Tom. 'File a missing person report – Sam Riley. Thirteen years old. You know what to do.'

'Of course.' Tom disappeared up the stairs at a run.

As they got into the car, Lexi remembered that the boys' choir's boarding house was within the cathedral precinct, while the school itself was on the northern edge of the town. 'Where did he go missing from?'

Amber shrugged helplessly and burst into tears.

'Okay, we'll go to the house first and check out his room. Can you call whoever called you and tell them to meet us there?'

Amber nodded and sniffed. By a supreme effort of will, she got herself under control and made the call. 'His housemaster will meet us there,' she said. 'Go up Burgate – there's a small mews on the right for vehicles to get into the precinct. He'll let the security guard know we're coming in.'

'Where's Grant?' Grant was Amber's husband and Sam's dad.

'He's away. I've called him and he's trying to rearrange his flight, but there won't be one now until the morning.'

'And Tasha?'

'I dropped her at a school friend's before coming to find you.'

'Good, well done.'

As well as driving and talking to Amber, another part of Lexi's mind was gaming out what might have happened. Could Sam really be Masher? She cast her mind back to the chatroom exchange between Masher and Nyx. She didn't know Sam well enough to able to say whether the short typed messages seemed typical of his voice – and she silently cursed herself for the years of estrangement between her and Amber. But could Nyx have targeted Sam? That was entirely plausible. He'd targeted Sam's friend Olivia, and Sam had been at the Tenterden festival.

Damn!

He'd been there with the choir, and both Amber and Grant had been in the audience – and she'd assumed that would have kept him safe enough. Evidently it hadn't.

'What is it?' said Amber, as they turned into the narrow lane leading to the cathedral precinct.

'What?'

'You pulled a face.' Amber's voice sounded higher pitched than usual. She was scared.

'Sorry. It's nothing.' She wasn't going to share her fears with Amber. Not before she had to.

A security guard waved at them from a small, green wooden cabin, and a barrier was raised to allow them access.

'Round here,' said Amber, pointing to the left. They followed a narrow road that took them past a couple of impressive-looking medieval houses that were now used as diocese offices, and round the eastern aspect of the city's magnificent cathedral – all the more imposing in the golden glow of the floodlights. 'There, that's Choir House, where the choristers board,' she said, indicating a short terrace of houses that looked more like sixteenth-century workers' cottages, built of red brick and local flint.

Lexi drew up in front of the building, and Amber led the way to one end where there was a stone porch shaped like a gothic arch with a white painted door.

Their knock was answered by a tall man with grizzled grey hair and a worried frown.

'Mrs Riley, I'm so sorry. Please come in.' He had a strong Eastern European accent.

Amber stepped inside. 'This is my sister, Lexi.'

The man's eyes widened momentarily as he took in the fact they were identical. It was a look both she and Amber had seen hundreds of times over the years, more so when their sister, Rose, had still been alive – triplets always caused a reaction.

'DI Lexi Bennett.' She needed the man to know that she was here in her police capacity as well as to support her sister.

'I'm Pavel Belka.' He put out a hand. 'Housemaster here.'

Lexi shook hands with him, then they followed him along a corridor that wound through the building and an extension built on at the back, until they came to a small office. There was a desk and two chairs. Belka looked around, perplexed.

'Let me go and fetch another chair.'

'No, please don't,' said Lexi abruptly.

Both Belka and Amber gave her surprised looks.

'We don't have time. When a person goes missing, every minute counts, particularly at the early stages.'

Amber's face crumpled, and Belka looked mortified.

'Of course. I'm sorry. What do you need to know?'

'When was Sam last seen, where, and by whom?'

'We know he was here at supper – a number of staff and boys saw him in the dining hall.'

'What time was that?'

'Six thirty.'

'And afterwards?'

'The boys have free time after supper. They can watch television, play computer games or play football in the garden, ride their bikes in the precinct...'

'But they have to stay within the bounds?'

'Yes, after supper they do. There are times when they can go out but not on weekday evenings.'

'Do you know what Sam did after supper?'

'So far no one remembers seeing him. We've spoken to his close friends and the boys in his dormitory, and of course we've tried calling him, but he hasn't answered his phone.'

'I've been calling too,' said Amber. 'No answer.' She sunk down onto the single chair opposite Belka's desk, dissolving into tears. 'Where is he?'

Lexi put a hand on her shoulder, but turned her attention back to Belka. 'What time was it when you realised he was missing?'

'Matron came to me to tell me at bedtime. The boys go up at eight thirty, lights out at nine. Matron always checks everyone's ready for bed and where they should be.'

'Can we talk to her?'

The housemaster made a quick call, and a minute later there was a knock on the office door. Lexi was expecting a comfortable-looking, middle-aged woman in a starchy white uniform, but quickly realised her ideas about boarding schools were long out of date. The woman who came in – in fact, Lexi would have described her as a girl – was anything but what she would have expected. Early twenties, if that, wearing jeans and a hoody, with a short-cropped pixie cut and a ring through one nostril.

'Mrs Riley,' she said straight away, rushing across the room to give Amber a hug.

'Oh, Lara,' said Amber, getting up to hug the girl in return.

'This is Lara Small, the matron here at Choir House,' said Belka. 'Lara, this is DI Bennett.'

Lara Small disengaged herself from Amber's clutching embrace and turned to Lexi. Lexi could see now that she'd been crying. Her eyes were swollen, and the end of her nose was red, almost raw.

'Tell me what happened,' said Lexi.

'I realised he wasn't around when the boys were getting ready for bed. I gave him five minutes – he can be a bit of a dawdler in the evenings – then I checked again. He's in Byrd, one of the smaller dorms, and I asked the other three if they knew where he was. They didn't. I knocked on the bathroom doors, but he wasn't there, so I ran down to the television room and checked the practice rooms – all over, really. There was no sign of him, so that's when I came and told Pavel.'

'Can we see his bedroom, please?'

Lara gave Pavel a concerned look. 'The other boys...'

'His dorm mates will be sleeping,' said Pavel.

'I wouldn't ask if it wasn't important,' said Lexi.

Amber looked from one to the other of them. 'Anything we can do to find Sam...'

'They probably won't be asleep,' said Lara. 'They're worried about him. I think it would be good for them to see that something's being done to find him.'

'Okay,' said Pavel.

'I'll need to ask the boys a few questions, too,' said Lexi.

Pavel's expression was pained, but he nodded in agreement.

Lara offered to show them the way.

'Where do you think he might be?' she said, as they climbed up a narrow staircase in single file.

'Hopefully not too far away,' said Lexi. 'How easy would it be for him to leave the cathedral precinct at night?'

Lara stopped at the top of the stairs and shrugged. 'It's like a gated community, so in theory he shouldn't be able to. But it's not a prison, and in the dark – I expect he could find a way to sneak out.' She started up another flight of stairs to the second floor.

'How has he been over the last few days?' said Lexi. She glanced back to see that Amber was gripping the banister, rooted to the spot. She held out a hand to her.

'He's not been his usual self since Olivia died. We've brought in a counsellor to talk to all of her friends, but I don't think Sam wanted to. Do you think it's to do with that?'

'It might be,' said Lexi, though not in the way Lara thought. 'Perhaps he just needed some time to himself. We'll get some uniforms out here to search the precinct thoroughly.'

Amber was crying audibly as they reached the top.

Lara stopped and turned to face them. 'Let me go first and tell the boys. I'll take them down to the television room, so you can check Sam's things.'

'Thank you,' said Lexi.

She gave Amber a hug. 'Let me do this. You wait here.'

Amber shook her head. 'No, I'll come with you. I'm more likely to realise if anything's missing.'

Three boys filed past them with downcast heads and sombre expressions.

'Hello, Archie,' said Amber, touching one of them on the arm.

The boy looked up and gave her a wan smile without saying anything.

Lara beckoned them into the room. 'That's Sam's bed, and his cupboard,' she said, pointing them out.

The room was small and cosy, with four small single beds tucked into the corners under the sloping ceiling. There was a row of cupboards along one wall, two small desks by the window, and another two in the centre of the room. Boys' possessions were strewn over every flat surface – books, clothes, musical scores and instruments, sports kit. There were stuffed animals on each of the beds – a huge lion on one, his mane matted and grubby, a collection of smaller bears on another, a dog, teddies. Teenagers they might be, but still small boys at heart, Lexi reflected.

On Sam's bed, there was a grey stuffed mouse wearing a red jacket. Amber went straight over to it and picked it up, hugging it to her chest and breathing in its smell.

Lexi pulled on a pair of latex gloves and started to go through Sam's things methodically – clothes, sports kit, dirty laundry, wash bag, textbooks, folders... everything she would expect to find. On the desk nearest his bed there was a laptop.

'Is this his?' she said to Amber, who'd been staring vacantly out of the window.

She looked round. 'Why the gloves? You think there's been a crime?' Panic laced her voice.

'It's standard procedure,' said Lexi, keeping her voice as low and as calm as she could.

Amber nodded, hardly mollified by Lexi's reply.

Lexi put the laptop into an evidence bag. She would need to get it to Greg Chambers as quickly as possible to try and find out if Sam had been visiting the dark web. Amber turned back to the window, still squeezing the mouse.

Lexi checked the bed, pulling back the tartan blanket, then slipping her hand under the pillow. She felt something with the tips of her fingers and shoved the pillow away onto the floor. A square of folded paper.

'Oh God...' Lexi's breath caught in her throat as a bad, bad feeling swept over her. She snatched the up the note.

'What have you found?' Amber's voice rose into hysteria.

It had been a mistake to let her come up here. Seeing Sam's personal belongings being searched was much too painful, and now this.

Lexi stared at the folded paper, to terrified to open it up. She turned away from Amber to hide what she had in her hand.

No mother should have to find this.

SIXTY

But as she turned it in her hand, she saw something written on the outside.

Aunt Lexi

Hardly daring to breathe, she unfolded it and then read it, still shielding it from Amber until she knew what it said.

Dear Aunt Lexi,

I tried to speak to you at the music festival, but Nyx was there and I got scared. And Mum's always around when I see you, and she mustn't know about this stuff. It would upset her.

You see, I know what happened to Olly – Nyx was persuading her to kill herself. I know who Nyx is and I've set a trap.

I've got to go now, but you'll soon get the answer.

Tell Mum I love her.

Sam

X

The words put Lexi onto an emotional rollercoaster – fear for his safety, frustration that he hadn't come to her, anger that he was almost certainly in danger. And the ice-cold realisation that, without a doubt, Sam was Masher. Nyx had been there, at the festival – Sam was confirming what they'd believed to be the case. If only Sam had said something there and then. They could have taken Nyx out of action.

But now, Nyx was about kill him.

'What is it?' Amber tried to grab the piece of paper from her.

'No, don't touch it.' Lexi's voice cracked. She held it up so Amber could read what her son had written.

Amber let out an agonised moan and staggered backwards, collapsing onto one of the other boys' beds. 'What's he talking about?' she gasped. 'Who's Nyx and what happened to Olivia? Why didn't he tell me what was going on?'

'To protect you,' said Lexi. 'It's complicated. Nyx has been manipulating kids into taking their own lives – Olivia, Shan Liang, Neil McGowan. And it looks like Sam has taken things into his own hands.'

'What?' The word came out as more of a wail.

But as much as Lexi wanted to comfort her sister, Sam needed her far more than Amber did at this moment. She couldn't waste a second. With shaking hands, she stuffed the piece of paper into another evidence bag and thrust it into her pocket. She picked up the laptop and rushed out of the room.

'Wait, wait...' Amber came running after her.

They crashed down the stairs, almost knocking down a small boy in a checked dressing gown.

'Sorry, sorry,' said Lexi, without stopping.

Amber squeezed past him without saying anything.

At the bottom of the stairs, Lexi saw the matron walking away from them at the far end of a corridor.

'Lara,' she called out.

The matron turned round and hurried back to them.

'I'm sorry – we have to go. I'll send a colleague to interview the boys.'

'You found something?' Lara looked down at the laptop in Lexi's arms.

'I don't know yet.' She wasn't going to tell Lara about the note. 'I'll also send some uniformed officers to search the precinct.'

They ran to the car and Lexi executed a high-speed turn to face the right direction for the road out.

'What did you mean when you said the kids had been manipulated?' said Amber, gripping Lexi's arm as she tried to change gear. 'Was Sam a part of that?'

Lexi shook her off.

'Is Sam in danger?'

What could she say? She didn't want to tell Amber that her son was in the clutches of a manipulative killer who wanted to push him into taking his own life.

'I need to call the station.' Lexi spoke to Tom in the incident room and tasked him with organising a search of the cathedral precinct around the school.

'I'll call in all our uniforms on patrol,' he said.

'And see if you can get the canine unit to come out – the dogs will do better in the dark. You can ask the matron at Choir House for some items of his clothing.'

'You think he's dead,' cried Amber.

'No, I don't. We use dogs to search for living people. Tom, who else is still at work?'

'Just me – but Colin only just left, so I could call him back.'

'Please do. Ask him to go to Choir House as quickly as

possible to interview Sam's dorm mates. I'm on my way back to the station with Sam's laptop, so can you get Greg Chambers in as well?'

'On it.'

By the time she'd finished speaking to Tom, she was pulling into the station car park.

'Amber, keep trying Sam's phone.'

Amber nodded her head. She was verging on the edge of hysteria, she needed a task to distract her from the horrors she was no doubt imagining. Lexi ran ahead and almost collided with Greg Chambers on her way into the incident room.

'Thank God you're here,' she said. She thrust the laptop at him. 'I need to know if Sam Riley was accessing the dark web and, if possible, if he ever visited the Club Edicius chatroom.'

'Of course.'

Greg planted himself at the nearest desk, gloved up and pulled the laptop out of the evidence bag. 'It would really speed things up if you had any idea of his login details.'

Amber appeared in the doorway, having trudged up the stairs more slowly. 'He uses his email address as his username,' she said, going over to where Greg sat. She leaned over his shoulder and typed it in. 'And I know his password.' She typed a string of letters and numbers. 'Grant insists on it – if either he or Tash change their logins, their laptops get confiscated.'

'Thanks,' said Greg.

Lexi watched him as he scanned through the applications, searching for Tor. It was a safe bet that Sam used different login details for accessing the dark web.

'Okay, he's got Tor,' Greg confirmed. 'But he's logged out of it, which means we won't be able to see what sites he's been visiting.'

'Then we have to assume that he's been in the chatroom.' She shot a look at Tom. He needed to understand what she was saying without her having to go into the details in front of Amber. He nodded at her.

'What chatroom?' said Amber.

Lexi took her hand and led her out of the incident room into the corridor. They stood facing each other, Amber's terrified eyes searching Lexi's face for answers.

Still holding on to her sister's hand, Lexi said, 'I think it would be better if you weren't here. I need to be able to fully concentrate on finding Sam...'

'I'm not stopping you from doing that.'

'I know you're not. But...' How could she put it? 'I need to be able to speak freely in front my team without being concerned that I might upset you.'

'Because you think he's dead already?' Amber's pitch had risen again.

'Because this is hard enough for you already, without hearing every small detail of the search efforts. It's too stressful.'

Amber took a deep breath, and Lexi saw her jaw tighten. 'I'm tougher than I look. He's my son – I need to be here.'

Being hugely aware that she couldn't give Amber any more time, Lexi stood firm. 'No. You wait in my office and, as soon as someone's available, I'll send you home with a family liaison officer to stay with you until Grant gets back. Right?'

Amber nodded, her lips tightly pressed together. Of course it was hard for her, and Lexi's heart went out to her – but finding Sam had to be her top priority. She went back into the incident room, leaving Amber settling herself in the other office. It was always tough, having to balance the needs of a case with the time needed by the victim's families, but when it was your own sister and your own nephew... Lexi had to steel herself. She couldn't afford to let either of them down.

Tom gave her a concerned look as she came back into the room. 'Okay?' he mouthed.

'I'm okay,' she said. She went over to the whiteboard, where someone had already pinned up a photo of Sam. He was in the red cassock and white surplice of a chorister, looking up wide-eyed with wonder, bathed in the amber glow of the cathedral lighting. Her breath hitched in her chest. 'Our current assumption is that Sam is Masher, and that he's arranged to meet with Nyx somewhere. He's already been missing a couple of hours, so time is running out. Nyx draws his victims to a public place where he can encourage or, more likely, push them into taking their own lives. What we need to do is work out where that might be. Sam left Choir House and would have gone somewhere either on foot or by bicycle. Call Colin and get him to find out if Sam's bike is missing.'

Tom pulled out his phone, but then he paused.

'If Nyx is meeting with Sam, what about Donna Mason?'

Since hearing that Sam was missing, Lexi had completely forgotten that Edward Mason's sister was missing too.

'He must be holding her somewhere, I suppose. Can you call Ridhi back in to co-ordinate the search for Donna?'

As Tom got busy on the phone, she went to her office to check on Amber, hating herself for what she was about to ask. 'Amber, if Sam wanted to go somewhere to be alone, where would he go? What were his special places?'

Amber stood up quickly. Lexi could see by her posture she'd changed – she'd pulled everything together to do what she could for her son. Her face took on a deep look of concentration.

Her voice was faltering. 'When we're at home, he loves spending time in the orchard at the bottom of the garden...'

Trees!

Lexi's heart skipped a beat.

'But he would expect you to be at home, wouldn't he?' said Tom.

Amber nodded.

'When he's not home?' said Lexi.

'There's a railway bridge nearby,' said Amber. 'Down one of

the lanes where we sometimes walk, the road crosses over the railway. When he was little, he used to love standing on the bridge and waving at the train drivers.'

'Would he still go there?' said Lexi.

Amber shrugged. 'We still walk that way sometimes.'

'Where else?'

'He loves the cathedral. He always has, and being in the choir is the most important thing in his life.'

'Is that under threat with his voice breaking?' said Lexi. His days in the choir had to be numbered.

'Yes.'

Lexi made a quick decision. 'Tom, go to the bridge. I'll go to the cathedral and direct the search there.'

'I'm coming too,' said Amber.

'No,' said Lexi. 'This is a police operation.'

'At least let me take Tom to the bridge. It'll be quicker.'

'No.'

Tom looked from one to the other. 'Lexi, she's right. And if Sam's not there or you find him first, I can take her home.'

There wasn't time to fight. 'Okay.'

They ran down the stairs and out to the car park.

'Call me when you're at the bridge,' said Lexi.

'Of course.'

They had to find him, and if he wasn't at either these two places, they would have lost valuable time.

'And let me know if you think of anywhere else,' she asked her sister.

Though, God knows, they'd probably be too late by then.

SIXTY-ONE

The cathedral was only a ten-minute walk from the station, but just two minutes in the Crossfire made more sense. There was virtually no traffic on the roads now, and she roared onto the ring road and then up Burgate like one of the boy racers the car had been designed for. Her brakes screeched as she nearly missed the tiny alley that gave access to the cathedral precinct, and she had to turn the wheel sharply to miss clipping her front wing on the corner of one of the adjacent shops.

'Calm down!' she said out loud, but really calm was the last thing she wanted.

The guy in the security box recognised her car and quickly raised the barrier for her.

Instead of taking the narrow road that led around the cathedral towards Choir House, she sped up the near side of the vast building to get to the main doors at the west end, slamming to a halt directly in front of them. There was no one here on this side of the precinct, though she'd seen torchlight through the trees on the far side.

As she got out of the car, her phone rang. Glancing at the screen, she saw it was Ridhi.

'What?'

'ANPR shows that Donna's car drove into Canterbury an hour ago.'

'Do you know where it is now?'

'Last sighting was on the ring road. Then it simply disappears.'

That wasn't surprising. Once a car was off the main roads, ANPR cover evaporated.

'Thanks. Keep trying to locate it.'

Did that mean Nyx was here, in the centre of town, or had he met up with Sam and then veered off to the railway bridge or somewhere else? And what of Donna? Was she with them or had he done something to her already?

She was standing in front of the huge cathedral doors and she couldn't think. Images swirled through her mind. Sam at the festival – Nyx had been there. The chaos in Donna's living room. The scrap of rope. The scrap of rope. The scrap of rope.

Why would that be there? Had Nyx dropped it when he took Donna?

Nyx. Edward Mason... Could he still be alive? Would he take his own sister?

Oh, God.

It all fell into place.

She knew who Nyx was.

She rushed at the huge doors, but of course they were locked. No lights were shining from the sentinel rows of stained-glass windows. She could hear no sounds from within the thick limestone walls.

There must be a way in.

There was another door, at the southwest corner, and she ran round to it. It was locked, too.

Back past the main door, panic welling inside her. The vast medieval building was like a maze, with cloisters and libraries, chapels and the Chapter House, built higgledy-piggledy over many centuries. As she ran around the south-east corner she was confronted by the long outer wall of the west side of the cloisters – no windows, no door, so she couldn't get in – but at the end of it, a narrow opening to a pathway and a sign pointing to the library. She kept running, her footsteps echoing on the stone slabs, her diaphragm finding the rhythm to push as much oxygen as possible deep into her lungs.

The path took her along the northern outer wall of the clois-ters. It was a narrow alley, so deep in the shadows of the building that she couldn't see the uneven paving ahead of her. She fumbled for her phone and switched on the torch as she ran – just in time. Was that a tiny doorway at the corner of the clois-ters? She stopped, went back a few steps and shone her torch onto an ancient door, so old the wood was warped and the door-frame crooked. There was a black iron handle, its surface pitted with rust.

Heart in mouth, she grasped it and pushed down on it. It moved slightly, but then stuck. Shoving her phone back into her pocket, she used both hands, bearing down with all of her weight. It groaned, then something gave with a sharp crack. Pushing her shoulder against the door, she applied more pres-sure. The wood scraped against the stone floor, just a few inches, before hitting the raised edge of an uneven slab.

Was it enough?

If she could get her head through the gap, she knew the rest of her body could follow. She peered through the space into darkness, but when she shone her torch through, she saw the vaulted ceiling and creamy limestone pillars of the cloisters stretching out in front of her. Good. From here she should be able to access the main part of the cathedral. She gingerly edged her head through the widest part of the gap that she'd forced open. It was a tight squeeze. The rough wood scraped her temples and crushed her ears. She swore softly under her breath as a sharp edge grazed her jawbone and splinters dug into the skin of her neck.

Her head was through. Putting one arm through the gap, she carefully twisted her body so her shoulders could follow her head, thanking her stars that the marathon training she adhered to religiously kept her frame slight. Her jacket caught on the metal latch that jutted out lower down on the door, and she cursed herself for not having thought of removing it before attempting this Houdini like feat. The fabric ripped and the rest of her plunged through the gap. Her body weight buckled the warped wood further and she fell to the floor with a clatter.

As the breath was knocked out of her, she bit her tongue. One wrist slammed down on the stone floor to break her fall, and one shin was crushed against the sharp edge of the doorframe, twisting her ankle as her feet tangled together in the gap.

She let out a yelp of pain and tasted blood in her mouth.

Breathe.

Take a moment.

But she didn't have a moment. She struggled to her feet, swallowing the blood in her mouth, gingerly feeling her jaw and brushing away the flecks of wood that clung to her hair, face and neck. One ankle objected strenuously when she put her weight on it, but she gritted her teeth and started limping the length of the cloisters in the pitch black. It was too dark to see the beautiful stone vaulting or the glory of the stained glass at the top of the gothic arches, but she didn't want to put her torch back on.

She trod as softly as she could on the stone floor, all the while listening for any human activity. The ancient building creaked and drafts whistled through gaps and under doors. The wind whispered around the columns of the cloisters, but it didn't tell her anything about whether Sam was here or not. Or Nyx. That was for her alone to discover.

Lexi had visited the cathedral so many times in her life that she knew where she was. In the southeast corner of the cloisters, there was a doorway which led up a set of steps into a small space known as the Martyrdom – the exact spot where Thomas Becket, the then Archbishop, had been murdered in 1170.

This door was, thankfully, unlocked but the hinges squealed loudly as she pushed it open. She stopped and waited, listening. Still nothing but the sounds of the slumbering building and no sign of any light inside.

What if he wasn't here? She might be wasting time that Sam didn't have.

The air felt cold – a slight draught brushed her cheek as she made her way slowly and quietly out into the north aisle, finding herself directly level with the choir screen which divided the vast length of the building across the middle. She stood at the top of the flight of steps that raised the choir above the nave, waiting for her eyes to become accustomed to the darkness, blacker than it had been outside or in the cloisters. Even when the moon was out the rainbow colours of the stained-glass windows allowed little light to penetrate.

Everything in the main part of the nave was still and quiet, so she turned and went through the carved stone arch in the rood screen that led to the choir. This smaller space was lined with the stalls where Sam and twenty-four other boys stood and sang so beautifully every Sunday, morning and evening. It was silent now, and Lexi felt the weight of history in the stones. She looked round. Tombs and sepulchres crowded in the shadows and the side chapels. Kings, knights, queens and bishops, stone cold dead. Ahead of her, the altar stood on a dais, covered by a cloth of gold, with tall gold candlesticks at either end.

She hurried past it, through the presbytery and up yet more steps to the Trinity Chapel at the very far end. The huge building was empty. There was no sign of Sam here, or Nyx. Thankfully, there was no body hanging from any of the medieval structures – stone arches and columns, wrought-iron railings and gates painted black and gold. The bodies in here were all carved from stone.

But that meant she'd failed to find Sam, and time was running out.

She turned to her left and started to run back in the direction from which she'd come, down the side of the Trinity Chapel and down the steps towards the northeast transept. She needed to get out and call Tom and Amber. Maybe they'd found Sam. Maybe everything was okay. But they hadn't called her to tell her yet. At the bottom of the steps, she pulled out her phone to check whether she had a signal or not. She had, but no missed calls.

Her heart was hammering, her blood pounding in her ears.

But from somewhere in the blackness that surrounded her, she heard a noise.

A scraping sound of wood against the floor.

Furniture being moved?

She heard it again. And realised it was coming from the crypt.

SIXTY-TWO

To her right, a narrow staircase led down into the crypt, the oldest part of the ancient building. A descent into hellish darkness, until she saw a glimmer of light. It flickered for a second and was extinguished. Had whoever was down here heard her boots clattering on the stone?

She stood still and waited.

A voice in the dark. Lexi strained to hear it.

'It doesn't matter what you do, no one will believe it...' Could that be Sam?

'Do you think I give a shit?' The woman's voice was all too familiar and confirmed what she'd realised outside the cathedral.

Donna Mason hadn't been abducted by Nyx. Donna Mason *was* Nyx. And inside, Lexi was beating herself up. She should have realised sooner why there had been something familiar about Donna, niggling away at the back of her mind – the frumpy dress. Similar to the woman who'd sat down next to her on the bench at Tenterden.

'Please let me down.' There was just the slightest tremor in Sam's voice.

'Don't be a coward, Sam. Olivia was a coward, and it didn't go well for her. She refused to put the noose around her neck, she tried to run away from me, she called for help. But of course, I couldn't let her get away. And I won't let you get away.'

Lexi couldn't wait to hear more. She had to act.

'Sam?' she cried. 'Sam, I'm here.'

There was no answer – from either Sam or Donna.

She pulled her phone out of her pocket, switched on the torch and pointed the frail white beam into the darkness.

The crypt was a maze of carved stone pillars supporting a vaulted stone ceiling. Its flagstone floor stretched away for what seemed like miles in every direction. There were dark alcoves hiding shadowy tombs and doorways – and in the dim light it seemed like one of those Escher drawings that repeats itself ad infinitum. But in the centre of the maze stood a figure.

At first she thought it was a giant, so tall did the dark outline appear, but as she ran towards it, the silhouette became clearer. It was a normal-sized person – no, smaller than most adults – standing on a chair. And stretching up from behind the head, she saw a rope leading up to a wooden cross strut between two pillars.

It was Sam, with a noose around his slender neck.

'Sam!'

But before she could reach him, someone else stepped out of the shadows to block her way. A slight figure, dressed in a black tracksuit, with a black baseball cap pulled down. The person from the telephone box – a woman. Donna Mason.

Nyx. She held up her hand and said, 'Stop!'

No longer in her frumpy corduroy dress, Donna Mason was ready for action, her long black hair pulled into a high ponytail, escaping from underneath the baseball cap at the back.

As Nyx, she'd enticed Olivia up to the top of the Westgate and then thrown her to her death. She'd helped Shan Liang tie his own noose to the beam under the Leas Cliff Hall – and then probably kicked away the bike. She'd met Neil McGowan at the ancient keep in the dead of night and only one of them had come away alive. And now she had Sam, and had put a rope around his pale, young throat, ready to throttle the life out of him.

Donna looked around as Lexi advanced towards them. She didn't look surprised.

'You made it,' she said. 'I was hoping you'd arrive just a fraction too late.'

'I'm sorry to have disappointed you. In fact, I should have realised earlier that it was you.'

Donna laughed. 'But you assumed Nyx was a man, didn't you? Don't you know who Nyx was?'

'Aunt Lexi?'

'I'm here, Sam.'

'Nyx was the Greek goddess of the night.'

His feet barely touching the chair he stood on, Sam wobbled. The chair creaked. Lexi lunged forward, ready to catch him.

But Donna Mason was in Lexi's path, arms outstretched to catch her. To stop her reaching her nephew. Lexi dodged to one side, but Donna was just as fast, and they smashed into each other, chest to chest, slamming breath out of lungs, their arms grappling. Donna caught hold of Lexi by the shoulders as Lexi tried to headbutt her away. She lost her footing and they both crashed to the floor. Lexi's phone was jerked out of her hand and skittered away across the stones, the torch going out as it hit the base of one of the pillars with a crack.

They wrestled, Lexi gasping for air as her muscles cried out for more oxygen. Donna, for all her slight frame, was stronger and heavier, and she had an iron grip on Lexi's upper arms. Lexi struggled. She raised her head, pushing up against the weight of Donna's body, until finally she was within reach – close enough to sink her teeth into her earlobe.

Donna let out a howl of pain, and Lexi sensed her rage switching up a gear. But Lexi's determination to save her nephew was just as fearsome, and she bit down harder. Donna wrenched her head to one side, tearing her ear from the grasp of Lexi's teeth. Lexi tasted blood in her mouth for the second time in a matter of minutes. She spat in disgust as she managed to wriggle out of Donna's grasp, kicking the other woman as hard as she could to push herself away.

It was pitch black. Lexi caught her breath and clambered to her feet quietly. She moved silently in the direction in which her phone had skidded away, sliding her feet along the floor to feel for it, her arms outstretched in front of her so she didn't walk into a pillar. She knew that Donna would be able to hear her. She could hear Donna's rasping breath a few feet away, and she seemed to be moving too.

'Aunt Lexi?' It was a dry croak of a word. 'Are you there?'

She reckoned Sam was approximately fifteen feet to the left of where she was now. She changed her course of action and started to move towards him and, as she did, she heard Donna moving quickly in the same direction.

Damn!

She had to get to him first, but she still had to be careful not to smash into one of the pillars.

A light went on in front of her. Donna had a torch of her own. She was holding it at waist height, directing the beam upwards and, in its yellow light, her features took on the ghoulish appearance of something from a horror movie. Blood was streaming down one side of her neck from where Lexi had ripped her earlobe, and her face was twisted into a demonic smile. But far more horrifying than that, she was standing directly next to the chair on which Sam was precariously balanced. And she had one foot up on the edge of the seat. It meant she would be able to kick the chair out from under him, and if she did that, he would be dead in an instant.

'Sam asked for my help. Now I'll give it to him.'

'No,' yelled Lexi, rushing forward.

'Yes,' Donna said, just as forcefully. 'Stop where you are, or Sam dies.'

Sam whimpered and one of his feet lost purchase. He wobbled and gasped as the noose took his weight until he was able to steady his feet again.

Lexi stood stock-still.

If she lunged forward, Donna would kick the chair away. If she stayed where she was, how could she save Sam? It was stalemate.

'He wants to die.' Donna's voice was barely a whisper. 'You know that, don't you, Lexi?'

'You've got that wrong.' Lexi spoke loudly and firmly. '*You* want him to die, but I'm not going to let that happen.'

'You're not?' Her tone was arch now, though still softly spoken. 'How do you think you can prevent it?'

Lexi took a small step forward, hoping that she was deep enough in the shadows for Donna not to notice.

'Get back.' The snarl told her she wasn't, and Donna rattled the chair with her foot, causing Sam to gasp. 'It's a long enough drop, you know. If I kick this chair away, Sam's body weight will snap his neck.' She said snap with such relish that Lexi wanted to be sick.

'You don't want to do this, Nyx.'

'Oh, but I do.'

'If you do it, I'm here as a witness and it will clearly be murder.'

'Once Sam is dead, I'll deal with you, DI Bennett. It'll look like a tragic double suicide.'

'You won't get away with it. The precinct outside is swarming with police.'

'Liar.'

'Go and take a look.'

'And leave you here to cut Sam down? I don't think so.'

'Please, Aunt Lexi...' Sam's distress was acute.

She had to do something to bring this to the right conclusion – and fast.

'You'll be better off dead, Sam.' Donna was whispering up at Sam but the words were for Lexi's benefit. 'You won't be a burden to everybody once you're dead.'

'Don't listen to her, Sam. Just hold on.'

The torch went out.

There was a crack of wood against stone. A strangled cough. The sound of feet walking away.

And in the pitch black, running to where she thought Sam was hanging, his life draining away, Lexi smashed right into one of the stone pillars.

SIXTY-THREE

Her head seemed split in two by a shaft of pain. She felt dizzy and stumbled, grabbing the slender pillar to stop herself falling forward headlong.

'Sam?'

A little way to her left, she heard a gurgling rasp.

In the opposite direction she heard footsteps running up the stone steps out of the crypt.

It didn't matter that Nyx was getting away. She had to get to Sam.

But she couldn't walk straight. Her head was spinning and her balance was off. She careened across the floor in the direction of his gasp.

Silence.

'Sam?'

Get a grip.

She kept moving, a warm trickle of blood tickling her eyebrow, then flooding into her eye.

She stretched out her arms, moving them from side to side, feeling for Sam's body.

'Where are you?'

Her left hand felt fabric, a firm kneecap underneath it. She had him. She stood directly beneath where he hung and clasped her arms around his legs, lifting him up to take the weight of his body so the pressure on his neck would be relieved.

The sound of a welcome gasp, then a cough, reassured her that she wasn't too late.

'I'm okay.' His voice was a dry rasp.

'Sam, thank God.'

Her skull was still gripped in a vice of pain. One eye was sticky with blood – there must have been a substantial gash on her forehead. But she couldn't wipe it away. She needed all her strength to hold Sam steady, to stop him from hanging. Donna must have been wrong about the length of the drop breaking his neck. She felt dizzy. She felt herself sway. If she fainted, Sam would die.

She bit hard on the inside of her cheek to keep herself alert.

Donna's footsteps had long since disappeared.

It was just the two of them, alone in the crypt, in the pitch black, both breathing heavily, Lexi clinging onto Sam as if his life were more precious than her own. And it was. An image of her sister, Rose, popped unbidden into her mind. The sister she'd left behind. The sister she'd let down. The sister she'd never seen again. She wasn't going to let that happen with Sam. She'd make sure he came out of this alive.

She was swaying. She felt lightheaded.

Her grasp on Sam's legs was loosening, her arms sapped of strength. Her legs felt weak.

Don't let go. Don't let him go.

'Help! Can anyone hear me?' She hollered as loud as she could, but she knew there was no one there. Just the two of them alone in the vast cathedral. Why hadn't she thought to order the uniforms to search here as well? Why hadn't they thought to do it themselves? She knew they would be radiating outwards from the cathedral, searching the nearby streets and parks, while she and Sam were in desperate need of help, deep within the heart of the precinct, so deep that no one would hear her shout.

How long had they been standing like this?

Lexi had lost all sense of time and space. It could have been hours. It could have been minutes. She struggled to resurface through a grey veil of pain. Deep breaths. She shifted from foot to foot and her mind kicked into gear.

'Sam? Can you hear me?' His head was drooped forward, but she could see there was slack in the rope above, so he wasn't taking the pressure of the noose across his windpipe or the arteries on either side of his neck. 'Talk to me, Sam.'

There was a slight movement in his body, then he emitted a low moan.

Good. He was definitely still alive.

Lexi considered her options.

She could stay standing like this until help came, but when would that be? It appeared no one had thought to search the cathedral, so maybe morning, whenever the earliest service was. She wondered if there were early morning cleaners. If she heard someone above or saw sign of a light, she could shout for help until they came. But could she stand here, holding Sam's weight, until the morning? And would he be okay?

It was barely midnight, she guessed. It was too long for them just to wait. She needed to get him down now, and she would have to do it on her own. But how? She glanced around. Even though her eyes were now accustomed to the lack of light, it was still too dark to see where the chair had landed when Nyx kicked it away, let alone the location of her phone, if it was still working after smashing into the pillar.

Taking her own and Sam's weight on one leg, she tentatively stuck out the other foot, moving it in a semi-circle to her side, hoping to hit the chair. Nothing. She tried it with the other leg. Same result. So it wasn't immediately within reach.

'Sam, can you put your hands up to the rope?' If he wasn't strong enough to loosen the knot at the back of his neck, perhaps he could put his fingers under the rope to relieve the pressure a bit.

With another groan, Sam moved his arms. He slowly raised one hand and feebly tugged at the rope.

'Are you okay?'

He grunted. 'Yes, think so.' His voice sounded strangled.

'This next bit's going to be hard. I've got to get the chair. It's the only way we can get you supported, and then I'll be able to climb up on it and undo the rope.'

Another grunt. He understood.

'But to get the chair, I'm going to have to let go of you for a few seconds.'

Sam's head moved. 'No, no, you can't.' There was raw fear in his voice.

Fear is contagious and the thought of letting Sam hang for even a few seconds terrified her. She gripped his legs tighter and tried to speak calmly.

'I promise, it'll only be a couple of seconds at most.'

She looked up at him, though all she could make out was the black silhouette of his head. Something warm and wet dropped onto her cheek. A tear. Sam was crying.

'Hold on to the noose with both your hands, so that your neck won't be supporting all your weight.' The boy sniffed. 'Do you understand?'

'Yes.'

'Can you be brave for me?'

'Yes.'

She felt his body move slightly in her arms as he readjusted his hands.

'We can do this, Sam. Are you ready?'

'Do it.'

She tried to remember the sound the chair made as it fell

away, which direction the noise had come from. She felt sure it was somewhere behind and beyond Sam.

'Okay. I'm going now.'

She let go of Sam's legs and ducked to the side of him, crouching low so that her outstretched arms would find the chair. Sam's body jerked as he took the strain and Lexi knew he would only manage a few seconds before he would need her support again. She swung round madly, but all she could feel in front of her was cold, empty air.

She lunged back and grabbed Sam's legs, from behind this time.

'Breathe, Sam, breathe.'

His body relaxed in her arms as she took his weight and lifted him enough for the rope to go slack.

'We'll try again.'

She knew he wouldn't want to, but she had to keep up the initiative. She was tiring fast, and Sam would only be able to give this a couple of attempts. It was imperative that she found the chair.

He didn't respond.

'Come on, Sam. You can do it. You've just got to hold it together for a few more seconds.'

His hands went back to his neck. 'Okay,' he croaked.

'Three, two, one.'

She let go of him gently so his body wouldn't jerk so hard. Then she crouched down again and systematically moved across the floor in a large semi-circle, covering the area behind where Sam was hanging.

Her hand found something hard. Wood. She grabbed at it – a chair leg.

'I've got it!'

She pulled the chair upright and ran with it back to Sam's inert form. As soon as it was in position underneath him, she guided his feet onto the seat of it. He would still be standing on tiptoes, but it meant his weight was supported. She steadied him with her arms around his legs until she felt certain he was secure.

'Okay, Sam?'

'Yup.'

'I'm going to climb up next to you and then I can undo the rope.'

Her heart was pounding with relief as she squeezed onto the seat of the chair beside him, gripping its back to steady herself as she got her balance.

'Sam, put your arms round me so you hold steady while I deal with the noose.'

He complied, but his grip was as weak as a child's half his age. The ordeal was taking its toll on him. Lexi had to work fast – it would be twice as hard to get him down if he passed out.

She put her hands up to the knot at the back of his neck and felt it. The noose had been created using a classic hangman's knot, with the rope coiled round itself several times before the end was pulled through a loop at the top of the coil. Even when she'd briefly had the torch on, the light had been too dim to see the colour of the rope. But she knew it was red – the same thick rope around the necks of both Shan Liang and Neil McGowan. And she also knew that hangman's knots were incredibly difficult to untie.

Gritting her teeth, she tried to work the end of the rope back through the loop at the top. But with Sam's weight intermittently pulling on it, the loop had been pulled in tight and Lexi's fingers couldn't gain purchase with enough strength to pull it loose.

Damn!

She couldn't see what sort of knot had been used to secure the rope to the beam above, but it was too high for her to reach anyway. She needed a blade to cut through the rope. It was going to be the only way to get him down.

'Sam, we need help. I can't loosen the knot.'

He answered with a small sigh.

'That means I've got to find my phone or run outside for help.'

However long it took her, Sam would be having to support his own weight on tiptoes. He was exhausted, but if he slipped or lost his balance, he would pull the noose yet tighter with disastrous results.

Don't think about Rose.

She couldn't think about the sister she'd left alone and injured in the forest. She'd run for help and by the time help came, her sister was gone. Forever.

That wouldn't happen this time, would it?

'Ready, Sam?'

A grunt.

'Okay, let's do this.'

Intuition told her where to search for the phone. She crawled across the floor in the dark, feeling with her hands.

'Hold steady, Sam.'

The flagstones were old and worn smooth, but there was dust and grit under her touch. She came to a pillar and felt around the base. There was nothing there.

No, wait...

She felt something sharp under the fingers of her right hand. A tiny sliver of glass? Frantically, she ran both hands across the slab stones surrounding the base of the pillar.

'I've got it!'

She grabbed up the phone and ran blindly back towards Sam. She clambered back onto the chair next to him. His strength was flagging and, as he slumped against her, their combined weight almost toppled them over. She pushed back to straighten their joint centre of gravity. Then she put both arms round him, still holding the phone in one hand.

Please, God, let it work.

She pressed the button on the side of the phone to activate it, and a dull glow emanating from behind Sam's back told her it had switched on despite the broken screen. She drew one hand to the side, so she could see it.

The home screen was lit up, showing the picture of autumnal woods of Virginia which she had on her lock screen. She pulled her hand closer and squinted at the screen. It seemed so bright after all the time in the dark.

Please...

Yes, there was a signal. It was weak, just a couple of bars, but all she needed was to get through to someone, anyone, who could raise the alarm.

Instinctively, she tried Tom's number.

Straight to voicemail.

'Call help now – we're in the cathedral crypt.'

Amber.

Straight to voicemail.

'Get help. I've got Sam, he's okay. We're in the crypt.'

There was barely any power left in the phone.

Someone had to pick up.

'Ridhi? You there?'

'Yes, boss. I'm at Choir House.'

'We're in the crypt. Get help. Bring something that can cut rope.'

'Have you got him?'

'He's alive.'

He was alive. That was all that mattered. Help was coming and they could both hold on for a minute longer.

SIXTY-FOUR

It seemed like spending forever in suspended animation, but finally Lexi heard voices and footsteps, and saw light flickering from the entrance to the crypt. She almost sobbed with relief. Sam was leaning motionless in her arms and more than once she'd stopped breathing to see if she could still hear his shallow breaths.

He was alive, just.

And Lexi, too – every sinew in her body was burning with the effort of supporting Sam's weight and keeping balance for both of them.

'We're here,' she shouted.

'Lexi!'

Never had she been so relieved to hear Tom's voice.

There were other voices and pounding feet on the steps.

The lights in the crypt went on and seemed far too bright, as Tom, Amber, Ridhi, three uniforms, the Choir House house-master and matron, and a man in a dog collar holding a bunch of keys all burst into the crypt.

'Sam, Sam,' she whispered urgently, 'your mum's here.'

It worked like a tonic. Slowly Sam raised his head and blinked as he looked around.

'Mum,' he croaked.

In the light, close up, Lexi could see his lips were dry and cracked, his face ashen, and around his neck, blossoming out from the pressure points caused by the noose, were dark purple bruises and red welts from the rope.

A uniformed PC helped her down, another immediately taking her place on the chair, supporting Sam. The third one held up a hefty rope cutter with black blades and red rubber handles. Between the three of them, they supported Sam as the one on the chair with him reached up above his head and cut through the rope.

Amber hovered close by, tears streaming down her cheeks. Lexi supposed they were tears of relief, but also at the shock of seeing her son with a noose around his neck.

Tom had found another chair and made Lexi sit down. He squatted in front of her.

'What happened? Did you find him here like this?'

'Nyx was here.'

Her attention was distracted as Sam was lifted down from the chair and laid gently on the hard floor. Amber knelt beside him, drawing him up into a tight embrace, saying his name over and over again.

One of the uniforms bent down and with the help of the other one, they very carefully cut the rope at the back of his neck so he was finally released.

'Treat that as evidence in a crime,' Lexi called out. 'This whole area is a crime scene.'

'Ridhi, take control of the area,' said Tom. 'Preserve as much as you can.'

She nodded her head and turned back to the PCs, starting to instruct them.

Tom turned back to Lexi. 'Nyx was here? Where is he?'

'She. Nyx is Donna Mason. Nyx hadn't abducted Donna – Nyx actually is Donna.' She wasn't sure if what she'd just said made sense, but Tom seemed to get it. 'When Maddie referred to Nyx as 'he', she was wrong – but we took it at face value.' Lexi was kicking herself inside. It had been a rookie mistake, and had probably cost them precious time.

A couple of paramedics came clattering down the steps. They immediately went to where Sam was still lying on the floor. Lexi stood up to go and talk to them but Tom placed his hands on her shoulders.

'Sit. You need to have that cut on your forehead attended to.'

Forced back onto the chair, Lexi wiped her brow with her hand. It came away sticky with blood.

'I don't have time. We need to go after Donna Mason. Her car is still subject to the APB, isn't it?'

Tom nodded.

'She won't go back home.' Lexi was thinking aloud. 'Where would she go?' The commonly held belief might be that a criminal always returns to the scene of the crime, but in Lexi's experience, they more often returned to a scene from their childhood. 'Have we got people searching her house?'

'Yes, we sent in the CSIs when we believed she'd been abducted.'

'Right, give them a call and see if they can find anything about where she lived as a child, anything about her family background.'

One of the paramedics came over to her. 'Can I clean that up and take a look, ma'am?'

Lexi nodded, suddenly exhausted, but all too aware that there was still much to do.

While the paramedic wiped the blood away from her forehead and around her eye, Tom went outside to get a better phone signal. She sat patiently as the paramedic worked, even though it stung – but rather this than a trip to hospital.

'We can't really stitch cuts like this,' he said. 'The skin's pulled too tight over the skull. I'll put a couple of butterfly strips across it, but I'm afraid you're going to have a scar.'

'Oh, great.' Lexi frowned and the cut hurt. 'No worries – let's just get it done. I need to be out of here.'

Amber came across to her.

'Thank God you found him,' she said. Her cheeks were streaked with tears and her nose was red.

'Is he okay?' said Lexi.

Amber nodded. 'They think he's fine, but they're going to take him to the hospital to be more thoroughly checked over. I can't thank you enough – you saved his life.'

Lexi breathed a sigh of relief. 'He was so strong. Give him a hug for me, Amber, and tell him I'll see him tomorrow morning.'

'Won't you come to the hospital with us?'

'I can't. When I got here, there was a woman here – Donna Mason. She runs a suicide cult and we need to apprehend her.'

Amber gasped, a hand flying to her mouth. 'A woman? She tried to make Sam do it?'

'I'm afraid so. I'll need to talk to Sam about how he put himself forward for the club.' The paramedic had finished applying the butterfly strips to her wound and was packing up his stuff. Lexi stood up. 'Look, I've got to go.'

She gave Amber a brief hug, then took the stairs out of the crypt two at a time. The lights were on in the cathedral now, and she could see that the southwest door was open. Outside, she found Tom, busy on his phone.

'The CSIs are going to email us scans of some paperwork they've found in Donna Mason's house,' he said, as soon as he finished the call. 'Details of where they used to live, where she and her brother went to school. Apparently, they were both born in Chatham...' He paused. 'I don't really see how this stuff is going to help us.'

'It probably won't,' said Lexi. 'But we don't have much to go on. She's bolted somewhere – and we've got to work out where.'

'One other thing they mentioned...'

'What?'

'They found a cache of mobile phones in Donna's wardrobe. One of the lock screens showed a picture of Olivia James. They think they're the phones of all the victims.'

'Donna's trophies. And her way of hiding the WhatsApp group from us.' Lexi felt sickened. 'What about ANPR? Any sign of her car yet?'

'Not so far.'

'Okay, let's get back to the station and look at what the CSIs send us.'

The Crossfire was still parked where she'd left it in front of the main doors of the cathedral. Tom's jeep was around the other side by Choir House.

'See you there,' he said, as Lexi got into her car.

The streets were empty and the town was quiet as Lexi drove slowly back to the station, deep in thought. There was something there, something in what Tom had said, but she couldn't put a finger on it. Maybe nothing. The most useful thing to them would be information from ANPR – real time information about where Donna Mason's car was headed. But she couldn't help feeling she'd missed something...

Then, as she turned onto the ring road, the realisation hit.

Chatham.

Born in Chatham.

Chatham hemp – the red rope.

Without a second thought, she drove past the turning which would take her to the police station car park and kept going. She drove out past Wincheap industrial estate and turned onto the A2 in the direction of Rochester and Chatham.

Sure, she was following a hunch, but her hunches were something she'd learned to trust over the years.

She pressed the accelerator to the floor and the Crossfire roared to life.

'Nyx, I'm coming for you.'

SIXTY-FIVE

She dialled Tom to let him know what was happening.

'Where are you? Are you all right?' Tom sounded perplexed as he answered the call.

'Fine. Following a hunch as to where Nyx is going.'

'We just got a hit on the ANPR – seems like she's heading up—'

'—the A2, right?'

'How the heck?'

Lexi laughed. 'Brain connections. When you said she and her brother came from Chatham it clicked with the fact that Emily Jordan thinks the rope came from the rope walk at Chatham Dockyard.'

Tom let out a low whistle.

'Can you look into whatever the CSIs sent over and see if there's any connection between her family and the dockyard?'

'Can I hell? I'll give it to Colin or Ridhi. I'm coming after you. There's no way you should be tackling Donna Mason on your own.'

'I was about to ask for backup, don't worry.'

'Yeah, right.'

'Just make sure we get any ANPR updates – if my hunch is right she'll come off at junction four for Rochester.'

'I'll be right behind you.'

By the time he'd given out the instructions, Lexi reckoned he'd be at least fifteen or twenty minutes behind her. But that was good enough.

Her dashboard clock told her it was close to two a.m. as she came into Chatham, an old seafaring town on the meandering estuary of the Medway. She drove slowly, checking parked cars and side roads for the white Volkswagen. She dialled Ridhi.

'Ridhi, have you managed to find a home address for the Masons when Donna and Edward were kids?'

'Nothing. They went to the New Road primary school, if that helps narrow the area down.'

She looked it up on her phone. 'Not by very much.'

'Just one interesting thing I found – I've got an image of Edward's birth certificate here. He was born in Medway Maritime Hospital – that's in the middle of Chatham – but the certificate gives father's occupation.'

'And?'

There was a note of triumph in her voice. 'You're not going to believe it but your hunch was spot on – he was a master ropemaker.'

'So he worked at the rope walk here in the dockyard?' She slammed the heel of her hand against the steering wheel. 'Of course! That's brilliant, Ridhi. Ten to one, that's where she's headed.'

'You nearly there?'

'Just approaching.'

'Wait for the sergeant, boss. Don't go in on your own.'

She hung up without promising anything. She didn't have time.

Chatham's historic naval dockyard sprawled for more than a mile along the eastern shore of the Medway. Once one of the country's most important dockyards, it had been decommissioned in 2011, and turned into a tourist attraction. The rope walk was a brick building, more than a quarter-mile long, where rope was still made using the original Victorian machinery. Donna's father had worked there, and Donna had provided rope from there for the suicides. It seemed clear that this was a place that meant something to her, somewhere that she might return to at a time of high stress.

Lexi drew up in front of the main gate. During the day it had a simple red-and-white striped barrier that was raised to let cars in and out through the red brick gatehouse, but now the solid wooden gates were closed across the road preventing access. There was, however, an open doorway in the gate for pedestrians to pass through. Fine – going in on foot would give her the element of surprise. She pulled her car over to one side outside the dockyard entrance, got out and went through the gate.

The sky was clear, and a half moon bathed the dockyard in weak light. The road descended from the gatehouse to become the main thoroughfare through a site that was almost a small town in its own right. Shipbuilding and submarine building pens, dry docks, vast hangers, a parade ground, the Commissioner's House with its walled garden, naval barracks, a modern visitors' centre – it all stretched out in front of her on the edge of the water. But she had only one destination in mind. The ropery was at the bottom of the slope, immediately to the left, a red brick, two-storey building reputed to be the longest built structure in Europe.

She walked down the slope, eyes peeled for any movement.
A dark figure loomed before her, standing stock-still in front of
the dockyard church. She blinked and then realised it was just a
carved figurehead from a sailing ship. The adrenalin had kicked
in and now her heart was racing, but that was good. She might
need to be ready to run at any moment, and if Donna Mason
was here, she'd need her wits about her.

At the bottom of the slope, she came round the corner of the
tall warehouse and got her first proper look at the rope walk
building next to it. She'd visited as a child, but she'd forgotten
just how jaw-dropping it was to see the squat brick building
stretching out in front of her for more than a quarter of a mile.
She let her eyes run along the endless wall, looking for signs of
light in any of the multitude of windows. She saw a faint glimmer, away at the far end – just a dull orange glow in one corner
of the huge gallery inside that ran the whole length of the
building.

Someone was here. Was it Donna? Of course, now she
should wait and watch until Tom arrived with backup, at which
point they could surround the building and make an arrest. But
how long would that take?

Something told her not to wait.

There were several doors along the length of the building. If
someone was inside, one of them must be open. The visitors'
entrance was closest to her – it led into a ground-floor exhibition
area, with one end of the rope walk above it, on the first floor. By
the time one had reached the other end of the long building, the
gentle upward slope of the ground meant that the rope walk
was now at ground level, and the doors at that end opened
directly into the long, narrow manufacturing space.

Lexi tried the visitors' entrance first. But the heavy glass
doors were closed and locked. She'd pretty much expected this
– along with the exhibition space, there was a small gift shop,
and that would mean a till and money. Of course it would be

properly locked up at night. She walked around the side of the building. Further along, a steel fire escape on the outside of the building led up to a double door on the first floor, a direct entrance into the rope walk.

She climbed the metal stairs with caution, placing her feet carefully to avoid any clanging noises. At the top, she could see that one of the two doors was a couple of inches ajar. She turned on her phone torch and, using her body to shield its light, examined the lock. It had been jimmied. Someone had broken into the building – presumably the same someone who had a light on at the far end of the long rope gallery.

She switched off the torch and slipped inside, standing still for a few moments in the shadow of the door to let her eyes become accustomed to the dark. The dusty air smelled of jute, almost like being in a barn full of hay, with a low note of machine oil underneath. Shafts of moonlight coming through the long row of windows on the building's west wall created pale rectangles on the wooden floor, but the rest of the rope walk blurred into shades of grey and black. A quarter of a mile away at the other end of the building, she could see the dull amber glow of the light, but it was too far off for her to be able to see anything.

Where she stood at the head of the rope walk, the silhouettes of machines loomed out of the shadows – huge engines that ran on metal tracks on the wooden floor, twisting lengths of jute and hemp into thicker and thicker ropes, strong enough for the rigging and mooring lines of the Navy's fleet of sailing ships. The Empire's industrial heritage, as if preserved in aspic, though still producing serviceable rope for yachts and boats, and a hundred other uses – including for the necks of Nyx's chosen victims.

But it was the middle of the night, and the machines stood silent.

Lexi unzipped her ankle boots and slipped them off.

Keeping close to the opposite wall where the shadows were deepest, she crept quietly on stocking feet towards the light at the far end of the gallery. She didn't know what Donna was planning to do, but she wanted to keep the element of surprise for as long as she could.

As she got closer, she could see more. A bare bulb hanging from the ceiling cast a pool of amber light at the very far end of the ropery, an area where the newly spun ropes were cut to the required lengths and wound into coils. Mounds of these coils lined the wall, and there was an old-fashioned bicycle resting up against them – the building was so long the ropemasters would cycle from one end to the other.

A dark silhouette was moving in and out of the light, a slight figure which looked like Donna Mason. Lexi couldn't make out what she was doing, but then she saw a flash of red.

Donna Mason was doing something with a length of red rope.

Lexi kept creeping closer, bending low to remain in the shadows.

Donna finished knotting a noose and tested it, holding the loop in one hand and yanking the rope at the top of the knot with the other. Satisfied, she took the long end of the rope and, as Lexi watched in horror, she slung it over a low wooden beam that supported the ceiling of the ropery. She knotted it quickly and skilfully to another length of rope which trailed into the shadows towards another beam. Then she climbed up onto a small wooden crate and slipped the noose over her head.

She was going to kill herself.

No!

There was no way Lexi was going to let that happen. Never. Donna Mason, Nyx, whatever she liked to call herself, was going to answer for her crimes. She'd murdered at least three teenagers, and had attempted to murder a fourth, and Lexi was determined to bring her to trial.

'Stop!' She emerged from the shadows and ran towards the light. 'Donna Mason, I'm placing you under arrest for the murders of Shan Liang, Olivia James and Neil McGowan, and for the attempted murder of Sam Riley.'

Donna Mason raised her head, and the echo of her laughter bounced all the way to the other end of the ropery.

SIXTY-SIX

Lexi sprinted the last few metres towards her.

'Stop,' said Donna, 'or I'll jump.'

Lexi pulled herself up short. If Donna kicked the crate away from under herself, the noose would tighten and she'd be dead. Lexi couldn't let that happen. She had to stall for time until Tom and the backup arrived.

'Why here, Donna? This is a special place for you, isn't it?'

'This is a special place for you?' Donna mimicked her in a childish, sing-song voice. Then she reverted to speaking normally. 'You're right. This beam... this is where Edward hanged himself.' There was a catch in her voice as she said her brother's name, revealing volumes about her emotional state.

'You said before that he'd taken pills.'

'Because it was none of your business.' Anger... to hide vulnerability. To hide the pain.

'It is now.' Lexi took a small step closer. In the weak light from the bare bulb, she could see the scowl on Donna's face.

'Tell me why you did it. Why you murdered those children.'

'They asked for my help. I helped bring an end to their suffering. I saw the pain that Ed went through and these kids are suffering in the same way. I'm their guardian angel. I take away the pain.'

'But you're the cause of their suffering. You undermine their confidence. Then you kill them. Was it that way with Edward? I think you pushed him to the brink, and found that you liked it too much.'

'Believe what you want.'

Donna raised a hand to tug on the noose around her neck and, as she did, her sleeve slipped up her arm to reveal a scabbed-over graze.

Lexi pointed at it. 'You did that at the Westgate, didn't you? When Olivia changed her mind and tried to get away.'

'What of it?'

'We've got skin traces from the wall. It'll match your DNA. A tidy piece of evidence for your murder trial.'

Donna Mason let out a short bark of laughter. 'Trial? It won't come to that, DI Bennett. Because tonight, one of us is going to die. Will it be you or will it be me? Or maybe even both of us?'

That couldn't happen.

'You failed to kill my nephew, and you won't kill me.'

'Then it'll be me that swings.' She wobbled on the wooden crate.

Lexi had to keep her talking.

'I think Edward was your first victim. Did you push him into it, just like you pushed Olivia and Shan and Neil? Just like you tried with Sam?'

'I assume you managed to get him down safely? And now you're basking in the warm glow of saving a life. Is that why you do it?'

'Do what?'

'Your job. Your godawful job, chasing after the worst humanity has to offer.'

'People like you?'

'I had nothing to do with Edward's death. My parents, my father in particular, put him under intense pressure. He hated Edward's aspirations to be a musician and punished him for them.'

'Why?'

Donna shook her head, then coughed as the movement made the noose tighten around her neck. She put her hands up to the back of her head, loosened the knot and tugged it off – she obviously wasn't ready to die quite yet.

Clambering down from the crate, she said, 'Music was my mother's thing. My father saw it as girlish, weak. He believed Edward should follow in his footsteps, become a master rope-maker. A man's job. He undermined and humiliated Ed at every opportunity.'

'And you weren't involved at all? Bullshit.'

Donna looked round until her eyes lit on a coil of red rope lying on top of a large pile of natural rope coils. She took a couple of strides across to the pile and picked it up.

Lexi was beginning to discern a pattern here. Donna wouldn't answer questions if the answer would show her in a poor light. Last time she'd come back with a counter question. But Lexi needed to control the conversation, so she wasn't going to wait to find out what she said next.

'I can't quite see the connection here, Donna. If, as you claim, you had nothing to do with your brother dying, why all the other deaths?'

She didn't answer. Instead, she returned to sit down on the crate and dropped the coil of rope onto the floor in front of her, holding one end of it.

'You helped Edward to die, didn't you? Or how else would you know exactly which beam he hanged himself from?'

'Sure – I was here. I helped him find the peace he craved.' Her hands were busy with the rope. She laid out two loops, side by side but facing in opposite directions, across her thighs. 'It was what he wanted.'

'Did your parents know you were here when he died?' Lexi was fed up with the lies and contradictions, but she had to spin things out until Tom arrived.

'Of course not.' The wooden crate creaked as Donna shifted her weight, winding a series of coils around the two original loops – a hangman's knot was taking form. She was making another noose. 'But they still blamed me for it.'

'Why?'

'Because they could. My father would never accept responsibility for anything. He had the gall to suggest that I'd bullied Ed. My mother was plain stupid. She believed whatever he told her.' She paused, counting the coils of her knot. 'I'm glad they're dead.'

'How did they die?'

'Of natural causes.' She glanced up, making eye contact. 'You won't be able to pin their deaths on me.' Then she fed the short end of the rope through the small loop that emerged from the coils, tugging the noose tight.

'And Club Edicius?'

'I help teenagers who're going through what my brother went through. They know what they want and I help them with it.'

'A public service? Heart-warming.'

'You wouldn't understand.'

'Try me.'

Silence.

Lexi glanced down to Donna's lap. The hangman's knot was finished.

'Tell me about Shan. You helped him at Leas Cliff, didn't you?'

'I help all of them.' There – that was the confession. Donna Mason had helped all of them to die. She was responsible.

'But you helped him physically, to put up the noose. I think you used the bicycle for him to climb up there. Then you took it away and he hanged. Did he really want to die?'

'I don't know what you're talking about. I wasn't actually there.' She was knotting the tail end of the noose to another length of rope that was hanging down from one of the cross-beams. 'I helped him through the chatroom. Made him feel better. Gave him the confidence to go ahead.'

'We've got the bike, and I think we'll find your prints on it.'

Silence.

'You killed him, didn't you? He didn't want to do it, so you intervened.'

'You can't prove a thing.'

'Believe me, I will. Tell me about Neil.'

'No.' Donna held out the new noose. 'Not unless... If you put this around your neck, I'll answer all your questions.'

Does she think I'm mad?

'You'll be quite safe,' she said. 'I just need you to feel the rope across your throat to understand.'

'To understand what?'

'The seductive power of choice.'

'I would never choose death.'

'Then you have nothing to fear.'

'Only you.'

Nyx smiled – for Donna seemed to have transformed herself into her alter ego. There was a change to the tone of her voice, and her body language suddenly radiated a sly confidence.

'This is how it works. I'll only tell you what you want to know – everything you want to know – if you play my game.' She pointed to the ceiling above them and Lexi looked up. There was a complex web of red ropes she hadn't noticed before, slung between two beams, running through loops and joined with elaborate knots. In some places, there were iron cogs attached to act as weights. She tried to trace the network with her eyes, but it didn't make sense to her.

A noise brought her gaze down. Nyx had climbed back onto the crate and was slipping the original noose back over head. She tightened the knot at the back of her neck. The rope from the noose led up to the network between the beams.

'Now you.'

The new noose she'd just made was hanging down from the same web of ropes, and there was a similar crate just nearby.

Lexi was beginning to understand.

'That's right,' said Nyx, as if she could read Lexi's mind. 'As long as we both keep our heads in the loops, we're both safe. But if one of us removes the rope...' She ran her index finger across the base of her throat.

'How does it work?' said Lexi. She was playing for time.

Donna pointed a finger up to the ceiling. 'You can see – the ropes run through a series of pulleys and counterbalances. Once your weight is balanced against mine, you can stop me from hanging and I can stop you. Or not, depending which way you want to play it.' She paused. 'And if you don't play the game, I'll check out anyway.' There was no mistaking what she meant by that.

Lexi could see that she was straining as the noose around her neck seemed to be tugging upwards – presumably due to the weights hanging from the web of ropes. With a bad feeling in the pit of her stomach, she climbed reluctantly onto the other crate and put the noose around her neck.

'Tighten the knot,' said Nyx. Her voice was a dry rasp.

With shaking hands, Lexi pulled the noose a fraction tighter, just enough so that her weight would take some of the pressure off Nyx's neck. She must be crazy. She knew she'd walked into a trap, but it was a risk she'd have to take if she wanted to ensure that Nyx remained alive to stand trial. She owed that much to Olivia, Shan and Neil. And Sam.

'Good,' said Nyx. 'You understand where we are now. A contest between equals.'

'That's not how I'd describe us.' Lexi couldn't keep the rank anger out of her voice.

'No, you're right. I was just being polite.'

Don't rise to the bait.

'You said you'd answer my questions.'

Nyx closed her eyes and leaned back slightly, causing a tug on Lexi's rope that nearly overbalanced her. 'Fire away. But don't say anything that might tempt me...' She wobbled on her crate again. 'If I go, you'll go too. Imagine – what a terrible discovery in the morning – a double suicide, you and me, hanging side by side.'

'Murder-suicide, don't you mean?' said Lexi. 'I have no intention of dying.' She felt the tension increase in the rope between them and tightened her grip on the loop around her neck. She wasn't entirely sure what would happen if Nyx kicked the crate away and hanged herself. Would she have time to pull the noose off her neck before the rope yanked her upwards? She didn't want to find out.

'Of course, you'd rather see me in court. But I haven't committed a crime. They did it themselves. All of them.'

'Forget it. The case against you is undeniable. Remember, I saw you in action with Sam.'

'Your beautiful nephew. He was having second thoughts about going through with it, but I managed to convince him. He's a desperately unhappy boy, and I was there for him.'

Lexi couldn't bear to hear her telling lies like that about Sam. There was no way she could have persuaded him. Hadn't she realised Sam was playing his own dangerous game? 'Tell me what you did to Neil.'

'Neil wanted to die, but he was a coward. I simply helped him carry out his wishes.'

'That's not how a jury will view it.' Lexi felt furious. 'Did it give you some sort of sick pleasure pushing these innocent kids to their death? Don't you feel one iota of guilt or regret?'

'Guilt and regret? No – it's what they wanted. But you'd know all about guilt, wouldn't you, Lexi?'

'You know nothing about me.' But the comment cut deep.

'I do. Sam told me – who you are, and what happened to you and your sisters. You know, there are a lot of articles about the Triplet Killer online. Apparently, you let your sister die to save yourself. I asked Sam about that and he confirmed it. You put your life ahead of hers. That's the sort of person you are.'

Lexi's world spun on its axis. Is that what Sam thought? That she and Amber had left Rose to die to save themselves?

'Poor, poor Rose.'

'Don't say her name. You don't know what you're talking about.'

'Why don't you join her?'

Lexi was taken back to the time just after it happened. How desperately she'd longed for Rose's return. And how, after months and months, she'd begun to give up hope. She'd thought about suicide in those dark, dark weeks. Sure. She'd thought about how she'd do it, and where, and who might find her. It was her fault that Rose was gone and she'd felt her parents' sorrow so acutely. She'd stopped talking to Amber and started drinking in secret. She'd longed for the oblivion death would bring...

Nyx jerked her head sideways, yanking on Lexi's rope. There was a triumphant smile on her face. 'Let me help you.'

Lexi started to cough. She felt starved of oxygen. Nyx was pulling the noose ever tighter. With legs like jelly, Lexi raised her hands to try to take the pressure off her throat, but it didn't help. Her head was starting to swim.

'Nyx?' She wasn't even sure that the word had formed in her mouth. 'Nyx...'

Nyx looked at her with an expression of satisfaction. 'You're doing the right thing. Do you think anyone will miss you when you're gone?'

SIXTY-SEVEN

Lexi kept coughing. She could feel pressure building behind her eyes, and she was becoming confused. Through the haze, she heard her phone ringing in her jacket pocket. She instinctively made a move to retrieve it, which was followed instantly by a sharp jerk on the rope.

'Don't answer it.'

She knew from the ringtone that it was Tom. He must be nearby. But could she hold on for long enough? She was starting to choke. Her feet wobbled on the wooden crate, which creaked under her weight. As she moved, the noose around Nyx's neck was pulled tighter. Nyx steadied herself. The base of the knot had been digging into the back of Lexi's neck, but now it relaxed a fraction as Nyx was no longer pulling on it so hard. Lexi was able to suck in a deep breath, her body grabbing at the oxygen.

She pulled herself together. She wasn't going to give up now.

'Why?' Her voice was a strangled rasp. 'Why do you do it? You... promised answers.'

'Like I said, I'm just helping them on their way. It's their choice, what they want.'

Lexi didn't believe her. 'You watched Edward die, didn't you? And if you hadn't done that, all the others would still be alive too.' She had to keep Nyx talking. If Nyx thought hanging herself was a better option than a life sentence, she'd do it. Soon probably. Tom's timely arrival would literally be a matter of life and death to Nyx. And, as a consequence, to Lexi.

'He wanted to die. He asked me not to stop him, so I didn't. And I don't stop the poor souls that find their way to me now.'

A plan was slowly unfurling in a corner of Lexi's mind, but could it work?

'Why didn't he want to be saved? I have to understand. Explain the whole business to me.'

'This world can be too much for some people. It was too much for my brother. And for Shan and Neil. And for Olivia – even though she got scared at the last minute.'

'That's not true. None of them wanted to die.'

But this line of argument was getting her nowhere. She needed to change course. Let Nyx think she was close to winning. If she made Nyx think that her manipulations had a chance of success, she'd keep going, keep pushing. Could it work? It would appeal to Nyx's vanity if she thought she might be able to persuade Lexi to jump off the crate.

'They thought death was the answer?'

'It can be... for some people. When you die, you can't suffer anymore.'

'Could it be the answer for me?'

Lexi could see the glint of Nyx's eyes in the dim light.

'Of course it could.' Her tone had changed from right-eousness to something more seductive.

'So why would I be better off dead?'

'You could let go of the guilt. You wouldn't be haunted by your dead sister any longer. You would be at one with her.

Wouldn't that feel better?' Nyx's expression softened. 'I know how you feel. We've both lost a sibling. We each shoulder some of the blame for it. It would feel right if we both went together, don't you think?'

Of course it wouldn't, but if Lexi could just convince her that she was winning the battle of their minds, Nyx might hold off from hanging herself for the next few minutes. She would relish the prospect of seeing someone else on the verge of taking their own life. She was addicted to the feeling of power it gave her. Leading someone vulnerable towards the end. Helping them on their way. Of course, she would want to help Lexi die. Her ultimate act of kindness.

But Lexi wasn't vulnerable. She was strong. Stronger than Nyx realised, and she could be just as manipulative.

She paused, as if considering Nyx's words. Then she gave a small nod, feeling the rough bite of the rope across her windpipe.

'How often do you dream about what might have happened to Rose after you left her alone in the forest?'

'Every night.'

'What would you give to be able to turn back the clock?'

'Everything. I'd give my life to save her.'

Come on, Tom.

'How much would it mean to you to have her forgiveness?'

The images Nyx was conjuring in her mind were hateful. Rose was gone, and there was nothing she could do to secure her sister's forgiveness.

'You think about suicide, don't you?'

'Often.'

'But you're a coward, aren't you? You can't go through with it.'

'It's not the right answer for me.'

'I could help you.'

Another tug on the rope. Lexi needed to stay in control of

the situation. She needed to steer the conversation back to Nyx's own vulnerabilities.

'Do you think your brother would forgive you for not saving him?'

Nyx's eyes widened. 'There's nothing to forgive. I wasn't the one who hurt him.'

'He might still be alive, but for you. Isn't that true?'

Nyx shook her head and the rope bit.

Lexi tensed her arms as her adrenalin surged. She would have split seconds to act.

'You're to blame for his death, aren't you?'

Nyx's anger was like a palpable wave crossing the space between them. Lexi braced her legs.

'No. My parents blamed me. But they were wrong.'

'You're lying.'

Nyx's jaw worked as if she was grinding her teeth. 'I'm not.'

'Why did he do it? And why here?'

'My father worked here for thirty years – he was a master ropemaker, and we lived just a few streets away. He was a harsh man and he had ideas about how he thought my brother should be. Not a musician. I told you, the musical talent came from my mother's side of the family, and my father had no time for it.'

Suddenly, it seemed as if Donna was back, with a need to unburden herself. Lexi remained silent, willing her to carry on.

'The rope was everything to my father. He assumed that at sixteen, Edward would leave school and take up an apprenticeship here. It wasn't what he wanted. He dreamed of playing in an orchestra. My father would beat him with a knotted rope and berate him whenever he heard him playing. In the end, he broke one of Edward's fingers. My brother killed himself here to make a point. Dad was a bully – it was his fault my brother killed himself, not mine. But still he blamed me.'

'You mentioned Barry Gray before.'

Nyx tilted her head to one side, which Lexi felt by a change in the tension of the rope. 'He was part of it, a minor factor. But it was my brother's relationship with my father that finally broke him.'

'And your mother? What part did she play in all this family strife?'

'She was weak. My father had worn her down over the years. Her health was poor by the time Edward died, and she never got over his death.'

'Did she blame you, too?' Lexi was starting to feel sorry for the young girl that Donna had been. But not for who she'd become. 'Help me understand you, Donna. Your brother's death must have been devastating. But now you watch other kids do the same.'

'I wouldn't expect someone like you to understand.'

'You're putting their families through what your family went through. That's not helping anyone.'

Donna screwed her eyes shut and clamped her lips tight. Was she confronting the paradox of her actions? Her fists were clenched by her side. The moment allowed Lexi to raise her arms unseen. She clasped the hangman's knot at the back of her neck and tried to loosen it.

'Your little online club has nothing to do with your brother's sad story or your pretend desire to help others like him. It's about your need for agency. Donna is weak, but by assuming the identity of Nyx, you become strong. Donna was bullied by her father and let down by her mother. No one bullies Nyx. Donna was abandoned by her brother. No one abandons Nyx, because she pushes them over the edge before they get the chance to.' She spoke slowly. She was regulating her breathing to stop her heart from racing.

Donna opened her eyes with a roar of anger, and saw Lexi's hands on the knot at the back of her head.

There was a flash of blue light at the windows at the far end of the rope walk. The backup had finally arrived.

Donna saw it too. And in a split second Lexi realised what was about to happen.

As Donna kicked the crate out from under her feet, Lexi's world went into slow motion. The rope at the back of her neck jerked sharply, instantly tightening the hangman's knot. She felt the rope constricting around her throat, crushing her windpipe. She couldn't draw breath. But in the same instance, she tugged the knot in the opposite direction. It wouldn't budge. It was too tight. Spots floated in front of her eyes and her lungs screamed for air. Her fingers were too slow, too clumsy, and she kept losing her grip.

I'm going to die.

No, she wasn't. She wouldn't let that happen. She thought of Sam and Tasha. She thought of Amber, from whom she'd been estranged for so long. Now they were a family again. She had so much to live for.

Her fingers grappled the rope for what seemed like forever, but finally she gained purchase on the knot and was able to loosen it just enough to be able to take a shallow breath. Never had the simple act of breathing seemed so precious. As the oxygen entered her blood, she fought for her life. Nails breaking, fingers feeling as if they might snap, she managed to slip the knot up the rope enough to be able to pull the loop up and over the back of her head. The rough fibres of the rope scratched against her jaw and cheeks as she dragged it forward and away from under her chin. The crate she was standing on creaked and rocked, then splintered with a loud crack. She let go of the noose and it whipped upwards. Donna's hanging body slammed to the ground, as Lexi landed hard on the wooden floor.

She coughed as the breath was knocked out of her, and her chest burned as she gasped to replenish the oxygen. She didn't have time to allow herself to recover. Still winded, she threw herself across the few feet to where Donna was lying. Her face was grey, and her tongue lolled out of her mouth. Lexi registered the blue tint around the edge of her lips – the noose remained tightly knotted around her throat and there was no movement of her chest to indicate she was still breathing. Her back was arched, and her arms and legs seemed to be rigidly straight.

Lexi pushed her roughly onto her front, so she could access the knot at the back of her neck. The drop from the crate had pulled it far tighter than the one that Lexi had struggled with around her own neck. Still gasping for air, she sobbed as she battled to loosen it – but she made no progress, and she could see the rope biting into the flesh of Donna's neck.

Please live.

If Donna died, it would be her fault, so overconfident of her ability to get them both out of trouble. It had been a mistake and now all of Donna's victims would be denied justice. Her fingers were raw and bleeding, but still she tried to undo the knot that spelled Donna's death sentence.

Footsteps sounded at the far end of the gallery.

'Lexi, Lexi, are you okay?' It was Tom and he was running towards her.

But there was more than one set of feet thundering up the length of the rope walk. She glanced up. Four or five figures were looming out of the darkness at the other end.

'Quickly, quickly.' Her voice cracked and her throat was raw.

Still she tugged at the knot.

'Get something to cut the rope,' she cried.

More lights went on, and she could see Tom, two uniformed PCs and two paramedics bearing down on her. Thank God someone had had the foresight to call the medics.

Tom veered from the centre of the floor to a rack of tools on one of the walls. He grabbed a pair of rope shears, then kept coming. As he reached her, she moved out of the way so he could squat down at Donna's side. The blades of the shears were thick and heavy, but he brutally forced one between the tight rope and the back of Donna's neck, ripping at her skin to get the blade into a cutting position.

Lexi held her breath as she watched him apply as much pressure as he could to bring the handles of the shears together. There was a rasping sound as the sharp metal sank into the twisted fibres. Tom grunted with the exertion, then sprawled to one side as the blade made it through. The rope fell away from Donna's neck.

And nothing happened.

Lexi had expected her to drag in a huge lungful of air, but her body lay inert, tongue still lolling, eyes bulging.

'Get out of the way.' One of the paramedics pushed her aside.

The other ran to Donna's other side, and together they flipped her over onto her back. 'We need oxygen, now. It's in my bag.'

Lexi saw that he'd thrown down his emergency response bag as he'd bent by Donna's body. She quickly unzipped it and located a small canister marked O2.

'And a mask,' said the paramedic as she handed it to him.

The other medic was checking Donna's airway. 'It's blocked – tracheal damage.'

'Tracheostomy?'

'Do it.'

Lexi stopped looking for a mask. They wouldn't need it if Donna was going to have a tracheostomy.

The paramedics worked fast. One of them made a small incision at the base of Donna's throat, then inserted a clear plastic tube. He immediately attached it to the oxygen canister, and used surgical tape to ensure the tubing was secure. Once that was done, the other straddled Donna and started CPR, placing the heel of one hand on her chest and covering it with the other, fingers interlocked. He began compressions, counting under his breath as he pumped up and down.

'Will she be okay?' said Lexi.

The medics ignored her, too busy to answer questions.

'Is there a door you can open at this end?' said the medic not doing the CPR, addressing the two PCs that accompanied Tom.

They shrugged. 'I'll find one,' said one of them. 'There must be a fire exit.'

The medic looked at the other PC. 'Bring the ambulance to this end of the building,' he said, tossing the ignition key at him.

The PCs scurried away to do as bid, and Lexi looked at Tom.

'Your neck,' he said. 'Are you okay?'

She put a hand up to her throat. It felt sore and bruised. 'I'm fine.'

As the first medic continued administering CPR, the second medic gave Donna a series of injections, continually checking for a pulse.

Lexi hardly dared breathe, waiting for what seemed like forever.

Finally, there was some sort of response.

'Got it. She's alive.'

They heard the ambulance drawing up outside, and there was a rush of cold air as one of the PCs opened a door.

'Right, let's take her in.'

Lexi could breathe again.

SIXTY-EIGHT

SATURDAY

As the ambulance siren faded into the night, Tom helped Lexi to her feet. She was shivering. She didn't know why. Perhaps it was the blast of cold air from the fire escape door, or maybe a reaction to what had just happened. Her legs felt weak. Her throat was sore, and her neck felt like she'd suffered whiplash. She supposed she had.

'Let me drive you home,' said Tom.

'Not yet. We need to get the CSIs in here.'

'The uniforms can secure the space, and Emily doesn't need us on hand to work a crime scene.'

He was right, of course. But it wasn't in Lexi's nature to leave the job to others, so they sat and waited in Tom's car for the crime scene manager to arrive. Lexi drank some water and, as the car warmed up, she gradually stopped shaking.

Tom gave her a few minutes before he spoke.

'What the hell happened in there?'

As she explained it to Tom, Lexi tried to make sense of it in her mind. 'It was like a challenge. A battle of wills.'

'You won.'

'Not if she doesn't survive – I'll only feel like I've won when I see her in court.'

'Well, in my book you're a winner. You saved Sam's life, and you apprehended a killer.'

Lexi didn't feel so sure. 'I think she wanted to be caught. She led me here, and she had that rope set up for a final show-down. I played right into her hands.'

'But she didn't get what she wanted. You're still alive.'

Lexi shrugged. She'd need to talk it through with Ed Harlow to properly understand what had driven Donna's twisted power plays. Her insistence that she was just helping people do what they wanted to do was clearly a monstrous lie. Maybe she was fooling herself about that, but she'd chosen her victims with care – vulnerable teenagers who were already under pressure – so they'd be more likely to succumb to the additional pressure she put them under in Club Edicius. She'd role-played at least half the charac-ters in the chatroom, a master of manipulation and suggestion. There was plenty to be unpacked, but it would have to wait.

Eventually, Emily Jordan and her team arrived.

Lexi took them into the rope walk and explained what had happened. Emily listened in silence, horrified by what Lexi had been through. Then she instructed her team on processing the scene.

'I'm sorry but I'll need your clothes,' she said, coming back to where Lexi and Tom were standing, 'for fibres and other traces.'

Lexi sighed. 'I've got some workout gear in my car.'

Tom offered to fetch it and while he was gone, one of the CSIs took photos of the marks on her neck, the wound on her forehead from the cathedral, and the state of her broken and bloody fingernails.

'You should get checked over by a doctor,' said Emily, as Tom arrived back with Lexi's sports bag.

'Honestly, I'm fine. I'm more interested in taking a shower.' She felt a desperate need to wash away the horrors of the night under a jet of searing hot water. 'Tom, we should get over to the hospital and see if Donna's ready to talk.'

She saw Tom and Emily exchanging exasperated looks, but she could rest and recuperate once the case was finally put to bed.

The Medway Maritime Hospital, where Donna Mason had been taken, was less than a five-minute drive away. Feeling more comfortable in a tracksuit and trainers, the journey just gave Lexi time to run a brush through her tangled hair. It made her suddenly aware of the gash on her temple that she'd forgotten about, as well as the bruising around her neck. She flipped down the sun visor to look in the mirror, but the interior of the car was dark.

'I don't expect they'll let us talk to her yet,' said Tom, turning into the hospital car park.

'We'll see,' said Lexi, but her expectations weren't high. 'In the meantime, let's get a police guard sorted for her ward. Then tomorrow...' She glanced at the clock on the dashboard. 'Today, I mean, we can formally charge her.'

'With?'

Lexi's head whirred through the evidence they had so far – the rope fibres they had found at the Westgate, the actual ropes that had been used to hang Shan and Neil, the rope with which Nyx had attempted to hang Sam, the snippet of fibre in her house and the ropes she'd used in the rope walk, plus the discovery of the mobile phones in her house. They cemented the link between the crimes, and her connection to all of them. But the precise charge?

'I'm not sure yet. Certainly, incitement to suicide – all that stuff online – and I believe we've got a strong case for assisting. But I think we can go further than that and get her for murder, for all three who died, and attempted murder for me and Sam.'

She didn't underestimate the work that this would involve, but she was determined to get the most just outcome for Olivia, Shan and Neil, and as importantly for their families.

They showed their badges at the entrance of the A&E department, and the woman on the desk confirmed that Donna Mason had been brought there and was still receiving emergency treatment.

'Sorry,' she said, 'it's been a chaotic night here.' Her words were borne out by the still-busy waiting area. 'I'll let the doctors treating her know that you're here, but you might be in for something of a wait.'

'Please let them know that we need to talk to someone as soon as possible,' said Lexi. 'And furthermore, they're not to discharge her or allow any visitors in to see her.'

The woman nodded, tired and not particularly interested. It was hardly unusual to have the police putting in an appearance in the emergency department.

While they waited, Tom sorted out a roster of uniformed PCs to stand at the door of the room where she was being treated. When a nurse came hurrying out of the room, Lexi waylaid her.

'Can you tell us how she is?' she said, flashing her ID.

The nurse shook her head. 'You'll have to wait for the doctor.'

Lexi went back to the row of plastic chairs where Tom was still busy on his phone.

Two hours and three coffees later, a young medic appeared in front of them. His face was hollowed out with exhaustion, his hair tousled and stuck to his forehead with sweat.

'You're the detectives waiting to see Donna Mason?'

They both stood up, and Tom nodded. 'Can we talk to her?'

As expected, the doctor shook his head.

'How long till we can?' said Lexi. There wouldn't be much point in hanging around here if they were going to have to wait hours for her recovery.

'I doubt you'll be able to talk to her at all.'

Lexi shuddered. 'She's still alive?'

'Yes.' He took a deep breath. 'But she can't breathe on her own. We've got her on a ventilator. When she arrived here, she was tachypnoeic with a low respiratory rate. Intermittent decerebrating movements and a blood oxygen level of sixty per cent. We administered oxygen therapy, thiopentone sodium and succinylcholine, but she developed pulmonary oedema.'

'In English?' said Tom.

'She's alive, but she's got fluid on her lungs. The compression of her airway and arteries by the rope caused cerebral ischaemia – in other words, her brain was starved of oxygen. Her decerebrate posture at the time of admission suggests severe brain damage.'

'Decerebrate posture?' said Lexi.

'Her head and neck were arched, and her arms and legs were rigid – it's caused by muscle spasms after brain injury.'

'How bad is the damage?'

The doctor shrugged. 'Only time will tell. We'll run some tests and monitor progress, but don't get your hopes up. I don't think she'll be talking any time soon, if ever again.'

'Damn it,' said Lexi, dropping back into the chair she'd just vacated.

The doctor left them. There were other patients more deserving of his help.

Lexi's mood slumped as the exhaustion of the past twenty-four hours finally caught up with her.

'It's my fault,' she said, as Tom sat down next to her. 'I handled it wrong.'

'Don't be ridiculous,' said Tom. 'She nearly killed you as well. And at least we can be sure of one thing – she won't have any more victims.'

It wasn't the best outcome, but it wasn't the worst either.

SIXTY-NINE

After a quick phone update, Maggie sent Lexi home for the rest of the day. Tom offered to take her back to the dockyard to retrieve her car, but she was too worn out to think about driving. Instead, he took her home, with a promise they'd go back for the car later in the afternoon, once she'd had a sleep.

A shower, some sleep.

It helped. But it didn't dismiss the feelings that she'd failed. Donna Mason should have been in a custody cell, not a hospital bed, and she blamed herself for that. Perhaps if she'd done things differently, it wouldn't have worked out that way. She shouldn't have risen to Donna's challenge. Hubris on her part had cost justice for Nyx's victims.

She picked at some food from the fridge, but she had no real appetite. She checked her watch a hundred times. Tom said he'd come back at four. She thought about calling him – if they went back to Chatham earlier, they might catch Emily Jordan and the CSIs still at work. But that didn't mean there'd be any additional information. Lexi had been at the crime scene, she'd been part of it. She knew what had happened and she'd already relived it in her mind over and over.

What could she have done differently?

All sorts of things, but there was no point in coming up with alternatives now.

Donna Mason was probably brain dead and she was to blame.

The doorbell rang. Clearly Tom had decided earlier was better too.

But it wasn't Tom – Amber and Sam were standing on the step when she opened the door.

She and Amber fell into an instant embrace, then she bent down and gave Sam the sort of swift hug that a thirteen-year-old boy could just about accept from a favourite aunt.

'Sam, how are you?' she said, ushering them inside.

'Well, you look like hell,' said Amber at the same time.

'Wow, thanks.'

'Sam, go and see if Aunt Lexi's got any Coke in the fridge.'

'Sure.' Sam disappeared into the kitchen and Amber pulled Lexi aside into the living room.

'I called the station to see what was happening and Tom told me. Are you okay?'

'I'm fine. I've had a sleep.'

Amber pushed Lexi's hair to one side to reveal the bruising on her neck. Lexi heard her sharp intake of breath. 'That looks anything but fine. And your forehead...'

Sam came in with a can of Coke. 'Last one,' he said to Lexi, plumping down on the sofa.

Lexi smiled at him. 'No worries. There are more in the store cupboard.'

'I'll get us a coffee,' said Amber.

Lexi sat down opposite Sam. She studied his neck. 'Matching bruises,' she said, pointing to her own throat.

Sam's body went suddenly rigid.

Idiot! thought Lexi. Of course, Sam would still be afraid.

'Listen, Sam. I went after Donna Mason – Nyx – and I caught her. She can't hurt you, or anybody else, ever again.'

He visibly relaxed. 'She'll go to prison?'

'We've got her in custody.' She didn't want to go into the details of exactly what had happened. 'You've got nothing to worry about.'

Amber came in with two mugs of coffee.

'Is it okay with you if I ask Sam a couple of questions?' she said to Amber.

Amber frowned. 'I suppose you need to talk to him about it.'

Lexi nodded. 'It's important we understand how Mason operated. Sam, can you tell me how you became a member of Club Edicius?'

Sam took a gulp of his Coke, then put the can on the coffee table. His hands fluttered nervously back to his lap. 'I knew about it from Olly. She told me about the WhatsApp group and the dark web stuff. I tried to persuade her to leave it and not to listen to Nyx but...' There was a tremor in his voice.

'Oh, Sam, we could have helped you,' said Lexi.

'Olly swore me to secrecy, and I'd never rat out on a friend.'

Lexi glanced at Amber. She looked distraught.

'Then what happened?'

'After Olly died, I was so angry. I wanted to go after Nyx. I was going to join the club and then expose what she was doing.'

Lexi gave him a nod, but inside she was furious. Not with Sam. His intentions had been good. But furious with the world in general for the existence of sick creatures like Donna Mason, those who preyed on young people with nothing but good in their hearts.

'How did Olly meet Nyx?' she said.

'At the Tenterden music festival last year,' said Sam.

So, they'd been right in suspecting this was her recruiting ground.

'And you?'

'I met her there too, only I didn't have much more contact with her. But when Olly got involved, I saw how Nyx sucked up to people in the WhatsApp group. After Olly died, I messaged her privately on WhatsApp and asked for her help. I pretended that I was upset about my voice breaking.'

Amber's hand shot to her mouth. Lexi understood – because it wasn't a pretence. Sam was telling the truth about that. No wonder Nyx had been all too ready to welcome him into the club.

'And she invited you into Club Edicius?'

'I was scared, but I wanted to bring her down for what she did to Olly.'

'Sam, I'm so sorry this happened to you – you know, I wish you'd come to me for help.'

'I was going to, Aunt Lexi.' He shook his head. 'But I wanted to get more proof of what she was doing. That was what you'd need to put her in prison, isn't it?'

'Yes, it is. But it was dangerous to try and take her on all by yourself. We were working on it, and we would have got the proof we needed.'

Sam shrugged. 'I didn't know that. I thought you'd just written Olly's death off as suicide.'

Lexi shook her head. 'We'd realised that something more was going on. She was forcing people to do it.'

'She tried to make me do it in the crypt. When I refused, she pushed me up hard against one of the pillars and put the rope round my neck. I couldn't breathe.'

Beside him, Amber burst into tears and pulled him into a hug.

'Enough now,' she said between sniffs, giving Lexi a pointed look over Sam's head. Sam was crying too.

Lexi nodded. 'Of course. Sam, you know, you were really, really brave when we were in the cathedral.'

Sam looked up at her, his expression brightening. 'I was?'

'You were. And you were brave to take on Nyx by yourself – but promise me and your mother you'll never do anything like that again.'

'I promise.' He looked at Amber. 'Mum, Aunt Lexi was a total badass last night.'

Amber smiled. 'I bet she was. But now she needs some rest. Sam, will you go and wait for me in the car?'

Sam sniffed and stood up. He came to Lexi for another brief embrace. 'I'm sorry, Aunt Lexi. Really, I am.'

'You've got nothing to say sorry for.'

'And thank you – you saved my life.'

'I wish I could have saved Olly's, too.'

Sam disappeared out to the car, and Lexi waited for Amber to remonstrate with her for upsetting him. But the expected tirade didn't materialise. She blew her nose on a tissue and went towards the door.

'Thank you, Lexi – I don't know what I would have done if you hadn't saved him. I don't think I could go on if I'd lost him.' She coughed and Lexi realised that she was trying to hide how much she was crying. 'I'm glad you're back.'

Lexi shook her head, close to tears herself. 'Me too.'

Amber blew her nose again, and they both pulled themselves together. 'What will happen next? Will there be a trial?'

'No. Donna Mason tried to hang herself last night. It looks as if she's suffered permanent brain damage, so Sam and the others' families won't get their day in court. It was my fault, and I apologise for it.'

'Thank God,' said Amber. 'I wouldn't want to put Sam through the ordeal of a trial.'

'But surely you'd want to see Donna Mason convicted?'

'I don't care – as long as she can't hurt any more young people, I'm happy. It might sound harsh, but I think this is the better outcome.'

She hugged Lexi and went out to Sam.

Lexi took the empty coffee cups back to the kitchen.

Was it the better outcome? Perhaps it was for Sam – and after all, wasn't he the one that mattered most? Donna had put him through hell and a trial would likely make him, and Olivia and Shan and Neil's families, relive the horror. A dysfunctional childhood and taking the blame for her brother's suicide had permanently warped her mind. Did she really think she was helping the kids she targeted? Perhaps it was how she rationalised doing something terrible that somehow made her feel better.

But they'd never really know now. Her brain was scrambled. Hardly justice.

Lexi wiped her eyes, washed up the cups and picked up her phone.

'Come on, Tom. We need to get on – I want to take another look at the crime scene.'

Donna Mason might never go to trial, but Lexi was still going to prove her a murderer. It was what she did.

A LETTER FROM ALISON

Thank you so much for reading *The Girl's Last Cry*. Whenever a reader chooses one of my books from the thousands of crime and thriller titles published, I feel that it's a real honour. I hope you enjoyed the time you spent with Lexi and her team, and that you'll feel inspired to read some more.

If you're interested in hearing about the next titles in the Lexi Bennett series, please sign up using the link below for details of forthcoming releases. Your email address will never be shared and you can unsubscribe at any time.

www.bookouture.com/alison-belsham

The Girl's Last Cry is the second book in the Lexi Bennett series. By the time you read this, I'll probably have finished writing the third one! Each time I write about Lexi, I get to know her a little better and her character develops into something deeper. She's so tough and determined to do right by the victims of the crimes she investigates – she leaves no stone unturned and, sometimes, throws caution to the wind as she gets the villain in her sights. I'm actually pretty proud of the person she's becoming! Kind, intelligent, empathetic and incredibly human. At the same time, with each outing she's faced with a more intractable problem to solve, a darker crime, a more vicious killer – for Lexi, the challenge is real, and I hope that's what makes these books a compelling read for you and all my other readers.

I have one small favour to ask of you. If you've enjoyed reading about Lexi and the team, I'd be hugely grateful if you'd write a review of *The Girl's Last Cry*. I'm intrigued to know what you think about Lexi and the case, and it would help new readers to discover one of my books for the first time. Feedback from readers is what makes all of the long hours and hard work of writing a book worthwhile – so give me a shout on Facebook, Twitter, Goodreads or my website.

Now, time for me to get back to work on the next Lexi story – coming your way soon...

Alison

xx

www.alisonbelsham.com

 facebook.com/alison.belsham.3

 twitter.com/AlisonBelsham

 instagram.com/alisonbelsham

ACKNOWLEDGEMENTS

Writing a book can seem like a very solitary undertaking when you're alone in the trenches. I watch the word count ticking slowly upwards – though on some days it goes down – and I wonder if I'll ever reach the end. But in those sorts of moments, I always remember that I'm not actually alone. Team Lexi is real and continuing to expand, and without the valued input from all these people I wouldn't be able to get my words in front of my readers.

First of all, huge thanks to my editor Ruth Tross. Ruth's input starts with the first glimmer of an idea for the next story and she continues to guide with an expert hand at every stage of the writing process. Her editing certainly makes me appear to be a much more polished writer than my first drafts would suggest, and she keeps tricky things like the timeline and who knows what when on track, for which she has all my gratitude!

Thanks are also due to the rest of the amazing Bookouture team – in particular to Richard King, Rights Director, Melissa Tran in editorial, Mandy Kullar in managing editorial, Melanie Price in marketing and the wonderful PR team, Kim Nash, Noelle Holten, Sarah Hardy and Jess Readett. Thanks also to copyeditor Dushi Horti and proofreader Shirley Khan, and to Lisa Brewster for designing the magnificent covers.

Also an essential member of Team Lexi is my agent Jenny Brown, whom I rely on for words of wisdom, encouragement and good cheer throughout the process. She's been incredibly supportive of my writing career from the very start, so I feel like it's a journey we're on together – with hopefully a long way to go still ahead. Thank you, Jenny.

Thanks to my wonderful writing companions Jane Anderson, Kristin Pedroja and Hannah Kelly for advice, celebrations and commiserations (actually, there aren't many of those!) and for regularly partaking of gin and cake.

Once again, Mark has earned my thanks for taking on the role of chauffeur in all my research trips to Kent – good company and a steady hand on the wheel.

Finally, a massive shout out to all my readers. Without you lot, there wouldn't be much point in the whole endeavour, so thanks from the bottom of my heart for picking up the books and reading them.

Milton Keynes UK
Ingram Content Group UK Ltd.
UKHW011832280723
425980UK00006B/200